# Costa Brava

DAVID KENNEDY

For my darling Rosy

Acknowledgements:

I could not have written this novel without the support of my wonderful wife, who pushed me into the project at the start, persevered with me throughout and did a brilliant first edit.
Thank you to Jim and Jojo Stephens for lending us your lovely alpine home, the perfect hideaway to get some writing done.
Thank you to David Walsh, my father-in-law, and Anuj Nayar, my first two guinea pigs, for being so kind and encouraging with your criticism.
A huge thank you to Will Young for his invaluable time and input in battering this into shape.
Finally, a thank you to Mel Atterbury for such wonderful proof read. Any mistakes or typos are now entirely my fault.

# ONE

The old man whimpered. He didn't want to. He still had his pride. Too much pain. He should have called the police. How silly. At his age. Why had he gone to check the fence? He'd thought they were wild boar. What could he have done if it had been a boar? Stupid old man. But a boar was more dangerous than these two. A half smile crossed his bleeding mouth. That was another mistake. The foreigner didn't like that at all. A crushing blow to what was left of his ribs. If only he weren't so old. Another blow. Something else cracked. Another question. The same question. Over and over again. He wouldn't answer them. He couldn't answer them. He had no idea what they were asking him. The old man felt his consciousness fading. Through all the pain he felt so sleepy. The big one slapped his face. He wished he were back home. It wasn't likely now. Back home in bed. He could just go to sleep. He heard them mutter something in their language. Strong arms picked him up, then the rush of the sea air on his face.

# TWO

There was a ping as the seatbelt sign turned off. The tall, stern-faced man in the front row unbuckled his belt and stood up. The impromptu gathering in the pub the night before had been a mistake and Alex Scott was eager to be out of the plane's tinned atmosphere. He retrieved a tan suede jacket and a battered leather holdall from the overhead compartment and turned towards the front of the plane. The stewardess finished deploying the stairs, smiled at him a little longer than necessary and indicated the open door. He thanked her and stepped out onto the steps.

The blast of pine-scented heat radiating off the tarmac hit Scott as he stepped out of the door. The grey London morning he had left was a world away from this bright, blue Spanish sky. Green, rolling hills surrounded the airport and behind them to the north loomed the majestic Pyrenees. He took a deep breath and started down the steps. The apprehension he had been feeling during the journey faded, as memories of the sparkling Mediterranean lightened his mood.

Once on the tarmac, he had a hundred-yard walk to the Girona Costa Brava Airport terminal building. The heat and the still air were stifling and he had to stop to take off his jacket half way. The last time he was here the airport had been smaller, a relic from the sixties, decorated with garish ceramic works of art depicting Don Quixote and other Spanish legends. It now seemed revitalised, more polished, all slate and tinted glass.

Scott entered the mercifully cool terminal building where a National Policeman in a spotless dark blue combat uniform waved him through passport control. As his fellow passengers ambled to the carousel, Scott made his way out through the automatic gates. He groaned when he saw the queue that was already formed at only one desk. Of course it was his car hire company. Sod's Law dictated that. Or Maybe Murphy's. Some annoying law at any rate.

A buzz from his pocket reminded Scott to check his phone. He had a text:

> Get taxi to house. Pl use car. Needs exercise. As does Salacia. Keys in usual place. Speak when you there. B

Well, it was a bit late now. He'd already paid for the hire car. No point in wasting it. Although the thought of leaving the queue and taxying it to the coast was certainly tempting.

Slowly the queue shortened, customer by customer. Did it really take so long to print out the hire agreement and sign it? Did every nuance of the insurance policy need to be explained to every customer? By the time Scott was up, he could have recited the patter verbatim.

Five minutes later Scott was climbing into a canary-yellow Fiat 500. The roof of the car came halfway up his chest. He put his holdall on the back seat, put the driver's seat as far back as it could go, and started the engine. With the air conditioning on full blast, Scott tootled out of the airport. A new ring road took him around and above the city then through the hills behind. How the place had changed. When he was last here, the city of Girona had been a small provincial capital, tucked away in the north-eastern corner of Spain, almost unknown to tourists. He remembered the old part with its bars and clubs. A small medieval town sheltering under the huge cathedral with a friendly provincial feel to it. Judging by the expanse of new apartment blocks the city had grown enormously. The satellite towns he passed had grown as well, but seemed half finished. Every little town he passed seemed to be surrounded by empty looking buildings, vacant shops and roads in grids with street lights but no houses.

Scott found the coast road more by luck than memory. The scenery became more familiar as he neared the coast. Pine and oak forests replaced pylons and street lights. Brick and concrete gave way to the stone of the numerous mediaeval villages nestling in the hills, each with its unique church spire. As he passed Palafruguell and took the road to the sea, the memories came thick and fast. An old nightclub that was now a hotel; the roadside restaurant they would go to for the simple *menú del día;* a bar he recognised which still looked the same, if a little more tattered.

Scott drove straight to Manolo's house. He remembered the way, despite his long absence, and took the little dirt road that led to the ramshackle breezeblock house with its kitchen garden and assortment of hens and goats. He sat for a moment in the car, dreading the reunion ahead.

The day before he had received a call from and old family friend, Bill Franklin. Scott had been at school with Bill's son and, over the years, Scott had considered the Franklins to be a second family. Bill had called asking for a favour. Manolo, the caretaker of Bill's house on the Costa Brava, had just died and Bill needed someone to look after the house and sort out a replacement. Scott knew the house and the area well, and, as a freelance journalist, he had no pressing reason to be in London, so had agreed on the spot. A few weeks relaxing on the Mediterranean had seemed a godsend in the London drizzle. Now, faced with the imminent reunion with Dolors, Manolo's widow, he was less enthusiastic.

Gathering his resolve, Scott squeezed out of the tiny car, pushed back the plastic fly curtain and knocked on the door.

'*Si, qui ets?*' said a weak voice in Catalan.

'*Soy yo, soy Alejandro.*'

A small round lady, head to toe in black, opened the inner door and two bony white hands reached out and encircled Scott's waist.

Between wails of sorrow, while still holding him in a tight embrace, Dolors told Scott the story of her husband's death. He had fallen from the cliffs. He was still young at heart. Only two days ago, Wednesday morning. God bless him. The cliffs he walked every day. What was she going to do?

For five minutes, they stayed in the doorway with Scott's arms wrapped around Dolors in an awkward hug as she alternated between burying her tear streaked face in his jacket and telling him about the accident. Finally, they retreated into the front room of the house. A simple room with a sofa, an armchair and a fake wood dresser with a lace doily on the top. A game show, in shocking pink, was in progress on the television. Dolors sat on the low-slung sofa, insisting that Scott took the armchair, made from fake leather with a handmade wool cover over the back. Between the sobs and the noise of the television, Scott had to lean over to hear what Dolors was saying.

Although Scott's Spanish had at one time been fluent, Dolors' mixture of Catalan and Spanish taxed his comprehension, but he got the gist. Dolors couldn't understand how Manolo had fallen from the cliffs. He knew the area like the back of his hand. He had been worried about people breaking in recently, and something about wild boar (or at least Scott thought she said that) or it could have been badgers? Then Dolors rattled off some numbers. It took him a while to realise that she was telling him a code, he assumed to an alarm.

Scott asked if she had some paper to write it down, she came back with a sheet paper, a key and what looked like a police report.

He wrote down the code for the alarm. She told him that the key was for the back door and the other keys were in the office in the house.

Scott had a cursory look at the police report that Dolors thrust at him, but apart from the word *'accident'* the report was meaningless to him. It was from the Catalan local police the *'Mossos d'Esquadra.'*

Dolors asked if she should come with him. Scott insisted that he was ok and that he would come over and check on her the next day or over the weekend.

After extricating himself, Scot drove the remaining kilometre to the Franklins' house with the windows open, enjoying the smell of pine, and the first glimpses of the blue of the Mediterranean.

# THREE

The coastal road wound through the hills above the shore. Scott took a smaller road that led down towards a large bay. On the far point he could see the old lighthouse that had been out of commission for decades. As the road curved round, a large white house appeared out of the trees on the next bend. The Can Daurat estate occupied the whole southern half of the bay. Its only neighbours were the sea and pine woods. It was one of the few still unspoilt stretches of coastline.

As he drew closer, Scott could see glimpses of the house and the cobalt Mediterranean beyond through the pine trees. The house was built in a typical Mediterranean style, whitewashed walls and terracotta tiled roof, with light blue shutters on the windows. Half the house was enveloped in ivy and bright purple bougainvillea.

Scott arrived at the gates, which were open, and drove up the circular drive to the front door. He was surprised to see a Range Rover parked in front. Pulling up in the tiny Fiat behind the large white car he got out to see a small grey suited man come round the side of the house.

'Hello, can I help you?'

'Ahh, es meester Franklin, no?'

'No, I'm not Mr Franklin. Can I help you?'

'I am looking for Mr Franklin.'

'Well, Mr Franklin isn't here, Mr Franklin is in London, but I can pass on a message, if you like.'

'Ahh, let me explain. I am Ferran Camps.' He held out a hand and a huge gold diver's watch appeared from the shiny grey sleeve. 'I have the ... eh ... the *inmobiliaria...* the real estate office in Begur, Camps International. Do you know?'

'I'm sorry, no.'

'An... and you are?'

'Alex Scott.'

'Meester Scott...*much gusto...* I have a client, *bery* rich, who would lie to buy this house. I would lie to make the offer to Meester Franklin.'

'Well, I don't think that the Franklins are looking to sell. But I will certainly pass on the message, and if you give me a card I'll ask Mr Franklin to give ...'

'It is urgent that I speak to Meester Franklin today. My client, *bery* rich, he want to buy immediately. We call him now? You give me his telephone?'

Desperate to get into the house, jump in the pool and relax, Scott was tired of this conversation and decide to cut it short.

'I'm sorry, but I can't bother him now. As I said, I'll pass on your message, but now I'm busy and need to get on with things. And by the way, I would prefer it if you didn't wander round the house uninvited.'

Ignoring Scott's last comment, he persisted. 'My client has *bery* much money, he will pay above market. But it is *urgente.* Can you *gib* me Mr Franklin telephone?'

'No I cannot *gib* you his telephone. As I have said, we will get in touch, if and when we are interested. Now I have to get on. I know where to reach you. Camps International. Goodbye.'

Scott headed off round the corner of the house before the man could reply, eager to lose *Señor* Camps. As he neared the side door he heard the Range Rover start up and the crunch of wheels on gravel.

Opening the door triggered a beeping from somewhere down the corridor. Trying the first door on his right, Scott saw that the old staff sitting room was now a little office. On the wall by the door was a small number panel above what looked like an intercom with a video screen. Scott punched in the code, the beeping stopped and the flashing red light turned to green. He looked around the room. There was a modern desk with a computer, an office chair, a bookcase of files and a safe on the floor. The monitor was divided into eight little windows, one of which showed the white Range Rover turning out of the front gate.

Scott pressed the button with a key on it on the intercom box and was pleased to see the gates start to close on the screen. The other windows all seemed to show rotating views of the grounds. There were views of the pool, the inside of the boathouse, the fence, the garage, and three more of different angles around the house. Looking more closely at the screen, Scott saw a little wheel and something that looked like a volume button. By clicking on an image, he realised that he could zoom in or out and move the angle of the camera. When he had last been here, front doors were left unlocked and cameras were unheard of. This sort of security seemed very up to date, and judging by the empty boxes in the corner of the room had only just been installed.

He checked in the drawer of the desk. As Dolors had said, there was a large bunch of keys. Next to it was the foot-long, old, iron key to the front door, its handle formed by an intricate interwoven C and D. He put the bunch of keys in his pocket. On the bottom of the drawer was a sticker with what turned out to be the code for the WIFI.

Scott left the office and wandered along the white tiled corridor into the kitchen. The house had metre-thick walls and was delightfully cool after the heat outside. As he entered the kitchen he stopped, overwhelmed with a rush of memories. The smell was just as he recalled - a mixture of olive oil, coffee and soap. He stood for a moment, inhaled deeply and marvelled how easily a smell could catapult him straight back to his childhood.

The kitchen itself hadn't changed much. It had the same earthenware pots and plates hanging over the old stove. The enormous American double fridge, with ice and water on tap, was new. Scott found a glass and filled it with some ice-cold water. Opening the heavy door, he realised a trip to the shops would be necessary.

He wandered through the rest of the house, soaking up memories that seemed to spring from every corner. When his parents died the Franklins, the parents of his best friend Charlie, had taken him under their wing during the summer holidays, and he had spent as much of his late teens here in this house as he had with his uncle and aunt in the UK. Since Charlie's death ten years ago, Scott had stayed close to the family but hadn't been back to Can Daurat.

The corridor from the kitchen was covered in Franklin family photos in big framed collages going back to the 1950s. He was halfway along the corridor before he saw his own first appearance. A photo of Charlie and him on the beach with some black sea urchins. Both were deeply tanned, Charlie's almost white blonde hair contrasting to Scott darker looks. He remembered that day. They had opened, cleaned and eaten them and lied about how delicious they were. How young and full of energy they looked.

As he walked along the corridor, he stopped to examine more photos. Some brought back memories he had forgotten years before. Charlie and himself losing their childish looks, becoming adults. Bill and Anne getting older. The group photos on the terrace with the never-changing view behind them.

He walked from the corridor into the drawing room. This large room ran most of the length of the house. There was a grand piano at one end which Scott remembered had

17

always been in tune but hardly ever played. He opened the cover and tried a few keys. The noise seemed deafening in the quiet of the silent house. Still in tune. He walked over to the floor-to-ceiling doors at the end of the room.

Scott opened them and walked out onto the terrace. The sun radiated off the terracotta paving. He walked to the edge and looked down over the garden.

The house was surrounded by formal terraced gardens which led down towards the sea. On the last terrace were the pool and pool house and beyond that the coastal path and rocks. There was a boathouse on the shore, just down the hill from the pool house. The property had about a kilometre of sea front, all the wild, rocky shoreline that gives the Costa Brava its name. Over towards the end of the garden there was a small promontory, surrounded by steep cliffs.

He crossed the garden, revelling in the smell of pine and jasmine and the chirping of the cicadas. He walked down the steps and along the sparking pool that was collecting pine needles at one end. Poor Manolo would have had a fit. Looking up, he noted the brand-new, shiny cameras that had been installed at the corner of the pool house, standing out against the more rustic whitewashed walls.

The pool house had a large reception area with a bar and wicker furniture with dated floral print cushions. It had been built sometime in the mid twentieth century, and in the back were changing rooms and showers. The bar hid the entrance to a staircase that led down to the boathouse.

Although the 'secret' door wasn't as invisible as he remembered, with the lock and hinges clearly visible, Scott couldn't help smiling as he remembered how exciting he had thought it as a child. He opened the door and fumbled for a moment to find the light switch. The stone spiral staircase was cut straight out of the rock and must have involved quite a feat of engineering.

As Scott descended the stairs, the salty, oily gasoline smell of the sea and boats rose to greet him. The boathouse had originally been built as a simple fisherman's boatshed on the water's edge. For centuries, the *Cami de Ronda*, the coastal path that followed the shoreline along the Costa Brava, had cut through the property between boathouse and the main house. When work was done in the forties or fifties to improve the path, the owners of the house had built a tunnel under the promontory and put a fence along the garden to keep the path separate. They built their pool and pool house above it and had built the staircase to join with the boathouse. Since then, the only way to the boathouse was either by the staircase or by sea. At the bottom of the stairs there was a short tunnel that ended in a wooden door.

From the outside the boathouse looked like a small shed on the water's edge. In fact, it was much larger, having been excavated into the cliff itself. The interior space was fifteen metres long by ten metres wide, the dock taking up most of the room. Hanging above the water on a gantry were two watercraft. On the left was the *Salacia,* a nine metre 1965 Riva Aquarama, and on its right Charlie's custom Bellini jetski. Scott went over to the winch on the wall and lowered the gantry, then tied both vessels up on either side of the dock.

What a contrasting pair they made: The Riva Aquarama, one of the most beautiful boats ever made, all varnished mahogany, white leather and sparkly chrome; the jetski, an ugly mix of black plastic and fiberglass, with garish stickers and angular lines. Beauty and the beast.

Scott went back to the house via the garage. He remembered the garage being full of a variety of cars, but now there was just one under an old grey cover. Scott pulled up a front corner to reveal a bright chrome bumper under a single, round, recessed headlight. Lifting it further revealed bodywork in deep racing green. Scott continued to pull, his grin working into a broad smile as he saw the unmistakable double winged emblem of an Aston Martin. So, Bill had finally bought the old Aston V8 he had always gone on about. It looked in great condition. Scott walked over to a bookcase filled with car manuals and found a large blue hardback book. An old parts manual. He took it off the shelf and opened it, to reveal a cut out interior with a set of car keys inside. He opened the right-side door to the Aston and sat in the driver's seat. It was vast, covered in soft leather, more an armchair than a sports car seat. In front of him was a huge wooden steering wheel. Dials of all different sizes were spread across a walnut dashboard. He put the keys in the ignition and was rewarded with the roar of the engine. He allowed the engine to tick over for a minute then shut it off. Well, he thought as he locked the garage, if Bill really wants him to keep it running, that's fine by me.

Back at the house, Scott went upstairs to the room he had always used and changed into swimming trunks. He came back down to the pool and dived straight in. He spent a while just floating on his back in the water, arms outstretched and looking up at the blue sky. How he had missed the Mediterranean.

After getting out and drying himself, Scott went back up to the terrace outside the sitting room. Leaning against the balustrade he took his phone and scrolled through his last emails until he found one from Juan Finat. Juan had been Charlie's and his best friend in the area, and over the years they had stayed in touch through the odd email, although they hadn't spoken for a while. Scott copied a number into his phone's address book and pressed dial.

'*Si… dígame!*'

'*Hola Juan, soy yo. Soy Alejandro.*'

'Alejandro! *¡Cabrón!* How are you my friend? *¿Dónde estás?*'

'Hey Juan! I'm at Can Daurat. I just got in. How are things with you? It's been a long time.'

'Ahh, you know. *Todo bien*. Kids and the wife! Not like *los tiempos pasados*. And you? *¿Dónde está la Señora Scott?*'

'*Una señora Scott?*' Scott smiled. Still being unmarried in your mid-thirties in London was relatively common, but here it was probably quite rare. 'Still on the lookout. What are you up to? What are your plans this weekend?'

'We are *en casa*. Isabel and the children are away *mañana*. With … *mis suegros*…my…'

'Your in-laws.'

'Yes, my fathers-in-law. But you must come to eat in the night? Today I can't... I have obligations. But tomorrow is good. You are free? How long are you here?'

'I'm not sure. I might be here for a while. Bill has asked me to look after things here. Do you remember Manolo? Here at Can Daurat?'

'Si, *claro*. Manolo. I heard he has died. Very sad. I remember him well. With the boat. That incredible… what was it…?'

'The Riva? The *Salacia*. She's still here. And Bill wants me to keep her running. Feel like a spin?'

'Yes. Of course.'

'When are you free?'

'What about tomorrow? I'm free in the day. We go out in the boat? And in the night, you come to dine *en casa*. Meet Isabel and the children.'

'That would be lovely. Ok, pop round whenever you want. I'll be here.'

'*Vale*. I come to Can Daurat at midday? I look forward to it. Hey... You should call Santi, he is here. And María. I will send you Santi's number.'

Santi and María, Santi's sister, were Juan's first cousins.

'Brilliant.'

'*Vale hermano, hasta mañana. Un abrazo.*'

'*Un abrazo, hasta mañana.*'

Scott's next call was to Bill Franklin in London.

'Yes, who is it?'

'Hi Bill, it's me, Alex.'

'Hello Alex, did you arrive safely? Did you get my message?'

'Yes, all good. I had already hired a car. I've just seen the V8. Beautiful. Are you sure you want me taking it for a spin?'

'Sure, sure. Please do. It need to be kept running. Just be careful. I trust you! How's everything there? Did you see Dolors?'

'Yeh, poor thing. She's in pieces. I got the keys from her. I see you've got a load of new cameras and security.'

'Yes, Manolo had been going on about people coming in through the fence from the *Camí* the last couple of weeks. My insurance asked for the cameras. And more lights. Manolo installed them on Monday. I hope he wasn't trying to install the lights on the cliffs when he fell. He told me I can see the footage online, but I haven't had time to work it out. '

'I saw a load of new stuff in the office. I'll have a look at it. It's so sad about Manolo. How old was he?'

'God, he was older than me. Must have been about eighty. Poor guy, what was he doing climbing around the cliffs at his age? He'd been with us forever. He had been at the house as long as I can remember. I think his father was the first guy my Ma took on at Can Daurat.'

'I forgot to ask Dolors about the funeral, do you know when...'

'It was yesterday. In Spain, they bury them quickly. Must be a relic of Muslim times. Or something to do with the heat.'

'Well, it's hot enough all right. I can't remember, is it normal for it to be so hot in June?'

'How hot is it?'

'Must be in the thirties.'

'Yes, it can get like that in June.'

'Well, I'm sorry to have missed the funeral. I'll drop in and see her again tomorrow. What do you want me to do about finding someone new?'

'There's no rush, as long as you're ok staying there. Dolors is well past retirement, but be tactful. She's probably got a pension, but I'll be happy to settle something on her. Can you sound out the situation? I know the house is theirs, my Ma gave it to them years ago, but if she wants to retire I'd like her to know we'll look after her.'

'Of course, Bill.'

'Can you try to find a new version of Manolo and Dolors? I'd prefer locals of course, but see what you can find.

'Now, I forgot to ask you when you were in London. Do you have a gun licence?' added Bill

'Yes, I've got an English licence, for shotguns and rifles.' Scott's uncle and aunt lived on the north coast of Scotland and once or twice a year he travelled up there to have a pop at some wild snipe or grouse and, once in a while, to cull the red deer. He also went on an annual boar hunt in Germany with an old school-friend.

'Great. I've got a few pieces in the house. I haven't used them for years, and they were on Manolo's licence. I think you will have to put them on your licence while I work out what I want to do with them. Can you find out from the police what needs to be done?'

'Yes of course. I'll have to get my licence sent out from the UK but that shouldn't be a problem. Where are they?'

'The gun safe. It's in the wine cellar. Manolo had the keys. You'll have to ask Dolors where they are.'

'OK Bill, don't worry about them. I'll sort all of that out.'

'Thank you. I knew I could count on you. You just have a bit of fun. We're thinking of coming out in August, but stay as long as you like.'

'Well, I've got a few ideas for articles that I can write from here, so if it's ok with you I'll stay until then. '

'Absolutely. *Mi casa es su casa* Alex, you're doing me a favour being there. If you need more fuel for the boat, I have an account in the gas station in the port in Palamós. Call me if you need anything'

'Speak…' But Bill had already rung off. Scott had forgotten to mention the estate agent. He'd tell Bill next time they spoke.

# FOUR

Scott wandered back into the house and went to look for the gun safe keys. In the office, he sat down at the desk and had a look at the computer. The screen was still divided into little windows showing different views of the house and grounds. One of the windows was showing the fence at the far end of the garden. As the camera panned right, Scott saw what looked like white tape fluttering in the breeze.

He walked back through the house and down the terraces. To the right of the pool there was some lawn, then the garden turned to pine wood. He walked through the trees until he came to the fence. It separated the garden from the public path that ran along the coast, and where the garden jutted out into the bay, the fence ran along the top of the cliffs. Along the top of this part of the fence there was a white and blue plastic tape with *Policía* written on it. Scott walked back until he came to a small gate which was next to the pool house. He opened the gate with the keys in his pocket and walked along the path towards the cliffs and the promontory. As the rocky shore became steep cliff, the path disappeared into a tunnel that went under the garden, and the fence rose up along the top of the cliff. Scott climbed up along the edge of the cliff and the fence. Below him he could see the boathouse off to the left. As he edged along he climbed higher and was soon high above the path. There was hardly any room to put his feet, and he had to hold on to the fence to stop himself from falling. Just before he got to the highest part of the fence, he found white tape in the mesh. Looking down, Scott could see the path below him and more white tape far below on the rocks.

Scott edged back down to the path. A scramble over the rocks got him to the base of the cliff. There, Scott found more police tape, bits of plastic surgical wrapping and a large dark stain that he thought looked like dried blood.

What on earth had Manolo been doing on the outside of the fence so high above the rocks? And at his age. Scott had only just managed it and he was forty years younger. Looking up, Scott saw that between him and the place where he had climbed along the fence, the *Camí de Ronda* came well away from the cliff. He frowned. Surely Manolo would have fallen onto the Camí before hitting these rocks?

Back in the house, Scott went straight to the office. He sat at the computer and clicked on the program's file history. A quick look revealed there were separate files for each camera for every 24 hours from midnight to midnight. The most recent ones were for that afternoon and by clicking on the time bar of a few minutes before, he could clearly see himself on the terrace talking on the phone. The recording history apparently started on the Wednesday two days before. Scott clicked on the first recording for the Wednesday for the camera by the fence. The timestamp showed 10am - well after Manolo's accident. If the cameras had been installed on Monday, surely there would be recordings from Monday onwards. If Manolo had fallen from the cliff on Wednesday morning, where was the recording?

Scott opened a yellow and white telephone book that was on the desk. He found and dialled the number for the *'Mossos d'Esquadra'* in Begur. Scott explained to the officer who answered that he was an old family friend of

Manolo, and asked if he could speak to somebody connected to the case. The office corrected him, it was an 'incident' not a 'case.' The officer in charge was not around but would give him a call in the morning.

Scott saw that he had received a text message from Juan with Santi's number. After a few rings, it answered.

'*Si. Digui'm.*'

'*Hola, ¿Santi?*'

'*Si, ¿qui ets?*'

'*Hola Santi, soy Alejandro. Alejandro Scott.*'

'*Hola Alex! ¡Coño! ¿Qué tal?* How are you? Juan told me you were here.'

'All really good thanks. How are things?'

'Good my friend. Good to speak to you. You are here for a while, no?'

'Yes, I'll probably be here for a month or two.'

'*De puta madre!* We go for a drink tonight? You remember María? She is coming from Barcelona. We are meeting *a las nueve.* Can you come?'

'Well,' Scott looked at his watch, 'it's half past seven now…. yes, I'd love to. I've got to pop to the supermarket but I can come straight on from there. Whereabouts?'

'Shall we meet at Café Royal? Do you remember it?'

'Yes, of course. In the *plaza.* Ok, I can be there at about nine.'

'*Perfecto. Hasta hora.*'

Scott felt his mood lighten. Although it was lovely to be back in Can Daurat, in the past the house had always been full of people. All on his own in the fading light, on top of the tragedy of Manolo's death, he had begun to feel rather melancholic and was grateful for a bit of company.

Santi had not been his closest friend, but had always been good fun. Scott could only just remember María. She was much younger than him, and they had moved in different circles.

Having made sure that the boathouse and the garage were locked, he set the alarm and left through the kitchen door. He had arranged to meet Santi in the main square of Begur which was a ten-minute drive from the house. On the way, he stopped at a large, new-looking supermarket and in half an hour had filled a trolley. How weird to be in Spain again. Although supermarkets superficially looked alike the world over, each country had its unique characteristics. Compared to London, here there were hardly any pre-cooked meals, condiments or packaged sandwiches; the fruit and vegetable section was enormous, with all the produce in piles and needing to be weighed. He stopped at the fish counter – this alone was the equal to most UK fishmongers – but decided against it. Anything he bought would be sitting in the car for the next few hours. Moving to the meat counter, the extensive array of hams had Scott stumped and, in the end, he just opted for the most expensive, which to him seemed a bargain when compared to London prices.

Scott put his shopping in the tiny boot and drove the rest of the way into Begur. Something had changed since the last time he had been there, and Scott found himself driving round and round tiny streets without getting to the main square. In the end, he gave up and parked the car in an underground carpark and walked the remaining few hundred metres on foot.

# FIVE

Begur was a medieval town, set back a few kilometres from the coast, with whitewashed buildings and cobbled streets. The centre had been pedestrianised, which explained his failure to get there by car, and the town seemed to have lost the dilapidated aura of faded grandeur that he remembered. It had been smartened up considerably and now rather reminded him of some parts of the Cote d'Azur or Sardinia. Everywhere he looked there were red and yellow Catalan flags with a blue triangle hanging in windows and balconies.

The Café Royal in the main square hadn't changed much. The square was teeming with people in the open-air tables, buzzing with chatting groups of friends. Although the sun had set, the air was still warm, all the girls were in light summer dresses and the men in shirtsleeves. There was an abundance of pastel colours, healthy tans and lithe limbs. He saw a familiar face at a table, waved and went over.

Santi gave him a big hug and kissed him on both cheeks.

'*Hola Alex*. How are you? You are looking well.'

'*Hola Santi*. You too.'

And he was looking good. In the past, Santi had been a tall, gaunt youth, with a slightly bad complexion and a bit of a nervous air, but since their last meeting he had filled out, had a healthy tan and a new aura of confidence.

'What would you like to take? *¿Una caña?*'

'Perfect.'

Santi ordered a small beer like his own from the waiter wandering amongst the tables and turned back to Scott.

'Had to park miles away,' said Scott. 'This pedestrian thing. Since when are no cars allowed?'

'Ah, that's only in July and August. I parked over there.' Said Santi pointing to a white convertible Alfa Romeo Spider which was parked under a no parking sign.

'And is it the fiesta now?'

'Yes, at the end of the month.'

'Is that why there are all the flags?'

'The flags?'

'In the windows.'

'Oh, those. No, they are *Estellades*. They are supporting independence.'

'That many? I thought here the independence movement was in the minority.'

'Things have changed since you were last here.'

The waiter put Scott's drink on the table.

'*Salud!*' They both said.

'So, tell me my friend. How are you? It has been a long time. I heard from Juan about Manolo. *Qué pena*. What a shame. *You* look well. Where have you been?'

'Based in London really. Well… at least recently. Before that I spent a few years all over the place. Spent some time in South Africa. And Asia.' Scott paused, blocking the unwelcome memoires that were attempting to invade his thoughts. 'But recently I've been doing a lot of freelance food and travel writing. I do most of my stuff in Europe. The occasional long distance trip if I can wangle it. What about you?'

'I was working in Barcelona for a few years. Then I came back here to work for the council. *Arquitecto.*'

'Congratulations. Hence the parking I suppose. Aren't you in charge of planning?'

'Yes, that is one of my duties.'

'That must keep you busy. There seems to be a lot of new building going on.'

'Well, things are a lot quieter than before. A few years ago, things were crazy. We have some new projects, but since the recession… I spend most my days looking at renovation plans.'

'Next step mayor?'

'Mayor?'

*'Alcalde?'*

'No, my friend,' laughed Santi, 'I am happy to be the architect.' Santi had either developed a new talent for sarcasm or he needed work on his lying ability.

'Juan said he's got married and has two girls. What about you?'

'Still *soltero*. And what about you?'

'Yup, me too,' said Scott.

As they were talking, Scott noticed a strikingly beautiful girl walking across the square. She was carrying a large old fashioned briefcase made of leather and a tubular case which seemed to be heavy. She had very long dark hair and was dressed in what Scott could only imagine was Barcelona chic – smart suede jacket and light blue shirt on immaculate figure hugging jeans, and white suede loafers. She was making her way through the tables in their direction, and it was only as she walked straight up to their table that Scott made the connection between her angular face and that of his companion.

'Santi….is that…' Scott started to say, looking towards the girl.

'María!' said Santi on spotting his sister and waved to her. She came over and kissed him on both cheeks.

*'Hola Santi. ¿Qué tal? Estoy hasta los…'*

'Hey María, you remember Alex? *¿El amigo de los Franklin?'*

'Hey Alex. Yes, how are you?' María leant forward to kiss Alex on the cheek. Taken off guard by such a pretty girl suddenly coming to kiss him, Scott leant forward too but to his left, so instead of kissing on the cheek they ended up bumping noses. An attempt to rectify his mistake resulted in a little nose dance before finally the ritual was accomplished.

'Hi María. I think the last time I saw you, you were still at school. How are you?'

'Good thanks Alex. A bit angry after the drive up from Barcelona. We were stuck in a *caravana,* a traffic jam, for two hours. I would have come tomorrow but Santi wanted these fucking papers from my mother's house today.' She turned to her brother. *'Oye, la próxima vez, vete tú a casa de mamá.'*

Turning back to Scott she said: 'I was saying he can collect the papers himself next time.'

'What you need is a large drink,' said Scott. 'What will you have?'

*'Una copa de cava. Gracias.'*

Scott ordered them all a drink.

'So, how are things? What are you up to?'

'I am an architect in Barcelona, like Santi. But I make real buildings not just *reformas.'*

'Everything you learnt, you learnt from me,' joked Santi. 'No, seriously Alex, María is a great architect.'

'Well here are the papers. What was the hurry?' María said to Santi.

'It is a long story.' He looked at Scott. 'I am working closely with a project…. there is a project to renovate some houses…' Santi looked across the square, 'I told the owner this morning that my grandfather, our grandfather, was the original architect and he got very excited. I said we had some old designs. I said we could compare them…. He might pay a lot of money for them.'

'Well if you sell this man the designs, don't tell Mamá. She thinks they are treasures.' She turned to Scott. 'Alex, our grandfather Albert Prats y Gaspart was an architect who was a friend of Gaudí, he was quite famous before the Civil War, I think there is a street named after him

32

somewhere.' She waved her hand as if to dismiss the notion. 'Well... he was shot in the war and our family lost everything.' She looked at the attaché case. 'He built many of the houses along the coast. And he built much of the Camí de Ronda. All my grandmother inherited from him were these papers. My mother thinks they are priceless,' she said, indicating the long tubular case and the attaché case. She opened the case and brought out a thick file of papers. From beneath the file a notebook fell on her lap. 'Oh *mierda*, I brought that. I meant to leave it with Mamá.'

'What's that?' asked Scott.

'It's the recipe book of my grandfather.'

'Recipes?'

'Oh, you know. Family recipes. Traditional dishes. My grandfather wrote them in prison. We had a tradition in our family of the men doing the cooking. I think it was originally a Basque tradition. Anyway, they are all very good. When my grandmother started the hotel, she started the restaurant with these recipes. The food was very famous.'

'That's interesting,' said Scott. 'What a lovely thing to have of your grandfather's. Can I have a look? I'm thinking of doing an article while I'm here on local food. Maybe I could use some of the recipes?'

'Yes sure,' said María. She handed the worn leather notebook to Scott.

'How lovely,' Scott said turning the pages with care. The pages were covered with handwritten notes and prose and the occasional ink drawn diagram. 'Is it in Spanish or Catalan?'

Santi replied. 'It is in *Castellano*. When my grandfather was in prison after the war, Franco made Catalan illegal – so to be able to write it he had to write it in *Castellano*. He wrote it while waiting to be executed.'

'How sad. Would you mind if I borrowed this for my article? I mean, I can take photocopies. I think it would make a really interesting angle.' He paused. 'That's if you don't mind, of course. I could come and make some copies next week.'

'You can take it now if you like,' said Santi, 'just please look after it or our Mother will kill us. She loves that cook book. Says it is priceless.'

'Ok Santi,' said María, 'I'm handing all the papers over to you. If you can sell the designs great. And Alex, please look after the book. But from now on they are not my responsibility.' She pushed some hair over her ear and turned to face Scott. 'So, Alex, you are a writer?'

'Yes. I do pieces on travel and food. I'm mainly based out of London.'

'Are you here to do the article?'

'Well…yes and no. Do you remember the Franklins? Charlie and his parents Bill and Anne? Their caretaker had an accident and died a few days ago. I've come out to help sort things out for them.'

'Of course, you were good friends with Charlie. I remember you and Charlie used to tease me about my English.'

'Sorry if we were horrid. Well. there's nothing wrong with your English now.'

'I remember when Charlie died. To die so young. So, sad.' She saw the look of sadness on Scott's face. 'So, Alex, will you be here for a while?'

'I think I'll probably stay until at least the beginning of August.'

'Great, you must come down to Barcelona to see me,' she said, putting a hand on Scott's forearm.

'I will definitely do that. How long are you up in Begur?'

'I'm here for the weekend but I have a dinner tomorrow and on Saturday I have a friend's wedding.'

'Ok, well I need to be in Barcelona in the week so I'll give you a call. What's your phone number?'

María gave Scott her mobile number which he put straight into his phone.

'Right, feel like another drink?'

*'Gracias amigo,'* said Santi. 'But I had better get home. I have a meeting very early tomorrow and I need to go through these papers first.'

'Thank you, Alex, but I have a lot to do tomorrow....' said María.

'Next time then. Let me get these.' He said and called for the bill.

They all kissed each other goodbye and Scott carefully put the cookery notebook in his jacket pocket. Scott insisted on paying and they all walked off in different directions.

It was about half past ten when Scott arrived back at Can Daurat. As he approached the house along the drive the security lights came on. He parked in front of the house and in ten minutes had transferred all his shopping to the kitchen and the pantry.

He realised that he hadn't eaten anything since the plane journey so took some of his new cheeses back out of the fridge and broke open a baguette. Selecting one of the red wines that he had just bought, he poured himself a glass and took his little makeshift picnic out onto the terrace by the pool. As he went outside the outside lights came on.

Well, he thought, María had certainly changed. Gone was the little girl that he remembered. He was rather looking forward to his trip to Barcelona. Pity she wasn't around this weekend.

After a few minutes of sitting still, the outside lights went off and Scott sat without moving, enjoying the darkness and the stars in the sky above, the noise of frogs in the woods and the sea breaking down on the shore. Looking out over the pool to the sea, he saw the lights of a container ship crossing the horizon. His thoughts came back to Can Daurat. And Manolo.

Why, in the most calm and serene place, did Scott have the feeling that all was not right? What had Manolo been doing at the cliff's edge? Why had he fallen where he had?

Why did the camera's recording only start after Manolo's accident?

# SIX

Scott awoke confused. Crisp cotton sheets. Ironed. Bright white light. The sound of the waves breaking. The smell of pine trees. He wasn't at home in London. As his eyes adjusted to the light, he began to realise where he was. The morning sunlight lit up the wall of his room with a golden glow. He looked at his watch: 6.30. The doors to the balcony were open and the light cotton curtains swayed in the breeze. He got up and walked outside. Below him stretched the garden, the pool and the pine trees with the sea behind. He blinked at the sun reflecting off the blue Mediterranean. It was a beautiful, cloudless day with a gentle fresh breeze coming in off the sea. This beat the view from his flat in Hammersmith.

Scott put on some shorts, a t-shirt and his running shoes and went down to the terrace by the pool. He worked through his daily wake-up routine of one hundred sit-ups and push-ups, then went out through the gate and down onto the *Camí de Ronda* for his morning run. Originally a fisherman's path, it was rebuilt around the civil war to help the *Guardia Civil*, the state police, in their patrols along the coast to stop smuggling. The picturesque path runs for 43 kilometres in and out of the coves of the rugged Costa Brava. Parts of it are just footpath, other sections have been built into tunnels and bridges. Scott ran south, occasionally running across beaches or through pine and

37

scrub oak woods. The morning began to warm up as the sun rose over the sea. He ran for half an hour, then turned back.

As Scott approached the house, he heard the noise of someone moving inside. How stupid to have left the house open. The terrace doors were wide open and his phone was upstairs in his bedroom. There was nothing on the terrace he could use as a weapon. Scott peered round the doors into the drawing room. The sound was coming from further inside. Dolors had mentioned the intruders. Could he make it to the phone? Scott removed his running shoes and silently crossed the drawing room heading for the stairs. If he could just get to his phone...

'*Buenos días Alejandro,*' came a voice from behind him.

Scott spun round to see Dolors coming out of the kitchen.

'Good morning Dolors, you gave me a shock,' he said, relieved it was her, but a little embarrassed having been caught sneaking into the house.

She was wearing the same black dress as the day before but had a white and blue housecoat over the top. Her eyes were still red and puffy, but she seemed less distraught and managed a smile reminiscent of the old her. Scott gave her a big hug and tried to explain that she needn't come into work, that she needed rest, that Bill understood. She replied that it was important to keep working and that breakfast would be ready in five minutes.

Scott ran upstairs to shower and change into swimming trunks and a t-shirt. When he came down Dolors had brought a tray with his breakfast out to the terrace in the sun. She fussed around him as if he were still the young teenager that she had first met two decades before.

Scott asked her if she would join him so she went into the house to get a coffee. She came back out and sat with him at the table on the terrace. There were a few awkward minutes rehashing the terrible accident, then talk moved on to her future. Dolors said that she had her pension, and that now Manolo was gone she would probably go and visit her sister in Barcelona, but she would like to stay in her house. She could keep coming in to Can Daurat as long as Bill liked.

Scott asked Dolors what she thought Manolo had been doing on the cliff. She said that he had been worried about intruders and wild boar. The fence had been broken a few times and the ground where the garden overhung the *Camí* had been turned over by boar rooting for grubs and acorns. So, he *had* understood her correctly the day before. Wasn't it very rare for the boar to come so close to the sea? Apparently, a large forest fire the previous year had pushed the boar into places where they didn't normally go.

Scott asked how they could get through the fence. Dolors said there were holes all along it and sometimes they forgot to close the front gates. She couldn't understand what Manolo had been doing climbing the cliff outside the fence. The police said that he hadn't suffered. The fall had broken his neck, she said as she crossed herself.

Dolors then started into a long story of how the coast was changing. You used to be able to leave houses unlocked. People had trusted one another. It was all different now, people had no respect for property. Too many newcomers. They had just installed new security and cameras. Dolors said that Russians had been buying up all the houses on the coast. Scott suppressed a grin as he remembered a similar gripe about the Arabs buying up everything years before. A Russian had bought the old lighthouse on the far point. That the same Russian wanted to buy Can Daurat. Scott told Dolors about the estate agent from the day before. She replied that he was working for the Russian. Manolo hadn't had time for him, that Bill would never sell.

Scott's mobile rang. It was Juan calling to say he'd be round in half an hour. Scott told Dolors that it was Juan, that they were going out on the boat. Dolors got up and disappeared inside, insisting on preparing them lunch.

Fifteen minutes later she came out to collect the plates from the terrace. Scott told her not to worry, to go home, that he would clean up. She resisted at first, claiming that she had to look after him but, despite her attempts to hide it, he could see that she was relieved. Scott told her that he was used to being on his own, that especially in these circumstances she need not come in.

Being waited on hand and foot was something that had always made him uncomfortable. Many childhood holidays had been spent with friends in their big houses full of staff and Scott had always found it a bit oppressive and much preferred the freedom of being alone.

He asked her where the gun safe keys were and she said they were normally in the office drawer.

Once she had gone, Scott found the key and opened the cellar door which was along the corridor from the kitchen under the main stairs. The wine cellar was all rough stone, hewn from the rock under the house. It felt icy compared to the heat of the day. Scott browsed the dust-covered bottles. Bill loved his wine. There was an amazing collection. Vega Sicilia, Pingus and Clos Mogador caught his eye. And in the next room Petrus, Yquem. Well, there certainly hadn't been any intruders in here.

In the corner of the second room was a large metal gun cabinet. Scott opened the heavy door and saw five guns. He took them out to have a look. There were three shotguns: a pair of 12 bores and a 16 bore. Next to them were a bolt action rifle and a double-barrelled express rifle. They were beautifully crafted weapons with detailed scrollwork on the metal and stunning deep walnut stocks. With care Scott took out one of the rifles and put it to his shoulder. He looked along the open sights at the bare lightbulb hanging over the door and realised the gun was rock steady in his arms. Not a wobble. It was a masterpiece of workmanship, perfectly balanced. Scott placed the gun carefully back in its felt-lined rack. The combined value of the five weapons was probably more than that of his flat in Hammersmith.

He looked in the drawer at the top of the gun cabinet and saw that there were a couple of gun cleaning kits and several boxes of ammunition. Scott remembered Bill being a keen big game hunter, with trips to Africa and South America. Scott had even been invited on one expedition to Tanzania when he and Charlie were seventeen, although his only weapon had been a 35mm Canon SLR. Bill was an enthusiastic hunter, but always insisted on going to hunt where stocks needed culling, and had been very derogatory about some of the dubious big game hunting in Africa where clients would shoot reared game in enclosed parks. Just one up from shooting ducks in a barrel, Bill had said.

Scott heard a doorbell ring. He locked the gun safe and the cellar door behind him. Going along the hall, he realised the front door must be locked. Shouting out that he was coming, he went back into the office to get the key. He looked at the computer screen and saw the front gates were open. Dolores must have forgotten to close the gates behind her. The front doorbell rang again.

Scott grabbed a huge iron key from the drawer and went back through the house to the front hall. Behind a set of glass doors was the ancient oak front door of the house. It opened with a groan. Behind it was the diminutive *Señor* Camps, with his Brilliantined comb-over and sparking diver's watch.

'Good morning *Señor* Scott.'

'Good morning, *Señor* Camps. Can I help you?'

'*Sí*, can we discuss further the offer of my client?' Camps was doing a side-to-side movement as if trying to get past him into the house, but Scott remained in the doorway, blocking his way. 'My client, he insist. He say that he will pay ten million Euros. It is a very good offer, *Señor* Scott. The house, she is worth seven maybe eight millions. You will tell Mr Franklin?'

'As I told you yesterday, Mr Franklin does not want to sell. I spoke to him yesterday and he was very clear.'

'But you will pass on the offer? Please? Ten millions?'

'Ok, I'll tell him. But I know what the answer will be.'

'The commission for the *agencia* is five percent, of course, as *intermediario*, *Señor* Scott, that commission is half for you. Two hundred and fifty thousand Euros.'

'Well, I'll pass on the offer. Now, really, I have to get going.' Camps opened his mouth to speak but Scott cut him off. 'Yes, I will definitely pass on the offer. Thank you. Goodbye'

With that Scott shut the heavy door and turned the key in the lock. He went back to the office and when he saw on the monitor that Camps had left he waited to check the gate had closed. Scott decided to go for a swim before Juan arrived. He walked round the large rectangular pool to the sea end where there was an ageing spring diving board. He dived in and swam a few lengths, then stopped as the phone in the pool house was ringing. Hoping the caller would give up, Scott stayed in the water. When they didn't, he climbed out of the pool and went into the pool house to the phone on the bar.

'*Sí, diga,*' said Scott, dripping water all over the floor. He had left his towel by the diving board.

'*Buenos días, Señor Scott por favor.*'

'*Sí, soy yo.*'

'Ah. Hello *Señor* Scott. I am Javier Belsario, I am the lawyer for *Señor* Olenka'

'Yes. Sorry, how can I help you?'

'*Señor* Olenka. He is buying Can Daurat. I am his lawyer. I would like to go over the details for the contract.'

'Look, I have no idea who *Señor* Olenka is. Or anything about a contract. This is the first time I have heard the name Olenka. Can Daurat is not for sale.'

'But *Señor*, *Señor* Camps said that…'

Scott had had just about enough of this as he could take 'I clearly told *Señor* Camps about ten minutes ago, that the house is not for sale. Please, do you not understand?'

'Can I come to Can Daurat? We talk? My client *Señor* Olenka is very wealthy. He… He says that he must have the house. What price would the owner want?'

'Look the owner has clearly said he doesn't want to sell. At any price. Now please stop ringing me. I will call you or *Señor* Camps if there is any change. Goodbye.' With that he slammed the phone down. Still dripping water, he walked back out into the sunshine.

The phone rang again. Scott, wheeled round, went back into the pool house and snatched up the handle.

'Look, as I keep saying….'

*'Hola?'*

'…I am fed up with you coming round, phoning, annoying me. THE HOUSE IS NOT FOR SALE!'

*'Hola? ¿Señor Scott?'* The voice on the end of the phone was deeper, different from the lawyer's voice.

'Hello, yes, this is Alex Scott, who is that?'

'Hello *Señor* Scott, it is Inspector Jaume Matas, from the *Mossos d'Esquadra*. You called me yesterday.'

'Oh, yes. I'm sorry. Sorry about that. Someone has been ringing… and I thought you were him. Yes, of course. Thank you for calling back.'

'I believe you represent *Señor* Franklin at Can Daurat. You have some questions regarding *Señor* Ruiz's accident?'

'Yes, I do. Can you hold the line one minute while I go indoors? The line out here isn't too good.'

'Er…*sí*…Yes, OK.'

Scott put down the phone in the pool house and made his way back to the house. He realised he had no idea what he wanted to ask the inspector and needed a few seconds to organise his thoughts. What did he want to know? He felt something was wrong but…he didn't really have anything concrete.

He picked up the phone in the sitting room

'Hello.'

'Hello *Señor* Scott.'

'Thanks for holding. Inspector…er…'

'Matas. Jaume Matas.'

'Inspector Matas. Thank you for calling. What I was wondering was this. Did you think…was there any reason to believe there was anything funny about the accident?'

'Funny?'

'Funny. Not ha ha funny. Odd. Strange. You know. Was there anything out of the ordinary? Well, if you can call falling off a cliff ordinary.'

'No *Señor* Scott. What happened to *Señor* Ruiz was a sad accident. He was an old man, and he fell. Did you know *Señor* Ruiz long?'

Scott realised that this was the first time he had heard Manolo's surname. To Scott he had always been just Manolo.

'I've known him for…' Scott thought, 'over twenty years. An old friend. I hadn't seen him for years, though. The owners of the house here asked me to come out…And… It's just that…. I had a look at the cliff, and it seems strange that Manolo… *Señor* Ruiz… would have been on the cliff, I mean, on the *far* side of the fence. I went there yesterday and even I found it difficult to get to. I can't imagine an eighty-year-old man climbing there. Why would he? And if he had fallen from the cliff, surely he would have landed on the *Camí?*'

'*Señor*, there was nothing suspicious when we arrived. *Señor* Ruiz had fallen and had suffered fatal injuries from falling to the rocks. *Señor* Ruiz would have felt nothing. It is a long fall.'

'But don't you think he would have landed on the path? The *Camí*. I looked down from the cliff and I am sure he would have landed there.'

'No *Señor*, we are satisfied that *Señor* Ruiz fell from the cliff to where we found him. If you have any other reason to suspect something?'

'Did you find out what he was doing on the cliff? I spoke to his wife Dolors, and she says there have been a lot of intruders along the coast. Could he have surprised an intruder?'

'An intruder? Has there been an entrance into the house?'

'An entrance?'

'An entrance. A robbery. Has something been stolen from the house?'

'Well, no. Not that I know of. Everything seems ok.'

'This is my point. There is no robbery. No entrance to the house. No sign of intruders. *Señor* Scott, I understand it is difficult to … to explain… when there is a death…. But it was an accident. *Señor* Ruiz was an old man. He shouldn't have been where he was on the cliffs. He fell. These things happen.'

'Er …but…But there are no recordings from before Wednesday at 10.'

'Recordings?'

'Video recordings. From the cameras. There were new cameras put in last week but the files only start on Wednesday. I think they might have been deleted. The files from earlier in the week'

'The files were deleted? You have evidence?'

'Well, no, not really.'

'*Señor* Scott, if there is no evidence, there is little I can do. Maybe the cameras start recording when they do. I am not a technical. Sometimes these things take time to activate. But *Señor* Scott, this was an accident. No more... As you say, there have been some robberies along the coast. Please, if you are concerned, if you need to call, this is my cellular number.' He read his number which Scott keyed into his phone. 'If you are worried you can call me directly. I must go now. Goodbye *Señor* Scott.'

Scott saved the number under 'Matas Police' in his phone contacts. Matas had not been much help, but he saw his point of view. If something had happened with an intruder, if Manolo had surprised someone who had pushed him off the cliff, Scott supposed it would be almost impossible to prove. Not without the camera recordings or other evidence.

# SEVEN

There was a buzzing noise from the office. Scott saw that the gate intercom was lit up and he could see Juan on the monitor. He pressed the button with the key on it and the gate started to open. He watched Juan get back into his car. Scott walked out the side door.

Juan parked his BMW next to the Fiat. He was the stereotypical Spaniard. Dark wavy hair, olive skin, wearing light jeans and a pastel blue sweater over a white shirt. He got out of his car and gave Scott a big hug.

'*Hombre*…it has been too long. How are you my friend?'

'Hey Juan. You're looking well. Yes, far too long. Come on in, let's get a drink.'

'Good idea. Hey, nice car! Yours?'

'Very funny. It's just a hire car.'

They walked back round the house and into the kitchen.

'So, my friend, what have you been up to?'

'Oh, you know. Work.'

'Still the same? *¿Periodista?*'

'Yeh. Same old business. I'm mainly doing food and travel articles now. It's fun… It pays the bills. It's safe and means I can be out here for a while.'

Scott opened the fridge and got out two beers.

'*Salud.*'

'*Salud. Gracias.* I needed that. So, poor Manolo. So sad. I saw him last week in town. He looked so young for… how old was he? *¿Ochenta?*'

'Nearly, he must have been late seventies at least.'

'Well he still looked the same as ever. You remember the fiestas years ago? Those were the days my friend. *Qué mala suerte.* Bad luck. Was it a *infarto….* er…the heart?'

'No, I've just got off the phone to the police. They say he fell off the cliff. He died from the fall.'

'*Joder.* How terrible. Manolo? Climbing the cliffs? At eighty?'

'Yes. What he was doing there, God knows. I had a look at the spot yesterday and nearly fell myself. There is something about it that doesn't make sense. I would have thought he would have fallen onto the path below. But the police say he fell all the way down onto the rocks. And he knew the shore and those cliffs like the back of his hand.'

'And… there is something weird with the new cameras here. Manolo had just put in a new security system, as there had been signs of people coming in. But I can't seem to find any recording from before Manolo's accident. There should be footage from Monday when they were installed.' Scott saw a confused look on Juan's face and realised he was bombarding him with his worries.

'But enough of that. Let's get some lunch together and get out on the sea.'

Scott picked up the rucksack that Dolors had left out for him from the side.

'And what's your news. Married and kids now, eh? How's that? Are you still working in Gerona?'

'No, we moved from Girona to Begur a few years ago, when my father died. I've got the hotel and Isabel opened her shop last year." Juan pronounced the name of the city in Catalan with an i instead of an e in Castilian. "The kids go to *guardería…er…*'

'Kindergarten?

'Yes, kinder...garden. In Begur. You will meet them this evening. And you? Still *soltero?* What happened to that girl you were with the last time you were here? *Era muy simpática.*'

'Yes, still single,' said Scott who was looking through the picnic rucksack. 'Still looking. Mmm... The last time I was here. Who was that? That was before Charlie died. Who could it have been? No idea.' He looked up at Juan. 'How's family life treating you?'

'My friend, it's different. Wonderful. But different. Hard work.'

'OK, that's lunch sorted,' said Scott who had been adding a couple of little packages from the fridge to the picnic bag as they spoke. 'Let's get a few beers and some wine and get out of here.'

Scott put some drinks in a cold bag with some ice, added a couple of towels from the linen cupboard next to the pantry, and they walked through the house towards the pool.

He handed Juan the bags and went back into the house, shut the outside doors and set the alarm. He came out the side door and joined Juan on the terrace. As they walked down the garden, Juan remarked on how long it had been since he was last here. Since before Charlie's death.

They walked through the pool house and down the spiral staircase into the boathouse. Juan let out a whoop of joy when he saw the *Salacia*. Scott retrieved the key from its hiding place and put the bags in the boat. Juan got in. Scott went to the front of the boathouse and unlocked the dock doors. He turned a winch which slowly opened them, light flooded in off the sea.

When the doors were open, Scott stepped onto the *Salacia*, turned the key and the twin V8 engines roared to life, the noise amplified by the confined space of the boathouse. He unhooked the mooring rope from the dock and edged the throttle forward.

Scott very slowly moved the Riva out of the boathouse, engaging and disengaging the forward gears, once or twice putting the left prop into reverse to help the turn. There were some rocks sticking out of the sea near the front of the boathouse and Scott was careful to keep well clear. Once the Riva had uninterrupted water in front, Scott visible relaxed and leant over to pull in the protecting fenders. Juan brought in the fenders on his side of the boat.

'Had to concentrate there. I'd rather not smash a quarter of a million-quid's worth of Bill's pride and joy on my first day here!'

'*A dónde vamos?*'

'Where to? Mmm... not sure. What's the name of that cave we used to go to? The one just north of here. Just nearing Aiguablava?'

'*Cova d'en Gispert. Si, buena idea,* let's go there.'

'First things first,' said Scott, taking a couple of beers out the cold bag. He opened them, handed one to Juan and sat down on the pristine, white leather driving seat. They were now coming out of the cove and Scott could see that they were all alone on the sea.

'Right. Accelerate to attack speed!'

Scott pushed the throttles forward and the boat leapt forward, straight onto the plane, easily scything through the tiny amount of swell. The Riva's twin V8 engines screamed. Talking was out the question as the boat sped over the waves. Scott grinned with a mixture of fear and exhilaration. He saw the speedometer climb quickly and settle at just over 40 knots.

They carried on up the coast past towering cliffs and rocky bays. In what seemed like no time at all, Juan waved at Scott and pointed to the left. Scott pulled back the twin throttles and steered the boat into a small cove. At the end of the cove was the entrance to a sea cave. Scott cut the engine and threw out an anchor.

'This is it, isn't it? The big cave?'

'Si. *Cova d'en Gispert. Dios mío,*' said Juan, whose carefully combed and gelled hair was now sticking up in a mess, 'what a machine. What a noise. Charlie called it the Rolls Royce of the sea. More like a Ferrari. *¿Te ayudo?* Can I help?'

'It's ok thanks. Let's just anchor here. We'll swim in later. No way I'm getting this thing too close to the rocks.'

Scott spread a towel on the back seat of the Riva and started putting out the food. There was a baguette, some tomatoes, some ham, a couple of local cheeses, half a roast chicken, and some salad. He opened a cold bottle of local rosé and gave Juan a glass.

'So, my friend. Tell me. What of your life? We haven't seen you in, what is it, ten years?' said Juan.

'I suppose so. Charlie died, what… nine or ten years ago? God, how time flies. It was weird yesterday... Coming through from the airport... brought back so many memories. Like I was last here only a few days ago. And it has changed so much. But still the same. Does that make any sense?'

Scott took a slug of wine.

'And it's odd being here on my own. I'll always associate Can Daurat with Charlie. With Bill and Ann, of course, …but I was always here with Charlie. Maybe that's why I haven't been back. When Bill asked me to come out and look after the house…. I wasn't sure...and with no Manolo…'

'I am very glad you came *hermano*. How long do you think you will stay?'

'I'm not really sure. Bill has asked me to find someone to look after the house, that will take a bit of time. It's going to be a bit of a nightmare with Dolors. I can't see her liking someone new taking Manolo's place.

'Well... Bill has said I can stay as long as I like. I've got a few jobs I can do from here. I've been wanting to write some stuff on this area for ages. Good excuse to go to some rather nice restaurants! I've got an idea for a local recipe article. And there are a lot of travel angles… So, I'll probably be here till the beginning of August at least. Bill said that he and Anne are coming out then and it might be weird being here with them, but I might overlap with them for a couple of days.'

'Well, tonight you will meet my family. I will try to get Santi to come.'

'I saw him and María yesterday. I popped into see them in Begur. How times have changed. He said he's really busy with work.'

'Yes, working for the council. He is now a respectable *político*. If that can be called respectable. He is the architect for the council.'

'So he said. So, he approves planning permits? That must be lucrative.'

'Hehe … we're not like Marbella here. Well, not any more. Santi is always complaining that he doesn't get any offers of 'envelopes.' Hundreds of Russians and no …. how do you say…?'

'Backhanders?'

'*Sí*…I like that. Back…handers.'

'So, there are a lot of Russians, eh? One has been trying to buy Can Daurat.'

'They are the only ones buying anything here. There is one guy who has bought many houses. *Un loco ruso*. He just bought the old lighthouse, the one we passed on the way here. Wants to do many changes. Santi has told him it is…*protegido?*'

'Protected.'

'Si. But he wants the *permiso de obras*. So far, he has started works at four houses, he starts the work, loses interest and moves on to another house. *¡Una locura!*'

'Sounds like the same Russian who made an offer of ten mil for Can Daurat… I got fed up with him and told him that Bill wasn't interested.'

'Ten millions? That's a good price.'

'And he offered me half the commission. It would have been two hundred and fifty thousand. That would pay a few bills.'

'You should try him at twelve millions and double the commission.'

Scott smiled at his friend's typically Catalan opportunism. 'Unfortunately, I don't think Bill would sell. He certainly doesn't need the cash, and he loves it here.

'He inherited it from his mother. I think she used to hang out with all the jet set crowd in the fifties. When the Costa Brava was *the* place to be. Didn't they make a couple of films with Liz Taylor or Ava Gardner and that lot along the coast here.'

'Yes, my father used to tell me about those days. My grandmother started my hotel after the war. The civil war, not the war in Europe. There was a time when many film stars came. And Dalí brought many people. My father was young then but remembered Bill's mother well. He said she was very elegant, quite the English lady.'

Scott held up the bottle and Juan held out his glass for some more wine.

'My grandfather was killed by Franco. They took everything. I think before the war many of these houses along the coast were belonging to my grandfather. He was an architect. He built many of them. We had many properties, he was an important man in Begur, not just in Begur, all of Spain, before the war. But he stayed loyal to *la Republica*. He was shot at the end of the war and we lost everything. Some lies about spying for the communists. He was an important architect. He had worked with Gaudí. He built much of the *Camí de Ronda* as well. For the public. You know the tunnels - his idea. Santi knows all about him. He did his project at university on him. That's why he became an architect.'

'Santi and María were talking about him yesterday. I've borrowed his food notebook for my article. Didn't know all that history. Thank God, we've never had to go to war. I can't imagine a civil war. What a nightmare. At least in a normal war you have two different sides. Civil wars are so much,' Scott paused, 'so much more personal. If that makes any sense. Did you ever have to do military service?'

'No, while I was at university it stopped. Thank God.'

'I can't imagine being in the army. Being ordered to shoot someone. I'm not sure I could do it. How lucky we are. Let's hope we never have to find out.'

They both sat there in silence for a moment. Juan got out his mobile phone and dialled. He spoke in Catalan which was in the main lost on Scott, who could only pick up that it was Santi he was talking to, that Scott was here and something about dinner that night.

'No. Santi can't come to dinner.' He said, having finished the call. 'He has to go and look at some works at one of the Russian's houses. *Señor* Alinca.'

'Ahh. That's sad. Could he have said Olenka?'

'Maybe.'

'Olenka is the man trying to buy Can Daurat. Olenka is the name the estate agent gave me.'

Juan shrugged. 'Santi wants to meet later for a drink.'

'Ok, great. Let's hit the town after dinner. I've been missing the nightlife in Begur. How is it. Same as ever? The square seemed quite smart yesterday.'

'It's changed a bit since you were last here. Many places have closed. More sensible. Like us!'

As they finished their lunch, Scott and Juan reminisced over times gone by, occasionally crying with laughter at the memories.

They decided to go for a swim into the cave. Scott made sure the ignition keys were hidden in the boat and the swimming ladder was in place and they both dived into the crystal-clear waters.

They swam the twenty yards towards the cave and then into the dark tunnel. The entrance was small but after a few metres the cave opened up into a chamber one hundred metres long and twenty or so high. They swam until they got to the end chamber where the roof soared into the darkness. Standing on the rocks, waist deep in water, Scott looked back along the tunnel.

'Hey Juan' said Scott, 'remember the cave we found along the coast, inland? The one we almost got stuck in?' Years before they had been exploring a cliff face and had found the entrance to a cave. They had explored it until they got to a point where they had had to squeeze themselves through a narrow gap. Scott could still remember the feeling of claustrophobia, of the rocks bearing down on him. The feeling of rising panic, about being held immobile underground.

'Yes. I'm not sure I'd fit there any more' said Juan, patting his stomach 'did you remember the story of the cave near here they used for the contraband?'

'Contraband? No...'

'*Sí,* it was all over the news. Big news in Spain. A tunnel was found from a house to a sea cave. They had made a train. For the *contrabandistas. Drogas.*'

'No, I didn't hear about that.'

'It was in the news for a long time. They found twenty tonnes of drugs. On the train in a tunnel. It was a kilometre long I think. From the cave to the house.'

'Really. Underground lairs and tunnels to the sea – sounds like a Bond film! Where was that?'

'Oh, not far from here. Towards the south I think. I think in the old days there were many caves used for contraband. Many of these houses were built for the *contrabandistas.*'

'Maybe that's what our Russian is doing with all his houses.'

'Maybe. Shall we go back to the boat? It's quite cold in here.'

'Right you are,' said Scott.

Back on the *Salacia* they sat for a while in the sunshine. Scott heard all about Juan's wife Isabel. They had met in Girona when Juan was working there and got married after a year of being together. They now had two children, Marta and Anna, both at pre-school. Juan was running the family hotel in Begur, which was open all year round. He was trained as a lawyer but seemed much happier with the family life and running a small but successful business.

After a while, the sun went over the hills and they decided it was time to head back. Juan proposed going to have a look at the Russian's lighthouse on the way. Scott pulled in the anchor and started up the engines

In five minutes, they could see the silhouette of the lighthouse. It was an old stone building, built right on the edge of a sheer cliff that rose straight up from the sea. As they came nearer, Scott slowed the *Salacia* down and they could see there was scaffolding attached to the cliff coming down from the lighthouse to the sea below. It looked like they had made a temporary jetty on the rocks at the bottom. As they neared the new makeshift structure, two men appeared and started waving their arms. They were both dressed in black boiler suits and had similar cropped haircuts.

'Let's go and see what they want,' said Juan.

'It looks like they want us to leave,' said Scott. The men were waving their arms.

'Fuck them,' said Juan, 'they don't own the sea.'

As they got to within a few metres of the jetty, they could hear the men shouting something in Russian.

*'Perdón? ¡No les entiendo!'* Shouted Juan back.

'Go. Go away' They had switched to English.

'Goay? *No entiendo. ¿Qué?'*

'Oh, stop winding them up,' said Scott to Juan, then turned to the men 'Good afternoon, can I help you gentlemen?'

'Go away. This is private property. No allow.'

'Well it's called the sea, and it's certainly not private property.'

'This belong Mr Olenka. No land.'

'No, it's no land, it's the sea,' replied Scott. The larger man took out a walkie talkie and said something in what sounded like Russian.

'I had no intention of landing. Come on Juan let's head off,' said Scott, turning the wheel on the boat.

'It really makes me angry,' said Juan. 'They come here, tell me that I cannot go where I like in my seas.' He turned and shouted: 'The coast belongs to all.' Then, turning to Scott, he said in a normal voice: 'It looked like they were building something there. Totally illegal. I'll get Santi to have a look. Ha. That'll fix their 'Goay...''

The rest of Juan's rant was lost in the growl of the engines as Scott accelerated off back out to sea.

In another five minutes, they were back at Can Daurat. Scott had to turn the *Salacia* around and to reverse into the boathouse, and in no time they had her tied up and were up on the terrace with a beer in hand.

# EIGHT

Scott awoke. Where was he? Something was causing him a lot of pain. Had he been in an accident? He moved his limbs. They all seemed to be functioning. He opened an eye and saw from the light coming through the curtains that it was well into the day. Big mistake. The pain in his swollen brain mushroomed. What had he been up to last night? He could only assume it was one of the worst hangovers he had ever felt. Well, not the worst, but certainly a contender. He swung his feet of the bed and sat up, his stomach lurching with a wave of nausea. What he needed was water, a lot of water. And orange juice. And bread. Cheese. Fat. Sugar.

Realising that he was still half dressed, Scott got out of bed. Keeping his eyes as closed as possible, he felt his way out of his room, down the stairs and along the corridor to the kitchen. He grabbed a glass from the cupboard and poured himself a glass of water from the fridge door. He drained it and poured another, then wandered along the corridor, through the sitting room out onto the terrace.

He pulled a chair into the shade under a wisteria plant, his mind attempting to piece together the night before. He remembered going round to Juan's hotel. Meeting Isabel, Juan's wife, and their two daughters. Then after dinner they had gone into Begur. But it was all blank from then on.

Scott saw his mobile was out of battery and went back into the kitchen and plugged it in to charge. It immediately started to beep and vibrate. He left it beeping and buzzing on the counter and walked over to the fridge. He stood staring at the contents of the fridge for a while. What to have? Something simple. He took out a paper wrapped packet of *pata negra* ham that was left over from the picnic the day before. Put a plate on the counter and ripped a large piece of bread off a baguette. He cut a tomato in half and rubbed it on the bread. Some olive oil and the ham. Scott grabbed a cup from the cupboard and managed to make a cup of strong black coffee from the high-tech coffee machine, more by luck than through any understanding of the blinking array of lights.

He took his plate and the coffee, wandered back out to the terrace and sat back in the chair in the shade.

What had they got up to last night? Scott was no stranger to a hangover, but it had been a very long time since he had felt this bad. He had the vague feeling of having done something that he shouldn't have done, the uneasy feeling of guilt. He finished his food and drained the coffee. Only one thing for it. Scott took of his jeans and dived into the pool.

Two quick lengths stripped a large part of the hangover away and Scott felt almost human as he climbed out of the pool. Feeling more up to it, he went inside to check his messages. It was half past two in the afternoon. He saw that he had called María at half past one in the morning. There was a missed call from Bill this morning, two missed calls from Juan, four missed calls from one Spanish number and two missed calls from another Spanish number. Not feeling like speaking to Bill, Scott decided to return Juan's call. After a few rings, Juan answered.

'Hey my friend, finally. Good *afternoon!*'

'Hey Juan.'

'What happened to you?'

'Ugh.' Scott groaned. 'Very good question. What *did* happen to me? What happened to last night? I remember dinner at yours but then…'

'Haha!' laughed Juan. 'You were *en forma,* Alejandro! Where did you go? What was she like? Have you seen Santi?'

'Where did I go when? What was who like? I have no idea what you are talking about…'

'Of course not! After *La Estrella*… you remember? You left with that blonde, *la sueca.*'

*'La Estrella?* We went there? What? I have absolutely no recollection. What blonde? A Swedish girl? Jesus. I have a complete blank. A blonde? The only thing I woke up with was a terrible hangover. Let's back up a bit, where did we go after yours? Everything after that goes a bit fuzzy. Oh, and thanks for dinner by the way. It was delicious. It was lovely meeting Isabel and the girls.'

'A pleasure my friend, you are always welcome. Ok, where did we go? From ours, we went first to *La Caja*, then we had a few drinks at *Gi 96*…We had a few *chupitos* with Ramón in his restaurant, then we went to *La India* for a couple of drinks. You tried to get my cousin María to come out. Finally, we went to *La Estrella* to see if Santi was there and that's where you met your *sueca.* I wanted to go to *El Globo* but you had disappeared with your new friend?'

'Christ. No wonder I'm feeling ropey. What were we drinking?'

Juan laughed.

'I told you not to drink the whiskey in *La Estrella*. Pere is a nice guy but he buys *garrafón.* It's a killer. I was on the beers. I told you.' Scott had a vague recollection of *garrafón* being local bootleg booze.

'Well, tell me better next time. I don't think I've felt like this since I was a teenager. I feel poisoned. Christ, I hope I didn't drive home. If I had got stopped by the police their machine would have exploded.'

'Relax, your car is still here, outside the hotel. '

'Thank God for that. Do I need to apologize to anyone? How bad exactly was my behaviour?'

'You were fine. No problem my friend. Always the gentleman. Did you go to *El Globo*?'

'You are asking the wrong person.'

'I was wondering if you saw Santi there.'

'I'm afraid I can't help you.'

'I've been trying to call him this morning but he doesn't answer. I rang his house but no answer there. I was hoping he had bumped into you. You didn't see him then?'

'I have no idea. Sorry, but I can't even remember going to *La Caja*, let alone what happened at the end of the night. I've got some missed calls from a couple of numbers. But… who was this Swedish girl?'

'I have no idea my friend. Very beautiful. You were talking to her in *La Estrella*.'

'Did you talk to her?'

'No, my friend, she only had eyes for you!'

'I hope I got her number. Beautiful, you say?'

'Very.' Juan laughed. 'One day my friend you won't be so careless with the girls. Especially ones like that.'

'Swedish, eh?'

'Well, she was blonde. She looked Swedish.'

'Well she wasn't here when I woke up. I better check to see who has called…'

'If you speak to Santi, can you ask him to call me?'

'Ok, no probs. I think I'm just going to recover for the rest of the day. Would you and Isabel like to come round for dinner next week? I'll try to get Santi along.'

'We would love to come. What day? Wednesday is bad for us.'

'Thursday or Friday?'

'Both are good for us my friend. I'll see when I can get the *canguro*, how do you say….?'

'Kangaroo? Sorry…er…. babysitter.' Scott's phone buzzed and he saw he had another incoming call, from a local number.

'Hey Juan, I'd better go. Got another call coming through.'

'Ok my friend. Maybe it's la *sueca*. We speak later, *un abrazo.*'

'Laters. *Abrazos.*' Scott said as he hung up. The incoming number was a Spanish number that his phone did not recognise. It was the number that had called four times that morning. Scott accepted the call.

'Hello?'

'Hello Meester Scott?'

'Yes, who is it?'

'Hello Meester Scott. Ferrán. Ferrán Camps. From the *agencia...*'

'*Señor* Camps. What?... How?... How did you get this number?' The last person Scott felt like talking to was this irritating little man.

'You give it to me. How are you Meester Scott?'

'What? Me... I'm fine thanks. Yes...what do you want?'

'Meester Scott, I have spoken to my client and he says he will pay eleven millions. But he must sign this week.'

'Eleven mil...What? Look, I told you.... I told your lawyer.... Mr Franklin does not want to sell. Period. Please. Stop calling me. And don't come round. How many time do I have to say...?'

'But Meester Scott, eleven millions is a very good price.'

Scott's head throbbed. 'I don't care if it's a very good price. I've told you. Mr Franklin does not want to sell. *No quiere vender. A ningún precio. Punto. Adiós Señor Camps.*' He hung up.

What was it with this bloody Russian? Scott had met a few persistent people along the way, but this guy was really starting to bug him. Just because he was some fat Russian billionaire who was used to getting his way.

He tweeted a compliment about Juan's hotel, then decided he'd better ring Bill back.

'Yes'

'Hi Bill, it's Alex. Sorry, I didn't get your call earlier.'

'Hey Alex. How is everything there?'

'All good thanks Bill.'

'You sound a bit rough. Big night last night?'

'Er...yes. You remember Juan?'

'Yes, of course.'

'I had dinner with him and his family last night, then we rather hit Begur a little too hard...'

'Send my regards when you speak to him. And to his cousin Santi. He is on the council now.'

'We were talking about you yesterday. Didn't your mother know all their family in the fifties?'

'Yes. I think they used to be *the* family in Begur before the civil war, but the old boy found himself on the wrong side at the end. When I was young there was only Carlotta. She must have been their grandma. She helped Ma buy Can Daurat. She had the hotel.'

'I was there last night. It's got very smart since I was last here. Oh, by the way, Santi had a whole load of his grandfather's architectural designs. He was going to flog some of them to a Russian who has bought a couple of houses. Did his grandfather not build this house? Would you be interested in the plans?'

'I think he had something to do with the house before the war. Sure, might be fun to have the plans. If you can send me a copy I'll have a look. How is Dolors?'

'She's ok. Still in pieces but bearing up. I tried to mention retiring to her but she was all the usual Dolors - going on about work being the point of life and all. But I think she was secretly glad when I said she needn't come in.'

'Well done. It's going to be tricky making the swap to someone new but I'm sure you'll manage.'

'Oh, Bill. There's an estate agent who keeps coming round. He's desperate to buy the house.'

'What?'

'There's a Russian who wants to buy Can Daurat. His agent offered eleven million and I turned him down.'

'Eleven million Euros. My. That's a good price.'

'Oops. Did I do the right thing?'

'Yes, of course you did Alex. No way I want to sell the place. But that's a lot of money for real estate prices at the moment. He must be loaded or stupid, or both.'

'I think he is one of those bonkers Russian oligarchs, he's bought the old lighthouse across the bay, and apparently two or three other houses. Starts work on them, knocks a whole load of walls down then moves on to a new place.'

'Well he's not getting to knock Can Daurat down. Manolo mentioned something about an estate agent.'

'I wanted to ask you something about that Bill.'

'Go on.'

'Something bothers me about the whole thing. I'm not sure what is it but something's not right. Too many little things out of place. Manolo was worried about something. Well, he must have been, as he put in the new security. Did he say what he was worried about?'

'He was worried that someone was coming into the garden. He said there had been a lot of break-ins along the coast. Why? What's bothering you?'

'I don't know. Probably being silly. Just a feeling…. The police are happy with everything. It's just…. don't worry. It's probably just me….'

'Well, keep the alarm on when you're out. And if anyone breaks in, don't be a hero. It's only a house. Nothing that can't be replaced. Not worth your safety. I think there are panic buttons now. If someone breaks in, just hit the button and get out. I don't want anything happening to you. Just remember it's all insured.'

'Ok Bill. Sure thing.'

'Call if you need anything. And you owe me eleven million euros. Bye Alex.'

'Bye Bill.'

# NINE

Scott entered the house and went into the office by the kitchen. He sat at the desk and had another look at the video files. There were now some new files from the previous day, but still nothing from before Wednesday.

On impulse Scott opened the browser and typed in 'olenka oligarch russian' and was rewarded by over twenty-two thousand results. There were some Facebook results and an Olenka twitter account. The top results were a Wikipedia reference to a Dimitri Olenka who was president of Zoloto OAO; an Alexei Olenka who was captain of the naval vessel Kursk from 1935-7; an Olenka Hotel in Sevastopol. He clicked on the result for Dimitri Olenka. This took the page to a recent article from the Financial Times on a Russian businessmen out of favour with the current regime. The article was based on two oligarchs in London who had taken up residence and were supposedly in semi-exile. Scrolling down the article, he saw the name Olenka and read that a Dimitri Olenka, president of Zoloto industries, had fled his hometown of Sevastopol for being in trouble with the government. He was thought to be based in Europe.

Scott did a search for Zoloto Industries and was rewarded by a Homepage in Cyrillic script with no obvious way of changing to a western European language. The company logo looked like a pile of gold ingots. Scott searched for Dimitri Olenka, and apart from the Financial Times article he had read earlier, there seemed to be a couple of Facebook pages, some more twitter pages and more Cyrillic pages. Clicking on the first Facebook link Scott was taken to a page of someone in their early twenties or late teens, so he went back a page and tried the next link. This page's 'owner' hadn't added a photo, and all the information was confidential.

Scott jumped as his phone vibrated on the desk next to him and began ringing. The screen showed a Spanish number that wasn't amongst his contacts. It looked like the other number that had called him a couple of times that morning. Scott let it ring a few times then answered.

'Hello?'

'Hey...' replied a female voice. 'Hey... it's me.'

It must be the Swedish girl from the night before.

'Hello? Who's that?' said Scott, hoping to get at least a name with which to start things off.

'Hey Alex. It's me. Remember. From last night?'

Wherever she was from, she spoke near perfect English, with only a hint of an accent.

'Hey. Hi...Yes... Sorry. Bad line. Couldn't hear you properly,' lied Scott. 'Hey. Of course. How are you?'

'Good. Did you get to bed OK? I called earlier but you didn't answer.'

Get to bed? He had no idea what she was talking about. Maybe she dropped him home. Or at least saw him just before he came home.

'Yes. Sorry about that. I've been on the phone all day.' Scott paused. 'Sorry about the state I was in. I hope I behaved myself.'

'You were charming,' she said with laughter in her voice, 'but a little ... er.... tired. Are we still on for this today or did you forget?'

Oh no, he must have made plans to do something. Better try to bluff it.

'Of course... What time did we say?'

'You did forget!' She wasn't giving an inch. That same attractive laugh in her voice.

'We said that we...would ...meet...Look, I'm sorry. You're right. I was very, er, tired.'

'We were going to go for a walk along the *Camí de Ronda*. You wanted to show it to me. You thought we could have some lunch and go for a walk.'

'Of course. Now I remember,' he lied, 'but it's so hot today. Instead of a walk, what about going out on the sea?'

'On the old speedboat you told me about?'

'Er...yes...exactly. We could have a bite on the boat. Whereabouts are you? Are you near the coast?' Although it meant he would be stuck with her with no escape route should things go badly, in that event he could always keep the engine running which would drown out most attempts at conversation. He still had some of yesterday's picnic in the fridge, and he could always come up with some excuse to cut short the trip. But so far, she sounded nice enough.

'I'm in Aiguablava. By the Hotel Aiguablava. On Fornells beach.'

'Perfect, I can come and pick you up at the little port. It's just round the corner from here. Or rather round the point. What's the time?' He looked at his watch. 'It's two-ish now, what about I pick you up from the port in half an hour?'

'I will be there. Shall I bring us some lunch?'

'I've got some food for a picnic here.'

'Don't worry, there is a little shop that does some great tapas next door. You will like them.'

'Ok, brilliant. I'll bring the drinks. See you in half an hour.'

Scott walked upstairs to his room, racking his brain for any memory of the girl. He had a vague recollection of talking to someone, but the memory was just a feeling. No images. She sounded agreeable enough on the phone. He liked the sound of her laugh. He wondered what she really looked like. Like many Latins, Juan had always had a fixation for any blonde girl per se, and in the past, he had become besotted with many supposedly beautiful blonde girls whom Scott had thought unremarkable.

Oh well, thought Scott as he walked into the bathroom, it's Saturday afternoon. Silly to be sitting at home licking one's wounds. The unshaven, bloodshot-eyed, shambling wreck that greeted him from above the taps convinced Scott that the brief swim had not quite worked the miracles he had thought. So as not to scare the poor girl, Scott decided to shower and shave before heading out to sea.

A quarter of an hour later, feeling much more human, Scott filled the cold bag with some ice, a couple of bottles of wine and some beers and water. Then he set the alarm, locked the house up and went down through the secret door to the boathouse. Despite the remnants of the hangover this second sortie from the dock was taken with more confidence and in no time at all he was skimming along the tops of the waves going north towards Aiguablava.

As he passed the lighthouse with its scaffolding jetty and tower, Scott saw the same two men from the previous day and gave them a wave. No reply. As he passed the point, he had to swerve round a very large motor cruiser which was coming the other way close to shore. It was an ugly ship, done up with gold and beige livery, and the skipper didn't acknowledge Scott's customary wave as the two vessels passed. A lot of unfriendly people about today, he thought.

He carried on north, passing the cove with the cave where he and Juan had been the day before, and as he rounded the point of Aiguablava he eased up on the throttle. High above him on the cliffs was the white 1960s *Parador* hotel.

Scott turned the corner and headed for the little fisherman's port in Fornells, across the bay from the *Parador*. As he navigated his way through the small fishing boats in the marina he looked at his watch and saw he was on time. He took the fenders out of a locker and attached them to one side of the boat and moored up at the quay.

He took out his phone and sent a message via Whatsapp to Juan:

> Seeing sueca. Do you remember her name?
> Help. Please

Scott was in the middle of organising the icebox in the little cabin on the *Salacia* when he heard someone call out.

'Alex?'

He raised his head up from the cabin. Great ankles. Long legs. Very long legs. Spectacular figure. The girl standing on the dock was certainly very beautiful, in a very Scandinavian way. So, Juan's judgement had been right after all. White blonde hair, fine Nordic face, eyes covered by dark fifties style sunglasses. She was wearing a pink tailored shirt and had white fifties looking trousers cut off under the knee. In one hand, she had a white leather handbag and the other was holding some sort of flat parcel.

'Hello. Can I come aboard?'

'Yes of course, come on...' Scott came up out of the cabin and held out a hand for her to hold. She was wearing inappropriate white shoes with high heels which he was relieved to see she took off before climbing aboard. As she got both feet on to the deck, he leant forward and gave her a kiss on each cheek.

'Morning. I mean afternoon. So, great to see you. Lovely day... Brilliant... What have you got here?' he said, relieving her of the parcel, which turned out to be a tray wrapped in paper.

'These are some tapas from the bar next to my house. You will love them.'

'That's very kind of you,' he said, taking them down into the cabin, 'I'll just pop them in here so they don't fall over.'

'What a beautiful boat. It is very old?'

'She's lovely, isn't she? I think she's from the sixties.' Scott couldn't believe he had forgotten meeting her the night before. She was really very pretty. 'Right, do you want to have a seat there?' He said indicating the passenger seat next to the driver's seat, 'and we'll get on our way. Do you want to give me your bag and shoes and I'll put them below? It's hot today, isn't it?'

There was a beep from his phone. A WhatsApp message from Juan:

> No idea my friend. You went away with her before I could ask. Força al canut

Scott untied the mooring ropes and eased the throttles into forward to take them out of the little port.

'Shall we get out of here and find somewhere with a bit of a breeze for lunch?'

'Good idea.'

He got the *Salacia* onto the plane and, once in the open sea, turned left to go north. The sea was a little bit rougher than on the previous day but the Riva cut through the waves with ease. As they motored along Scott occasionally looked over at her and smiled. She seems to be enjoying the ride, as the wind blew her fine hair all over the place.

They motored north past the long Pals beach and the Islas Medes. The islands were surrounded by a circle of yellow buoys that marked the limits of the nature reserve that they had to go round.

They carried on north for a few minutes until Scott found what he had been looking for. There was a large cove surrounded by steep cliffs. Half way along a cliff there was what looked like a large sea cave. There appeared to be several boats lining up at the entrance to the cave.

As they got to within twenty metres of the boats, Scott cut the throttle and put the engine in neutral. From this viewpoint, light could be seen in the depths of the 'cave.'

'It's a natural arch. Have you been here before?'

'No, this is my first time on the sea.'

'What, first time *ever*?'

'No, I mean, on the sea here. On the Costa Brava.'

'Right... ok... It's natural arch. It must have been a cave for years until the sea slowly wore its way through to the other side. It's called *Roca Foradada*. Those boats are trying to get through to the other side.'

'Will they succeed? It looks too small.'

'They'll make it. We could make it in this. But it's a bit rough at the moment. I don't want to damage this boat. Shall we head up the coast a bit more and we can come back through it later?'

Scott took them back out to sea and they carried on up the coast for two coves until they got to one that had amazing blue-green aquamarine water. There were no other boats. There were medium sized cliffs on the shore with a little sandy beach in the sun.

'I think this will do,' said Scott. He threw out the anchor and then cut the engine. 'I love this little beach. It's only accessible from the sea. We can swim in and have a look later.

'OK. First things first. What would you like to drink? Would you like a glass of wine, we've got some beers, water?'

'What are you having?'

'Well, I need a large glass of water. Then I was thinking of a cold glass of rosé.'

'What a good idea. Can we sit on the cushions?' She pointed to the large white leather cushions that covered the back of the boat.

'Yes of course, you sit there and I'll get the drinks. Are you hungry? Shall we get out the tapas?'

As the girl climbed up onto the back of the boat, Scott brought up the tapas, a bottle of water and a bottle of local rosé wine. He poured them both a large glass of water, and downed his glass in one, then poured two glassed of wine and joined her up on the cushions.

'Now, you must forgive me if we cover much of the same ground as last night. I'm afraid I was stupid and was drinking spirits at that bar we were at. *La Estrella*. The owner buys his alcohol from Andorra. It's basically moonshine, poison. Works destruction on the head and the memory.'

'Is that why I have such a terrible head today? I have been feeling awful.'

'You too? Thank God… I mean… Not thank God you're feeling awful. But… well….'

'I've been feeling very …. shaky. This morning I thought I had eaten something bad.'

'I felt awful too. Thought the world was about to end. Thought it was just me. I really don't know why they sell the stuff. It really is poison. My friend Juan… do you remember him?'

'Yes, your friend in the bar.'

'Yes, Juan, I spoke to him today and he was laughing at me for drinking spirits there. He says it's all contraband. Oh, well, we live and learn. Drink up your water and you can start on the hair of the dog.'

'Hair of the dog?' She said with a concerned expression on her face.

'It's an old English saying. In medieval times, people thought that if you were bitten by a dog, you needed to put a hair from the same dog in the wound and then you wouldn't get any diseases. It means the best way to treat a hangover is with alcohol.'

She drank her glass of water and accepted a glass of rosé from Scott.

'Here is to the hair of the dog. *Budmo!*'

'Cheers! Budmo?'

'*Budmo* is what we say back home when we toast. Or *Dybosia!*' Something in the slight rolling of her Rs had made him think she was Russian, but he wasn't familiar with either of those words. He had a great friend who had lived in Moscow for years and had been out there a few times. And had made many toasts.

'Every foreigner thinks that in the Ukraine we say '*Na Zdorovie*' as they do in Russia.'

Me too, thought Scott. So, she was from the Ukraine. Not Sweden. Nor Russia. 'Well, *salut y força al canut* as they say here.'

'Doesn't that mean strength to your...er...penis?' He was sure she blushed.

'Ah, you already know that toast!' Laughed Scott. 'Well, everyone thinks so. But originally it meant something like heath and wealth. The *canut* was a medieval money purse. Normally made from a bull's testicles! But nowadays, yes you are right, everyone thinks it means that.' Including Juan, he thought.

'Shall we open the tapas?' Scott passed the girl the tray and she pulled off the paper wrapping. Inside was a cardboard confectionary tray filled with little bite sized rectangles.

'These are made by the shop next to my house. They are homemade bread covered in different toppings. Try one.'

Scott tried one that turned out to be foie gras. It was spectacular. He tried another. It was covered with spinach, goats' cheese and pine nuts. Another had *escalivada,* a mix of roasted peppers and aubergines. There was one with a type of tuna paste, and another one with pickled anchovy and an olive paste.

'Wow. These are amazing. What an incredible selection. Thank you for getting them. Far superior to what I was going to rustle up.'

Scott refilled their wine glasses.

'So, I'm sure I asked you last night, but what are you doing here? Are you on holiday?'

'You really can't remember?' She laughed. 'No, I am here on work. I've been here a few weeks.'

'Oh. What sort of work?'

'I work for a Russian company. In relocation. There are a lot of Russians coming to the Costa Brava. I studied at university in London, the European Business School. Do you know it?'

'The one in Regent's park?'

73

'Yes.'

'I know *of* it.'

'Well, when I finished there I got a job with a Russian company in London, but I always wanted to live somewhere warmer, so this relocation job seemed perfect.'

'What did you do in London?'

'I was working as a PA for an executive in a commodities company.' She put down her glass. 'And what about you? You said you were a journalist?'

'Yes, I write mostly travel and food articles. Do you go back to the Ukraine much? Are your family there?'

'My parents are in Kiev. But I don't go there much. The place is in a mess. It's better here. About where do you write travel articles?'

'Well, I've done a lot of articles in Europe, of course. It's so easy to get around now, there's a lot of demand for tourism info. I did a few pieces on walks in forgotten historic places... well, places off the beaten track. The Pyrenees, with all the Cathar castles in France; the Carpathians... Last year I did a fun article on bath houses across Europe. Now and again I try to do something that takes me further afield. I've been to Africa a bit. To Asia.'

'And you are writing an article here? You said last night that you were looking after the house, and something about someone dying. I don't remember well...'

'Yes, it's really sad. Manolo, the guy who used to look after my friends' house, the owners of this boat, died on Wednesday. He fell from a cliff. Killed himself.'

'He killed himself?'

'No, I don't mean he killed himself as in suicide. I mean the fall killed him. He fell from the cliffs in front of the house.'

'How sad. It's a beautiful house. Well, the outside anyway.'

'Did you drop me off last night?'

'What? You don't remember? You were trying to get me to come in for a nightcap.'

'And you…?'

'It was too late and I had to get home. But it was a nice idea.' She said with a coy smile.

'I'll have to try harder next time.'

'Yes.' She said, holding his gaze. 'You must. You came out a few days ago, no? To look after the house? Why?'

'Yes, well, it's a long story. I had a great friend, Charlie, who died many years ago. We were at school together. Had been best friends for years. I used to come out here to the Costa Brava to stay a lot when I was younger. I know the house and the area well. A couple of days ago Charlie's father needed somebody to come out and look after the house. Someone who they could trust. So, they asked me. And I can move at short notice. I'll probably stay here till the summer. Thought I might write a couple of articles on the area.'

'And your family? They are in England?'

'What's left of it. Well, in Britain. My parents died years ago, and I've got an uncle and aunt who live up in the north of Scotland.'

'Oh, I'm sorry.'

'Don't be sorry. You didn't kill them. Sorry. That's a bit crass.'

'They were killed?'

'It was a long time ago. They died in a car crash. In the Alps. We were all going skiing and a lorry hit some ice and then hit us. We were knocked of the road. I didn't have a scratch.'

'How old were you?'

'It was just before my sixteenth birthday.'

'How awful.'

*'C'est la vie.* These things happen. Anyway, the Franklins, that's the people who own the house here, they were amazing. Use to invite me everywhere. They became like a second family. Charlie, their son was a great guy. God, the trouble we used to get ourselves into here. Then Charlie

died and...' Scott paused. 'Well, that's all a bit morbid. More wine?'

'Yes please.' Scott poured them another glass of wine.

'And how is the relocation business?'

'Oh. It's OK. Not difficult really. At the moment, I am trying to find a large house on the coast. Do you know of any?'

'What, to rent or for sale?'

'Both. I have some parties coming out soon. One needs a big house like yours. Fully furnished. For a month. And another wants to buy.'

'I can ask around for you.'

'Thank you. That's really kind. Your friends. Would they be interested?'

'I can ask. But I seriously doubt it.'

'They are English? From London like you?'

'They are from London but they are Americans. Well, they have a house in London. They have houses everywhere.'

'The people who want to rent, they will pay well. They are coming out this next week. Could you ask them for me?'

'But where would I go?'

'Well... You could stay at mine.' The same coy smile.

'Well, that's a very tempting offer.' Hello, thought Scott, things are definitely getting interesting... 'But I'm afraid they'll say no. The house is full of their things. It's more a family home than a holiday home. And they don't need the money.'

'What do your friends do?'

'Bill Franklin made a packet in banking years ago. Now he runs loads of companies and sit on lots of boards.' He stood up. 'Now, it's getting rather warm. Fancy a swim? Shall I get you a towel?'

Scott climbed down through the cockpit and went into the little cabin to get out a couple of towels.

The girl, whose name still eluded Scott, had taken off her shirt and trousers and only had on a smart fifties-style white bikini that hid nothing of her spectacular figure. If only Juan could see this, thought Scott.

He removed his shirt and shorts and they sat on the cushions in their swimsuits with their wine.

'Did you see those islands we passed on the way up the coast?' he asked her.

'Yes.'

'They are an amazing nature reserve. Called the *Islas Medas*. It's got some of the best diving in the Mediterranean. Do you dive?'

'Scuba? Yes. Well, I have my PADI. I learnt last year. I went to Egypt, the Red Sea. Very beautiful.'

'I don't know the Red Sea. Never been to Egypt. Well, the diving here is great. The Medes is the largest dive centre in the western Mediterranean. I was thinking about going there for a dive. It's really unspoilt. Most of the coast here has been ruined by boats anchoring. Like we are doing now. Along this coast, the sea bed is a virtual desert. The anchors have scraped all the life off the rocks. But in the Medes there is coral, loads of fish and wildlife – it's like being somewhere on a reef. It's sad really, seeing what the coast should be like. But great diving. And loads of caves to dive. Would you like to come? We can fill some tanks and dive from this.'

'Well…I'm not really very good. I've only just done my PADI.'

'Don't worry. We won't do anything too deep. You need to have a licence, like your PADI, to dive there. I have dived there loads of times. There are a couple of scary caves but we can steer clear of them. It'll be fun. I'll look after you. You on?'

'Ok, if you are sure. When were you thinking of going?'

'What about someday next week?'

'OK that would be great.' She said with a smile.

'So, have you seen much of the area?'

'Not really. I spent a night in Barcelona when I arrived, then came straight up here to Begur. This is my first time out on the sea. It is the most beautiful coast. I had never heard about it before.'

'I agree. I think it beats the Côte d'Azur and the Costa del Sol hands down. They are the most famous stretches of coast but it's so much more beautiful here. I think it's the little coves and beaches. And it is relatively unspoilt. In August, it gets a little busy like anywhere now in the Mediterranean, but this time of year it's incredible.' He paused. 'Right, feel like a swim to the beach?'

'In a minute. I've just got to make one call. To my boss.'

'Working on a Saturday. That's industrious.'

'Sorry about this… won't be a second.' She got down from the cushions, retrieved her phone from her handbag, made a call and had a brief conversation in what sounded to Scott like Russian. Scott didn't understand any of it, apart from her mentioning his name.

'All good?' He asked her when she had finished.

'All fine. Do you speak Russian?'

'Not a word.'

'It was my boss. Asking me to check my emails. To see if the clients have been in touch. I said I was out on the sea with you. What a bore. Won't be long.'

She started typing on her phone.

'Oh no. I can't seem to get data on my phone. It's my new sim card - I've been occasionally having problems connecting. Would you mind if I quickly checked my emails from your phone? Would that be ok?'

'Yes of course. No problem. If it works. We might be getting no data where we are. I'll check.'

Scott got his own phone from the cabin, unlocked it and opened the browser. It opened up on the last page he had been on – the results for a search for Russians on the Costa Brava. He deleted that page and did a search for Islas Medas. A google page showing results appeared after a second.

'Everything seems to be working fine. Here. It's open on the browser.' He said, handing her the phone.

'Thank you, Alex. That's really kind. I won't be too long.'

'Don't worry, I'm on some European data package. Use all you want. Oh, I haven't saved your number to my phone, could you put it in the address book?'

Scott left her tapping away on his phone and cleared up the remains of their lunch and put the glasses in the cabin. He got the wooden ladder out from under the cushions in the locker next to the engines and attached it to the back of the boat.

When she had finished on the phone she returned it to Scott and as he put it away in the cabin, he had a surreptitious glance at his list of calls. Now, instead of a Spanish mobile number, 'Natalya mobile' was the last number. Now he had a name.

He took the keys out of the ignition, and hid them along with his phone in one of the cupboards in the cabin.

'All done?'

'Yes, I'll race you to the beach.' With that she took off her sunglasses and dived in. Scott climbed up onto the cushions and dived in after her. She was a strong swimmer, and Scott had to push himself to catch up. They swam the 20 or so metres to the small beach, then walked up a few metres and flopped down next to each other on the sand.

As she turned round, Scott was struck by the brightness of her green eyes.

'Wow.'

'What?'

'Your eyes, they are so green.'

'And yours are so blue.' She moved her face closer to his.

'Gave me a shock. You had them hidden under your sunglasses. Are they always that green?'

'Yes. Are yours always that blue?'

'As far as I know.'

'This is beautiful.'

'Very beautiful,' he replied without taking his gaze form hers. 'It's lovely here. So unspoilt. There is no access from the land. It's stopped it becoming ruined.'

'So, no one can disturb us?' She raised an eyebrow.

'Not unless they come by sea. And there are no boats about.'

She leaned over and kissed him.

# TEN

It was half past seven when the shade from the setting sun covered the beach and they decided to swim back to the *Salacia*. They climbed up the wooden ladder and he handed her a towel.

'Here you go. I suppose we'd better get going before it gets dark.'

'When is that?'

'Sunset should be in an hour or so.'

'Oh, will we see the sunset over the sea?' she said with excitement in her voice.

'Unfortunately not. The sun sets over the land in the west. This coast is best for sunrise.'

'Well, maybe we should stay here till then?'

'I'd love to. But I'm not sure about the weather. Wouldn't want to be out here all night if the wind got up. But we could do a night on board some other time.'

Scott brought up Natalya's clothes from the little cabin.

'Here's your stuff. It'll get cooler once the sun goes over the hill.' He handed her the clothes and brought in the wooden ladder while she got dressed.

'Shall we try that arch on the way back?' She nodded. Scott put on his shirt, started the engines and pulled in the anchor. They returned the way they had come, and approached the natural arch from the north. By now all the other boats had gone and they had the place to themselves.

Scott manoeuvred the *Salacia* into position and they slowly navigated the arch. As they entered the tunnel, and the gentle swell of the sea brought the roof of the arch to within a metre of their heads at its lowest point. The arch was about fifteen metres long, and they drove through without talking, Natalya resting her hand in the small of Scott's back, with only the gentle gurgle of the twin engines reverberating around the confined space.

'See, no problem,' said Scott once they were through, letting out his breath.

'Do we have to go back now?' she said as they emerged from the arch. 'It's been so lovely. Could we not just anchor in a safe place?' she said and kissed him.

'There is nothing I'd like better,' he said when they broke apart. 'But I really need to get her back on a mooring. The weather here can change so quickly. It's not called the Wild Coast for nothing.'

He pushed the throttles down and they sped off south. They passed the Medes Islands and the long Pals beach and, in no time, came round the point of Aiguablava. The sun was now well below the horizon, and the sky was an amazing mix of pink orange and blue. He navigated the rocks at the entrance to Fornells harbour and pulled up at the same quay where he had met Natalya.

'Well, here we are.'

'Would you like to come back to mine? I could make us some dinner? Could you not leave the boat here? I'm sure it will be safe.'

'That's a lovely idea. But I'd better get her back home. I tell you what. Why don't I pop her back and I can come and join you for dinner?'

'Would you like me to ask if you could leave it here? It would save you having to go back. I can ask at the hotel, I'm sure they will know.'

'Don't worry. I won't be long.'

'But I'll only be a second. I'll quickly go and ask.'

'No really.' He insisted. 'I'd prefer to get her back to Can Daurat. She's a very valuable boat and if anything happened to her…. I'm just not sure about leaving her here. No, I'd better get back.' He was flattered by her insistence that he stay. She seemed put out by the thought of him leaving her, if only for a while.

'But don't worry, I'll be back here in no time. I'll pop over in…damn… completely forgot. I left my hire car in Begur last night. Could you come and pick me up from the house? Then I can pick up the hire car from Begur later.'

'You would like me to come over to the house? Ok. No problem. Look. It's so beautiful. The sky. I'll come and pick you up if you have a quick drink with me now. At the hotel. The terrace will be amazing in this light. It's been such a lovely afternoon, don't let's end it quite yet.'

'Ok,' conceded Scott, 'but just one drink. I've got to get her back before it's gets dark or I'll never get her into the dock.'

'I'm so glad,' she said, her manner lightening. 'Let's have a cocktail.'

She gathered up her things and Scott held her hand as she stepped onto the quay. He tied up the *Salacia*, making sure the fenders were the only parts rubbing against the concrete of the quay. He realised he had forgotten to bring any shoes. So, he grabbed his phone, his wallet and the keys and joined Natalya barefoot.

'I hope they don't mind bare feet in the bar.' He said as they walked along the port towards the hotel that made up most of the buildings of the small fishing village. They walked the twenty or so yards up the hill and through a little gate that took them up some steps onto the terrace of the hotel. From here they had an amazing view of the whole of Aiguablava bay.

'Now, what would you like?' asked Scott, looking round for a waiter.

'I'll order from the bar,' she said. 'I need to go to the toilet. What would you like?'

'A vodka fizz would be great. Just ask them to make a Gin Fizz with vodka.'

'I will have one too,' she said and walked inside. He watched her walk to the bar and lean over to talk to the barman. She then disappeared into the hotel. Scott sat at one of the tables on the terrace. He marvelled at how a day can change. This morning he had been sitting nursing a terrible hangover fully intending to spend the rest of the day in bed or moping around the house, and here he was in a beautiful bar about to have a sunset cocktail with a spectacular girl who was great company and certainly taken with him. What a great way to pass a Saturday afternoon.

She came back to the terrace and they sat there talking. Scott occasionally cast a worried look at the ever-darkening sky.

'What's taking that barmen?' he said after they had been sitting for about fifteen minutes. 'It can't take that long to make a drink. And there is no one else here.' He walked to the doors of the bar and waved at the barman, making a drinking motion and then palms apart motion. The barman waved back mouthed '*ahora mismo.*'

By the time the barman brought the drinks and an impressive selection of olives and nuts, the sky was lapis lazuli blue scattered with a few bright pink clouds.

'I'm afraid I'm going to have to neck this and get going or I'll never get the boat back in,' said Scott.

'It's about nine now, would you be able to come and pick me up from my house at ten, ten fifteen?' he said, draining his glass and standing.

'Er… yes…of course. Are you sure you can't stay?'

'Great. I'll see you then.' Scott gave Natalya a quick kiss, went into the bar and paid their bill, then ran down the little lane towards the port. He turned to wave but she was on her phone and not looking in his direction. The street lights were just coming on. Scott edged the *Salacia* off the quay and out into the open sea. Once he was out of the port and away from the street lights his night vision improved, but he estimated he only had a quarter of an hour before total darkness. This was cutting it bit fine.

Rounding the point before Can Daurat he saw that the big motor yacht from earlier on in the day was now moored in the bay off the lighthouse's makeshift jetty. He carried on round the point and saw a glimpse of the whitewash of the house in the trees up ahead. The hill above the house was now in shadow and loomed over the bay.

As he approached the boathouse he slowed right down. Although he felt confident he could navigate back into the dock, the light was bad and he didn't want to make a mistake in the fading light. Nearing the channel, he noticed a speed boat near the shore, fifty yards along from the boat house. It was six or seven metres long with some sort of driving console in the middle. He couldn't see anyone on it, it should certainly not be moored there.

As he slowly navigated the pitch-black water, he wished he had left a light on in the dock to guide himself back in. He put out fenders on both sides of the *Salacia* and entered the channel at the slowest possible speed. When he judged himself to be in the right place he turned the wheel, put the right engine into reverse and held his breath as the fifty-year-old Riva slowly turned, its mahogany hull inches away from the unforgiving pale pink rock, now a cold grey in the gloom. When the bow was pointing at the black gaping mouth of the boathouse dock, he put the right throttle into forward for a second or two before cutting both engines and gliding in to the dock. He reached out into the darkness with the boat hook and it held, which was enough to stop the momentum of the boat. He took up the stern rope, stepped up onto the dock and tied the rope onto the nearest thing he could feel, which he assumed was a cleat, but by now he couldn't see anything in the dark.

Once he was sure the *Salacia* was tied up to something that wasn't going to move, he felt his way towards the door where the light switches were. The bright halogen lights completely blinded him for a second.

He made sure the *Salacia* was tied up properly, albeit facing into the building, and shut the dock doors. Now that's done, on to the evening's entertainment, thought Scott as he ascended the spiral staircase. Compared to many girls he had known, Natalya seemed remarkably keen for a first date. Well, to be accurate, it was their second date. She had seemed so unwilling for him to leave. He didn't want her getting too attached. She was a charming girl, very pretty and attractive, and as long as she didn't start taking things too seriously, he couldn't think of a better companion with whom to spend a few weeks. Just the memory of their lovemaking on the beach put a spring in his step.

Scott turned off the lights in the pool house and walked out onto the dark terrace, expecting the outside security lights to come on. But they didn't. He was sure they had been working the other night, and he could remember turning the switches on. As he crossed the terrace towards the house he realised that none of the outside lights had come on.

Then he heard a noise from over by the cliff. Not a natural noise. A scape of metal against something. Either rock or more metal. He froze and listened. Nothing. He waited. Nothing. Maybe he had imagined it. In his bare feet, without making a sound, he walked across the tiled terrace towards where he had heard the noise. As he entered the trees, he slowly felt his way, trying to make as little noise as possible. He strained to listen out for anything above the distant roar of the waves far below. He had just decided that it was nothing, and had turned to go back to the house when he saw a blur come out of the darkness and something very hard hit him across the head.

# ELEVEN

For the second time in twenty-four hours Scott awoke with a splitting headache. This time he was lying in the dark, on grass and pine needles. He could hear the sea close by, and frogs croaking. Where was he? And why did his head hurt? He tried to remember. He remembered going out on the boat. He remembered Natalya. They had been out on the boat. They had swum to the beach. He could definitely remember the beach. He remembered their cocktail at the hotel. His tricky arrival back in the dock at dusk. The outside lights had not gone on. He had gone to investigate a noise. Then nothing.

He looked at his watch, the luminous dial showed quarter to ten. He couldn't have been out of it for more than a quarter of an hour. He looked around. He was in the pine trees at Can Daurat, on the seaward side of the pool, over by the cliff.

He sat up and it felt like his head exploded. He gingerly touched the back of his head and found a bump with what felt like some clotted blood. Either he had fallen or something had hit him very hard. He got to his feet by holding onto the nearest tree.

Another blast of pain racked his head, and, feeling slightly sick, he paused, holding on to the tree before heading towards the pool house. He walked barefoot over the pine needles trying to get his thoughts together. As he stepped onto the paving, the pool house's outside security lights came on, bathing the terrace and the pool house in light. These had definitely not been working before. He walked into the open door of the pool house. No one there. He poured himself a large glass of water at the bar.

Something had hit him across the back of his head. He could remember the feeling that something was rushing out of the dark. Someone had hit him with something hard. He had been walking towards the cliffs and the fence, investigating a strange noise. Maybe this is what happened to Manolo. Thank God he hadn't gone the same way. He picked up his phone and was about to dial 012 for emergencies when he remembered he had the policeman's number on his phone. What was he called? He typed in 'police' and 'Matas police' appeared. He dialled.

'*Si, digui'm!*'

'*Hola*, hi… is that inspector Matas?' Scott was not feeling up to having this conversation in Spanish, and he remembered that Matas' English had been very good.

'Yes, who is this please?'

'Hi, it's Alex Scott. We talked the other day. About Manolo. *Señor*….er….' He couldn't remember Manolo's surname.

'Ah yes. *Señor* Scott. *Señor* Ruiz's accident. Yes. We spoke yesterday.' Matas sounded irritated. The first time they had spoken he had seemed helpful enough. 'How may I help you? It is late; I am not at the *comisaría*.'

'I have just been attacked. Here at Can Daurat.'

'Attacked? By whom?'

'I don't know. I heard a noise in the garden and I went to look, and all of a sudden I woke up in the trees with a big bump on my head. I was over by the cliff. Where *Señor*… Where Manolo was when he supposedly fell.'

'And the attackers? Are they there? What happened to them? You saw them?'

'No. It was dark. But it wasn't long ago. I'm not sure how long. Maybe only a minute or two. They might still be here. But the lights are working now.'

'The lights?'

'The security lights. They came on when I came back towards the house. But they weren't working earlier. They go on with movement. So, no one has walked by here in the last few minutes. But they might be in the house.'

'Ok, calm down. Where are you now?'

'I'm in the pool house.'

'I know it. Lock the door and I'll be over in five minutes. Don't go up to the house. I live very near, five minutes away. It will be quicker than calling for … er… backup.'

'Thank you.'

'Just wait where you are. Lock the door. I'll be there soon.'

He rang off. Scott went to the doors but decided against locking them. They were floor to ceiling glass doors, if anyone wanted to get through them they wouldn't provide much security. He checked the door to the staircase which was shut. He remembered there was a games cupboard next to the bar. Opening the door, he thanked God the Franklins were American and selected a shiny aluminium baseball bat. Well, if they came back, at least he had something with which to return the favour.

He went over to the bar, thinking that he could always hide in the boathouse below. That's if the intruders didn't know about the staircase. Had the secret door been open when he got back? No, he was sure he had opened it himself. His eyes went to the shelves next to the door. Whisky. Just what he needed. He picked up a tumbler and poured himself a couple of fingers of a nice looking sixteen-year-old Lagavulin. He sat on one of the wicker bar stools, keeping his eyes on the windows and the doors to the garden. The peaty, medicinal taste of the whisky made him feel much better. He had just poured himself a top up when his phone went. It was Natalya.

'Hey Natalya.'

'Hi Alex. I'm just on my way over.'

'Er…. wait. Don't come over. Something has happened. There was someone here when…The police are coming round.'

'What? What do you mean? What has happened?'

'I got attacked. Hit on the head.'

'What? Are you all right? Are you hurt?'

'I'm fine. Just a bump. But they may still be here. Don't come over now. The police are on their way.'

'But…' Natalya started to protest.

'I'm fine, really. I'll call you in a while. I'd better go now.'

'Are you sure? Call me. I'll come straight over. And Alex?'

'Yes?'

'Be careful.'

He hung up the phone. The security lights had just come on again.

# TWELVE

*'Hola! Hola! Señor Scott?'*

Scott went to the window and saw a sprightly looking, grey-haired man in his forties with an automatic pistol in one hand and a torch in the other, who was coming round the side of the house.

'Inspector Matas! Over here!'

Matas put his torch in his pocket and walked across the terrace and down the steps towards the pool house, the gun lowered but not holstered.

*'Señor Scott.'* He said coming through the doors. 'Jaume Matas. Are you OK?' Scott saw his eyes flick to the baseball bat in his hand, then to the bottle of whisky and glass on the bar.

'Well, apart from a bump on the head. Yes.'

'Let me see.' Matas came over to Scott and had a quick look at his head. 'You are all right. Now, you said someone hit you. Did you see them?'

'No. I was walking over there... out in the garden.... I went towards the fence. The cliff.'

'Did you see who hit you?'

'No. It was too dark. I ... er...something hit me. Then I woke up on the floor under the trees.'

'Ok, let's be calm. I need to check the area. Have you seen or heard anyone?'

'No. Since we spoke, there hasn't been anything. The lights haven't come on or anything. Not until you arrived.'

'Ok. You wait here. I will check the house. Don't move from here.'

Matas shone the beam through the trees. The tiny, powerful torch lit up everything up to the fence. Then he walked back up the stairs and disappeared round the side of the house. Suddenly the noise of frogs stopped. A couple of minutes later he appeared again from the other side of the terrace, this time with just the torch in his hands. Scott saw he had holstered his gun. He came down to the pool house.

'Well, *Señor* Scott, I have checked around the house and there is no sign of anybody and no sign of break in. Will you come with me, we can check inside?'

'This way,' said Scott, leading the way round to the kitchen door. At the door, Matas held out his hand. Scott passed him the keys. Matas opened the door, and they heard the beeping of the alarm.

'Please, the alarm,' said Matas, standing to one side. Scott went into the office and punched in the alarm code.

'Well, it doesn't look like they got into the house,' said Scott turning on the lights as they walked in to the kitchen. 'There are sensors on all the ground floor doors and windows, the alarm hasn't gone off. Maybe I disturbed them before they could break in. It's odd the lights weren't working when I arrived.' Scott paused. 'Thank you for coming round. Can I offer you anything? A coffee? Water?'

'Thank you. But I must be getting home. *Señor* Scott, I realise... the death of your friend... it is very sad. But there has been no entrance here. You say you did not see anyone?'

'Well, no, I didn't actually *see* anyone. I couldn't... it was dark. But I felt something. Well, someone hit me over the head. I didn't just fall over...'

'*Señor* Scott, I think you are upset about your friend. You have a drink too many... yes?... You fall...'

'Hold on a second, the whisky… I… that was after I was hit. Look, I got back just as it was getting dark. There was a boat moored just along the shore. They must have come from that. It is easy to climb up the rocks to the garden. I came up from the boathouse and the garden lights weren't working. They definitely weren't working. They must have turned them off.' Scott paused. 'As I came out from the pool house I heard a noise. It wasn't a natural noise. A scraping noise. Or a metallic noise. Anyway, something didn't fit. It came from over by the cliffs. By where Manolo died. I went to have a look. As I was walking through the trees, someone hit me on the head.' He put a hand to the back of his head. 'When I came to the lights were back on. I went straight to the pool house. That's when I had a drink. That's when I called you.'

'*Señor* Scott, this is a small town. I heard that you were very drunk last night. There was a complaint, but I saw your name and I spoke to the person. I explained that you were upset. But you need to…'

'What? What are you talking about? What complaint?'

'There was a complaint that you were drunk and not in control. I was in the *comisaría* and I spoke to the person. But you need to calm down. You…'

'That's absolute bollocks. OK, I had a few drinks with some friends. But there was no complaint. Who complained?'

'I cannot tell you that. But I can tell you it was a member of the public who…'

'I can't believe this. If I don't know who it was, how can I defend myself? This is ridiculous.' Scott was stunned. He had just been attacked and now he was having to account for *his* behaviour when out the night before.

'*Señor* Scott, the complaint was not… after I spoke with the person they did not pursue the matter. There is no need to worry.'

'I'm not worrying. But this is all total nonsense. Who was it? And it has nothing to do with what happened this evening. Someone was on the property and hit me.'

'I'm sorry, but there is no evidence. Everything seems to be correct here. Can I ask you, before your er...accident, have you been drinking today?'

'Well, I had some wine at lunch. But that's... Look, I didn't fall. I was hit. I can remember seeing something coming out of the dark. I *definitely* did not fall. And the lights. How do you explain that they weren't on? And then they were. Wait a sec. The cameras. The light could have been turned off from outside, but the cameras are controlled from inside the house. Let's look at the camera footage. That will show us.' Scott pulled Matas into the office and sat in front of the computer. He moved the mouse and the screen came alive.

'This will show us. There is footage from all over the garden.' Scott told Matas, who had come into the office and was standing behind him. He opened the file that held the recordings. There was nothing from that afternoon.

'What? I can't believe this. There are no files. I know I left the cameras on. I checked before I left. I can remember making a point to do it.'

Matas shrugged and was about to say something but Scott interjected:

'The cameras. Don't you think it's rather strange that twice the cameras have failed to record something? Both times when they were needed? Why are there recordings from any time since they were installed, *except* from when Manolo fell and from this afternoon?'

'*Señor* Scott, I am not a technical person. But if the cameras are not recording, maybe you did not turn them on. That does not signify, how do you say it, foul play? The cameras are controlled from here, no?'

'Yes.'

'Well, when we came in, the alarm was on. So, someone would have had to enter the house, turn off the alarm, then

94

turn off the cameras, then put the alarm back on. And for what reason? Nothing is stolen. I'm sorry *Señor* Scott, this is not probable. Look, I came over as I live close by. I find you drinking whisky having fallen over. There was no attack. I am not angry but I must get back to my family. Please... no more of this.'

'*Señor* Matas, listen.' Scott took a deep breath to calm himself down. 'I can assure you I am not drunk. I don't know who complained, but today I saw the person I was with last night and she can corroborate that there was no bad behaviour. Certainly, nothing that needed a 'complaint.' I may have had some wine over lunch, but not enough to confuse being hit over the head. I am not making it up. There is something strange going on here but I have no idea what it is. There is something not right about Manolo's death. I can't believe it's a coincidence that he so called 'fell' from the cliff and a couple of days later I am attacked in nearly *exactly the same* spot. I agree with you that none of this makes sense, but I know what I saw. The lights were turned off when I arrived back from the sea and when I left I can remember making sure everything, that is the lights, the cameras and the alarm, was turned on.'

'*Señor* Scott,' said Matas, 'I think I have been more than patient with you. It is late and I am going home. Please stop with these fantasies of yours. I am sorry for your loss, but enough. *Basta ya!* We are busy, we do not have the time. If you waste more police time we might have to take matters further. So please, no more wine, no more cocktails, no more whisky, no more ridiculous stories. Please could you open the gate, I climbed over it to get in and I have left my car on the road. Goodnight *Señor* Scott.'

Matas left by the kitchen door. Scott went to the office and opened the gates. He went back to the desk and watched Matas walk down the drive and out the gates on the screen and then closed them.

He was pretty certain he hadn't told Matas about the cocktails at the hotel.

# THIRTEEN

Scott called Natalya after Matas' departure and, after a brief explanation of events, she insisted on coming over. Armed with his baseball bat and a powerful torch, he then made a quick circuit of the house, garages and garden to check nothing was missing or had been broken into. He walked through the trees towards the sea. When he reached the fence by the cliff he shone the torch down towards the shore. The strong beam of light lit up the boathouse with its closed doors over to the left and, shining it further along, he saw the speedboat had gone. He heard a car horn from the road and ran back up to the house and opened the gates. He walked out and round to the front of the house.

Natalya's little VW Polo crunched to a stop on the gravel and she was straight out of the car and fussing over Scott. She insisted on going straight inside and examining his head in the kitchen. She had changed into a light summer dress and espadrilles with laces tied round her ankles. Scott gave her a kiss and she told him to behave while she looked at his head. He put his arms round her waist but had them swatted down. After lots of protesting that he was fine, she asked to hear the whole story. He started to describe the events, then thought it would be easier to show her where it all happened. He took her through the house and out onto the terrace.

'This is a beautiful house. Where were you attacked?' asked Natalya.

'Down there,' said Scott, pointing to the trees next to the pool house. 'There, under the trees. Don't worry, the policeman checked there was nobody around anymore,' he said, on seeing her worried expression. 'I came up from the boathouse. It's down below there, on the shore line.' He pointed down towards the pool. 'You come up from the boathouse through the pool house. Anyway, when I came back, the outside lights were all off. It was very dark. I heard a noise somewhere over there and when I went to have a look, well… someone hit me over the head.'

'Are you sure? Could it have been low branch, or a falling…?'

'Please Natalya, I went through all of this with the policeman, someone hit me. But what I can't work out, is why? Nothing seems to have been taken. And it doesn't look like anyone has been in the house. The car is in the garage. I suppose I could have surprised them… before they managed to do anything.' He paused, staring down towards the sea. 'Maybe someone had left something. If Manolo, that's the caretaker who died, if Manolo had surprised someone and his death wasn't an accident… maybe they pushed him off the cliff… maybe they left something when that happened… and had come back to remove any evidence.'

'It is so sad. Where did he fall from?'

'Almost the same place, just over there. Do you see the fence? Well, they found his body at the bottom of the cliff just beyond that. I just don't know what Manolo could have been doing the *other* side of the fence. After tonight I'm certain there is something not right about the whole thing.' Scott looked at Natalya and decided to stop labouring the point.

'Now, I'm sorry Natalya, all this has rather got in the way of our dinner plans. It's past eleven now. Do you still feel like going out? It's the last thing I want to do. What about a bit of supper here?'

'That sounds lovely. But what about your car?'

'Oh, I can leave that at my friend's hotel. He'll call if it's in the way. I can get it tomorrow. I've got some food here. Do you like beef?'

'Er…yes. That would be great.'

'Well, let's go inside, we'll fix ourselves a drink, try not to fall over drunk and somehow club ourselves to death, and get a bit of dinner on the go.'

They went into the house. Scott opened a bottle of Priorat red wine he had bought the day before and handed Natalya a glass. She sat on the counter in the kitchen as he busied about getting their dinner ready. He peeled some potatoes, cut them up into little cubes, put them in an oven dish with some olive oil, garlic and thyme, then put them in the oven.

'You like cooking?' asked Natalya as he ground some pepper onto the large piece of fillet steak that he had taken out of the fridge.

'Love it. When I was younger, I flirted with the idea of being a chef, but in those days the whole food industry wasn't as sexy as it is today and I ended up going into journalism. But I did do six months working in a restaurant in my gap year before university.'

'Where was that?'

'In London. It was hell. Nearly put me off food altogether. The heat, the stress, all with a psychopathic chef shouting at you. I've never really got to grips with the whole shouting thing. Why you can't be asked to do something nicely…'

Scott placed a few broccoli stems in a steamer and put it by the stove. He browned all sides of the filet in an iron skillet on the gas stove and then put it in the oven.

'The thing about a restaurant kitchen is that you only learn to do one thing at a time. Not cooking as a whole. I had to chop things. And even that was a luxury, most people start on dish washing. A friend of my parents got me the job. But it's turned out to be useful – I'm now pretty good with a knife. He had started chopping an onion and some garlic.

'Let's eat in here.' He took some cutlery out of a drawer and placed it on the large, pine kitchen table that took up one end of the room.

'Do you like cooking?' he asked

'Not really. I like eating though.'

Natalya was wandering around the kitchen with her wine glass, looking at the pictures on the wall, the shelves with their selection of cooking books and various souvenirs from different part of the world. 'Do you always cook for yourself? Most men I know just order things in.'

'Well, I don't know if round here you can order any delivery service. When I'm in London, I suppose I cook at home more than most. The thing about cities is you have so much more choice to go out. Am not too keen on delivery services. Even if the food is good it always arrives looking tired. If you want to eat at home, you might as well cook. But I love going out. London's got such a great load of new restaurants. And my work takes me to some incredible places. I've got an article to write on a hotel in Barcelona that I was thinking of doing next week. Would you like to come and try the restaurant? It's got a Michelin star; the food is meant to be exceptional.'

'Wow. Yes. Sure. It all depends on my work. As long as I don't have to, er, show any clients around or be here for a specific reason, I can always escape.'

Natalya told him how she had been meaning to get to Barcelona but hadn't had the opportunity.

A few minutes later, Scott took the meat out of the oven. He gave the potatoes a shake, and shut the oven door. He took the meat off the pan and wrapped it in tin foil. He placed the steamer on the stove.

'So, what are you doing now?'

'Just letting the meat sit for a bit. It's been in for fifteen odd minutes, which should be enough. The broccoli is steaming and I'll just make a bit of a sauce for the meat.'

He put the chopped-up onions and garlic into the pan from which he had taken the meat and put it on the stove. He went over to a cupboard the other side of the kitchen and came back with a bottle of brandy.

'What are you doing with that?'

'It's just some brandy to deglaze the pan.'

'Deglaze?'

'Getting all the cooked bits off the bottom of the pan. It's where all the taste is. I'll pop some brandy in the pan when the onions and garlic are cooked and then add a bit of red wine. Talking of wine….' He picked up the bottle and approached her glass.

'I don't really want to drive over the limit.' She said with her hand over her glass.

'Do you have to drive? I was rather hoping you'd stay here tonight.'

'I was hoping you would say that,' she said, smiling as she uncovered her glass. 'Yes, I'd love another glass.'

Scott poured them both some more wine.

'You're not worried about the attack? Them coming back?' she asked.

'Well, I'm probably not going walking round the garden in the dark without that bat, just in case. Whoever it was could have hurt me more when he or they had the chance, so, no, I'm not too concerned. They've gone now. I probably just surprised them when they thought I was out of the house. After all, the boat was out, my car isn't outside. And I came back at dusk from the sea – any later and I wouldn't have made it. It's just very weird. What they were doing here? It must have been the owners of that boat.'

'What boat?'

'Some sort of speedboat. A large one, with a distinctive console. It was moored just down along the shoreline when

101

I got back.' Scott poured a generous slug of brandy into the skillet and then tipped it so that the gas flame licked the side of the skillet. The alcohol from the brandy burst into flames.

'Wow! A pro!'

'It looks more impressive than it really is,' said Scott as the flames died down. He added some red wine from the bottle and left the skillet bubbling. He went over and opened the foil wrapped meat. He then sliced the fillet. The meat was well cooked and brown on the outside but reddish pink in the middle.

'How do you like your steak?'

'Um, medium?'

'I think it's a crime to overcook it, especially fillet. So, this is blue to medium, I was going to give you the better-done slices, but I can cook it a bit longer if you'd prefer it that way.'

'No, that looks great, thank you.'

Scott divided the meat onto two plates, put the broccoli and some little cubed roast potatoes from the oven on each, and finally poured some of the sauce on top of the meat. He put the plates on the table, and pulled out a chair for Natalya.

'This looks amazing,' she said, taking her seat, 'I'm hungrier than I thought.'

'Probably the sea air.'

'Or maybe the unexpected exercise this afternoon.'

'Yes, that too,' he said grinning. 'Cheers.' They clinked glasses.

'Very pleased to have met you, Mr Alex Scott.'

'Likewise, Natalya, how very glad I am to have met you last night. How *did* we meet last night?'

'You still don't remember?'

'Well, what with my hangover this morning and being clonked on the head, it's a miracle I can remember my own name.'

'You came up and talked to me at the bar.'

'Were you there with friends?'

'Well, I was meant to be meeting a friend. But she never showed.' She took a bite of her steak. 'This is incredible. So tender. I think this is the best steak I have ever had. You are an amazing cook.'

'Well, thank you. But the meat is good. Nothing to do with the cooking. This is all very simple. But often the best things are.'

During their meal, they managed to polish off the rest of the bottle of wine, and talked about Natalya's time in London, her university and her experiences there.

After their steaks, Scott apologised for not having any dessert, and Natalya declined the offer of coffee. Scott offered to show her the house, which ended up in them going directly to his room.

# FOURTEEN

Scott awoke as the first rays of sunlight came into the room. He saw the curve of Natalya's shoulder and smiled. Leaning over he gave the shoulder a kiss and Natalya buried herself further under the sheet. He climbed out of bed and put on some shorts and a t-shirt. He looked at his watch, it was quarter to seven. He went out onto the balcony. Another glorious morning on the Costa Brava. He stretched in the morning light and a pain on the back of his head reminded him of the events of the previous night. Feeling the bump with his hand, he noted the swelling had reduced a little, although it was still painful.

He went back into the bedroom and picked up his trainers and socks and closed the shutters to keep out most of the morning light. Once downstairs he put on his socks and shoes, left a note on the kitchen table and went out into the garden. After his morning exercises, he crossed the garden towards the little gate onto the *Camí de Ronda*. On the way, he walked by the spot where he had been hit. The whole area was covered in pine needles and it was impossible to see if anyone had left footprints. Even in daylight, he could not see the spot where he had fallen. There were certainly no low branches that he could have walked into by mistake. Then something caught his eye. Over by the fence, the ground looked as if it had been disturbed. The pine needles weren't scattered around on top of the soil, they were mixed in with the earth. Some of them were sticking up out of the ground half buried. It looked like the marks animals make when they have been digging but flatter, as if someone had tried to correct any sign of disturbance.

He could see why Manolo had thought wild boar had been coming in. They come out of the deep forest to root for fungi and grubs, and dig up the ground with their tusks. What they don't do is flatten the earth afterwards.

He had a close look at the lock of the gate to see if there were any marks of someone trying to gain entry, and realised that although the new fence was in good condition, it wouldn't take too much effort to climb, and wasn't a great deterrent to somebody determined to get in. Shutting the gate behind him, he decided to run north along the *Camí*, in the direction of the lighthouse. As he ran, he went over the events of the previous days. Running was his meditation, it gave him a time on his own to focus, without outside interference.

Manolo's death. He was sure something was not right. Why had he been there? And how had he fallen as he had? Scott was sure he would have fallen onto the path and not down onto the rocks. What had he been doing there? Could he have surprised someone, just as Scott had? He was an old man, maybe instead of knocking him out, they had hit him too hard and by accident killed him. Then whoever it was could have thrown him off the cliff to make it look like a fall and cover up the fatal blow. That would explain him falling to where he had been found. They would have had to have thrown him out, over the Camí, but it would make sense. Had the keys to the house been on Manolo? Or the house might have been open when he 'fell.' Maybe the intruders got access to the office and deleted the camera recordings. Then set it to record again later. If they had the keys, could they have made a copy? The alarm code. He must check the office to see if it was written down anywhere. A spare set of keys and the codes would explain all his questions about the cameras and the security lights. He should check with Dolors whether the house had been open when the police arrived.

What it didn't explain was why someone would want to break into the property and then do nothing apart from root around under some trees. As far as he knew, nothing obvious had been taken from the house. There were some valuable pictures and works of art, and from a cursory look there were no empty patches on walls or spaces devoid of furniture. The car and the *Salacia* were there. The wine and the guns appeared untouched.

If Manolo's death wasn't accidental what other possible reasons, apart from robbery, could there be? Could Manolo have been in trouble? He knew a story of a housekeeper who had got hooked on prescription morphine and had ended up on heroin. In the end, he was caught stealing valuables to fund his habit. That seemed unlikely. Manolo had always been squeaky clean. He had stuck to one glass of wine a day with his lunch and Scott had never seen him touch any stronger alcohol, let alone drugs. He had never known him to gamble. An argument or fight over gambling or drug debts seemed unlikely.

The path had brought him round the bay then climbed to the height of the lighthouse. On his right were thirty-metre sheer cliffs down to the sea. He could see across the bay towards Can Daurat. From here the garden fence was clearly visible. He hadn't paid it much attention before, but he supposed that his current position would be equally visible from the end of the garden at Can Daurat. He was now next to the lighthouse. In fact, the end of the garden at Can Daurat was the only place that had a clear view of these cliff tops and the lighthouse itself.

He started to run again. What if Manolo had seen something that he shouldn't have? Maybe Manolo had been killed to silence him. Could his attackers have come back in the boat he had seen the night before to retrieve something they had left behind?

He came to the wall that surrounded the lighthouse. It was old and bits had crumbled away. This section of the path curved inland to go around the lighthouse which was right on the cliff edge. As he passed the entrance gates he heard the noise of drilling and hammering. Impressive for contractors to be working at eight o'clock on a Sunday, thought Scott. About fifty metres along the path there was a bearded hiker sitting down doing something with his backpack. As Scott approached he kept his head down and lifted a hand in reply to Scott's *'Buenos días!'* without looking up. The path started to descend sharply with an alarming drop straight down to the sea on Scott's right. Erosion had battered the path and in places it was slippery with gravel and he had to watch his footing.

Scott carried along the path for another twenty minutes. He passed through a couple of idyllic bays with tiny beaches. No one was around at this time of the day and there was a light mist over the water which gave the scenery a mystical air. When the path turned inland and joined a road he decided to turn back. Running up the steep incline to the lighthouse had Scott pouring with sweat and gasping deep breaths by the time he reached the top. He just managed an *'adios'* to the hiker who, probably a birdwatcher, had assembled a camera with a long lens. He ignored the valediction.

The run back to Can Daurat was all downhill from the lighthouse. In the bright light of the morning, his worries lessened. He would check with Bill that there was nothing taken from the house and he would keep an eye out for the speedboat he had seen. The first thing he had to do was to change the alarm codes and any security passwords.

He reached the fence and the gate and, as he slowed, he could hear chatting coming from just round the corner. He passed the gate and carried on down the *Camí*. He rounded a bend and was confronted by a group of men in hard hats and high-viz jackets milling round the tunnel that took the *Camí* under where Can Daurat's garden stuck out into the promontory. The men were closing the path with red and white plastic tape with *'Ajuntament de Begur'* written on it.

Scott said good morning and asked what was going on. The one who seemed to be in charge, who hadn't shaved and smelt strongly of brandy and black tobacco, told him that they were shutting the tunnel. Apparently, someone had seen part of the tunnel falling, or loose, or something like that - Scott got a bit lost on the explanation, and the council had decided to close that section of the path. He said there were lots of parts of the path that had been closed. Mainly due to erosion.

This would stop his southbound runs. He asked the workmen how long the path would be closed for. He replied that they were only there to close it, that he should ask at the architect's office in the council.

Scott turned back up the path and went through the gate into the garden. How different it seemed in the light. He walked across the dew-covered grass and the cool tiles of the terrace and blinked as he went from the light of the terrace to the darkness inside. Hearing noises from the kitchen he called out.

'Morning!'

'Good morning. In here!' said Natalya. She was standing by the coffee machine with a cup in hand wearing his shirt from the night before.

'Hey. How was your run? I got the note.' She was fiddling with the buttons on the machine. 'How do you turn this on?'

'Great. Sleep well?' Asked Scott as he reached round her and flicked the on the switch.

'Yes thanks.'

He kissed her.

'Ew! You need a shower!' she said, pulling away from him.

'Ok, I'll be back down in a minute. Do you want any breakfast? There's bread here,' he said opening the bread bin, 'and there is some cheese and ham in the fridge. This cupboard has all the jams and honey. Here, I'll get you a plate.'

'Don't worry, you go and have a shower.' She said. He gave her a peck on the cheek and went upstairs for a shower.

When he came back downstairs, the kitchen was empty. He walked outside to the terrace and Natalya had set up one of the tables with coffee, milk, toast, jams and honey and a plate of cheese and ham.

'So, the run was good?'

'Yes,' he said as he sat down opposite her.

'Where did you go?'

'Just up the *Camí*. You know the *Camí de Ronda?*'

'Yes. It's the path that runs along the coast.'

'Well, it runs along the end of the garden over there. There's a little gate that opens on to it. I ran that way for a while,' he said pointing north. 'It's really beautiful. The only two buildings on this stretch of coast are this and the lighthouse on the far point, the other side of the bay. It's really quite wild. When I got back they were closing the tunnel under the garden.'

'What tunnel?'

'When they built the *Camí* here, they made a tunnel that goes under the garden. Only for about twenty metres. It goes under that bit that sticks out,' said Scott, pointing to the promontory. 'There are some men from the council closing the tunnel. They said it was unsafe or something. It's annoying. To go south, without using the tunnel, you either have to go by sea or climb over the fence on the south part of the property. It looked fine to me yesterday.' Natalya didn't seem overly interested, Scott decide to change the subject.

'Well, it's another lovely day. Have you got any plans?'

'It all depends on work. If there is a client about. I'll call them a bit later. What about you?'

'I've got a few things to sort out here in the house. Later, I want to get out on the sea and see if I can find that speedboat that was tied up here last night. They must have had something to do with whoever hit me. Want another coffee?'

'No thanks. I'm good. I'd better get home and do a little work.'

'Could you drop me off in Begur? I suppose I'd better collect my hire car.'

'Yes, of course.'

'Feel like a swim to wake up?'

'I haven't got a bikini.'

'Neither have I,' said Scott with a grin.

# FIFTEEN

It was midday by the time Natalya dropped Scott off at Juan's hotel. He popped into reception to see if Juan was around, but neither he nor Isabel were there, so he left a note and headed back to Can Daurat in his hire car.

In the office, Scott found some instructions for changing the cameras' security codes but none for the alarm. He retrieved his laptop from his room and went out onto the terrace by the pool. The WIFI reception wasn't great and, after an annoying wait watching a little circle go round and round on the screen, his browser found the website of the hotel in Barcelona. He looked through it, and when he was satisfied he had understood their branding concept, he retrieved the manager's mobile number from an old email. Pierre Sambat, the French General Manager, spoke excellent English, and after a brief chat to introduce himself, Scott outlined his ideas for the infomercial. It was to be in the form of a traveller's article, on the surface an account of a food-lover's renewed acquaintance of Barcelona and its gastronomy, but really a plug for the hotel and its starred Michelin restaurant. The article was to be placed in a luxury lifestyle magazine.

When Sambat realised Scott was staying an hour up the coast on the Costa Brava, he suggested coming down to do the article the next day. There had been a table cancellation for the following evening (otherwise the restaurant was fully booked for six months) and if he wanted he could stay the night. It was no problem to bring a guest. They agreed to meet in the early afternoon.

After speaking to Sambat, Scott called Natalya and left a message asking her if she was free to come to Barcelona the following day. He then caught up with a few emails. He emailed an editor in London to inform him of the article on traditional Catalan recipes. He accepted an invitation from his uncle to go up to Scotland in the autumn to cull some deer. His phone rang.

'Hey, I got your message.' Natalya.

'Hey there. I just spoke to the hotel. I'm going to head down tomorrow. Feel like joining me?'

'I need to check with work. What's the hotel called?'

'The Arena Bloc Hotel.'

'And you said the restaurant has a Michelin Star?'

'Yes. It's called the Balconera. Looks good.'

'Well, let me check and I'll get back to you. What are you up to?'

'Just pottering about. A bit of work. You?'

'I've got to get a report finished for a client by tomorrow. I think it'll take me all day.'

'Ok, well, if you finish, give me a call. Speak later.'

'Bye.'

Scott then called Santi and left a message asking him to call back. He found a few websites dedicated to domestic employment and spent half an hour reading offers from employees and employers. There were many more people looking for work than offering it. To test the water, he set up a new Gmail account, then posted an offer for a 'Caretaker on the Costa Brava' on two of the most professional looking sites. He wasn't specific about the location, but gave a general job description. By the time he had finished posting the second announcement, his Gmail account had twenty-seven new messages.

Scott went back into the kitchen and put an egg on to boil. He gathered together some ingredients: a tin of tuna in extra virgin olive oil, some raw green beans, a few lettuce leaves, a tomato, and half an onion. He mixed everything except the egg in a large bowl and added a dressing of olive oil, balsamic vinegar, some mustard, salt and pepper. He then peeled the hard-boiled egg, cut it in half and added that. He opened a tin of olives and a tin of anchovies and added a few of each. He poured a glass of water and took the bowl, a fork and his glass of water back out to the terrace.

His new Gmail account had two hundred and fifty-eight new messages. He decided to shut his computer and enjoy his lunch in peace.

Just as he was finishing his salad, his phone rang. It was Juan.

'Hey, my friend, how are you?'

'Hey Juanito. All good.'

'Why did you take that beautiful car away from my hotel?'

'Yes, I thought it added a certain air of class!' Scott said with a laugh. 'I thought the canary yellow went particularly well with the red.' The outside of Juan's hotel was painted a deep burgundy.

'You said in your note that you have had *un incidente.*'

'Yes. I was attacked last night.'

'What? Where? Are you ok?'

'Just a bump on the head. I came back to Can Daurat and someone hit me over the head in the garden.'

'*Coño!* What did they take?'

'That's the strange thing. They didn't take anything. Well, nothing that I have noticed.'

'I can't believe this place. These sorts of things are happening more and more. You were lucky. Many times, they wait for the owners to return to get them to show where they keep their money. I have a friend, he and his wife were tied up... and, with a knife...'

'Well the weirder thing is that I think they came by boat.'

'By boat? Pirates?'

'Ha ha. Very funny. I was out yesterday on the *Salacia*. When I got back it was just getting dark. There was a speedboat tied up on the rocks along the shore a bit. It must have been them. When I came to afterwards it was gone.'

'That's clever. Difficult to be chased by the police. How many of them were there?'

'I don't know. I didn't see them.'

'What do you mean?'

'I didn't see them. The lights were off in the garden. I went to have a look and someone hit me over the head. That's the last thing I remember before waking up.'

'Well, at least they didn't get any vital organ!'

'Very funny.'

'Did you not see them *at all?*'

'Nope. Very annoying.'

'And they stole *nothing?*'

'As far as I can tell, no. But they had turned the outside lights off. Oh, and the cameras didn't record anything. But I'm sure they had been on when I left.'

'Like with Manolo. No?'

'Exactly. It's as if someone had deleted the recordings. But the alarm in the house was on.'

'You should change all the codes.'

'Already done. Well, most of them. I need to get the alarm instructions off Bill.'

'You should have called. We would have come over. What did the police say?'

'I rang the inspector who is in charge of Manolo's case. Inspector Matas. Do you know him?'

'Matas. Yes. I know him. He is the *jefe* of the investigation department.'

'Well he came round. I don't think he believed me. He thought I had just hit my head while drunk. He said something about someone complaining about my behaviour in Begur on Friday night when we were in town.'

114

'What? Friday night?'

'He said someone complained about my behaviour. That I was out of control when drunk. You didn't mention anything like that.'

'Alejandro, I told you. You were *un caballero*, a gentleman. Yes,' he laughed, 'you were in good spirits, but no, there was no 'out of control.''

'He said someone tried to lodge a complaint with the police. *Una denuncia.*'

'*Una denuncia?* No. I don't believe it. Unless it was the *sueca's* boyfriend! Hey, how did that go? You saw her yesterday, no?'

'She's not Swedish. She's Ukrainian. And yes, I saw her yesterday. She's a nice girl.'

'So, will you see her again?'

'Might do.'

'You fucking English. Coming here and stealing all our girls!' Juan said laughing.

'She's Ukrainian. How can she be 'yours?''

'Beautiful, no?'

'Yes very. For once your terrible judgement was right. I don't mean Isabel, of course.'

'So, this Matas, what did he say about the attack?'

'I think he thought I had made the whole thing up. That I had fallen over and done it myself?'

'Done what?'

'The bump on my head.'

'OK. But …'

'The fact was that nothing had been taken nor broken in to. When he arrived, the lights were working again. The cameras didn't show anything. Can't say I blame him really.'

'If you had rung me, I would have called *Sargento* Duarte. He's in the *Mossos* in Begur. He would have believed you. Not like this inspector.'

'Yes. I think next time I'll avoid Inspector Matas. Hopefully there won't be a next time.'

'Hey, talking about Duarte. He will retire soon. What about suggesting Duarte to Bill? You need someone for Can Daurat. He's totally *de confianza,* trustworthy. Well,' he laughed, 'as much as a policeman can be trustworthy. I had a beer with him last week and he was complaining about his retirement. Didn't know what to do with himself. I don't know why I didn't think about him on Friday.'

'Sounds great. I've been dreading the interview process. I put an ad online today. It seems to have received twenty-five billion replies already. What's up with your country. Has no one got a job?'

'Where did you put the ad?'

Scott mentioned the two websites.

'Yes. I tried those once for help in the kitchen. For the hotel. They are free. You get many, many replies. I think I received over a thousand replies. In the end, I went to an *agencia.*'

'Well your guy Duarte sounds ideal. Can you give me his number?'

'I will send it to you. Hey, Bill might even know him. He was in the *Guardia Civil* before the *Mossos.*' The *Mosos d'Esquadra*, the Catalan regional police force had replaced the *Guardia Civil* in the 1990s. The *Guardia Civil,* who still carried echoes of the Franco regime, maintained control over external matters such as border controls and the coast.

'Brilliant, thanks, that would be a great help.'

'Are we on for Thursday?'

'Thursday?'

'Dinner at yours? You said…'

'Of course. Yes. I'll try Santi again and ask him. Have you spoken to him?'

'I saw him briefly yesterday. He's very excited about something. Running round like *un loco* for his Russian. This man Alinca.'

'Olenka. I tried to call Santi earlier.'

'Well he's been up at the *faro* near you.'

'The lighthouse? I ran past it this morning. There was lots of work going on. What is he doing?'

'Something to do with our grandfather's plans. He was too busy to explain.'

'Have you met this guy Olenka?'

'I've seen him around occasionally. One of these super rich.'

'All above board?'

'Above board? What do you mean?'

'I'm not sure. But could there be anything dodgy going on at the lighthouse?'

'No idea. You'll have to ask Santi. He's been there enough. He should be checking they do everything correctly.'

'I wasn't thinking about the building work.'

'What do you mean.'

'Not sure. Might just be me being silly. Being attacked, Manolo's death,' he paused, 'it's got me wondering. Probably nothing.'

'Right my friend. Listen you take care. You can always come and stay with us. I had better go and check on my girls. Are you sure you are ok?'

'Yes. Thank you.'

'I'll send you Duarte's number. Good luck with the Russian. Are you seeing her again?'

'Ukrainian. Different country.' He paused. 'Yes, probably.'

'If you are in town drop in for a coffee or a beer. Bring her with you. Otherwise we'll see you on Thursday.'

'See you then. *Un abrazo.*'

Scott hung up and dialled Dolors' number. Dolors told him that the house had been open when they found Manolo, that his set of keys had been on the table in the office. She had locked up after the police and the ambulance had left. She thought there should be a spare set of keys to the house in one of the office drawers. She said

117

all changes to the alarm had to be made through the alarm company.

After hanging up, Scott walked round the house to the front where the alarm box was installed on the wall facing the road. He could just make out a name and a telephone number on the brightly coloured yellow and blue box. He dialled the number and selected 'Accounts' from an automatized list of calling options. The employee who answered told him that, to change the keycode for the alarm, he needed the account holder's written permission: to correctly answer the security question: and to call during normal office hours.

He went back down to the pool terrace and opened his computer. Ignoring his new Gmail account, that now had four hundred and thirty-two messages, he sent an email to Bill asking him to send him authorisation to change the alarm codes. He didn't mention the attack in the email. Scott retrieved the keys from the kitchen, his camera bag from his room, locked up and went back outside to the pool house. He remembered seeing a pair of binoculars in the sports equipment cupboard. He took them and a wooden baseball bat that was in the cupboard and went down the secret stairs to the boat shed.

He opened the dock doors and this time remembered to turn the dock lights on, just in case he had to return in bad light again. He had to reverse the *Salacia* back out, but in daylight the channel out seemed larger and he turned easily and headed out into the open bay. As it was Sunday, there were a few boats about, but the bay was still pretty clear and, pushing the twin throttles to full forward gear, Scott felt the reassuring press of the leather seat into his back as the beautiful craft was hurled forward by its huge 350 horsepower V8 engines. He was about to clear the far point before he remembered the purpose of his trip and slowed the *Salacia* down to an idle.

He took the binoculars out of their soft leather case and had a look at the new scaffolding construction that linked the jetty to the lighthouse on top of the cliff. Apart from the jetty itself, which was a flat platform, bolted straight into the rock where it met the water, it looked just like scaffolding on the side of a building. The construction was three or four metres wide and went straight up the thirty or so metres to the top of the cliff. Grey net tarpaulin covered the structure. As far as he could make out, a series of ladders and what looked like a shaft of some sorts went up through the scaffolding. Heavy tarpaulin covered the top but he could see the outline of what looked like a hydraulic crane.

From sea level, he could only see the top of the lighthouse, and, although there were sounds of construction work coming from the top of the cliff, he couldn't see any activity. He took his camera out of its bag, changed the lens to a 300mm zoom, and snapped a few photos. The *Salacia* was not in gear, but the light southerly breeze had brought her round the point and he could see the large motor cruiser anchored in the lee of the headland.

She was an ugly ship. Too many sharp angles for Scott's taste. He preferred either the faded elegance of pre-war motor cruisers or the flowing beauty of modern sailing yachts. She was large, at least fifty metres long, with a white hull and tall white superstructure. The metal details, instead of being the usual chrome, were covered in either brass or gold leaf and the seating upholstery was beige leather. As the *Salacia* drifted further round the point he saw that there were what looked like a pair of jet skis under tarpaulins on a flat deck at the back of the ship, which he assumed could double as a helipad. There was a crane at the back of the deck which looked like an add-on and ruined the silhouette of the vessel. Moored to the stern, at the boarding platform, was a speedboat in the beige and gold livery of the mother ship. Its size and the shape of its driving console tallied with what Scott remembered of the boat from the night before. He had though it grey or blue, but the light had been bad. Although it was the right size, it was impossible for him to be sure it was the boat he had seen. He took a few photos of both the tender and the ship. With the powerful 300mm lens he took a close-up of a scowling crewmember who waved his arms at Scott in a shooing motion.

Feeling less than his usual marine cordiality, Scott raised a middle finger at the man and took a few more unnecessary photos of the ship.

He put the engines into gear and carried on up the coast. As he came round the point into Aiguablava bay, he was confronted with the sight of dozens of boats moored up on the buoys in the bay. He only now realised quite how many speedboats there were on this part of the coast. Of the thirty or forty boats moored in the bay at least five or six could have been the boat he saw the night before.

It was a quarter past five when he got back to Can Daurat. It was still a lovely afternoon and, after the events of the previous few days, he was looking forward to relaxing by the pool with a novel that he had been neglecting. He couldn't shake the feeling of apprehension as he did a tour of the house. All seemed as he had left it. The incident from the night before had shaken him more than he had realised. He checked the camera recordings in the office and all appeared to be in order. He got his book and a towel and a sun lounger out from the pool house. He dragged it to a sunny part of the terrace and sat down on it. He had only got through a couple of pages of his book before his thoughts started wandering back to the recent events. He still felt as confused as before. He left his book on the lounger and went back into the house to get a glass of water. He brought his laptop and phone back outside and went through some emails. Bill had replied saying he would send him the authorisation the next day when he got to the office.

Natalya sent a WhatsApp message saying that she could come to Barcelona the next day but that she would have to work for the rest of the day. He replied that he would be round to pick her up around midday. He was looking forward to going to Barcelona. He hadn't been there for over ten years but, in the past, it had been one of his favourite cities. He went to a restaurant review website to find somewhere to have lunch. He saw that the restaurant Balconera was ranked seventh best in Barcelona. He found a few tapas bars that were highly rated and finally settled on one in *Barceloneta*, the quarter between the beach and the old port, which had great reviews. He rang it was told that they didn't take bookings, but on a Monday, there shouldn't be a problem with a table for two if he didn't mind a little wait.

He spent the rest of the afternoon alternating between trying to read his novel and doing a bit of work on his laptop. When the sun went down over the hill, he went inside and cooked himself and early supper of chicken breast and salad. He went up to bed to read but soon fell asleep.

# SIXTEEN

Scott awoke to a grey morning. The air was cooler than usual and he thought the clouds signified rain. He completed his morning exercises and once more ran past the lighthouse, on a few bays, and then back. There were still noises of banging and drilling coming from within the old building.

At half past nine he received an email from Bill with authorisation to change the account details with the alarm company and the code word for the alarm. He forwarded the attachment on, then rang them up and, after a laborious process to identify himself, managed to change the codes. He learnt from the employee that they kept a record of all activity on the alarm and they sent it by post each month to Can Daurat. Scott asked to be sent a copy of the last month's activity by email, and gave them Bill's secretary's email address to send future monthly reports.

During the night, he had received a text message from Juan with a P Duarte's .vcf file. He imported the file into his phone's address book and dialled the mobile number. After a couple of rings, it was answered.

'*Si, diga'm!*'

'*Hola. ¿Señor Duarte? Soy Alejandro Scott, un amigo de Juan Finat. Me dejó su teléfono.*'

'*Si, hola Alejandro. Ya me llamó ayer.* How are you? I speak with Juan yesterday.'

'Juan said that you might be interested in coming to work at Can Daurat. I don't know if you knew Manolo?'

'*Sí, claro que sí.* Yes, I know Manolo well. We have many histories. Very sad his accident.'

'Well, Mr Franklin will need someone to do Manolo's work. Juan suggested that you might be interested?'

'Yes. He tell me. Yes, I am very interested. But not possible now. In July. I er... I stop work in July. Until then policeman. Sorry, my English is not so good.'

'No *Señor* Duarte, it is excellent.'

'Pablo, *por favor.*'

'Ok. Pablo. Well, could we meet to talk about this? When would be good for you? Are you free at all this week? I'm off to Barcelona today but I'll be back tomorrow.'

'Tomorrow I am working. Wednesday in the morning?'

'Wednesday would be great. Can you come here?'

'Can Daurat. Yes. No problem. I know well.'

'Shall we say at ten?'

'Ten, no problem.'

'*Hasta entonces!*'

'*Hasta el miércoles.*'

Scott wrote a brief email to Bill, telling him about the potential caretaker, the new alarm codes and that he was off to Barcelona for a night, but that he would call in the next couple of days.

He packed his small travelling bag with his laptop, camera, washbag and a change of underwear. Realising most of his clothes needed a wash, he decided to wear his last clean shirt and to do some shopping in Barcelona. He locked and alarmed the house, and went down to the boathouse and garages to check they were properly secure.

While he was approaching the hire car it started to rain. Large warm drops of rain, like in the tropics. The patter of raindrops increased to a roar and Scott took shelter under the eaves of the garage building. The little Fiat 500 would be a nightmare to drive on the motorway in this weather. It was too small to be hurtling along the motorway in the wet. What he needed was something bigger. With larger wheels. And maybe a great big V8 engine.

He removed the old cover from the Aston Martin and put his overnight bag in the back. He opened the garage doors with a clicker that he found in the glove compartment, and turned the ignition. With his foot firmly on the brake pedal, he put the car into gear, there was a shudder from the car. Scott disengaged the handbrake next to his right leg, then moved his foot to the accelerator pedal. The huge car surged forward and Scott braked, the car coming to an abrupt stop, the wheels squeaking on the polished concrete floor of the garage. All right, he thought, at least the brakes work. He texted Natalya to say he was on his way over, then gently pressed down on the accelerator and eased out of the garage and down the drive and out of the front gates, making sure they closed behind him.

After a few minutes of driving along the winding coastal roads, Scott felt he was getting to grips with the car, although he was erring towards caution due to the rain.

In ten minutes, he arrived in Aiguablava. Natalya had suggested he park in the hotel's car park. The rain kept up, so Scott rang Natalya to ask where her house was but she said she would be with him in a moment. Ten minutes later she opened the door and passed him her bag which he put on the back seat. When she had shut the door, she leant over and gave him a kiss.

'Ahh, I'm soaked!' She said, wiping her face with her hands. 'Hey, I *like* the car!'

'Well, you look great. Thought I take this out for a spin.'

'I like it!' She leant back into the leather upholstery. 'I feel I am in an armchair.'

'Right, off we go,' said Scott.

'It's a pity it's raining,' she said, 'this is my first time in Barcelona.'

'I checked the forecast, and I think the weather is better there,' said Scott. He drove back the way he had come on the previous Thursday and headed south once he arrived at the motorway. With the noise of the rain and water they drove in silence for a while, Scott enjoying every minute of driving the classic sportscar. About half way to Barcelona the weather cleared. They were just passing Hostalric, a mediaeval town surrounded by a crenelated wall and its acropolis bathed in sunlight. Behind it loomed the Montseny mountain.

Natalya questioned him about Barcelona. He regaled her with a few stories of adventures in his youth, most of them involving Charlie. On the way into Barcelona they passed the *Sagrada Familia*, Gaudi's nineteenth century masterpiece, which was still under construction over a century after it was started. They drove down the *Paseo de Gracia* towards the *Plaza Catalunya*, the main square and symbolic centre of Barcelona. Scott turned off into a side street where he found the entrance to the Hotel Arena Bloc's underground car park. He managed to negotiate the very narrow car park in the wide Aston and they took their bags to reception. The manager was busy so they decided to go straight out for lunch.

It had stopped raining and the street was packed with thousands of tourists; kiosks selling flowers and birds; hawkers selling fake designer handbags, belts and sunglasses. Every fifty metres or so there was a different performer in some weird pose: a statue of Liberty; a gold Aladdin on a flying carpet; something that looked like a pile of rubbish. All motionless until someone from the crowd dropped a coin in their bowl. Then the torch would move, the statue open its eyes. Aladdin rubbed a lamp. Scott was tempted to stay, to see what would happen to the pile of rubbish, but was sure the eagerly expectant audience was just fodder for pickpockets and anyway, as he said to Natalya, lunch beckoned. After being pestered by a succession of street vendors selling very cheap-looking lager, Scott steered Natalya off the Ramblas into the *Plaça Real*.

The elegant square was the embodiment of a Mediterranean city. Graceful arches encircling the square provided shade to numerous cafes and restaurants. In the middle of the square was a gurgling fountain and tall palm trees.

'This has changed since my day,' said Scott. 'When I first came here every other person was a junky or a dope seller. You were taking your life into your hands. I once saw someone stabbed on the table right next to me. As teenagers, we used to think we were quite the hard arses by just being here.' Looking round the square, Scott could only see tourists. Lots of families and children. There were smart cafes and what looked like a boutique hotel. 'Yup, they've certainly smartened this up. I suppose that's the way of things. We used to go to a grotty dive on the first floor over in that corner.' Scott pointed to a corner of the square to his left. 'You had to ring on a buzzer and they would let you in. It was like being in someone's flat. Probably was just someone's flat. You could smoke what you liked, there was a pool table. It felt very bohemian. Over there. Ha.' He paused. 'Looks like it's still there. See the second floor. Look, over there.' On the second floor where Scott was pointing there were a series of floor to ceiling windows that were open with people leaning out and milling round. 'I can't believe it. It looks like it's still going.'

'Are we going to eat here?' asked Natalya.

'I thought we'd head to Barceloneta. It's only ten minutes' walk and it's not so touristy. Well, that's what I read anyway. There's a restaurant that I want to try.'

They walked off up one of the side streets and into the maze of the mediaeval quarter the *Barrio Gótico*. The tall stone buildings seemed to lean inwards and blocked out most of the sun and the streets were dark and cool. The stone paving felt sticky underfoot and there was a lingering smell of alcohol and rubbish.

'At night, all these streets are packed with little bars and clubs. Teeming with people with plastic glasses going from bar to bar. I remember they used to wash the streets down with large hoses in the mornings just as you were trying to get home. Looks like it hasn't changed much.'

After a few minutes, they came out onto the *Passeig Colom*. The wide, ordered avenue was a marked contrast to the disarray of the old quarter. In front of them was a huge marina with very large yachts. The clouds had disappeared and the air was fresh after the recent rain, the port sparking in the sunlight.

'This avenue is named after Christopher Columbus. There is his statue,' he said, indicating a tall column with a statue of a man pointing out to sea at the top. 'He's pointing in completely the wrong direction. America is the other way.'

They crossed the avenue and walked along the side of the marina.

'This port has changed a bit since my day. I remember lots of little fishing boats and small yachts. It looks like the big boys have kicked them out.' Some of the yachts looked more like cruise liners. Most of the flags flying of the backs were the red and blue of the British Red Ensign and Scott saw that many were registered to Bermuda and Barbados.

'I don't see the point in these monsters. It must be like staying in a rather tacky hotel. You certainly wouldn't get the feeling that you were at sea.'

They were passing a huge yacht that had five upper decks, a helicopter on the back and at least fifteen staff all in livery busy cleaning the ship.

'Give me the *Salacia* any day. Well, I suppose if you gave me this I could buy a few hundred *Salacia*s.'

They reached a corner of the marina and walked away from it, into a grid of small streets of very narrow apartment blocks. After a couple of intersections, they came to a busy restaurant with five people standing outside. One of them was a waiter, who told Scott that a table for two would be about a quarter of an hour. They wandered a few streets further and came out onto the beach. They saw a beach bar fifty metres away and walked up to it and Scott ordered two mojitos.

Although it was a Monday, the beach was packed. Judging by the amount of pale skin on show, most were tourist enjoying their first sunbathing of the year. There was a relaxed and cheerful atmosphere to the crowd, and it was easy to forget they were in a major city.

They drank their cocktails then wandered back to the restaurant. After a short wait, they were shown to their table. It was a simple place with Formica-topped tables and odd plastic chairs. The tables were packed close together and they had to apologise to squeeze past to get to theirs. The waiter who had seated them came back with a pad of paper in his hand and read out the fish on offer, almost shouting above the din of the restaurant. Natalya asked Scott to choose for her. He proposed getting a selection of dishes to share and settled on clams, prawns, and some grilled cuttlefish to start followed by seabass baked in salt.

The food was very simple but delicious. The seafood was all cooked in the oven or *a la plancha*, on a flat metal grill, and the seabass came to the table still covered in its mound of salt. The waiter cracked open the salt and served each of them half the fish. They talked about Natalya's childhood in Kiev and more stories from her time in London at university. She was nostalgic about those days but when Scott asked about her decision to move to Russia and her current job she seemed evasive and changed the subject. She asked Scott all about his time in Barcelona and he ended up retrieving memories of his late teens that he had spent with Charlie that he hadn't thought of in years.

After lunch Scott still had an hour and a half to kill before he needed to be back at the hotel, so he took Natalya to see the Santa Maria del Mar cathedral in the Borne district, next to the old port. There was a service being held, but they slipped in the back and had a quick look round.

'That's so beautiful,' said Natalya, once they had left the church and were standing in the little square in front of it in the sun. 'Really simple but beautiful.'

'It's one of my favourite churches,' said Scott. 'It's incredible to think of the impact it must have made in the fourteenth century. All the buildings around it would have been so small. The stone to build it was all carried on the backs of the quarry workers as a religious offering. I think it was an influence on Gaudí when he designed the *Sagrada Familia*. If we've got time tomorrow, we should really go and see that.'

They started walking through the Borne district, which was now filled with trendy bars and little boutique clothes shops. Scott bought a couple of shirts at a small store along the way. When they got to the *Via Laietana*, Scott suggested to Natalya that she wander round the *Barrio Gótico*, the oldest part of the city, while he went for his meeting with Sambat and they could meet back at the hotel in a couple of hours.

# SEVENTEEN

The five-star Arena Bloc Hotel had been newly renovated and took up a whole city block. The architect had kept the old nineteenth century façade but had completely rebuilt the inside. Scott entered the automatic doors and crossed the marble foyer to the reception desk. He asked for Sambat, and was asked if he minded waiting a few minutes. He wandered over to the concierge's desk and flicked through a few leaflets on Barcelona, before crossing the hallway to look at the bar. The decoration was modern: bare concrete walls with polished concrete floors and metal pipes, with the whole effect softened by blood red velvet curtains from ceiling to floor and similar velvet upholstery in the banquettes that ran along the side of the room. The bar looked adequately stocked and although there were no customers, there were three bar staff working away.

Scott turned round to the sound of approaching footsteps. An energetic looking man in his mid-forties was crossing the hall with his hand extended.

'Alex Scott? Pierre Sambat. Nice to meet you.'

'Nice to meet you,' echoed Scott, shaking his hand.

'Sorry to keep you waiting. We just had an important client check in and, well, some clients, they insist on being shown the hotel by the manager.'

'No problem at all. I was just having a look around.'

'Excellent. Now, you are staying with us, no? Have you received your key?'

'I arrived before lunch and left some bags, but no, I haven't checked in yet. But don't worry no rush.'

'Ok. Good. If you like I can show you the hotel, then we can sit down for a few minutes and you can ask me any questions? I am afraid then I must get on with some other work, but I can leave you in the capable hands of my reception staff should you need anything. You can ask them any questions, and we have a database of photos which you might like to go through. Now the chef has prepared a meal for you. You said you would be two people, no?'

'Yes, if that's ok.'

'No problem at all. As I said yesterday, the Balconera restaurant is normally full, but we had a cancellation. In fact, we had two cancellations. Our client who I was just checking in insisted on trying the restaurant at any cost. Thankfully I can fit him in too.'

'That all sounds great.' Said Scott. 'Well, lead on.'

Sambat showed Scott round the hotel. On the ground floor, there were two restaurants: the Balconera, which had a similar modern/minimalist design as the Canelo Bar; and the Bar Lacone, which looked to be a fusion of bistro, tapas bar and café. In the basement, there was a Spa which included Moroccan style hammam, steam baths and sauna.

They caught the lift from the basement straight to the top floor. This was dominated by a large terrace with a pool and a bar. There was an amazing view of the rooftops of Barcelona, to the north you could see the towers of the Sagrada Familia basilica, to the south the Montjuic hill and on the landward side the Tibidabo hill with its funfair and church perched on top. They took a seat at one of the tables under an umbrella.

'So, what do you think of our hotel?' Said Sambat, and then, without waiting for an answer, asked, 'What sort of angle will the article take?'

'Ostensibly, the article is about the experiences and impressions of a travel writer coming back to Barcelona after many years away. I'll do a quick paragraph on some of the major changes to the city, then get onto the two biggest – the increase in quality in hotels and the food revolution in Catalonia. I'll, of course, use the Arena Bloc and the Balconera as the shining examples of this. Daniela in the group's head office told me to liaise with you on marketing focus. Who are you looking to attract?'

'Well, our corporate marketing team seem to be doing an excellent job. Barcelona has some of Europe's largest trade fairs and we have a very well-connected marketing department. Where we feel we are lacking, is in the private sector. We would like to attract more of the top tier private tourists. At present, they go to the best-known Barcelona hotels, the Palace, the Mandarin Oriental, the Arts.'

'Ok.' Scott paused. 'How about I include in the article that the hotel provided or organised a limo service that took my 'wife' round the sights and to the shops? I will of course mention the hammam and the spa. Let's see…Have you any colourful member of staff I could mention as a great source of local info? The idea that, by staying here, you are somehow bypassing the usual tourist experience and receiving extra personal attention, might be an added draw.'

'I suppose Miguel, one of our doormen, would be good for that,' replied Sambat. 'He looks the part, he is quite a character. Big moustache, always impeccable, and he gets on well with the clients. He is on this afternoon, I'll get him to come and see you.'

'That sounds great,' said Scott, 'anything we can add to the article to differentiate the hotel from the competition is good. Of course, the restaurant and the Michelin star is a great draw. Anyway, when I've got the article written I'll pass it by you and your marketing guys and you can see if you want to add anything or make any changes.'

'Ok, good.'

'Some celebrity gossip always works wonders. Do you have any stories that I could add?'

'Not much one could print I'm afraid. Well, let me think…' Sambat paused. 'We have had a rock star's birthday party here last month.' He mentioned a current media favourite. 'She took over the whole top two floors. It was reported in the press at the time, so we aren't breaking any confidentiality by reporting it.'

'Great. I can definitely use that.' He thought for a moment. 'If I can have a quick word with the chef this afternoon, I think I'll have enough to go on.'

'No problem at all. You should be able to catch him about this time. Now, if you will forgive me,' Sambat said standing up, 'I must get back to work. I fear the new arrival will need some more attention.'

'That difficult?'

'That difficult,' concurred Sambat. 'What is it with these young millionaires? This one rang this morning and asked for a very specific bottle of champagne and I need to check if my supplier has found it. He wanted to land his helicopter on the roof. As you can see we don't exactly have somewhere to land,' said Sambat, opening his arms wide. 'I had to send him to the Juan Carlos Hotel… And then send a limousine to pick him up from there.'

'He arrived by helicopter? From the *airport?*' The drive from Barcelona airport to the centre of town was only fifteen minutes.

'No, from up north somewhere. Now, do you want to come back down with me to reception. You can get your room key, visit the kitchen and I can get someone to show you the photos we have on file.'

They went back down and Scott spent the next two hours talking with the chef and checking the hotels photo database. He met with Miguel the doorman and took some photos; the large droopy moustache was too good to not be included in his article.

Natalya arrived at the hotel at six and called Scott from the lobby. He went down to meet her, they retrieved their key and bags from reception and went up to the room. It was a small suite made up of a huge bedroom, with a large bathroom and separate lavatory. There was a complementary bottle of cava in an ice bucket. Scott made a mental note to thank Sambat, poured a couple of glasses and they went out onto the small balcony that overlooked the tree lined avenue below.

Natalya told him about her afternoon. She had wandered round the *Barrio Gótico* and been to see one of the Gaudí houses on *Passeig de Gracia*. The *Casa Batló* was designed around the theme of St George and the Dragon, the saint being the patron of Barcelona, and was the most visibly stunning of Gaudí's nineteenth century masterpieces. The roof mimicked the scales of the dragon, with the chimneys signifying the St George's lance. Scott had never been into the house, as in his day it had not been open to the public, and let Natalya take him through the mass of photos she had taken with her phone of the interior, with its original décor and furniture.

Scott told Natalya their table was for nine, so they decided they would head down to the bar early for a cocktail. Natalya went for a shower and Scott opened his laptop to catch up with some emails, but soon decided to join her in the shower.

.

# EIGHTEEN

They made it down to the Canelo Bar just before nine, Natalya was looking stunning in a simple black dress and Scott had put on one of the shirts he had bought in the Borne district that afternoon. The room was busy, with most of the banquettes full and about ten people milling around the bar area. At the bar, they had a look at the cocktail menu and Natalya opted for a Bellini while Scott tried the Canelo house cocktail: a mix of rum, vodka, tequila and cinnamon. The cocktails were very good, and they were about to retreat to a banquette when a couple walked into the bar. The girl, who was taller than her companion, had a stunning figure and long, dark hair, looked up to catch Scott's gaze as they neared the bar. The surprise on her face mirrored that on Scott's.

'*María!*'

'*Alejandro! ¿Qué haces aquí?*'

'We're having dinner here in the Balconera. I'm doing some work for the hotel.' He said, kissing her on both cheeks. 'How strange bumping into you. How lovely to see you.'

'*Igualmente. Qué casualidad. ¿Me presentas a tu amiga?*'

'Of course. María…Natalya. Natalya, María.' Natalya held out her hand which María took but leaned forward and kissed her on both cheeks.

'And…?' Scott said looking at her companion.

The man was in his twenties, of medium height, with close cropped blonde hair and bright blue eyes. He was wearing a black and white Versace shirt, grey slacks and sparkling gold trainers. He had a slight build and an effeminate air about him.

'Dimitri Olenka.' Then she said in English: 'Dimitri, can I introduce you to an old friend, Alejandro Scott? They are having dinner here at the same restaurant.' Scott held out his hand to Olenka who gripped it harder than necessary and pulled it towards him as he shook it. So, this is the billionaire, thought Scott.

'Alejandro, Dimitri has come to Barcelona for the night and kindly asked me to dinner,' said María.

'Pleased to meet you,' said Scott.

'Would you guys like to join us for dinner?' Olenka had a Russian accent with a slight American twang to it. He

'Thanks, but we already have a table.'

'Natalya.' Olenka nodded to her and said something in Russian.

'You know each other already?' Scott asked.

'Er…yes,' replied Natalya, who looked lightly taken aback. 'Mr Olenka is a…. a partner… in the company I work for.'

'Call me Dimitri, please.' Olenka said in English.

'Well, what a coincidence,' said Scott. 'Everyone knows each other. And I think I know your lawyer Mr Olenka.'

'Dimitri, Please.'

'Dimitri. I think he rang me trying to buy my friends' house. We're neighbours. I'm in the house along the coast from your lighthouse. Can Daurat?'

'Ah, yes of course. The blue and white house. I asked my lawyer to make an offer. It was a good price. You should have accepted. Too late now. I am no longer interested.'

'Well, the house wasn't for sale anyway,' said Scott, feeling irritated by the Russian.

'Now, María, I think a drink is in order. What is that?' Olenka said pointing at Scott's cocktail.

'It's their speciality, it's got cinnamon in it. It's good.'

'Two of those.' Olenka said to the barman, pointing at Scott's drink again.

'Was the wedding fun?' Scott asked María.

'Yes thanks. How was *your* weekend?' asked Maria, her gaze moving to Natalya.

'All good, it's been great to be back,' said Scott, ignoring the innuendo in María's comment. 'I tried to call Santi, but got no answer.'

'He's been very busy with Mr Olenka. They have been doing a lot of work at the lighthouse.'

'I know. I've been passed a couple of times and there is loads of banging going on.' He turned to Olenka. 'You are doing a lot of work on the lighthouse? Are you building a jetty at the bottom of the cliff?'

'So, you are in the white and blue house next to my lighthouse?' said Olenka, ignoring Scott's question.

'If you mean Can Daurat, yes.'

'And you are, what? The caretaker?'

'No, I am a friend of the owners. I have come out…'

'Last week, I wanted to buy it.' Olenka said to María. 'But now I am no longer interested.'

'My friends don't want to sell.' Scott said.

'Well, I have gone off the idea anyway.' said Olenka. 'They should have accepted when they had the chance.'

'Well. That's life isn't it,' said Scott, thinking the conversation was going nowhere. 'Well, Dimitri, it was nice meeting you. María, *hasta pronto.'* Scott picked up their drinks and walked with Natalya over to a banquette.

'You didn't tell me you knew Olenka.' Scott said to Natalya when they had sat down. 'When I talked about the lighthouse you never mentioned him.'

'Er…I…I didn't know it was his place. I have only met him…. a few times. He is a partner in the company. He doesn't really mix with us.'

'What an arse,' said Scott, then saw how miserable her expression was and added: 'Sorry, he's your boss and all, but…Didn't want to get stuck having dinner…' Scott paused as Natalya's gaze suddenly looked up at something behind him.

'I've told the waiter to put you on my table,' announced Olenka from just behind Scott.

'I'm sorry. What?' he said wheeling round to face the Russian.

'I told the waiter we will eat together. He will put us all together.'

'Really, there's no need. We wouldn't want to intrude…' started Scott.

'Not at all.'

'I am actually here for work, so I'm afraid it won't be poss…"

'Don't worry about it. I'll clear it with the manager. He'll do anything I say. It's no problem,' interrupted Olenka, 'and I'm buying the wine. This way at least you will drink something good. Natalya, you would like to join us?'

'Yes, we'd like very much to join you,' replied Natalya, with what Scott thought looked like a fake smile. As Olenka walked back to get María she whispered to Scott:

'Sorry Alex. I'd rather be alone. But…. He…is my employer. Do you mind?' She put her hand on his.

'Ok, well… OK. Of course not,' lied Scott.

Olenka and María brought their drinks over to their banquette.

'So, Dimitri, are you here in Barcelona for long?' asked Scott when they had sat down.

'Just one night. The Costa Brava is pretty, but it's a little boring. I felt like the company of a beautiful lady and here I am.' Olenka said with a lascivious look in María's direction.

'And what brought you to the Costa Brava.'

'I had heard a lot about the coast and the area. I decided to make a few investments.' He said. 'I came over a few weeks ago.' He indicated María. 'With the help of María's brother Santiago, I have been redeveloping some properties.'

'Is that your line of business in Russia?'

'No, it's just a side line. I'm in commodities. Oil. Gas. Gold. There are many fortunes in Russia in oil. Russia is the best country in the world for commodities. What business are you in Alech...Alech...'

'Alex, just Alex is easier.'

'Ok, Alex. What business are you in?'

'I am a journalist.'

'A reporter. Is that why you are in the Costa Brava?'

'Well, I can work from here.'

'And so, what are you investigating here?' Olenka seemed wary of Scott.

'Just some food articles. I'm writing a piece on this hotel. That's why we are here.'

'Ahh, a food hack.' Olenka seemed to relax. 'Then you will like the restaurant tonight. There is a six-month waiting list. I am told it is impossible to get a table for... for normal people. I called the manager from my helicopter and he arranged a table for me.'

'I heard there were a couple of cancellations,' said Scott.

'We've all finished out drinks, shall we go through?' Olenka stood and indicated the door from the bar to the restaurant.

On the way, Scott spoke to María in Spanish.

*'So, this guy, what's his story?'*

*'My brother asked me to go out for dinner with him. Do you remember the plans I brought to Begur? He bought the lot. A lot of money. He has bought some of the houses my grandfather built. My brother has gone mad over this guy. Thinks he will make a fortune. Asked me to show him a bit of Barcelona. Who's the Russian?'*

*'Ukrainian. She's a friend. I met her over the weekend in Begur.'*

*'She's pretty.'*

*'Strange us all being here. Did Juan tell you I'd be here?'*

*'No. Dimitri called me this morning and said he was staying here. It was a complete surprise to see you here.'*

*'Well I said I'd see you this week.'*

*'Did you call me late Friday night?'*

*'Er…Yes. I was with Juan and we wondered if you…'*

The restaurant was half-full, with a couple of tables in the middle unoccupied. There was a quite murmur of gentle conversations and a gentle clink and clatter of glassware and cutlery. A waiter took them to the middle of the room to a large round table that could happily have sat double their number. Olenka had called the waiter over.

'We want to move to that table.' He said, pointing to the table next to it which was laid for six people. As for as Scott could see there was no difference between the two tables.

'I'm sure we'll be fine here.' Said Scott.

'No, it's no problem,' said Olenka. Then to the waiter: 'Yes, we'll sit on this table.' He pointed to a chair for María and sat down in the chair next to it. The waiter who was standing next to María pulled out her chair. Scott shrugged and held out a chair for Natalya. Once they were seated the waiter changed over the menus and removed two placings, then placed a centrepiece made of crystals and rock in the middle of the table.

'We have made a special menu for today. Has anyone any allergies or dietary needs?'

'Do you have any caviar?' asked Olenka. 'I would like some caviar and some cold vodka.'

'Er… sir…the tasting menu is prepared especially. I will ask the chef,' replied the waiter.

'Just a little to get our taste buds going,' said Olenka, winking at Scott. 'And bring me the wine list.' The waiter went away and immediately another waiter came to their table. He introduced himself as the sommelier.

*'Señor* Sambat said Mr Scott was to have the wine tasting menu. I prepare a special list to complement the food. We have some…'

'No, I'll choose the wine,' interrupted Olenka. 'My treat. They never give you the good stuff on these menus.'

'I don't know,' said Scott. 'I'd say nowadays restaurants are pretty expert at combining the food with the wine.' He turned to the sommelier. 'Thank you, we'd like to try your selection.' Then to Olenka. 'Thanks for the offer Dimitri but I think we will stick to what was prepared for us.'

'Suit yourself,' said Olenka, *'we,'* he paused to look at María, then turned to the sommelier, 'will start with the bottle of the Krug Clos d'Ambonnay 1995 that I believe should be cold by now. And you can decant the best bottle of Pingus that you have.'

'Yes, of course sir,' said the sommelier.

'I always ask ahead when I go to a hotel.' Olenka spoke directly to Scott. 'They never have any decent champagne. The wine list here looks drinkable though. I had the manager show me a copy when I arrived.' There was a moment of silence, Scott picked up his napkin from the table and put it on his lap.

'So, Natalya,' said María, 'how long have you known Alejandro?'

'Well, we just met last weekend. I am working in Begur. Do you know it?'

'Yes, of course, my family is from there. What work do you do?'

'The lovely Natalya works in a, er, relocation agency of mine,' said Olenka looking at the Ukrainian. Then he turned to Scott. 'Great business. I believe we Russians are the only people buying any property these days.'

'I have heard you have bought various properties Dimitri. Are you thinking of settling here or is it for development?' asked Scott. 'What are your plans for the lighthouse?'

'Where is that waiter with the champagne?' said Olenka ignoring Scott and turning round in his seat. 'It can't take this long to open a bottle. Balconera?' he said, looking at the cover of the wine list. 'What does that mean?'

'Something to do with a balcony.' Said Scott. 'Although I can't see any balconies in here. There is nothing even resembling a…'

'They're anagrams,' said María.

'I'm sorry. What are anagrams?' asked Scott

'Balconera… Arena Bloc… Canelo Bar. They are all anagrams. Of Barcelona.'

'And the Lacone Bar,' said Scott. 'Clever. How did you know that?'

'I thought it was pretty obvious,' said María smiling at Scott.

'Aren't we the clever one,' teased Scott. The waiter had returned with a bottle of champagne and an ice bucket. Olenka insisted everyone would like a glass so the waiter returned with four very fine champagne flutes on the table and opened the bottle. He poured everyone a glass and left the bottle in the bucket.

'Krug made this from one field of pinot noir in 1995. They only made around 5000 bottles. Superb,' declared Olenka, swigging at his glass. They all tried theirs.

'What do you think Alex? You, the food hack?' Olenka said to Scott, the question sounding like an insult.

'Amazing. Incredibly smooth. Delicious.'

'Is it very expensive?' Natalya asked Scott.

'Last month I paid three thousand euros for a bottle, but as I had to get the hotel to find me this it cost me double,' said Olenka in a loud voice that carried across the restaurant.

*'Joder, seis mil euros. Para una botella. ¡Vaya jilipollez!'* María said to Scott, then, having said what an arsehole he was for paying so much for a bottle of wine, turned to Olenka and said in English, 'I was just saying how delicious it is.'

The waiter brought out the start of what turned out to be a spectacular tasting menu. In all there were ten dishes, starting with the chef's take on a fusion of traditional tapas and Japanese cuisine. Then there followed a succession of delightful dishes with everything from a cherry gazpacho to roast suckling pigs' ears in an acorn fed ham mousse. When the bottle of champagne was finished, a bottle of Pingus 2001 was opened for Olenka, who promptly decided the wine was too cold and asked for another one. The sommelier took the bottle and came back with another. He offered some to Natalya and Scott, who thanked him but turned him down, choosing to follow the recommendations of the restaurant. With each course a different wine was produced for them. They were all delicious, and Scott could see Olenka eying each new arrival with what looked like jealousy despite the bottle of wine he and María were sharing.

Conversation was stilted. Scott made an effort with Natalya but she was very quiet throughout the dinner, which he took for shyness in front of Olenka. María chatted away with Scott about Begur, Charlie Franklin and old times. This seemed to irritate Olenka, who seemed more interested in proving his knowledge of all the most exclusive resorts and destinations in the world than holding any real conversation. Scott judged him to be in his late twenties or early thirties, but he spoke with the confidence of the very rich. Everything he said was said as a statement of fact, as if there was no possible alternative position. It had always bugged Scott that the combination of financial success and a sycophantic entourage made the very wealthy believe that their opinions on anything and everything were somehow superior to those of other people.

The menu ended with a dessert and a cheese course. In the break before the dessert, Olenka went off to the toilet. It was a relief to be free of his oppressive company for a few minutes.

On his return Olenka called over the waiter and ordered a bottle of 2001 Chateau d'Yquem. By this stage in the proceedings Scott was feeling the effects of the wine and Natalya had a rosy glow to her face. María seemed totally sober and a little bored. Olenka, perked up after the trip to the toilet, launched into a series of self-congratulatory anecdotes. They were served a delicious chocolate mousse, made with caramel sculptures and a frozen hazelnut cloud. Olenka hardly touched his, and the two girls declared themselves full after the desert, so Scott alone ate the last dish of the menu, a surprisingly light cheese soufflé combined with a salted fresh fruit 'cake,' on his own.

They decided to go back into the bar for coffee. Olenka took the girls through while Scott went to the kitchens. He congratulated the chef and the sommelier on their triumph, and thanked them for their effort. The chef said the hotel would email Scott some professional photos he had had taken of a couple of the dishes for the article.

Scott went from the kitchens along a corridor to the lobby and then into the bar to join up with the other three. As he crossed the lobby he passed a man whose face was vaguely familiar. He thought he had seen a flash of recognition on his face, so he stopped, intending on turning round to say hello, but the man had carried on past him and, realising he could not place the face, he decide to carry on into the bar.

They were sitting at a table with coffees and Olenka was nursing a large balloon cognac glass. As Scott sat down, María finished her cup of coffee and declared:

'Well, Dimitri, thank you very much for a lovely dinner. Now I must be heading home. I have a meeting early in the morning.'

Olenka put his hand on her arm.

'No, María, stay please. The night is still young. Come on. You must show me some of Barcelona. Santiago said you would.'

'Thank you but I really must be going.'

'Come on, it's not late. It is only half past twelve. Come on, I insist, stay for a drink.'

'No Dimitri,' said María, this time with a bit of irritation in her voice, and pulled her arm from under his. 'I am going home. Thank you for dinner. Natalya, nice to meet you,' She leant over to Natalya and gave her two kisses, 'and Alejandro, see you soon.' She gave Olenka a peck on the cheek, then as she kissed Scott goodbye said to Scott in Spanish: *What a bore. Just because he has my brother jumping through hoops, doesn't mean he owns me. See you soon.'*

Olenka's gaze followed her as she walked across the bar, then went to Scott.

'What a beautiful lady. If she weren't so stuck up! Eh? So, my friend, you will join me? Have a cognac.'

'Thanks, but I'm bushed. After this coffee, I think I'll call it a day.'

'I have some restorative, if you would like? Very good!' Olenka said to Scott, tapping his nose.

'Thanks, not really my thing.'

'It's great stuff. Try some.' He started to rummage in his pocket.

'No, really, it's not for me,' said Scott as Olenka produced a small bag of white powder.

'I love this country.' Said Olenka. 'You can get anything you want. Natalya...' He said something to Natalya in Russian.

'Scott, shall we stay for one more drink?' She said when Olenka had finished. 'I would really like a vodka and soda.'

'Ok, one more drink then.' Scott called over a passing waiter and asked for a vodka and soda and a whisky with water. The waiter showed him the whisky list and, feeling like something light, Scott asked for a Glenmorangie 10-year-old.

Over the following twenty minutes Olenka made two more trips to the toilet and by the time Scott finished his drink, he was sick to death of the young oligarch, his continual one-upmanship, his bragging about wealth and his inexplicable belief that they were somehow best buddies. When Natalya finally finished her drink, Scott thanked Olenka for his generosity and led her off, with Olenka still protesting the night was young.

In the lobby on the way to the lifts, Scott saw the man he had seen earlier. He still couldn't place him and the man turned away again. In the lift, Scott let out a sigh.

'Thank God that's over. What a bore.'

'I'm sorry Alex. He was insistent that we had dinner with him. I'm sorry if…'

'Don't worry. What's done is done. It would have been nicer to have just had dinner with you, that's all.'

'María is very beautiful. Have you known her long?'

'Since I was a teenager. Her cousin is an old friend…actually, you met him. Juan. The night we met. Remember/'

'Yes, of course.'

'My friend Charlie and I used to hang out with Juan and María brother Santi a lot. María was just a kid then.' They had arrived at their floor. 'Did I not mention that a Russian was trying to buy Can Daurat. The house I'm staying at?'

'Sorry? What?'

'The other day. Didn't I mention that there was a Russian trying to buy Can Daurat? When you said, you did relocation?'

'I don't think so.'

'And I never mentioned Olenka?'

'I don't think so. I'm sure I would have remembered.'

'Was Olenka the one you said was looking for a house?'

'No, that was a family from St Petersburg.'

'Ok,' said Scott, opening the door to the room. 'And you didn't say to work you were coming to this hotel?'

'Why? No. I mean, I don't think so. So what, why the questions?' Natalya was upset.

'Ok. Calm down. It's just a bit odd him coming to the same restaurant on the same night as us. Forget it.'

Natalya walked into the bathroom and closed the door. Scott walked over to the window, opened it and went out onto the balcony. There were hardly any cars on the streets at this time, and the tree-lined avenue was bathed in the orange glow of street lamps. All the lights in the buildings in front were off except for one window which had the blue flickering of a television. Over the top of the building in front he could just see the top of the *Tibidabo* hill. He could remember the view from up there being spectacular.

He heard the click of a door latch and saw Natalya come out of the bathroom. She slipped off her dress and got straight into bed. Scott went into the bathroom. As he brushed his teeth he realised he was being silly about Olenka. Natalya obviously felt Scott was judging her by association. Nothing an apology couldn't solve. As he climbed into bed he realised Natalya was already asleep. He whispered her name but got no reply.

Rolling onto his back, Scott looked at the orange glow on the ceiling coming in from the open balcony door. Suddenly it came to him. He knew where he had seen the man in the lobby. He was the hiker he had seen outside the lighthouse in Begur.

# NINETEEN

The telephone woke Scott. It was eight thirty. He hadn't asked for a wakeup call.

'*Si, dígame.*'

'Mr Scott?' An English voice.

'Yes.'

'Mr Alex Scott?'

'Yes, that's me.'

'Good morning Mr Scott. You don't know me. I'm Peter Taylor. I work for the Financial Times.'

Scott had a parched mouth and a throbbing in his head. Not the worst, but still a hangover by anyone's standards.

'Sorry…how can I help you?'

'I am a friend of Josh Hill.' Hill was a colleague of Scott's in London. 'He told me you work together.'

'Yes. Well. Sort of. How did you …?'

'I have something very important I'd like to discuss with you. Could we talk?'

'Look. It's not great timing. What's this about?' Scott looked over at Natalya who was still asleep.

'It's really very important Mr Scott. I wouldn't bother you if it weren't. It won't take up much of your time. I urgently need to speak to you.'

'Well, today is a no-no. If you give me your phone number, I'll call you tomorrow or later on in the week and we can talk.'

'It really has to be now Mr Scott. It concerns your friend *Señor* Ruiz.'

'*Señor* Ruiz?' Scott paused. 'You mean Manolo? What do you mean it concerns him?'

'I can't say over the phone, Mr Scott. If we could just meet, I'll explain. Please, call Josh, he'll back me up. We really must meet up. Today.'

'I can't meet up, I'm in Barcelona.' Scott then realised that the caller must know this as he had called the hotel phone.

'So am I. I am in a hotel round the corner from yours.'

'Ok, I'll call Josh. If he says you're ok I'll call you back. Can you give me your number?'

Peter Taylor gave him an English mobile number which he keyed into his mobile phone.

'Give me an hour or so and I'll call you.'

'Thank you, Mr Scott. And please, don't tell anybody about this.'

'Ok I won't.'

'I'm really serious. Please don't tell a soul I have rung you. Don't mention my name to anyone. Apart from Josh. I don't think I'm exaggerating to say this is life or death.'

'Ok, I won't tell anyone. Let's speak in an hour.' Scott said putting down the phone. Feeling rather fazed by the call, Scott rubbed his eyes, then rolled over and gave Natalya a shake.

'Good morning! Time to wake up!'

'Morning' Said Natalya from under the sheet. What time is it?'

'Eight thirty. Come on wake up. Feel like breakfast?'

'Oh, after last night I don't think I'll ever eat again. What's the plan? When shall we head back up the coast? What time do we have to leave here? Can't we go back to sleep?'

'Well, I thought we'd have some breakfast, then… I might have a meeting that I'd forgotten about. Just have to call to see if it's still on. If it is I shouldn't be more than an hour. I can get that out of the way, then we could either head back up to Begur, or we could spend the morning in town. You must see the Sagrada Familia.'

'Ok. Let me wake up and have a shower. Are we having breakfast here in the room?'

'Why not? You jump in the shower and I'll get us some breakfast. What do you want?'

'Just some coffee for me.'

'And orange juice?'

'Lovely'

'Scrambled eggs?'

'Ugh, no!'

'Sausages and mushrooms?'

'Shut up. Just coffee, and orange juice.' Natalya got out of bed and walked into the bathroom. Scott picked up the phone and dialled the number for room service. He ordered breakfast for two. When he heard the shower running he picked up his phone, found Josh Hill's number and rang it. After a couple of rings, it was answered.

'Yo!'

'Hi Josh. It's Alex Scott. You sound very lively for this time in the morning!'

'Hi Alex. Been up for hours. It's our second one. He's not sleeping too well. Bit of colic. So,' he paused, 'Peter called me last night asking about you.'

'A Peter Taylor rang me just now. Wanted to meet up. Here in Barcelona. Said you knew him.'

'Yes, he's a mate. His son's the same age as Bella,' Scott had to assume Bella was his daughter, 'they're at kindergarten together. I've known Peter for a while though. Good man. Good journalist. Found out that you had written some pieces for the paper and rang me to see if I knew you.'

'He says it's really important. Life or death. Mentioned a friend of mine who died recently.'

'Look, if Peter says that, then it's probably the case. Never known him to go off the handle.'

'He's being very cagey. Won't speak over the phone and all.'

'Hear him out, will you? I'm sure he'll be able to explain. He's a good man.'

'Ok Josh, thanks for that.'

'No problemo amigo. How's the weather in Barcelona?'

'Usual. Clear skies. Sun. Probably too hot. How's London?'

'Oh, fuck off. Good to speak, Alex. Let's go out for a pint when you're back.'

'Ok, Thanks Josh.'

The shower was still running so Scott call the number Taylor had given him. It answered on the first ring.

'Hello. Yes?'

'Peter Taylor?'

'Did you call Josh? Can we meet up?'

'Yes. I can see you in an hour or so. I've only got an hour. Where do you want to meet? Why not come to my room?'

'No, that wouldn't be a good idea. Why don't you come here? I'm in the Hotel Berlin, just round the corner. If you turn right out the front of your hotel and take the first street on the left, it's straight in front of you. Can't miss it. Room 306. Come straight up.'

'I'll be there.'

'And Mr Scott….'

'Yes, I know. I won't tell anyone. See you then.' Scott hung up. He heard the shower stop. The bathroom door opened and Natalya came out wearing a towel and sat at the table by the window. She appeared rather distant.

'Look Natalya, I'm sorry about last night. Didn't mean to give you the third degree.'

'Third degree? What's that?'

'I mean … You seem a little cross…Maybe I was…'

'It's just,' Natalya paused, 'Last night *you* seemed cross with *me*. I'm sorry we had dinner with Mr Olenka. I'm sorry I asked you to...'

'Ok, don't worry about it. I was just pissed off that I had to spend the evening with a bore spouting crap about himself instead of having a lovely dinner with you. Let's write it off as a work dinner. We'll make up for it with a really lovely dinner, just you and me.' He held her gaze. 'Ok?'

Scott got out of bed and went over to where she was sitting.

'I'm not sure we have made the full use of this room yet.' He said, leaning forward to kiss her. Natalya's arms reached up round his neck, her towel falling down to the floor, and there was a knock at the door.

'Room service.'

'Damn' said Scott, as Natalya gathered up her towel and skipped into the bathroom. Scott put a towel round his waist and opened the door. There was a liveried waiter with a huge trolley on wheels. He asked Scott where he wanted it and Scott pointed to by the window. Having navigated the room, he unfurled two panels to make the trolley a round table, then proceeded to take from underneath a series of silverware jugs and plates with domes on them. He brought up two glasses of orange juice with little paper covers. He laid two plates, cups, saucers and cutlery, then placed the room's two chairs at the table. He then brought up a small vase with a carnation in it. He removed the domes with a flourish to reveal an assortment of croissants, pastries and toast.

Scott felt in his jeans pocket and found a five euro note and gave it to the waiter who asked him to sign, thanked him then left.

'Has he gone?' said Natalya from the bathroom.

'Yes.' She came out.

'I thought you were only getting coffee? What's all this?'

'Breakfast,' said Scott. 'We've got coffee, orange juice. A croissant or two.'

They sat at the table in their towels with the morning light streaming through the window. After breakfast, Scott had a shower and then told Natalya he had to go out for his meeting. He said he'd only be an hour, she should wait there and then they could go and do a bit of tourism.

The Berlin was a small three-star hotel that occupied one building in the next block to the Arena Bloc. Scott said good morning to the receptionist and asked for *Señor* Taylor in room 306. The receptionist just pointed to the lift that occupied the old stair well of the building. As Scott stepped from the lift on the third-floor, automatic lights came on in the corridor. It was painted white and had a grey carpet and the occasional framed print of Barcelona along the walls. Room 306 was at the end. Scott knocked at the door and heard a scuffle and then:

'Hello?'

'Hello? Mr Taylor. It's Alex Scott.'

There was the clunk of the door being unlocked and then opened. Scott was not surprised to see the man he had spotted in the lobby of the Arena Bloc the night before. It was the same man that Scott had seen outside the lighthouse, but without the beard.

'Hello, hello. Come in. Please.' Scott came in the door and Taylor locked it behind him. He waved him in. There was a small bathroom, a cupboard of sorts and the bedroom that was in the corner of the building. Most of the room was taken up by the twin beds which were place side by side, allowing just enough room for a table and chair and a small mini bar under the table.

'Peter Taylor,' he said, holding out his hand, 'pleased to meet you.' Taylor was shorter than average, slightly overweight, with close-cut brown hair that was greying at the temples. He had an oval face with bright brown eyes that sparkled out from a nest of laughter lines. He was wearing an orange shirt and jeans, with only socks on his feet.

'Alex Scott,' said Scott shaking his hand.

'Sorry about the space. Lucky I didn't bring a cat along, eh? Now, grab a seat, would you like the chair or the bed?'

'I'll take the chair if that's ok,' said Scott.

'Of course, of course.' Taylors grabbed a bundle of files and papers that was on the chair and placed it on the bed which was already covered in paperwork. There was a laptop on the bed with its power cord plugged in under the table. Scott had to squeeze past Taylor and step over the cord to get to the chair.

'Sit down, sit down. Please. Can I get you a drink? Not sure what's in the mini bar. A water, or a coke?'

'I'm fine thanks,' said Scott, sitting down in the chair. 'I've only got an hour or so. Could you start by telling me what on earth this is all about? What is this about Manolo?'

'Of course. Let me just put on the telly.' Taylor pressed a button on the remote control and the television came on. He increased the volume a little. 'Just in case someone is listening at the door.

'Well. Where to start?' He looked from side to side as if looking for a physical starting point. 'I thought I saw you recognise me yesterday in the hotel. I thought Olenka was on to me.'

'Is this about Olenka? I saw you in the lobby. It was only after that I realised where I had seen you before. You were hiking next to the lighthouse in Begur. But you had a beard.'

'Ahh, that's where you recognised me from. Thought I saw a flash of recognition in your face last night. I wondered where I had slipped up. Thought the beard was quite a good disguise.'

'I was running past the lighthouse a couple of days ago. You were outside it getting your camera out.'

'Very observant. I didn't recognise you. *Now* I remember.'

'What has Olenka got to do with Manolo? Was he involved in his death?'

'Not only involved. Responsible. I believe it was murder. Shall I start from the beginning?'

'Go on,' said Scott.

154

'Ok. I, as I'm sure Josh told you, I write investigative pieces, mainly for the FT. A while ago I wrote an article on Russian oligarchs who were on the run from the state. I don't know how much you know?'

'Not that much.' Scott admitted.

'After the break-up of the Soviet Union in 1990, Russia saw the largest privatisation boom in history. Before 1990, all industry was state owned. With their new capitalism post 1990, these state-owned industries issued shares that were physically distributed to the population. Peasant farmers and workers who had no concept of corporate structure or shareholding were given bundles of shares and told to get on with it.' Taylor took a sip from a cup on the side table.

'Like a pack of vultures, the oligarchs of the future went around buying up these share certificates at a fraction of their real cost. They were being sold on the street in Russia in bundles by the kilo. Few knew their real value, so shares were sold to buy bread, to buy eggs, whatever. How could a simple worker know the value of one share in the newly privatised aluminium company he works for? These young businessmen, many of them in their twenties, made untold fortunes in the space of a few years. The Moscow stock exchange and the Commodities exchange just gave these bright opportunists an arena in which to increase their wealth by consolidating their holdings in the newly privatised companies.' Taylor paced as he spoke, but due to the size of the room could only take a pace and a half before turning round.

'While the regime tolerated the wholescale rape of the country by these newly named 'oligarchs,' it had two conditions. Firstly, no politics. As soon as an oligarch dips his toe in politics without the express wish of the premier, it's off to the gulag with you, and I'll have your cash now, thanks. That's why the richest man in Russia, aged thirty-four and chairman of Yukos, ended up languishing in chokey. He made the mistake of getting involved with his

'Open Russia' foundation. It was only in 2013 that he was released from prison and went abroad. His fortune had gone from $15 billion to $500 million. No prizes for guessing where that money went. He's started to get involved in politics again in exile in Switzerland, so look out for a sudden accident or weird radiation poisoning. The second requirement of the state is that a percentage of their wealth goes to their wonderful premier. It doesn't matter where they are based, Moscow or Belgravia, everyone pays his share.'

Taylor turned to Scott.

'Are you sure you don't want a drink?'

'I'm fine, thanks. What has this all got to do with Olenka?' asked Scott. 'And Manolo?'

'Olenka's grandfather was some form of naval officer from Sevastopol. Commander in the Russian merchant navy before the war. Got zapped by Stalin in one of the purges. His son Alexei, Dimitri's father, was the port manager in Sevastopol and managed to get his grubby paws into a share of most maritime commerce going through the port. He was about to retire in the early nineties but managed to hold on in his position long enough to make the most of the privatisations. Little Dimitri was brought up a prince with not only every finger in a different commodity pie, but his toes too. He's into oil in Kazakhstan, gold in Siberia and anything else he can get his grubby hands on. His company Zoloto industries has holdings in numerous companies all over Russia and the old Soviet republics.

'All these holdings have been acquired through bribery, corruption, extortion and theft. Any complaints and the problem just disappears. Either the courts throw it out or, as has happened in many cases, the complainer is physically thrown out. Literally. Out of the window. It's a speciality of one of Olenka's lieutenants. Mikhail Spralov. Huge great big thug with a shaved head. Looks like the comic villain.'

'I think I've seen him,' said Scott, remembering the boat trip with Juan.

'But there is nothing *comical* about him. Ex-KGB killer. I had a contact at Zoloto. A nice man. A good man. Became a bit of a friend. He managed to get his hands on some incriminating documents. Passed them on to me. They found out and next thing I hear he has 'fallen' from his flat while cleaning his windows. In winter. No one in Russia would ever open the window in winter, let alone clean it.'

'Do you think Manolo....?'

'Your friend Manolo is just another in a long line of people who have had strange accidents. The fact that Olenka had just moved in next door is more than a coincidence.'

Scott looked at his watch. He had said to Natalya that he would only be an hour.

'Can I stop you a second, Mr Taylor?'

'David, please.'

'I've just got to call someone.'

'Please, go ahead.'

Scott took out his mobile and dialled Natalya. He told her that the meeting was dragging on, that he wasn't sure how long he would be. Maybe she should start without him? He suggested a walk up the *Paseo de Gracia*. There was the *Taipes* museum, and she could visit the *Pedrera*, another Gaudí building just up from the *Casa Batló*, then head towards the *Sagrada Familia*. He would be as quick as possible and would join her when he could. He asked her to leave their bags at reception. He hung up and said to Taylor:

'Sorry about that. Now, what problem would Olenka have with Manolo?'

'I'm coming to that Alex. You don't mind if I call you Alex, do you?'

'Of course not.'

'So, young Olenka is king of the castle in Sevastopol, he behaves himself and keeps out of politics. Just feathers his gilded nest with more and more money. But he is lazy and hasn't been making the expected payoffs, so much so that he has to go into temporary exile in western Europe. Olenka, being a commodities man, is heavily involved in the derivatives market and comes up with a tidy solution to get the money to the premier.

'His plan was to buy options from one of the premier's Panama-owned companies. He spent a hundred and fifty million dollars buying these options, which give him the right to sell oil to the premier at a very low price. The price is way below the foreseeable price for oil, so, in essence, the options are worthless. All he has to do is let the options expire and he has paid a hundred and fitly million to the premier for some worthless options. And all legal and above board. Payoff successful.

'But Olenka was greedy. He wanted to have his cake and eat it. He has hedged his 'loss' with the premier by doing the opposite, in an attempt to recoup the money spent on the premier's options. He has tried to compensate by *selling* similar options to everybody else. And I mean everybody. The options he has been selling were considered so worthless he has had to sell a lot. Many times the number of options he bought off the premier.

'But then the oil market collapsed. Few had seen the effect fracking would have on the US market. Stock piles grew, production grew, Saudi kept pumping and the price of a barrel of oil fell through the floor. Suddenly, Olenka's 'worthless' options that he has bought for a fortune are worth many times the amount he paid for them. But so are all those options he has sold. The crash in the market has made him a fortune from the options he bought from the premier, but he will owe twice that to the market.'

'Wait a sec,' said Scott. 'If he has sold a load of options to the market, how does that make him lose money?'

'If I sell you a 'put' option, an option to sell, I am selling you the right to sell me oil at the agreed price. So Olenka has sold the right to sell oil, i.e. he is obliged to buy at what was a very low price, but what now is higher than market price. When the options expire, Olenka will owe the difference between the option price and the market price to those he sold the options.'

'Ok, I'm with you… just,' said Scott.

'Olenka is basically broke. And instead of paying the premier his hundreds of millions of 'tax,' he has burnt him for hundreds of millions. The options expire at the end of the month, this Friday. I estimate by close of business on Friday, the premier will owe Olenka six hundred million dollars, and Olenka will owe the others around double that. If Olenka is to pay the markets, and return the premier's money, he will need twelve hundred million dollars just to stay alive. By Friday.'

'But what has that got…?'

'Nearly there,' interrupted Taylor. 'Now, why isn't Olenka panicking? He must have a few million in cash. And Zoloto is worth a few hundred million. But it's not liquid. He'll never be able to sell in a week. And his exposure to Kazakhstani oil will have reduced Zoloto's value. Anyway, I'm not sure it would cover this sort of debt.

'So, what the hell is he doing on the Costa Brava, when the proverbial shit is fast approaching the fan? He's swanning around buying houses, buzzing around in his chopper, having dinner with you in five star restaurants.' As Taylor spoke he waved his hands in the air.

'He has known for weeks that this was going to happen. But all he does is start investing in property on the coast here and spend all his time apparently renovating the buildings.

'I did some digging, and Olenka has just had a rush-job done on the *Rusalka*, his yacht. It's currently moored off the Costa Brava.' Taylor went to his suitcase and pulled out the camera that Scott had seen him with on the *Camí de Ronda*. He showed Scott a photo of the beige and gold liveried yacht.

'Yes, I've seen her. She's at Begur,' said Scott.

'It's just arrived on the coast from having a refit in Marseilles. I got a colleague to do a bit of rummaging and, apparently, the order was to alter the docking bay on the ship. To change it into a cargo hold. The order was to strengthen the floor to hold forty tonnes. And fast. Olenka paid the shipbuilders way above the odds to do the work in a week. And slap a crane on the back.'

'So, my question to you,' said Taylor, 'is, what weighs forty tonnes and can make billion dollar profits?'

'Drugs,' they both said at the same time.

'Exactly,' said Taylor. 'I can't think of anything else which could potentially provide such a massive cash profit. I did a few numbers. Take a kilo of cocaine. What's that worth? Apparently, you can buy a kilo of cocaine in a South American port for five or six thousand dollars, so let's say six million a tonne. Maybe less than that in quantity. What's a kilo worth in Europe? In Spain, it sells for eighty dollars a gram. That's eighty thousand dollars a kilo, eighty million a tonne. Allowing for a bulk sale, lets halve that to forty million a tonne. That's a profit of thirty-four million dollars a tonne.'

'So, forty tonnes... '

'That's around one point three billion.'

'That would cover his debts and give him a bit extra.'

'Exactly.'

'And you're thinking Begur is his point of entry?'

'Look,' said Taylor, searching through his papers and pulling out one sheet, 'I had a look at containers being shipped by Zoloto industries. Managed to get a source to leak the details. There's a container ship, the *Persiana*, a Panamanian container ship bound for Genoa. Its origin is Cartagena in Colombia. On it are two forty foot containers belonging to a subsidiary of Zoloto industries. Apparently, they contain tractor parts. Total weight fifty-six tonnes. Look at her proposed route.'

He showed Scott another paper with a map and a ships trajectory.

'Comes right past the Costa Brava on Thursday night. Or, there is the *Sudbury Hill*, a container ship that has just come through the Suez Canal. Destination Southampton. Another subsidiary of Zoloto has a similar cargo on board. Three forty foot containers with sixty-five tonnes. Something like tractor parts too. They were loaded at Karachi. Now that isn't a million miles from Afghanistan. The *Sudbury Hill* will also be passing the Costa Brava on Thursday night. Apparently, heroin use in western Europe is on the up. I looked at the figures and they are almost identical to cocaine, if anything slightly more lucrative.

'Security in European ports is very tight. Since we've been on high terrorism alert, the checks and controls in the ports have intensified. It's pretty risky trying to get anything into them. But what if the *Rusalka* went out to meet a ship? I would have thought it wouldn't take more than an hour or so to transfer forty tonnes. A billion and a half buys a lot of complicity.'

'What do you think this has to do with Manolo's death?' asked Scott.

'I have been digging into Olenka and his affairs for a while now. I first came across him when I was doing a series of articles on oligarchs in London. Since investigating his business I have had one source die in an 'accident,' heard of three other suspicious deaths, your friend included, and found numerous accounts of extortion, fraud and theft. I think your friend Manolo must have seen or overheard something that made him a threat. If Olenka is thinking of bringing in forty tonnes of narcotics, he's got to unload it somewhere.'

'And he's just built a jetty and crane at the lighthouse. It would be simple to off load there,' said Scott.

'Exactly. Your friend Manolo must have seen something.'

'I was sure there was something suspicious about his death. The way he supposedly fell. None of it made sense.'

'And death by falling is Olenka's man Spralov's favourite *modus operandi*. When Olenka started buying property here and I heard there had been an accidental death in a fall, I knew something was going on. Came straight out here from Moscow.'

'Olenka has been trying to buy Can Daurat. The house I'm staying at. It is the only house that has a view of the lighthouse. Apparently, he has bought other properties. He wanted an immediate sale.'

'Sounds like Olenka. If in doubt, throw money at it.'

'But now he says he isn't interested. I got attacked the other night. Came home and was hit over the head. I thought it looked like the *Rusalka*'s tender. I must have surprised them.'

'You got attacked? You're lucky to be here. I suppose two accidental falls would be too much of a coincidence. Attract too much attention.'

'But, Peter, why did you contact *me?* Surely the police would be better.'

'I can't go to the police. Not yet. Haven't got any evidence. At the moment, all I have is proof that Olenka is in for a fall himself. You can't start asking Interpol to stop container ships and search them. Not from a hunch. Not without proof. When I saw you having dinner with Olenka last night, I thought you might be his buyer in Spain. Having a last-minute meeting, to dot I's and cross T's as it were. Then I heard you speaking English. English accent. Well educated. Hardly your typical buyer of a billion and a half of drugs. So, I started digging and the nice receptionist let it slip that you were a journalist writing a piece on the hotel. A quick Google and I saw you were a colleague of Josh's. He's an old mate of mine. My son goes to kindergarten with his daughter. He confirmed that you were above board, said you were out in Spain doing a friend a favour, as their housekeeper had just died.' Taylor clicked his fingers. 'It all fell into place. The house where the guy fell. Neighbour of Olenka. *That* was your connection.'

'But I had never met Olenka before. It was a coincidence that we were at the hotel together.'

'Do you really think so?'

'How could he have known I was coming to Barcelona?'

'Did no one...?'

'Natalya.'

'The blonde?'

'Yes. She knew. And she works for him. Indirectly. But why would Olenka want to have dinner with me? I'm his neighbour. So what? What's so interesting about me?'

'That I can't tell you. You're his neighbour. Could you have seen anything?'

'I haven't. I suppose I have been poking around a bit. Taking photos. I've rung the police over Manolo's death. But why did *you* contact me?'

'I need your help. You are in a unique position to have a look from the inside. He seems interested in your company. Might as well make the most of it.'

'I hardly know the guy. Only met him yesterday.'

'He was quite chummy with you last night. Any chance you could get an invite to the lighthouse. Have look around?'

'I don't know...'

'Look, at the moment, I can't get close to Olenka. His goons know me from Russia. I was hanging round Zoloto too much. Wandering past with a beard was about as close as I want to get. And as you can see beard is gone. And I nearly got spotted last night. Well, I did get spotted, I suppose, by you.'

Taylor reached out hand grasped Scott's forearm.

'You are his neighbour. You have just had dinner with him. He won't be suspicious of you, if anything he wants something from you. You have an excuse to be toing and froing past the lighthouse.'

He let go and stepped back and leant against the table.

'If you can help me, maybe we can get the man who killed your friend. Just keep an eye out for anything suspicious. As soon as I think the drugs are on board the *Rusalka*, I can call the police.'

Scott took a moment to respond.

'I'll have a think about it. Ok, if he's responsible for Manolo's death, I'd like to see him caught. But from the sound of it, things could get dangerous...'

'I just need someone to keep an eye on him for the next few days.' Taylor pleaded.

Scott came to a decision. 'Ok, look. Why don't you come up and stay at Can Daurat on Thursday? You've got a ringside view of the lighthouse. Maybe we could do a trip or two out in the boat.'

'Really? Are you sure? That'd be great, really great.'

'And I can ask around locally. I can try to press my friend Santi for some answers. He's the local planning man. He might know what they are doing. Seems to think he's going to make loads of cash, apparently. But I can't see him being into drugs. Well, you never know. People change. You think it will happen on Thursday?'

'It has to. From Friday, close of business, Olenka is going to owe over a billion dollars. And the premier is going to have to pay him hundreds of millions of dollars. He's going to go ape. Olenka must have a plan up his sleeve. Otherwise why the cargo hold? The cranes? I can't think of anything else that makes sense. I'm sure one of those container ships is the carrier. And they both pass by on Thursday. He *has* to settle his options debts by close of business on Monday.'

'That's leaving it a bit close, isn't it?'

'Well if you have a boat load of cash, there are a number of places within two days' cruise that would be happy to accept a deposit. Gibraltar, Malta. Even Tripoli.'

'Ok. As soon as we know he's got the drugs we call the police. Do you have any contacts?' asked Scott.

'Not here. I have a few in London and Moscow. Spain's not really my turf.'

'I might have one,' said Scott, 'There is an inspector who looked into the death of Manolo. He thinks I'm a drunk getting over excited about an accident. Apparently, he's quite senior. If we had proof, it would be a pleasure to prove him wrong.'

'Mmmm,' mumbled Taylor, picking up his camera and scrolling through the photos, 'doesn't look anything like this, does he?' he said, showing Scott the screen. There was a photo of Matas and Olenka at the lighthouse.

'Oh no. Yes, that's him. Inspector Matas.'

'He's been up to the lighthouse a few times. Seems very chummy with our man. And that was just in the couple of days I was there. I think your inspector may be in Olenka's pocket. So, he's in charge of your friend's case then?'

'Yes. And I called him when I was attacked. He said he didn't believe a word. Probably because he knew it was true.' Scott paused. 'I thought there was something funny about him. Well, we can't go to *him*.'

'What about the coast guard?'

'Matas is *Mosso d'Esquadra*. In theory, it's the *Guardia Civil* who are in charge of customs, the sea … things like that. I can ask discreetly...'

'So, you're in?' Taylor was visibly excited.

'Look, I'll give you a hand. I don't want to end up like Manolo.'

'Neither do I. It might be a once in a lifetime scoop, but no article is worth risking your life. I just need to keep an eye on him. If the *Rusalka* does a night voyage on Thursday and comes back low in the water, we'll know we're right. Call the police straight away. Cocaine or heroin, who cares. Yes?'

'Ok. I'm in,' said Scott.

'Great.' Taylor held out his hand.

# TWENTY

Scott looked at his watch. It was quarter to eleven.

'Look Peter, I'd better be going. Got this girl, the blonde from last night. I might be able to get some info out of her about the whole lighthouse project. She works for one of Olenka's companies.' Scott started to make his way to the door.

'Do you want to come up to Begur on Thursday midday? If you really think Olenka is going to be bringing in forty tonnes of drugs on Thursday night, we can keep an eye on the place and if the *Rusalka* comes back low in the water, we can call the police, customs or DEA or whoever. How does that sound?'

'That sounds great.' Taylor held out his hand again. 'Now Alex, remember, be careful around Olenka. The death of your friend Manolo is not the first accident to happen round him. His thug Spralov has no qualms about chucking any perceived threat out the window.'

'I'll keep that in mind,' said Scott shaking hands for the second time.

'Seriously, he's very dangerous. A complete psycho.'

'I promise to keep well clear of him. But I *can* ask around and see if we can't get some more info. I really must dash now. You've got my mobile number?'

'Yes, you called me earlier.'

'Ok, good. Right then. See you on Thursday.'

'See you on Thursday Alex. And thank you.'

Taylor shook Scott's hand again, and let him out of the hotel room. Walking out from the air-conditioned hotel into the midday sunlight reminded him how long he had been talking to Taylor. He found some shade under a tree and dialled Natalya. She had been at the Sagrada Familia for half an hour and sounded a little annoyed.

Scott hailed a cab, and from the browser on his phone bought an entrance ticket for the next available slot which was in fifteen minutes. As he got out the taxi in front of the south side of the building, he was struck by the awe-inspiring impact of the soaring towers and organic design of the hundred-year old church that was still being built. He texted Natalya and she said she would meet him by the lift to the towers.

After a brief queue, he made it in and went through the nave of the church following the signs for the lift. He couldn't help but stare upwards at the soaring columns and graceful lines of the roof and walked straight into a short Chinese tourist whom he hadn't seen. He apologised and hurried towards the lifts. Natalya was there waiting for him.

'Hey Natalya, sorry the meeting went on so long,' he said and gave her a kiss. 'I couldn't get away earlier. How has your morning been?'

'I went to the *Pedrera*. It's not as good as the *Casa Batlló*. Then I had a coffee and came here.' Her face brightened. 'This place is incredible.'

'Amazing, isn't it? I can't believe how much they have done since I was last here. It was just a building site with some towers before. Now it's really a cathedral. Have you been up the towers?'

'Not yet. I was going to go up when you texted. Shall we go up?'

'Yes. Ok.' They joined the queue for the lift.

'They think it will be finished in ten years' time,' said Natalya. 'Nearly one hundred and fifty years after it was started.'

'Did you know Gaudí was run over by a tram?' said Scott.

'What?'

'He was run over by a tram. One of the greatest ever architects. And he was run over by a tram. Quite an ignominious way to go.'

'Igno...?'

'Embarrassing. It's pretty daft to get run over by a tram. They run on rails.' Natalya was still looking blank. 'Doesn't matter. Did you know he designed the whole building using an upside-down model with string and weights?'

'I've seen it. It's downstairs. In the museum.'

'So clever. I suppose nowadays everything like weight distribution and stress is calculated by computer modelling. But he was way ahead of his time.'

They squeezed into the lift. As the lift started up, Scott caught Natalya's eye and he could see the beginnings of a laughter in her eyes. A Japanese tourist next to her made a weird hiccup noise and he could see her straining not to giggle. He hoped she wasn't involved in Olenka's operation.

The view from the top of the tower was spectacular. Natalya, now an expert after a visit to the museum in the basement, pointed out that they still hadn't built the main tower, which would be even higher.

They decided to take the stairs down. A decision Scott soon regretted. The tower steps were in the form of a traditional spiral staircase but without the central column. In its place was nothing, a hole that went the whole way down. The handrail on the wall was little comfort and after a couple of flights they were both feeling a little dizzy as well as vertiginous.

'Right, I need a coffee. Or a beer,' said Scott when they had made it down. 'Are you done or do you want to see some more?'

'Let's go,' said Natalya. 'Are you ok?'

'Fine,' replied Scott. 'It's not vertigo. I just hate heights.'

They left the *Sagrada Familia* and walked a few blocks in the direction of the centre of town. They came to a café they liked the look of and sat at a table outside on the pavement under a shade. Natalya ordered a water and Scott a *café con hielo*.

'So, you had a good meeting?' asked Natalya.

'Interesting.'

'Was it to do with the hotel?'

'No, another project that I think I might get involved with. Nothing to do with hotels.' Scott decided to steer the conversation onto Olenka. 'That was an amazing dinner last night.'

'Yes delicious.'

'I'm would much rather just have had dinner with you. I suppose Dimitri *is* your boss.'

'Well, he's an investor, I don't exactly work for him.'

'Of course not. How long has your company been here? Are there other offices?'

'Well, I started work a few weeks ago, but Niki, who is my boss, has been in Begur for a few months.'

'And Olenka is an investor. Do you know how long he has been involved?'

'I have no idea,' said Natalya, 'I assume for quite a while.'

'What's his story? Olenka. He must be loaded. But he's young, must be in his twenties.'

'Er…I don't know. I don't know much about him.' She looked away as if to close the discussion, then turned back to face Scott. 'Your friend María is nice. She said she is an architect.'

'Yes. The same as her brother, Santi. He's the planning officer for Begur council. Have you come across him yet?'

'No, I don't think so. Why would I?'

169

'Well, if someone wants any work done to a house they need to get planning permission. Santi's in charge of that. Have none of your clients needed that?'

'Er...well...no. Not yet. I have only been here a short while.'

'Well, you will. I'll introduce you. Apparently, he's very busy with all Olenka's renovations at the moment. How many houses does he own here?'

'I don't know Alex.'

'That was strange coincidence us all meeting in the hotel like that.' Scott was watching Natalya carefully.

'Yes.'

The waiter brought her water and an expresso in a cup and a little glass with ice for Scott. He put some sugar in the coffee, stirred it and then poured it in to the glass with ice.

'What time are we heading back to Begur?' asked Natalya. 'I'll have to call the office. They needed me in this afternoon.'

'Well, I thought we could jump in the car and head up whenever we want.'

'I think I've got a meeting at four or five.'

'I'll get you back by then.'

They finished in the café and strolled back to the hotel. As they were walking along Gran Via they passed a shop selling security devices and gadgets. They were just a block from the hotel, so Scott asked Natalya to carry on, he said he needed something for Can Daurat. He went into the shop and after ten minutes emerged with a package. Back at the hotel, Scott spoke briefly to the receptionist, wondering whether she was the one who gave out his personal information to Taylor.

They retrieved the car and headed back up to the Costa Brava. They drove for most of the way in silence, both lost in thought. Scott dropped Natalya off at her work and headed home.

# TWENTY-ONE

After the night in Barcelona and the morning's revelations, coming back to Can Daurat felt strange. The surroundings were so familiar, so associated with happy memories, but now Manolo's murder had barged its way to the front of his thoughts. Scott's imagination raced with images of the old man being bundled off the cliff. All for something his ageing eyes had seen, or his worsening hearing had overheard.

After unlocking the door, Scott turned off the alarm and went into the kitchen. He got his computer out of his bag, poured a glass of water and went out onto the terrace to try to catch up with some work. It was another sweltering day and Scott sat in the shade where it was cooler and he could see the screen on his computer.

In the middle of answering a boring email, Scott raised his head to think, his gaze unfocussed, when he suddenly realised something was wrong. The garden looked different. There was the pool, the pool house, the trees. That was it. There was no fence. The garden went from grass to sky. Wondering what had happened, Scott slowly walked down the steps and towards the promontory. The fence was gone. So was most of the cliff. A large area of garden was now a pile of rock and earth spread out over the rocks below.

It looked like half the garden had fallen into the sea.

'What the …?'

Scott went to what was now the edge of the cliff and looked down. It looked like a landslide. The fence had not broken and was now suspended in the air above the collapsed part of garden. In amongst the rubble he could see scattered bricks and what looked like the remains of an arch. The tunnel. The *Camí de Ronda*. This was the tunnel that had been taped off. Thank God they had noticed. It had looked pretty secure to Scott. He hadn't believed the council's work to be necessary. He had been wrong.

Scott went back to the terrace and picked up his phone. He dialled Santi's number but it went straight to answer machine. He left a message, then searched on the browser on his phone and found the number for the council. He followed an annoying series of automated questions before getting through to the receptionist.

*'Hola. Buenas tardes. Can you put me through to Santiago Hernandez?'* he asked in Spanish.

*'I'm sorry, he is away for a few days. Can anyone else help you?'*

*'Could I speak to someone in …er… whoever is responsible for council works.'*

*'That would be the architect's office.'*

*'Yes, them please.'* She transferred the call.

*'Yes. Good afternoon, this is the architect's office.'*

*'Is Santiago Hernandez about?'*

*'The architect is away for a few days. Can I help you?'*

*'Well, I am calling about the tunnel. On the Camí de Ronda. Can Daurat. Near the old lighthouse.'*

*'Yes?'*

*'It's collapsed. The whole lot has collapsed.'*

*'And what do you want us to do?'*

*'To come and mend it. It's the council's responsibility.'*

*'Ok. I'll make a file for it. Where did you say?'*

*'The Camí de Ronda. There is a tunnel that goes under the garden at Can Daurat. It has collapsed.'*

*'You are the owner?'*

'No, I er... Yes. I am.' Scott thought it better to lie. 'I would like the council to come immediately and repair it. It's dangerous. Anyone could fall.'

'Right,' she said, and Scott could hear the crackle of paper being unfolded, 'you say the Camí de Ronda under... Can Daurat?'

'Yes, that's it.'

'Well. I can give you a telephone number. They will be able to help you. Let me just get it.'

'What do you mean?' asked Scott. 'Isn't this the architect's office?'

'Yes. But that part of the Camí de Ronda belongs to the Coastal Department. It's not Council responsibility.'

'But it must be. The Council closed the tunnel a few days ago.'

'No, it did not. That must have been the Coastal department.'

'It was the council. I talked to the workmen, saw the sign. I talked to them on Sunday.'

'That is impossible, it was not the council. It's not our jurisdiction. I would know about any closure, I'm the architect's secretary, I prepare all the paperwork. And we do not operate at weekends.'

She then gave Scott the number for the coastal department. He tried the number a couple of times but it was busy.

Scott retrieved his keys and unlocked the little gate which was now attached to a fence that after five or six metres had been pulled over and disappeared into the landslide. About ten metres of fencing had come down where the tunnel had collapsed. He walked out onto the Camí, turned right and walked round the corner to where he had met the workmen the two days before. The tape closing the path was still there, most of it was buried under a pile of earth.

Scott went back up to the house and dialled Bill's mobile.

'Alex, how're things? How was Barcelona?'

'Er…all good Bill.' Scott paused. 'Well, not exactly. Do you remember your garden?'

'Yes.' Bill paused. 'What's happened?'

'Well, it looks like half of it fell into the sea.' Scott then described the scene. He told bill about the council workers on the Sunday closing the tunnel off, and the conversation he had just had with the secretary.

'Now why doesn't that surprise me?' Bill said. 'Typical bureaucracy, doesn't know its arse from its elbow. Are the pool and the boathouse ok?'

'Yes, they are fine. It's further along. The point. You know, the bit where the tunnel runs under the garden. It looks like that bit on has fallen down.'

'Ok. Well, doesn't sound like anyone was hurt or we would have heard something. Going to cost a fortune to put back. That point was built before the war when they made the *Camí* a proper path. If it's the Coastal department's jurisdiction, try to make them sort it. Can you check what's covered by the insurance company? Dolors should have the details. I know the garden is covered in the policy. Don't know if this is covered though.'

'Ok Bill, I'll keep you updated.'

'Can you take some photos and send them to me?'

'Yes of course. Bill…'

'Yes Alex.'

'What's your knowledge of the Russian derivatives market?'

'That's an odd question. Well, let me think. We sometimes use it to hedge operations in Russia, mainly fuel costs. Personally, I try to steer clear. But an interesting market. Very volatile. Why?'

'Do you remember I mentioned there was a Russian trying to buy Can Daurat? Dimitri Olenka. I'm doing a bit of digging into him. Well, someone mentioned he's a bit overexposed on the derivatives markets, and I was wondering if there was any way of checking?'

'I can ask my manager in Moscow.' Bill pronounced the second syllable like the animal. 'He is pretty plugged in to most things. Should be able to find out something. What's this about?'

'I met a journalist who's writing a piece on him. Seems to have done his homework, but I'd like to do some checks myself.'

'Yes, no problem. Text me his name, any details you have and I'll see what I can do.'

Scott wondered whether or not to tell Bill about the link between Olenka and Manolo's death. He knew how fond of Manolo Bill had been, and while on the surface Bill appeared a benevolent father figure, he had glimpsed the ruthlessness that had created his business empire. He decided to wait on calling out the heavy artillery until he was sure of the facts.

'Everything else ok?' Bill asked. 'You got the alarm authorisation I see. We received an email from the company with last month's record. Much better system. Thanks.'

'No problem.'

'Ok, Alex, I'll see what I can do on that Russian info. You take care. Bye'

'Bye Bill.'

He tried Santi again and got the answer machine. Then he called Dolors. After a little preamble, he explained about the garden. She was flabbergasted and said she would come over right away. He told her there was no need. That everything was under control. In the end, she relented, but made him promise to call her if he needed anything. She told him the name of the insurance company. He asked her if she knew a policeman in Begur called Duarte. She said yes of course. She and Manolo had known him for years, he used to be in the *Guardia Civil*. Scott asked her what she thought of him taking over the odd jobs in the house. This brought forth a flood of tears and sobbing and memories of Manolo. In the end, Scott had to tell her that he was going to talk to Duarte to sound him out. The last thing Scott wanted was Dolors finding out he had talked to Duarte without informing her.

After he spoke to Dolors, he went back to his emails. He, too, had an email from the security company. He had a look at the attachment and saw it was last month's statement. He replied to the company, thanking them for the information, and asking for an advance on this month's report which would show the last two weeks. Scott walked to the end of the garden, took some photos of the damage and texted them to Bill with Olenka's name.

Scott found the number for Can Daurat's insurance company and arranged for a visit to the house to assess the damage.

He opened his browser and saw the Gmail address he had set up for the caretaker adverts now had over a thousand emails. He logged out without reading any.

Scott spent a couple of hours researching Taylor's information. Transparency International rated Russia the worst of the twenty-eight countries surveyed in the 2011 Bribe Payers Index. There were loads of articles on the premier's wealth, estimations of which ranged from ten billion dollars to two hundred billion. Apparently, the official version had him owning just an eighty square metre apartment and four cars. No shareholdings were in his name, and his part ownership of many of the companies in Russia's biggest industries was pure speculation by journalists and the opposition. What seemed accepted by all was his zero-tolerance of dissent and his heavy-handed approach to any insubordination.

Scott searched for David Taylor and read a few of his articles. He had written the piece in the Financial Times that had mentioned Olenka as an oligarch on the run which Scott had read a few days earlier. Taylor wrote exposés of financial crimes and bad corporate governance. He had written an interesting article about various dictators around the world and their staggering accumulation of wealth, concentrating mainly on Saddam Hussein, Gaddafi and Mobutu. His articles were well researched, calmly analytical, with logical conclusions and not inclined to flights of imagination or speculation.

Scott thought about calling Natalya, weighing up the idea of involving her. He liked her, enjoyed her company and physically he found her very attractive, but he couldn't shake off the feeling there was more to her relationship with Olenka than she had said, and the coincidence of the meeting in Barcelona was implausible. He doubted that she was actively involved in any major criminal activity, unless she was a much better actress than he gave her credit for.

In the end, he sent her a message asking her if she was free to come over that evening or if she wanted to do anything in town. She replied that she was tied up with work, but that the next day she was off all afternoon if he wanted to do something. Scott remembered their conversation on the boat at the weekend and, on the off chance he could persuade her to go diving, went down to the boathouse and put some scuba cylinders on the compressor to fill.

Later, back in the house, Scott tried Santi but it went to answerphone again. So he dialled María's number.

'*Si, diga.*'

'*Hola María, soy yo. Alejandro.*'

'Hey Alejandro. How are you? It was good to see you last night.'

'Yes, great to see you. That food was amazing. I'm not so sure about your friend.'

'*Qué pesado.* What a bore. The things I do for my brother.'

'I have been trying to call Santi. Do you know where he is?'

'Yes. I spoke to him this afternoon. He is crazy busy with that bore Dimitri. Apparently, Dimitri arrived early this morning from Barcelona very *resacoso*...er?'

'Hungover.'

'Yes, hungover. And they have been on the project all day.'

'There's been a landslide here at Can Daurat and I wanted to ask Santi what the council will do about it. I wanted to ask him something else as well. Is he on his mobile? Can I reach him anywhere else?'

'No, he's not at home. Try his mobile.'

'I've been trying that. If you speak to him again can you ask him to call me. It's really quite important.'

'I'll be seeing him tomorrow.'

'In Barcelona?'

'No. Begur. He's asked me to come and help him with his project. Says he needs my help, it's urgent.'

'María?'

'Yes?'

'I'm not sure about Dimitri. I'd be careful if I were you. I wanted to warn Santi too.'

'Don't worry. I'm a big girl. I can deal with men like Dimitri.' María paused. 'But thank you for worrying.'

'It's not just you that I was worried for. Dimitri might be involved in something illegal. Bad.'

'What, a Russian millionaire doing something bad? Alejandro, you surprise me.'

'No María, I'm serious.' Scott paused. 'This could be dangerous.'

'Look, I'm just going to Begur to help with some plans. Anyway, Santi will be there. I'll be fine.'

'Please get Santi to call me. Urgently. It's really important.'

'Yes Alejandro. Now I have to go. *Besos.*'

'Bye María. *Besos.*'

Scott hung up the phone concerned that he should have been more open with María. He had promised Taylor that he wouldn't tell anyone, but María and Santi were old friends and if Olenka was about to bring in forty tonnes of drugs, he didn't want them damaged in his wake.

Scott send a message to Duarte, reminding him of their meeting in the morning. He picked up the binoculars and went to the new edge of the garden where the fence had been. He looked across the bay at the lighthouse. He looked down to the base of the cliff to the jetty. There was the beige and gold tender of the *Rusalka* tied up. It looked so like the boat that had been moored nearby the night he was attacked. The *Rusalka* was anchored some way off. After ten minutes of watching her he saw a crewmember come outside for a cigarette. Hardly a major criminal enterprise.

The light was fading and Scott decided to leave his investigations until the next day. He was looking forward to trying out his recent purchase.

# TWENTY-TWO

Scott decided not to run past the lighthouse. He wanted to go there later with Taylor and didn't want to be seen hanging round the area. After his exercises, he climbed the fence behind the garages and made it down to the *Camí de Ronda* to the south of the landslide. He went to have a look at it. He could see marks of digging and pickaxes amongst the rubble that now blocked the path. They must have tried to move it, he thought, but it was a huge job. It would probably need mechanical diggers.

He ran south for half an hour. It was another lovely cloudless day with hardly a breath of wind and, at seven in the morning, there was not yet anyone about on the Camí de Ronda. As he ran through other tunnels he looked to see if there were any cracks or signs of collapse, but all looked in good shape to him.

On his way back, he veered inland a kilometre or so before the house and approached via the main road. The gates were open and Dolors' car was parked by the side kitchen door.

*'Buenos días!'* Scott called out.

*'What a shock! Good morning! Where have you come from?'* replied Dolors. Scott gave her a kiss hello.

*'I have just been for a run, along the Camí. Did you see the garden?'*

180

'Yes. What a disaster! What's happened? The garden! What will Mr Franklin say?'

'I've already spoken to Bill. I spoke to him yesterday before I spoke to you.'

Dolors then started a long monologue on Manolo's death. It was all garbled, in a mix of Castilian and Catalan, with references to the spot from where Manolo fell and the significance of the ground now falling away. Apparently, it involved God's will, but Dolors didn't appear any happier for that fact.

After a few minutes, Scott managed to persuade Dolors that everything was in hand, that he would get the garden put back as it was, either through the council or the insurance. He assured her that he was fine, that the house didn't need cleaning and he could manage to make himself some food. It was a quarter to nine, and while Duarte wasn't due to arrive before ten o'clock, he would rather they didn't cross paths just yet. Although Dolors had said Duarte was a friend, he thought it best not to interview her husband's replacement in front of her.

In the end, she left at a few minutes after nine o'clock, and Scott had time to shower and shave and prepare a few questions he wanted to ask in the interview.

At ten o'clock on the dot, the front gate buzzer rang. Scott opened the gates and went out to meet Duarte. He was younger than Scott had expected, probably in his mid-fifties. He had greying dark-brown hair, olive skin and was clean shaven. He was dressed in a short-sleeved shirt and tie, grey slacks and some very polished brown leather moccasins, which made Scott feel a little underdressed in his shorts, shirt and flip flops.

'Hola Señor Duarte, Buenos días. Alejandro Scott.'

'Mucho gusto Señor Scott, Pablo. Pablo Duarte.'

'Por favor, llámeme Alejandro.'

'You prefer we speak in English?' asked Duarte.

'*Spanish will be fine.*' Although Duarte's English had been good on the phone, Scott thought they would communicate better in Spanish.

They commented on the brilliant weather as they walked round the house to the terrace by the pool. Scott had previously brought out a jug of water and two glasses to the cast iron table. Scott offered Duarte a chair.

'*Very sad what happened to Manolo. I was a friend of his, his and his wife Dolors.*'

'*Yes, she told me.*'

'*My colleagues tell me he fell from the cliff. Was it over…. What has happened here?*' Said Duarte pointing to the fallen part of the garden.

'*There was a…*' Scott couldn't think of the word for landslide in Spanish, '*…fall of earth. I was in Barcelona.*'

'*Lucky you weren't on it when it fell. This old path. It was built in the thirties. They really need to rebuild many parts of it.*' Scott offered Duarte a glass of water which he accepted.

'*Now, you said on the phone that you might be interested in working here.*'

'*But not until July. I retire from the Mossos in July.*'

'*Yes, of course. I remember. Do you know the Franklins?*'

'*Señor Franklin I know from sight. I remember his mother, very much a lady, from when I started in the Guardia Civil. The children I do not know. There is a son, no? And a daughter?*'

'*Just a daughter. There was a son. But he died a few years ago.*'

'*Yes. Now I remember. Very sad. It was on a boat? Yes?*'

'*In Greece.*' Scott looked across the garden at the horizon. Charlie's accident in Greece. That had seemed a lifetime before. Turning back to Duarte he said: '*Of course, it will depend on Mr Franklin, but I can outline a little of what the job will be, the hours, pay etc.? Is that ok with you?*'

Scott then ran through the list he had compiled of duties a caretaker would be required to perform, from odd jobs round the house, to keeping control over the security and keeping the various motors running. Duarte said he had been brought up on the sea, so care of boats wasn't a problem, and he was a bit of a *'manitas'* – he loved odd jobs and fixing things.

Scott found himself getting on very well with Duarte, and thought he would fit in well with the Franklin family. His being an ex-policeman wouldn't hurt the security either. Duarte said he would be happy with the salary, and he even proposed his daughter, who was married and lived in Begur, as a substitute cleaner if, or more likely when, Dolors didn't feel up to continuing work.

After they had covered all the ground Scott felt necessary, their conversation changed to Duarte's current job.

*'You used to be in Guardia Civil, no?'* asked Scott.

*'Yes, but I was one of the first to become a Mosso in 1996.'*

*'I get a little confused with all the different police forces.'*

*'Well, is it simple. There is the Guardia Civil, the state police. Then there is the Mossos d'Esquadra, the Catalan regional Police. Then you have the Policía local in towns, unless it is a city, then you have also the Policía Urbana.'* Duarte smiled. *'Well, maybe it is not so simple.'*

*'Is there any difference between being in the Guardia Civil and the Mossos?'*

*'The work is basically the same. All that has changed is the uniforms, the language. And it means I can stay here in Begur.'*

*'And how long have you been Sargent?'*

*'Fifteen years.'*

*'You never wanted to do other things?'*

*'Like what?'*

*'I don't know. The drugs squad, detective. You know.'*

*'What here? In Begur?'* Duarte laughed. *'No, I have always been content where I am.'*

'Is there much organised crime?'

'No, not much. We have some trouble with Gitanos. They are a closed group. They have the control of the illegal drugs and weapons. We are lucky, no mafia here. No, for that we have the politicians!'

Scott laughed with Duarte. 'And drugs? I heard there was a big bust a few years ago. Something about a tunnel.'

'Yes. But many years ago. In eighty-eight. I was still in the Guardia Civil. That was incredible. This old masía,' masías were the local stone country houses, 'it had a cave underneath. They had carved a tunnel that reached the sea. It had an electric train for bringing the drugs. There was a Panamanian trawler that dropped the drugs off and they used to bring them in like that. We found nearly twenty tonnes of drugs. I think it is still the biggest ever drug's bust.'

'Cocaine?'

'No, in those days they were bringing in hashish.'

'Is there much trafficking nowadays? Being a coast with a history of smuggling and all.'

'No, not really. They get most of the smuggling in Galicia and the south. We control the ports carefully here. You might get someone unimportant bringing in small quantities, but all the ports now have dogs, scanners and the newest technology.'

'Is there much consumption?'

'Here? Are you joking? It's everywhere. All the kids are at it. Sometimes I think Portugal has the right idea.'

'Why, what do they do in Portugal?'

'Nothing. Drugs are not illegal. They are not legal, just not illegal. It lets the police do other, more important work. Sometimes I think of the thousands of days of work we put into stopping these kids doing what they will do anyway…how we could better spend our time…'

'I have a colleague who is writing a book on the European drug's trade. He's been asking me questions *about the scene here. Is there anyone at the police I could ask?'*

*'Here in Begur?'*

*'I've come across an inspector Matas. No disrespect but we didn't see eye to eye. But please keep that to yourself.'*

Duarte laughed. *'That is because he is an arse. You might be better off asking the Guardia Civil in Palamós. They will have information for your friend. There is one, Lieutenant Robles, I will call him. You should speak to him. He was many years on the drugs squad.'*

*'Thanks, that would be a great help.'*

They talked for ten minutes more, Scott told Duarte that he thought it was all looking good for July, but of course the final decision would be with the Franklins. He suggested a trial period in August. If that all worked out well then it could become permanent.

Scott thanked Duarte for coming round and said goodbye to him at his car.

He then dialled Natalya, who was at work but confirmed that she was still free for that afternoon. He asked her if she felt like coming out on the *Salacia*, as it was such a lovely day. He suggested they could try a quick scuba dive. She sounded pleased, said that she would love to and that she would be round at his at one.

He dialled Bill.

'Alex.'

'Hi Bill. Have you got a minute?'

'Fire away.'

'I just had the soon-to-be-ex-policeman around. Pablo Duarte. I liked him. I think you will too.'

'That is encouraging. Was he keen?'

'Seems to be. Wants to do something in retirement. He must be in his fifties. Happy to be paid what you were paying Manolo. He says his daughter is in Begur, could ask her if you needed someone to take over from Dolors. All in all, rather convenient.'

'That's really good Alex. Thank you'

'Bit of luck really, finding him. So, I told him he could start in August for a month, then you can see how you find him.'

'Perfect. Need I do anything before?'

'I don't think so.'

'Great. Any news on the garden? What did the insurance say?'

'I haven't spoken to them yet. I'll call them today.'

'Let's me know what they say. Oh, Alex?'

'Yes Bill.'

'My Moscow manager Alexei got back to me about your Russian. Give me a minute…' There was some tapping on a keyboard. 'Yes… Dimitri Olenka…Zoloto?'

'That's him.'

'Well… Alexei says he's in a lot of trouble. Says he hasn't been… keeping up certain political contributions…mmm doesn't sound healthy… Hold on…' Bill paused. 'Ok…Apparently, he has promised to settle all debts by…by the end of this month.'

'Any idea how?'

'No…He doesn't say. He says he knows someone who is owed a bundle and your man has told him he will have the funds to cover it by the end of the month. Your Olenka has been telling everyone the same thing apparently. He'll settle at the end of the month. Does that help you?'

'I'm not sure.'

'I can get him to do some more digging if you want.'

'Thanks Bill, don't worry.'

'A pleasure. How is everything else?'

'All good.'

'How is the *Salacia?*'

'Beautiful as always.'

'Been diving?'

'Not yet. But I was thinking of going out this afternoon.'

'Please be careful Alex. Don't dive alone.'

'Of course not, Bill. I'm going with a friend.'

'You take care. Bye Alex.'

'Bye Bill.'

Scott found Taylor's number on his phone and dialled.

'Hi, Peter, it's me, Alex.'

'Hi Alex. What up? Any news? Is there much activity from your neighbours?'

'It all looks quiet on the lighthouse front. Then again, it's all covered by screens. I'm going to pop over there and have a look. And going out on the boat later, might have a nose around.'

'Just be careful. Remember, stay well clear of heights.'

'I will keep my distance. I have just heard some news from Moscow. My friend, who owns the house and does some business there, asked one of his directors about Olenka. He said that Olenka has been telling everyone he owes money to that he'll have the money by the end of the month.'

'Interesting.'

'And you're sure he couldn't raise the money through his businesses?'

'Not the amount that he owes. No, if he can make the money by the end of the month it's not through any business of his that I have seen. This coupled with his being here, spending all his time here, I think we're definitely on the right track.'

'Are you still on for coming up tomorrow?'

'Yes, of course. I should be with you round midday. I know the house. I passed it the other day. The blue gates, no?'

'Yes. Just ring the buzzer and I'll let you in.'

'Brilliant, see you *mañana*. And Alex, thank you.'

'*Hasta mañana* Peter.'

It was a quarter past eleven. Scott dialled the number he had rung the previous day and spoke to the Coastal department. No one there knew anything about the tunnel collapse. He called the insurance company and he was told to email an account of the incident with photos attached to the claims department.

Scott walked as far as he could towards the end of the garden and looked at the lighthouse through the binoculars. The *Rusalka* was still moored a hundred metres off the jetty, but the tender was now next to her. There wasn't much movement from the scaffolding tower, but from this distance Scott could not hear whether any work was underway on the property.

Scott went back inside and retrieved his purchase from the day before that was charging in the kitchen. On the way back to the hotel he had gone into a spy shop, after telling Natalya that he would meet her back at the hotel. It had been crammed with gadgets, mainly cameras hidden in different household objects. Scott had been tempted by a pair of night vision goggles, but in the end, had settled for drone with a camera. It was very small, had a long range and battery life (or so the assistant has assured him.) More importantly, at four hundred euros, it was not half as expensive as Scott had thought it would be. He saw one military grade spy drone for sale for two hundred thousand euros.

Instead of the usual four propellers, Scott's drone flew with two plastic wings which fluttered like a hummingbird. That was what it was made to look like, with its body covered in green and yellow stickers.

Never having flown a drone before, he had thought it better to buy one with GPS controlled flight and automatic return. It was controlled by a handset which reminded Scott of remote control cars when he was a boy. It had a couple of joysticks and an extendable antenna with a bracket on the top to which you had to attach your mobile phone. This provided the screen from which you could see either a map view of its position or the view from the camera. Scott put the battery he had charged overnight in the body of the drone, placed the drone on the terrace tiles on its four support 'legs' and turned the power switch on. The wings 'flapped' twice and a light blinked on the handset.

Scott clipped his mobile phone into the universal bracket and plugged the jack into the base of the phone. After following a few steps to download the right application, he opened the program and he could see through the camera of the drone. The camera pointed forwards and down, and the angle could be physically adjusted. He bent the camera angle a little further down, and now all he could see on his phone's screen were the poolside tiles.

His maiden flight was a great success. He managed to do a circuit of the house, recording the view. As the drone circled the house, it passed by his bedroom and he could clearly see his jeans on the floor by the bed through the window. He nearly crashed it into some trees, but once he realised that if he let go of the controls the drone hovered in the same place, his flying became more relaxed and controlled. Once the drone had come round the house and he could see it hovering over the garages, he hit the 'home' button and it came straight back to his position on autopilot, then slowly settled back down. It landed in nearly the same spot as it had taken off. On 'home' mode the view through his phone screen had changed to the map view, and he could see the satellite view of the house with a little zigzag line around it showing the flight path that the drone had taken. He went upstairs and retrieved a small rucksack from his bedroom.

He locked up the house and walked along the Camí towards the lighthouse. When he was one hundred or so metres away, he left the path, walking into the woods away from the cliffs. It was thick with scrub oaks, pines, the occasional cork tree and some annoying creeper with heart shaped leaves and thorns that caught his clothes. After twenty metres, he found a large outcrop of rock. It turned out to be two huge boulders. By putting one foot on each boulder he managed to get himself up onto the top of the larger one, which was already hot from the sun. It had a flat top about three metres in diameter, and best of all had a large scrub oak, that would hide him from being seen from the lighthouse. Scott unpacked his bag and assembled both the drone and the handset. Once connected his phone told him the battery was at eighty three percent.

The sun was straight overhead, there was hardly any breeze and Scott could hear the waves breaking on the bottom of the cliffs far below. Although the drone was marketed as silent, the whirr of its wings sounded very loud to Scott. He let the drone stabilize, then sent it in an upward trajectory in the direction of the lighthouse. The drone passed over the oak tree and out of Scott's sight. Looking at the screen on his phone, all he could see were trees passing before the camera. The display told him the drone was at ten metres. He supposed that was ten metres above take off altitude, as he was thirty or so metres above sea level. He kept the joystick pressed forwards. Suddenly the *Camí* came into view and before Scott could react the drone was out over the sea. There was just a blue screen on his phone until the camera's autofocus readjusted and he could see the water and the waves below.

Scott let it hover, then he pushed the right-hand joystick on the handset to the left. His view rotated until he could see the middle of the cliffs. He advanced slowly, adding a bit of height to the drone to widen his field of view until he could see the lighthouse's wall on the right of the screen. He turned to the right and advanced. Scott soon had a clear view of the grounds of the lighthouse and then the building itself. Or rather what was left of it. It looked like all the grounds had been dug up, and while the outer walls of the lighthouse were left intact, it was missing the middle of its roof. As the drone flew over Scott could see right down into the building. It looked to him like it had been hit by a bomb. He couldn't see any standing interior wall and the floor seemed wrecked.

The drone had now overshot the lighthouse. It took a few seconds of searching until Scott got his bearings again. The drone was over the sea again, on the far north side of the lighthouse. He brought it back at a slightly lower altitude. It flew over the seaward wall and Scott stopped it. The camera was showing a digger at work. It was moving rock and earth from one pile to another.

He turned to the left to look at the main building. There was a gaping hole on the seaward side, with tyre tracks from the digger running into the building. Suddenly Scott noticed two figures in the bottom right of his screen. They were pointing straight at the camera. One of them looked like the man he and Juan had met on the jetty the week before. The display said battery seventeen percent.

He pulled back on the left-hand joystick and the drone flew backwards in an arc, keeping the lighthouse in sight. He saw the two men run across the grounds of the lighthouse following the drone. Realising it would lead them straight to him, Scott changed direction. He pushed the toggle into forward and up and flew straight back over the lighthouse. Once he was over the building he brought the drone down to four metres and veered left on a slow arc. He hoped the drone was now curving inland from the coast, although all he could see was flashes of green tree and the occasional rock. The battery sign was now flashing red. Hoping the drone was out of sight of the two at the lighthouse, Scott pressed the 'home' button.

The screen on his phone suddenly changed from the camera view to the map view, showing the whole journey in green from where Scott was on the large rock, the trajectory over the water, over the lighthouse, then round the building and back over the house. He thought it looked like a drunken ant trail. There was a straight line turning into a dotted one showing the drone's trajectory back towards where he was. Suddenly the green dot, which had been moving along the line, flashed a couple of times then stopped moving and stayed a constant red. The battery meter showed 0%.

He was sure the men at the lighthouse had seen the drone. Hopefully they would have thought it was returning north, away from his position. Manolo had seen something

191

and had ended up dead. These cliffs suddenly seemed alarmingly high.

Scott put the controls in the backpack and made his way back through the woods towards the *Camí*. The creepers kept catching on his clothes, and at one stage he found himself surrounded by a huge blackberry bush. When he managed to disentangle himself he had to retrace his steps to get round it. Finally, he saw the *Camí* through the trees. He was about to step out onto it when he heard talking in what sounded like Russian. He dropped down behind a juniper bush. The two men from the lighthouse were coming along the *Camí*. They were arguing which way to go. They came to within a few metres of Scott. The large bald one, who fitted Taylor's description of Spralov, was pointing south along the path, in Scott's direction. The other one was pointing with his hand in a casting motion towards the other side of the lighthouse. They turned to look the other way. Spralov had something under his shirt at the waistline. Was it a gun? What else would you tuck into your waistband?

Spralov then lit a cigarette. In the still air, Scott could hear every move he made, the crackle of the cigarette box's wrapping, the noise of the wheel of the lighter and the sound of the intake of breath. A trickle of sweat ran down Scott's face. The acrid smell of tobacco overpowered the rosemary and pine. Scott looked at his watch. It was a quarter to one. Natalya would be around any time now and might ring at any moment. Very slowly he took his phone out of his pocket, conscious of every little sound. He turned his phone on to silent mode. Not daring to move any more, Scott remained in his crouching position.

The two started talking in Russian. Scott made out the name Olenka, something that sounded like 'Doorot' and, he wasn't sure if he were being paranoid, but what sounded like 'Scott.' They carried on arguing. Ten to one. Scott's legs began to shake from the awkward position he was in but he dared not move. The smaller one seemed to tire of the argument, saying something which Scott took to be 'Have it your way, I'm off,' turned his heel and walked back up the *Camí*.

Spralov scowled, turned to be looking back down the path, and finished his cigarette. Then, muttering something to himself, he, too, retreated up the path. When he was sure he had gone, Scott let out his breath that he had been holding in. He waited an extra couple of minutes then stood up, stretching his legs after crouching for so long. He came out of the scrub onto the path. It was nearly one o'clock. He didn't have time to go and search for the drone. He didn't want to have to walk straight past the lighthouse either. He checked his phone, the app still showed the location of the drone on the map. He would have to come back and get it later.

Scott ran back along the path, and was back at Can Daurat by a quarter past one. As he came up through the garden his phone vibrated. It was Natalya. She was at the gate. He let her in and she parked in front of the house. She looked stunning in a light cotton dress. He was surprised at how pleased he was to see her. As she got out the car, she asked:

'Hi Alex. Hey what happened to you?' Scott realised he was red in the face and sweating.

'Oh, I've been down on the *Camí*. I didn't tell you. There has been a landslide. Over by the cliff.'

'A what?'

'Landslide, or the tunnel collapsed. Or both. The garden has half fallen away.'

She kissed him. 'Yuck. You smell.'

'Sorry,' said Scott, 'I'll have a quick shower.'

'Can I join you?' said Natalya, kissing him again.

# TWENTY-THREE

'I'm hungry,' said Natalya, 'what time is it?'

'It's two fifteen.'

'Can we eat something here?'

'Yes, of course. Then I thought we could go out on the boat. It's too hot on land. Try some diving.' He sat up. 'Right, this time I really *will* have a shower.' Scott said getting out of bed.

Twenty minutes later Natalya came downstairs to the kitchen. Scott had a saucepan of water on the boil and was grating some cheese. On the counter next to him was a blender, full with a red liquid.

'What are we having?' asked Natalya.

'Well, I thought we'd start with some gazpacho. Have you had it before? Followed by some pasta.'

'Yes, I love gazpacho. Are you making it?'

'Yes. It's very simple. Just whir up some tomatoes, onion, peppers, cucumber, garlic and oil. Basically, it's a liquid salad.' Scott went to the freezer and got a few cubes of ice out which he put in the jug. 'We can drink this from glasses. I'll just do this pasta and we can eat.'

'Alex?'

'Yes Natalya.'

'This afternoon, can we just go out on the boat, and get away from everything?'

'That *is* the idea.'

'I mean, let's leave our phones behind. Then no one can call us. Really get away from it all.'

'Ok, if you want. We can't go without the radio. It's wired into the boat.'

'Please Alex, I just want to forget work for an afternoon. Just be the two of us.'

'Of course,' said Scott, realising this was important to her. 'We'll be totally on our own. There is a bay round the point where no one goes. I thought we could try a bit of diving there.'

'Diving?'

'Yes. You said the other day you had your PADI.'

'But it has been a few years. I'm not sure if I remember how to do it.'

'Don't worry. We'll stick to very shallow water. Just have a swim around. Like snorkelling with tanks. Then we can do a proper dive some other day.'

Scott put some thick tagliatelle in the saucepan, gave it a stir and put a lid back on. He got a tin out of the cupboard and put some oil in a pan on the stove.

'What's that?'

'Cockles. I saw them in the supermarket and couldn't resist.'

'What are they?'

'Cockles? Little clam like things. *Berberechos.* They love them in Spain. Sometimes tins can cost fifty to a hundred Euros. These are just cheap ones. I'm making a cheat *Vongole.*' Scott started chopping an onion and some garlic.

'Right, can you pour us both a drink?' he pointed to a bottle of white wine, with condensation running down the outside, which was next to two glasses. He sweated the onions and garlic in a pan, then added a few cherry tomatoes and some parsley and the cockles. Then he seasoned it with a little salt and pepper.

'Ok, that's done. Couldn't be simpler.' He picked up his glass of wine and clinked it with Natalya's. 'Cheers.'

'Cheers.'

They took their lunch on a tray into the shade on the terrace. Scott brought up their dinner in Barcelona with Olenka but Natalya was reluctant to talk about the subject. When they had finished lunch, Natalya sat in the sun on the terrace while Scott got the equipment together. He filled two large kit bags and took them down to the boathouse and put them in the *Salacia*. The tanks were in the boathouse next to the compressor, so he checked three tanks were full and put them in the boat.

Back on the terrace, Scott asked Natalya if she were ready. He closed up the house and led her into the pool house. She looked confused for a moment until Scott pushed back the secret door and showed her the hidden doorway to the spiral steps.

'Why the secret door?' she asked.

'I don't know. Just for fun, I suppose.' He led the way down the spiral staircase. The walls were hewn out of the rock. There were lights every two or three metres and Natalya descended slowly in her heels with a hand on Scott's shoulder. Half way down they stopped at an alcove cut into the rock with a trompe l'oeil of a window looking out onto the bay. In the middle of the bay were a couple of old ships with masts and rigging. The picture was faded with some paint peeling off the plaster and Scott remarked that it didn't really look very convincing.

They got to the bottom of the stairs and walked along the short tunnel. Scott went straight to the end of the dock and opened the sea doors. Natalya kicked off her shoes and Scott helped her into the boat before locking the door to the stairs. He untied all but one rope and was about to get in when Natalya reminded him that they were leaving their phones behind. She handed him her bag and he took his mobile out of his pocket and put them all under a towel on the side workbench.

'They will be safe here,' he told her. He climbed in, started the engines, untied the boat and moved out of the dock.

As they came out into the bay, Scott saw the lighthouse and it's scaffolding in front of them.

'Your boss's place,' said Scott, pointing to the lighthouse. Natalya said nothing.

He pushed the throttles forward and the *Salacia* surged. They went north, back the way they had gone a few days before. This time Scott slowed the *Salacia* once they had passed the point with the lighthouse and steered in towards a small rocky bay behind. There were steep cliffs in the typical beige/pink rock of the Costa Brava, with signs of scrub oak and pine trees above them.

'There's no beach here so there are hardly ever any boats.' Scott said once he had slowed down to an idle. 'Most of the seabed along the coast is barren, scraped clear of any life by all the boats anchors. As this bay is hardly ever used, we might get to see something other than just rock.' Scott neglected to add that from here he could also keep an eye on the *Rusalka*. From their position, they could just see her, moored off the lighthouse. He would not be much use as a lookout once they were underwater, thought Scott, but he should keep on eye open as much as possible to help Taylor, just in case the Russians suddenly upped anchor and headed out to sea.

Scott steered the *Salacia* towards an orange buoy which was bobbing on its own in the middle of the cove. He retrieved the boat hook and, as the boat glided up to the buoy, he caught it and cut the engines. Holding onto the buoy he climbed onto the front of the boat and tied her on.

'Can anyone tie up here?' asked Natalya.

'I'm not sure. I think this buoy must belong to a property up there somewhere,' he said, looking up towards the rocky cliffs. 'Well, we're not doing any damage. Not as much as if we had anchored. I can't see the harm in us mooring here for an hour or two.' Scott put out the swimming ladder and started to take the equipment out of the bags.

'It's so lovely in the sun, can we wait a bit?' asked Natalya. She looked nervous.

'Of course.' Scot paused. 'Look, if you're not sure about it, we don't have to go diving. Let's just go for a swim if you'd prefer that.'

'No. I'll be fine. I think.'

'It really will be just like snorkelling. But with more freedom.' Scott looked over at the control panel by the steering wheel. 'The depth gauge is reading twelve metres. I think that's as deep as this bay gets. If, at any stage, you feel you want to stop we can come straight up. You won't need to stop to decompress. From that depth, you can come straight up on the air in your lungs, just always remember to keep blowing out air as you come up.'

'I remember that. I'll be fine. But can we wait a bit?'

'Yes, of course.' Scott picked up one of the bags he had brought on board. 'Want some water?'

'Water?'

'I've got some wine too, if you'd like?'

'Water's great.'

Scott poured a couple of glasses of water. He joined her on the seat at the back of the boat.

'Is everything ok? You seem…worried about something.'

'No, it's just that…I'm a bit nervous of diving. Maybe I will have a glass of wine.' She finished her glass of water and Scott poured some wine into it.

'There's really nothing to be scared about. We'll put on the kit, make sure you're happy. We can go down the mooring rope very slowly. If, at any time, you feel like stopping, we can come straight back. It'll be fun. It's a glorious day and the water is crystal clear.'

'Alex, I need to talk to you about something.'

'What? Yes, of course. What is it?'

'It's about my job and Mr Olenka. I need to tell you something.' Natalya bit her lip. 'You *do* like me?'

'Yes, of course I do Natalya.'

'Well, I haven't…' She paused. 'I haven't been…Look, Alex. I really like you.' Her bright green eyes suddenly welled with tears. 'I think I am in love with you.'

'Nata…' Scott felt completely thrown. He didn't know what to say.

'No, let me finish. I think I am in love with you. That is why I need to tell you…' Natalya looked up at Scott and wiped away a tear from her cheek.

'Don't worry, you can tell me. What's up?' He reached out and held her hand.

'Alex, do you promise you won't be cross?'

'Cross about what? Of course not. What is it?'

'My job. Mr Olenka. I need to tell you…'

She stopped.

'Is there something about Olenka you need to tell me?'

Natalya took a deep breath.

'When me met. Last week in the bar. Well…' She pulled her hand away. 'I was told to get to know you.'

'What?' Scott paused. 'What? In Begur?'

'Yes. I was told to go to the bar to get to know you. Your friend Santi had mentioned to Mr Olenka that you were going to the bar. You were asking questions about Mr Olenka and he wanted to know more about you. I… I didn't mean to…'

She stopped again.

'You didn't mean to what?' Scott tried to keep his voice as gentle as possible, despite his feeling of betrayal.

'I didn't mean to fall in love with you.' She said, looking away at the shoreline.

'But you *did* mean to lie to me,' said Scott.

'I never wanted to lie to you.' She sounded miserable.

'So Olenka told you to get to know me. What did he want to learn?'

'He said… He said you were a journalist asking questions about his business. In Russia, he is always being harassed by journalists. He told me to get to know you. To keep an eye on you and tell him what you knew.'

'And were you told to sleep with me?' Scott couldn't keep the hurt from his voice.

'No. Not that. I think I exceeded my brief.' She smiled, then sniffed and wiped away another tear. In a feeble voice, she carried on. 'I really like you. I wouldn't...'

'Ok. Do you really work for a relocation agency?' Scott thought he might as well try to get some straight answers.

'If you count having only one client. Then yes.' She said, looking up at him.

'Olenka?'

'Yes. He told me to rent or buy your house if possible.'

'Tell me about Manolo?'

'What?'

'Manolo. The caretaker of Can Daurat. Who died. The supposed accident?'

'I...er...I don't know anything about that.' Natalya seemed confused by his question.

'Well, last week I certainly wasn't asking questions about Olenka. I was talking to the police about Manolo's death. I didn't even know Olenka's name. The supposed 'accident,' you must have heard something about that.' Scott voice had become raised, his tone accusatory.

'I promise, Alex, I have only heard that it was an accident. It was *you* who told me about it. On this boat. When we went out for lunch.' Her eyes pleaded her innocence but Scott pushed on.

'But you must have heard something about Manolo's death from Olenka. If he wanted to buy the house.'

'Only that he had died. I was not involved in the approach to buy the house. That was the estate agent. Mr Camps. He spoke to your friend Manolo.'

'And you heard nothing from Olenka about his death?'

'No, nothing. I promise you.'

'Do you know this man Spralov?'

'Mishka Spralov? Yes, of course I know him. He is Olenka's... how would you put it? His bodyguard? He is in charge of security. He frightens me, he frightens everybody. You have met him?' There was a concerned look on her face.

'Well, no. Not exactly. Do you think he could have had something to do with Manolo's death?'

'Mishka? But it was an accident…'

'I'm not too sure about that. Have you ever overheard anything about Manolo or his death? Please, the truth.'

'I promise you Alex. If I had, I would tell you. I don't remember hearing them talk about it at all.' Scott stood up and leant against the side of the boat.

'Ok.' Scott wanted to believe her. 'Now, what did Olenka tell you to do once you had met me?'

'He told me to get to know you. He called me that night to say you were at a bar. To go there and get to know you. To try to get close to you. He wanted to rent your house. He wanted to get you away…'

'Yes? He wanted me away from Can Daurat? Was that why he wanted to rent it? To get me away?'

'I don't know. He just tells me what to do. I am not told why.' Natalya looked like she was about to cry again. 'He said I was to try to rent the house off you. For my 'clients.' When I said that we were going out on the boat, he said that was good. To keep you out as long as possible.'

'Why does he want me away from Can Daurat?'

'I don't know Alex. He didn't tell me. All I know is that lately he has become more and more stressed. Sometimes he is up, sometimes he is down.'

'What is he doing at the lighthouse? There seems to be a lot of work going on?'

'I don't know. I have not been allowed in.'

'Is he building something there? Has it got something to do with his businesses?'

'Alex I don't know. I don't think so. He must be building a house. He likes everything to be just as he likes it.'

'But he has other properties?'

'Yes. He has two other houses along this coast.'

'And is there work going on there?'

'Not so far as I know.'

'So, aside from getting to know me... by the way you should ask for a raise, good job... what else do you do for Olenka?'

'I am in charge of his property portfolio. That is why I got the job here.' Then she added after a pause: 'Nothing I am ashamed about.' There was a flash of anger in her eyes.

'Our coincidental meeting in Barcelona? That was arranged?'

'I'm sorry Alex. I didn't think it....' She paused and bit her lip. 'Yes. But...When I told Mr Olenka we were going to Barcelona to a hotel, he asked which one. I only found out he had arrived in Barcelona that afternoon when you were in your meeting with the hotel. He told me he was going to arrange for us all to have dinner. To make you agree to it.'

'Why did he want to have dinner with me?'

'I don't know Alex. I think when he heard you were a journalist... He doesn't like journalists... Maybe he heard we were...'

'You told him we were sleeping together?'

'No. I wouldn't... I meant he knew I was staying with you in Barcelona.'

'Is there anything between you and ...?'

'No, nothing like that. He is my boss but I think he might want to... But no.'

'I don't think he came to Barcelona out of jealousy. He could have just told you to stop your 'work.' That you are *so* good at.'

'Alex!'

'Sorry. But this is all a bit of a shock,' lied Scott. While he and Taylor had suspected something like this, Scott wasn't sure how to take the information about her feelings for him. He didn't like seeing her so upset, but thought now might be a good moment to try to get some more information on Olenka.

202

'So, he wanted to buy or rent Can Daurat, but then changed his mind?'

'Yes.'

'But he didn't want me around?'

'I don't know Alex. Maybe because you are a journalist. In Russia Mr Olenka has had a lot of trouble from journalists. He is a bit paranoid.'

'I thought his business was commodities. Why would he worry about a journalist looking into his business here?'

'I don't know Alex. Maybe he just doesn't like journalists.'

Scott looked up and around the bay.

'Have you been on that?' He said, pointing to the *Rusalka* in the distance.

'No. Why would I?' She replied, looking confused.

'That's the *Rusalka*, your boss' ship.'

'Oh, I didn't know. No, I have never been on board. This is the first time I have seen it. I think it just arrived in the area a few days ago.'

'What is she doing here?'

'The ship?' She seemed confused by the question.

'Yes.'

'It's Mr Olenka's ship. It is here for the summer.'

'The sailors on board don't like anyone getting close. Could he be up to something with her?'

'Up to what? With who?'

Scott sat back down on the seat next to her.

'It seems strange to me that Olenka doesn't want anyone near the lighthouse nor the ship. He wanted me away from Can Daurat, which is the only other house on the bay.'

Natalya, confused by the direction of Scott's conversation, returned to her confession.

'Alex, I'm really so sorry I lied to you. About our meeting. Are you very angry?'

'Angry?' Scott decided to ease up on her. 'No, I mind that you lied. But not angry. In fact, I should probably thank Olenka.'

'Really? Not angry?'

'Look Natalya. So what? You were told to meet me by your boss. Ok, so you lied to me about that. And the coincidence of bumping into Olenka in Barcelona. I can't say I'm particularly happy that you did, but I don't think that's the worse crime in the book.' She was looking down and he lifted her chin.

'I had a feeling something was odd about Olenka being at the hotel. Too much of a coincidence us meeting like that in Barcelona. I'm pissed off you didn't tell me, but there's no harm done. Are you absolutely sure you haven't heard anything about Manolo?'

'I promise you Alex. I have heard his name mentioned, but that is all. I think it was you who told me. I work for Mr Olenka but I do not work in his inner circle. If I had heard anything about your friend I promise I would tell you.'

Scott looked at Natalya. While a part of him was screaming warning signals to be cautious and not to trust her, another part of him just had to look at her tear-streaked, remorseful eyes and he felt his resolve give. He knew he couldn't trust her completely, but if he was careful what he let on to her, the damage she could do was minimal, and maybe she could be useful in getting some more information on the operation at the lighthouse. And she really was very pretty.

He leant over and kissed her lips. Then kissed each tear streaked cheek.

'Ok Natalya. Let's forget the whole 'how we met' story. I think Olenka is up to something strange at the lighthouse. Will you help me find out more?'

'What do you mean 'something strange?''

'I don't know,' lied Scott, 'but he doesn't want anyone to know what he's up to at the lighthouse; he wanted me out of Can Daurat; there are things about Manolo's death that I don't understand. It might be nothing. He could just be a paranoid, press-averse millionaire, but there are some things I would like to check. Will you help me?'

'Of course, Alex. Whatever you need.'

'Can you find out what the ship's, the *Rusalka*'s, movements will be in the next few days?'

'I could ask one of the crew. We could go by the ship this afternoon.'

'Well,' Scott paused. 'I'm not sure about that. I don't really want Olenka finding out that I've been asking questions about him. Is there anyone else you could ask?'

Natalya thought for a moment.

'I could ask Anna, she's Mr Olenka's PA. She would know.'

'What's your relationship with her?'

'She is nice. We chat occasionally. About Russia, Ukraine.'

'Why don't you tell her you've been out on the sea. Ask about the *Rusalka*. Say you saw her today.'

'Ok. And you want to find out …?'

'If she's going to go out to sea in the next few days. Most importantly tomorrow night.'

'If *who* is going out?'

'I mean the ship, the *Rusalka*.'

'Tomorrow night? Why tomorrow night?'

'It was something Olenka said in Barcelona,' lied Scott.

'Ok. Of course Alex.' She seemed confused but desperate to make it up to Scott.

Scot debated whether to ask Natalya about Taylor's suspicions about drug dealing. She appeared sincere when she said she knew nothing about Manolo's death.

'Do you think Olenka could be involved in drugs?' He asked her.

'Yes, well, it is pretty obvious that he likes cocaine.'

'Yes. He's not shy about offering it around either. No, what I meant was… Do you think he could be involved in, shall we say, the supply of drugs?'

'Dealing?'

'Well, I was thinking more importing.'

'Is that why you are interested in the boat?'

'Well, if he were involved, it would be a good way to smuggle stuff in.'

'Alex, Mr Olenka would not be into that. Yes, he likes to take drugs but not that. At least I have never heard any such thing. Mr Olenka is well known in Russia, and there are a lot of stories circulating about him. But I have never heard anything like that. He is famous for his business empire, the oil and gold, and he has a turbulent social life, but I have never heard a rumour like that.'

'It's probably nothing. Just something that crossed my mind. Forget I mentioned it.'

'Do you still want me to ask about the boat?'

'Yes please. But I don't want you getting into any trouble with Olenka. Only if you can ask her in a normal conversation.'

'Ok. About meeting you in the bar? You don't mind. Really?'

'Really. Just no more lies. Please. And I really like you too.' He said, and gave her a kiss.

'Right, let's forget all that business. What better way than to jump in the sea! Let's go for a swim. It'll clear out heads. We can have a quick dive and then head back home. I'll cook you something delicious for dinner.'

Natalya looked with a worried expression at the calm water next to her.

'I promise it will be fun. It's shallow here, we'll just potter around beneath the boat.'

Scott went into the cabin and brought up two scuba tanks and then the two large bags. He took a wetsuit out of one of the bags.

'Here, try this on for size. It's a girl's small. It should fit,' he said, handing it to her. As Natalya stripped off to her bikini and put on the wetsuit, Scott prepared the tanks with their buoyancy jackets and octopi: depth gauge, compass, regulator and auxiliary regulator. Once she had the wet suit on, Scott helped her with the zip up the back, kissing her neck in the process.

'See, fits perfectly. Now do you want to try on a mask?' He handed her a bag of masks of different sizes. 'Put the mask against your face and breath in through your nose. If the mask sticks it fits.' He retrieved another smaller bag filled with neoprene boots.

'What size feet are you?'

'Thirty-eight.'

He handed her some boots and a weight belt that he brought up from the cabin.

'Ok, you're all set.'

Scott took a little red flag with a white diagonal line on it and attached it to the little mast by the windscreen.

'To warn other boats we are diving,' he explained. Once he had struggled into his wetsuit and collected all the different pieces of equipment, he helped Natalya on with her jacket and tank and then put his on.

'Right, inflate your jacket.' He reached over to her jacket and pressed the button to inflate it. 'That's so you don't sink like a stone when we get in.' He then took her through the different parts of the equipment, but she remembered it all well and needed few reminders. They put on their fins and Scott helped Natalya to the side of the boat so she was sitting with her back to the sea.

'Ok, remember this? Just hold on to your mask and regulator, keep breathing calmly and lean backwards. You'll fall straight back into the sea. Don't worry, you'll float. Get your bearings and we'll meet at the buoy.'

He took her regulator out of her mouth and gave her a kiss. He put it back in, and as Natalya put her hands to her face to hold her regulator and mask, Scott stepped to one side. She looked at him, her eyes wider than normal, and her lips crinkled around the regulator as she tried to smile.

'Off you go.' He said and she leant back. The weight of the scuba tank pulled her back, her feet flipped up and she fell straight into the water with a huge splash. There was a bit of commotion and flapping of fins and then the buoyancy jacket righted her.

'You ok?' He asked, leaning over the side of the boat. The reply was a thumbs up, quickly corrected to the proper diving 'OK' sign, made with thumb and forefinger. 'See you at the buoy.' He said, pointing to the front of the *Salacia*. Scott put on his fins, checked everything was in its place. He looked over the boat and saw the keys were still in the ignition. He flopped across the boat in his fins, removed and placed them in a hidden cubby hole.

He flopped back, checked Natalya wasn't there in the water beneath him, checked his mask and regulator then flipped himself backwards over the side.

Scott had to fight the involuntary feeling of panic as he hit the water and his world changed into bubbles and water. He made himself relax and breath slowly and the bubbles cleared and he felt himself righting to the vertical. He gasped as the cold water seeped into the wetsuit. In front of him was the *Salacia* and his vision was half above and half below water. Once stabilised, he swum on his back along the hull towards the bow of the boat to join Natalya at the buoy.

# TWENTY-FOUR

Natalya was waiting at the buoy.

'Just follow me and enjoy yourself. The only important thing is to remember to keep breathing out when you are coming up. Don't worry, you'll be fine,' Scott said.

He held the buoyancy jacket's inflator in his left hand above his head and pressed the deflate button. He watched Natalya do the same. As the air left their jackets they sank under the surface. Immediately their world changed. All Scott could hear was their steady breathing, and the gurgle of bubbles whenever they breathed out. The bright daylight went as they descended into a blue-green world. His eyes adjusted to the change in light and he could see Natalya in front of him, holding onto the buoy's mooring chain. Looking down he could just make out the shapes of rocks below. As they sank he pinched his nose with his right hand to equalise the pressure in his ears and saw that Natalya was doing the same. They slowly ran their hands down the chain of the buoy until he felt his fins touch the seabed.

Sinking to his knees, he looked at the depth gauge that was hanging down his left side. It read fourteen metres. He looked up. High above them he could see the bright blue of the sky and the hull of the *Salacia* at the top of the chain. The surface seemed very far away. His air gauge read two hundred and fifty bar. On the *Salacia,* he had told Natalya to tell him when hers reached one hundred bar. He leant over and checked it, which read the same as his. He caught her eyes and he made the 'OK' sign with thumb and forefinger. Natalya replied the same way. He wiggled his fingers like two legs swimming, made a circle movement with his hand and pointed away from the chain of the buoy. He saw her eyes crease and her lips pull back on the regulator in a smile.

Scott inflated his buoyancy jacket with a little air, just enough to give him neutral buoyancy, looked at the compass on his depth gauge and headed due south, towards the cliffs. Looking behind him he saw Natalya was following him. They kept about a metre and a half off the seabed, which under the buoy was covered in patches of sand and long seaweed, but soon became dotted with large rock formations and boulders. Scott swam down to the base of a huge rock and saw it had an overhang. He opened one of the Velcro pockets in his buoyancy jacket and took out a waterproof torch attached to a thin string. He turned it on and pointed the beam under the rock. The yellow light brought out the natural colours of the rock and the dull green changed to a mix of greens, reds and browns. He saw a bit of movement and he lit up a lobster.

Scott turned around and beckoned Natalya over. When she was next to him he handed her the torch, after untying it from his jacket, and pointed to the hole under the overhang. After a few moments, Natalya backed out from the rock. He pointed to his eyes then made a scuttling motion by wiggling his fingers. Natalya gave him the thumbs up and smiled. He took the torch back and put it in the jacket pocket. While putting it away he felt something else in the pocket, which turned out to be a piece of white plastic with a pen attached. He took the top off the pen and tried writing on the tablet.

'LOBSTER?' he wrote. He showed the tablet to Natalya and she nodded her head, smiling. He put the tablet back in the pocket and they swum on. They went round the large rocks and came across another flat patch of sand and seaweed. Scott swam down and sat on the sand. Natalya swam over and after a wobble and a lot of air bubbles she, too, settled down next to him. Scott took out the tablet and wiped the writing off with his thumb.

'ALL OK?' he wrote. Natalya nodded. 'HAVING FUN?' Another nod. He looked at his watch. They had been underwater for fifteen minutes. He checked his compass and carried on in the same direction. After a few minutes a wall of rock loomed out of the green. The water was very clear and he estimated the visibility to be about twenty to thirty metres. The cliffs in front of him went straight up from the seabed to the surface. Scott headed for a part of the wall that had a deep fissure. Then they turned left along the wall, still swimming along just above the sea bed. There was the occasional grouper that passed them and the wall was covered in sea life. When Scott brought out the torch and shone it on the wall there was a blaze of red as the torchlight brought out the bright colours of the anemones and tiny pieces of coral. As they swum along they passed over starfish and sea cucumbers.

After following the wall for about ten minutes, Scott checked his watch. They had been underwater for just over half an hour. His air was at just over one hundred and eighty bar, he reached over to check Natalya's which was a little lower. He made a circular motion with his finger to Natalya who turned round. They swam at a gentle pace back along the wall to the large fissure and then away back towards the boat. Scott saw movement out of the corner of his vision. He beckoned to Natalya to come alongside him and pointed at the sea bed. She shrugged her shoulders and frowned, so Scott swam forward, holding onto her arm, keeping his other arm pointing at the seabed. Suddenly the area of rock and sand he was pointing at came alive, and Natalya started. The octopus swum off along the sea bed, releasing a cloud of black ink in its wake.

They carried on swimming north and Scott heard the unnatural metallic whine of an engine that sounded close. He looked up but could only see the blue white expanse of the surface. After a few minutes, Scott was able to see the distinctive large rock where they had seen the lobster in the distance over to their left, and realised that they had veered slightly too far out into the bay. They swam over to the rocks and, after a few more metres, could see the chain of the buoy going up from the seabed to the surface. The noise from an engine increased and Scott looked up. Some speedboat passed over them.

They swam along the sea bed until they were at the bottom of the chain. Scott looked up and could see the hull of the *Salacia*. He motioned Natalya to come up to the chain and to sit.

'LETS WAIT - BOAT ABOVE,' he wrote on the tablet. The last thing he wanted was to get caught in somebody's propeller. 'HAD FUN?' he wrote. Natalya nodded. He put both hands together and made an octopus like motion. She gave him the thumbs up sign. He made a patting motion with his hand, to show they would wait, and held up all five fingers and then tapped his watch. He checked the time, they had been underwater for just over an hour. His air was on one hundred bar. Natalya's was on eighty. Lots to spare. Better to be safe and wait until the boat was far away and there was no danger of being run over. Looking over to the sandy seabed he saw the white body of a dead starfish. He swum over to get it, thinking Natalya might like it as a souvenir.

Scott had just picked the starfish up when everything turned to chaos. What felt like a wall of water hit him in the back. In a cloud of sand, he tumbled over and over, his mask and regulator ripped from his face. Scott only just held his breath as he tumbled along the seabed. Just as quickly as it had come, it was gone. Scott felt down his right side and found his regulator. He put it back in his mouth and felt the relief as air flowed once more into his lungs. With his eyes closed he felt about his head for his mask. He tried not to panic. As he had tumbled his mask had been pushed down his face and was hanging round his neck. He placed the mask over his eyes and breathed out through his nose, filling the mask with air. His heart thumping, Scott forced himself to remain calm and to get his breathing under control. He blinked, his eyes smarting from the seawater. He was in a cloud of slowly descending sand particles. In front of him, as the disturbed sand started to settle, he could begin see the seabed stretching out into the green gloom. He turned round. There was now some large object standing on the seabed. Scott couldn't understand what it was until he recognised the top tapered into a point. It was the *Salacia*. She had come straight down and was now sitting with her stern on the seabed. His heart pounding in his ears, Scott thrashed his fins, praying he would find Natalya safe the other side of the sunken boat. He reached the *Salacia* and swum round the hull. As he came round, there was a cloud of dark water with sand and bubbles everywhere. He swam into the cloud and felt arms flailing about. He held onto an arm, and pulled himself close. Natalya was struggling, eyes wide in her mask. At least she still had her regulator in her mouth. He held her shoulders, trying to calm her down. She was making a whining noise. He caught her gaze with his own, trying to convey calm. She made another whimper and looked down.

The stern of the *Salacia* had come down across her legs. The dark cloud was blood billowing up. He looked back at her eyes, trying to hide his own terror. He held her frightened gaze with his and grasped her shoulders, willing her not to panic. Very slowly he took his hand off her left shoulder and motioned for her to be calm. Her wide, staring eyes kept his gaze as she nodded. He pointed to her legs and tried to indicate that he was going to try to free them.

Scott couldn't see where her legs went under the boat, there was too much blood in the water, but he felt down them until his hands reached wood. Touching a thigh, he heard a muffled scream from Natalya. The boat was pressing down on her, but she was bleeding profusely as the cloud of black kept billowing up, despite Scott's attempts to wave it away.

Scott tore off his fins and expelled all the air from his buoyancy jacket. He could then firmly plant his feet on the seabed. He held Natalya's hand as he took in the situation. The *Salacia* was vertical on her stern. Resting directly on Natalya's legs. He prayed it had only cut a vein. If it were an artery, Natalya didn't stand a chance. He had to get her legs out. He knelt and began to dig the sand away around her legs. Each time he touched her she flinched. He knelt behind her and as gently as possible pulled at her waist. There was another, louder scream from Natalya followed by a swirling cloud of black blood. It was no use. She was pinned under the boat. He knelt next to her. He turned her face towards him. Her eyelids flickered and her eyes rolled. Then her eyes shut. Her mouth opened and, in a stream of bubbles, her regulator fell out of her mouth. He snatched it back into her mouth and pinched her cheek. Natalya's eyes opened, and her mouth gripped the regulator again. He heard her take a breath and saw the bubbles as she breathed out.

Holding her gaze with his, he pinched her cheek again and saw that she flinched. Opening his eyes wide he pointed at his mask. Natalya opened her eyes wider and nodded. He pointed at her legs. He made a pulling motion. He pointed at the deck of the boat that was in front of them and made a pushing motion. Natalya nodded.

Scott got to his feet. He looked up. The *Salacia* reached half way to the surface. He would have to try to push it, let its weight carry it over. He would have to be quick once it toppled. Once the weight was off Natalya's legs, he would pull her out and get her to the surface as quickly as

214

possible. She had to stay conscious. If he inflated her jacket and she rose to the surface unconscious, her lungs might explode as the air in her lungs expended as it rose. It was a risk, but if he didn't get her out from under the boat she would certainly die.

He tapped her on the shoulder to warn her what was coming and pushed with all his strength against the boat. The boat began to move and he heard Natalya's scream again amidst a mass of bubbles, and he could see the black cloud expand out of the corner of his eye, but he kept pushing. He thought the *Salacia* was about to topple over when the boat pushed back and settled vertically as it had been before.

Scott looked down and saw Natalya's regulator had once again slipped from her mouth. He bent down and thrust it back in between her lips. He felt her teeth gripping the regulator mouthpiece and realised she was still conscious. The *Salacia's* cabin in the bow must still be full of air. It was that which was keeping the boat vertical. If he could get the air out, then maybe he could push the boat over. There was the danger that it might topple onto Natalya rather than away from her. Even without the air it might not fall. And even if it did fall it might not free Natalya. What was certain was that if he did nothing, Natalya was going to die. There was no time to get help.

Scott swam up towards the forward hatches on the front deck. Swimming in scuba gear without fins felt awkward and slow, adding to his feeling of helplessness. When he arrived at the hatches, he tried to open them but they were shut from the inside. He swam back down and up through the entrance to the cabin by the steering wheel. As he had thought, there was a large pocket of air in the cabin. He surfaced in the dark with something soft and heavy pressing on his head. He took out the torch from his pocket and turned it on. He had surfaced under the now soaked sofa cushions which were floating on the water in the bottom of the upended cabin. He pushed the cushions aside and shone the beam around. Above him were the two hatches.

By standing on a bit of shelving and the cupboard drawer from under one of the sofas, Scott managed to climb up the cabin. He was nearly within reach of the latches when he stopped. He could not move a centimetre closer. He struggled against the weight of his scuba tank and all the equipment. Balanced precariously, he shone the torch around and realised that, somehow, he had got entangled with a rope and it was this that was stopping him from climbing higher. He dropped back into the water. Try as he might he couldn't get the tank past the rope, so Scott removed his buoyancy jacket. The air in the cabin was still breathable, although it smelt heavily of petrol, and Scott climbed quickly up to the level of the hatches.

Scott wrapped the lanyard of the torch a couple of time round his wrist, and then with both hands undid one of the butterfly clasps. After a couple of turns, he could hear the noise of bubbles from the escaping air. He freed one latch and started on the other one. Once he had turned it a few times, the hatch blew open and he felt air rush past him as it was expelled from the cabin. He did the same with the second hatch. He dropped back down and grabbed hold of his scuba equipment as the water rushed up past his head. In the cramped confines of the cabin he found it impossible to put back it on, so he put the regulator in his mouth and swum down holding the tank and jacket in front of him.

As the air left the cabin, the boat started to shift. He had just got out when, very slowly, the boat began to fall over. He pulled his equipment free of the rope and swum away from the *Salacia* as she fell. There was a great cloud of sand as the weight of the boat settled. Scott put his arms through the buoyancy jacket's armholes and flipped the tank over his head, fastening the Velcro belt tight once it was on. He swum straight to where Natalya had been. The boat had fallen on its keel, and Natalya was lying horizontally on the sea bed. He couldn't see what shape her legs were in for the black cloud of blood. He looked at her face and saw her regulator had fallen out. He held her by the shoulders and pulled. She was free of the boat.

He reached forward to her buoyancy jacket and pressed the button to inflate. Then he unlatched her weight belt which fell to the sea floor. He grasped her regulator and shoved it in her mouth, pressing the button on the front to force air into her mouth. He saw the flicker of her eyeballs move behind her eyelids. They were rising now and Scott pressed the button to inflate his own buoyancy jacket. As they rose to the surface, Scott kept his hands pressed to Natalya's face, holding her mask and regulator in place.

Scott remembered to keep breathing and was relieved to see a steady stream of air leaving Natalya's regulator. He hoped that was the air leaving her lungs as it expanded as they ascended.

They broke through the surface. Scott was blinded for a moment by the sunlight. He pulled his mask down round his neck and looked at Natalya. Her face was sheet white. He pulled off her mask and shouted her name. There was no reaction. He pressed his finger to her neck but between the cold of the water and their bobbing motion he could not feel a pulse. He looked at her body. Her legs were floating on the surface, in what looked like an unnatural angle, there was a rip in her wetsuit about mid-thigh seeping blood that suddenly seemed very red in the sunlight. Keeping hold of Natalya by gripping her left arm under his armpit, Scott undid his own weight belt and managed to pull off the lead weights. He wrapped the belt around her thigh above the tear in the wetsuit and pulled it as tight as possible. He had nothing to twist his tourniquet but he hoped it was putting some pressure on the artery.

Scott tried slapping Natalya's face, but there was no reaction. He looked round. The nearest rocks were about thirty metres away. Looking out to sea Scott prayed for a boat but there was just the flat horizon. He started to swim for shore, holding on to Natalya with his left hand and paddling with his right. He cursed himself for losing his fins. They were about half way towards the rocks when Scott heard the noise of an engine. He turned round and could just see a small motorboat crossing the bay about hundred metres out to sea. Scott shouted 'Help!' then *'Ayuda!'* then 'Help me!' while waving his right arm. He saw a girl in a bikini of the back of the motorboat wave in his direction but the boat carried on south and disappeared round the point.

Scott carried on towards the rocks. Most of the shoreline of the bay was steep cliff but he headed for an area that looked like it had flat rocks and a way of getting out of the water. When they reached the shore, Scott found a rock to stand on so he was knee deep in the water. He undid Natalya's buoyancy jacket and let it and the scuba tank float off. As gently as possible be picked Natalya up and put her on her back on a rock that was out of the water. He didn't like the look of Natalya's legs. As he had lifted her up, the neoprene had felt soft and squishy, and one leg had flopped in an unnatural angle. At least the blood had stopped a bit. Remembering an old school first aid course, he loosened the tourniquet. There was a gush of blood out of the rip in the wetsuit. He tightened the belt once more, then took off his own buoyancy jacket and tank.

'Natalya,' he shouted. 'Wake up. Natalya!' He slapped her in the face. There was no reaction. Her white cheek felt cold and lifeless. He once again put his fingers to her neck. He couldn't feel anything. He put his ear to her mouth. Over the lapping of the water he couldn't hear a thing. Unzipping her wetsuit, Scott started pumping her chest. He pumped ten times then pulled her mouth open and blew into her cold lips. Then he pumped her chest again. He had repeated the process a couple of times when he heard the noise of another engine. Looking over his shoulder he saw another motorboat crossing the mouth of the bay.

He jumped up onto the rock and waved both arms in the air.

'Hey! *¡Ayúdame!* Help me! *¡Ayuda!* Please! Help me!' he shouted. He saw someone on the boat wave at him, then go forward in the boat towards the driver. The driver looked in his direction and suddenly it was turning towards him.

'Yes! Over here! Help!' shouted Scott. He dropped down to his knees and started pumping Natalya's chest again. After ten pumps, he breathed into her mouth. Then pumped again.

'Please wake up! Come on Natalya! Wake up! Come on!' he shouted. The boat was nearing the shore. It was a seven-metre speed boat with open fore and aft decks. There was a man at the driving console and another man and a woman in bathing suits. The boat came to within a few metres.

'Help me please!' shouted Scott. *'Ayúdame por favor. Hemos tenido un accidente. Mi amiga está... está muy mal.'*

'You are English?' asked the driver. 'I can call for help.'

'Yes. Please! There's no time to wait. I need to get her to a hospital urgently. Thank you. Thank you.'

'Of course.' The man said. 'We'll pick you up.' He looked over the side at the rocks. 'I can't get the boat right up to you.'

'We'll come to you,' replied Scott. One of the passengers had put out the swimming ladder at the back. Scott climbed down onto the rock he had been on before. He held Natalya in his arms and turned round.

'Can you get any closer?'

The driver nudged closer. He picked up a boat hook.

*'Manel, ayuda al chico!'* He said to the male passenger. 'My friend will help you.' While the driver kept the boat off the rocks with the boathook, his passengers leant over the side of the boat with outstretched arms.

There was still a metre between Scott and the boat. Holding Natalya in front of him, he pushed off from the rock. Their neoprene wetsuits gave them extra buoyancy and after a second he felt Natalya pull away as the passengers on the boat took hold of her. Scott let go and swam to the stern of the boat to the diving ladder. He was up the ladder in seconds and rushed help the two passengers who were leaning over the side of the boat.

'You and I, we lift her?' said the man. Scott took the place of the girl who was holding Natalya's shoulders. He put his hands under her armpits and nodded at the man who was holding her legs at the knee.

'Lift!'

They struggled to lift her clear of the water, finally Scott got her torso over the side. As Scott stumbled backwards Natalya fell into the boat. She hit the white deck with a smacking noise and there was a gush of bright red blood from the tear in her wetsuit.

'Go! Please. We must go now!' pleaded Scott to the driver, who put the boathook down, turned the wheel and pushed down the throttles.

'I must call the coast guard,' said the driver, looking down at the now red deck of his boat. 'Tell me, what happened?'

'We were diving. The boat sunk. On top of us. It was on her legs. We were just diving. Fifteen metres. I don't know if she is breathing. Please, hurry!' implored Scott as he fell to his knees. He again felt for a pulse but could not feel anything with his numb fingers. As he started CPR again he heard the driver calling the coast guard on the radio. After a moment, he turned to Scott.

'We will go to Palamós. They are expecting us.' With that the driver pushed the throttles right down and the boat leapt forward.

# TWENTY-FIVE

It took them twenty minutes to reach the port of Palamós. Scott kept pumping Natalya's chest and breathing into her mouth. Occasionally they hit a wave from the wake of another boat and Scott was thrown against the side of the boat. Natalya's blood was now all over the deck of the white fibre glass boat and the two shocked passengers kept their distance. The man offered to take over the CPR but Scott carried on without replying. Occasionally he shouted at Natalya to wake up. He remembered the importance of keeping the blood circulating. All he needed to do was to keep pushing oxygenated blood around her system. Even if her heart had stopped. Keep circulating the blood until he could get her to a defibrillator.

They came round the point into Palamós port. Looking up, Scott saw the bright yellow of a helicopter on a quay. They headed straight for it. There was a *Guardia Civil* launch tied up next to it and a group of about twenty people waiting. As they pulled up, the male passenger put out two rubber fenders and then threw a rope to one of the policemen who pulled the boat in. Two men in bright green jumpsuits climbed down into the boat. A policeman handed them down a large holdall.

As one knelt and felt for a pulse, the other turned to Scott and asked her name. His companion checked her pulse and called her name.

'*Qué ha pasado?*' The other man asked Scott.

'*We were diving.*' Scott replied in Spanish. '*Only fifteen metres. We were about to come up. Our boat sunk on top of us. It fell on her legs. She couldn't get out. There was a lot of blood. I got the boat off her legs. We came straight up. She doesn't respond. I have tried to...*' Scott made a pumping motion with his hands. '*I couldn't feel any...heart,*' he said, not knowing the word for pulse.

'*She is English?*'

'*No, Ukrainian.*'

'*Ok. Does she speak Spanish? English?*'

'*Er...I don't know. English.*'

'*What are you called?*'

'*Alex.*'

The man turned to his colleague. He handed him a pair of scissors and he cut into the wetsuit at the waist, allowing him to expose Natalya's torso. One put a hand to her neck, then pumped her chest. He tore open a clear plastic bag, took out a plastic mouthpiece and blew into Natalya's mouth. The man said something else and they opened the holdall.

'Ok Alex,' he said in English. 'We are going to try to start Natalya's heart. Please, stand back.'

'Is she going to be ok?'

'We will try. Please, stand back.'

The man took two paddles attached to wires out of the holdall and the other cut off Natalya's bikini top. Her skin looked like marble to Scott. White and cold. He placed the paddles on her chest, the other one did something in the holdall and Natalya's body arched, then fell back to the deck. He pumped her chest a few more times, then they tried the paddles again. Her body arched and smacked down back onto the deck. Scott saw the look and the almost imperceptible shake of the head that the one holding the paddles gave his companion as he felt for a pulse.

'Ok Alex. Now we need to get her to a hospital.'

'Will she…?'

'We have tried to start her heart, but there is no response.'

'Can't you…?'

'We will keep trying in the helicopter. We must be quick.' He said something to a policeman standing on the quay and they passed down a plastic stretcher. The two ambulance men put Natalya on the stretcher, wrapped a blanket round her and fastened the Velcro straps. They passed the stretcher up to the policemen on the quay and climbed up after it.

Scott climbed up after them and made his way towards the helicopter. The two ambulance men placed the stretcher on the floor of the cabin and one climbed in, the other spoke to one of the policemen on the quay.

*'We will take it to the hospital, but…'* Scott overheard him say. He had used 'it' instead of 'her.' Scott walked up to the helicopter, but a policeman stopped him.

*'Please sir. Leave them to do their job. There is no room for you in the helicopter. I need you to give me some details.'*

*'But… I must go with her,'* Scott said, *'she is….'*

*'She doesn't respond. I'm sorry. They will keep trying, but I need you to give me some information. To help them. You can do nothing in the helicopter. Please, come with me. Then we will get you to the hospital.'*

*'Yes, of course,'* said Scott, in a daze. The policeman gently held him at the elbow and led him away from the helicopter. They shut the doors and when another policeman in front of the pilots gave them the thumbs up the engine revs increased and the rotors started to move. Soon the rotors were just a blur, then the engine noise rose to a roar and the helicopter slowly lifted off the quay. It hovered at about three metres, then it started to rise again. Its nose came down and it sped off across the water and up over the building on the landward side of the port. It was soon a speck in the distance.

*'Please. Come with me,'* the policeman said. After the deafening roar of the helicopter, the port seemed very quiet to Scott. Another policeman had climbed down into the boat they had arrived in and was talking to the driver, taking notes. Scott started to walk towards the boat, but the policeman steered him away.

*'I need to thank...'* Scott started to say.

*'Don't worry. They will be here. We need to get the information. Quickly.'* At the end of the quay was a building which looked like the superstructure of a boat, with portholes for windows, decks with railings, radar and masts rising from the roof. It had *'Servicio Marítimo de la Guardia Civil'* written on the side of the building with a coat of arms of a shield with an anchor and a crown.

*'It is your wife?'* asked the policeman as they walked along the quay.

*'My wife...? No, just a friend. We were diving. It wasn't deep. I told her to wait. I didn't want to come up with another boat in the area.'* Scott was finding it hard to focus. His legs were shaking. He couldn't get the image of Natalya's white face out of his mind. He held on to the door frame as they entered the building.

The little office had three desks, all covered with paperwork. There was an array of different VHF radios in their chargers along the windowsill. The policeman took a seat and motioned towards a chair. Scott sat down. His neoprene suit squelched as he sat down and he heard water drip onto the floor.

*'Sorry about...'*

*'Don't worry.'* The policeman looked at his computer screen, then clicked a few times with his mouse.

*'Ok. My English, it is not good. Castellano is ok?'*

*'Yes, no problem,'* replied Scott.

*'Good. Now, can I have your friend's name.'*

*'Natalya.'*

*'Natalya.'* He typed with only his two index fingers. *'Surname?'*

'Er...' Scott realised he did not know her surname. *'I don't know her surname. Does that matter?'*

The policeman raised an eyebrow.

*'Ok. No problem.'* He said in a gentle tone. *'Does she have any identification on her?'*

*'I only met her a few days ago.'* Scott felt guilty that he didn't know her surname. *'We were diving. The boat. It sunk. We haven't anything.'*

*'Do you have a telephone for her family? Friends?'*

*'No. Nothing.'*

*'Ok. No problem. Her identification. It is sunk?'*

*'Yes.'* Scott was finding it hard to concentrate. *'No... Wait... She left it at home.'*

*'At home?'*

*'At my house. Well, it's not my house. The place I am staying. She left her handbag there. If I can get home I could take her bag to the hospital. Where are they taking her?'*

*'They have gone to the IC unit in Girona. They will be there very soon. I need some information from you. Your name please.'*

*'Alexander Scott.'*

*'Alexander. Scott,'* he repeated, typing. *'Your identity document? Passport?'*

*'Passport. But sorry, I don't know the number from memory.'*

*'Ok, your address.'*

*'Can Daurat. Carretera del faro, Begur.'*

*'Can Daurat, Begur. Is that your permanent residence?'*

Scott gave him his London address.

*'Telephone?'*

Scott gave him his mobile number.

*'Your relationship to the...to Natalya?'*

*'Friends. I only met her a few days ago.'*

*'Tell me about the accident. You were diving?'*

*'Yes.'*

*'Where?'*

'In a bay, just north of the lighthouse at Begur.'

The telephone rang. The policeman answered it in Catalan. He said 'si' a couple of times then the person on the other end spoke for a while. He looked at Scott as he listened. He said:

'D'acord. Merci. Fins ara.' He drew in his breath.

'Alexander. I am sorry to tell you that Natalya was declared dead on arrival at Girona Trueta Hospital. I am very sorry.'

'What? No, she can't be.'

'I am so sorry.'

Scott slumped in his chair, stunned.

'I thought it would be fun.' Scott said in English.

'Pardon?' The policeman looked with worry at Scott's ashen face.

'Sorry. I said I thought she would have fun. I thought it was safe. It wasn't deep.'

'I am sorry Alexander, this must be very difficult, but I need to take down some details. Then we can get you to the hospital.'

'I don't need to go to the hospital. Not now.'

'All right. I need some details, then we can take you home, yes?'

'Yes, I would prefer that.' Scott realised he had to pull himself together. 'What do you need to know?'

'We will need her name and details.'

'If you come back with me to Can Daurat, her handbag is in the boathouse.'

'Ok. Can you tell me about the accident? You said your boat sank?'

'Yes. It sunk on top of us. We were diving. Nothing deep, just swimming round. We were waiting at the bottom of the buoy. Do you know the little bay, just north of the lighthouse by Begur? The orange mooring buoy there?'

'Yes, I know it.'

'We were moored to that. I don't know if we are allowed to. We weren't there long. We were waiting at the bottom of the chain. There was another boat on the surface. I didn't want Natalya to surface under another boat. I thought we had time. I thought it would be safer to wait.'

'And the boat sank?'

'The boat, the Salacia. My friends' boat. She came down on top of us.' He paused. 'I swum off to get Natalya a...' Scott's voice cracked. 'Suddenly there was a lot of sand everywhere. The boat had sunk. It was on top of Natalya. I tried to get her out but her legs were trapped. She was losing consciousness. I had to get her up. I got her legs free and we came straight up.'

'Ok. One moment' The policeman's two-fingered typing needed to catch up. 'Ok. Carry on.'

'We came up. I got her to some rocks. I tried to feel a ...' Scott put two fingers to his neck.

'Pulse?'

'Yes, pulse. But my hands were so cold. I tried to pump her heart. She didn't respond. Then the boat arrived. We got her on the boat and we came here.'

'Your friend's boat? She is old?'

'Yes. But old as in classic old. In great condition. A Riva. An Aquarama.'

'I know her. A beautiful boat. She sank? Why do you think?'

'I don't know. I floated her last week. She was fine. She had been in the water for a few days. There was no water coming in. I would have seen it.'

'Ok. That will be for the inspectors. How much fuel was on board? This is for the environment department.'

'Well, I don't know. I think the gauge was at about a quarter. I haven't filled her up yet.'

'Ok. Do you have the paperwork, the licence, your licence, the insurance papers? Do you have them at the house?'

'Yes. I think so. Unless they are on board the Salacia. But I can get copies.'

'Ok. Are you sure you don't want to go to hospital?'

'Yes. I am fine.'

'Ok. Why don't we take you back to...' He looked at his screen. 'Can Daurat? The house, it has a jetty? We can land by boat?'

'Yes.'

'It is the house before the lighthouse? The big white house? With the boathouse?'

'Yes, that's it.'

'We can go to your house by sea, and we can leave a marker buoy where the boat sank. To warn other boats. And you probably want to claim the salvage, no?'

'Salvage?'

'Before someone else comes along and claims it.'

'What? Yes. Ok.'

'We will mark the wreck. I will arrange a company to lift the boat. As there is a death involved, we will then take the boat for inspection.' He clicked a few times on the computer's mouse and the printer started. 'We need to bring some paperwork...' He picked up a radio from a charger.

'Let's go to the boat.' He picked up the sheets of paper from the printer, stamped them with a rubber stamp, and put them in a clear plastic folder.

Scott stood up and shivered.

'Are you all right? Do you want a blanket?' asked the policeman. 'I'm afraid I don't have a change of clothes. I have a blanket if you would like?'

'No, thank you. I will be all right.' replied Scott.

He followed the policeman out of the building and along the quay. There was a group of people gathered near the police patrol boat and the speedboat that had brought them to Palamós. The driver of the boat was talking, hands gesticulating. As Scott and the policeman reached the group the man on the boat looked up and stopped speaking. The group parted in silence. Scott walked up to the edge of the quay. He walked up to the speedboat as the policeman went to the police launch.

*'I am sorry about your boat. The blood.'* Scott said to the driver of the speedboat.

*'It's nothing. I am very sorry about your friend.'*

*'I have to go back home with the police now. Can I have your details? I know Natalya's family would like to thank you for your help.'* Scott felt his voice cracking again. *'I would like to thank you, properly, but now I have to go.'* The driver of the boat climbed up onto the quay.

*'Carlos Darder.'* He held out his hand.

'Alex Scott.' As Scott shook his hand, Darder reached his left hand round Scott's shoulder and gave him a hug.

*'You did everything you could. I am so sorry,'* he said to Scott, who had to fight back the tears.

*'Thank you for helping us. Can I have your details?'*

*'Don't worry about that now. I keep this boat in the marina here. Ask at the office. They have my details. We can meet up under better circumstances.'*

The two passengers from the boat waved to Scott. He walked through the silent group of onlookers to the police launch. It was painted white and green. The policeman was waiting for him. As they climbed down on deck, the policeman on board held out his hand.

*'Teniente Robles.* I am sorry for your loss.'

'Alex Scott.'

*'Alexander lives at Can Daurat. You know, the big white house just before the lighthouse,'* said the policeman from the office.

*'I'm sorry, I don't know your name,'* Scott said to him.

*'Sargento Puig. Are you ok? Are you warm enough?'*

*'Yes, thank you.'*

*'Ok, Sargento, let's go.'* Robles then switched to English again. 'Ok Alex. We will take you to your home. The *sargento* says the girl's documents are at you house, no?' Scott nodded. 'And as it is close, you will come with us to mark your boat? Yes?' Scott nodded again. 'Are you ok? Do you need a blanket?'

'No, I'm fine. Really. Thank you,' said Scott.

229

'Ok. Well, please, sit here.' He motioned to a bench in front of the driving console. Scott sat down. The sergeant handed him an emergency life preserver, which looked like a red garland to be put over the head, then untied the boat from the quay and the lieutenant manoeuvred the patrol boat away across the port. They kept at a slow speed almost idling until they came out past the breakwater. Then the noise of the engines increased to a roar as they came up on the plane.

# TWENTY-SIX

As the police launch sped across the almost flat surface of the sea, Scott gazed at the horizon, stunned. He needed to call Bill. Arrange to get the *Salacia* out of the water. Call the insurance company. Maybe he could check Natalya's phone for a number. He thought she had mentioned her family in Kiev. Her mother certainly lived there. He could ring Olenka. Santi would have his number. Or get it from the awful Camps man. Or he could just walk up to the lighthouse. They would need to make arrangements for getting the body back home.

How had the *Salacia* sunk? Had he left a plug open? He was sure there hadn't been any water in her. Boats don't just sink.

Scott couldn't get the image of Natalya's face out of his mind. The pain in her eyes. Her trust in him as he had motioned for her to be calm. The tears when she had told him about lying to him, told him she was in love with him. The awful slapping sound of her body landing in the boat. Her legs at that terrible angle. Her beautiful, long legs. Her cold, white skin as the medics tried to resuscitate her. He had only met her a few days before but her smiling face had already become very familiar. He would never see it again. She would never giggle in a lift again.

Scott's attention was brought back to the present as they came round the point before Can Daurat. The sergeant

231

slowed as they neared the boathouse. The police launch was a good few feet shorter than the *Salacia* and he easily navigated in.

The doors were open. It had only been a few hours since they had left. It felt like a lifetime ago. He looked at his watch. It was a quarter past seven. As they entered the boathouse, Scott stood up to help but the sergeant motioned for him to sit and, once the boat had bumped along the dock, got out holding a mooring rope which he tied to one of the cleats. Scott removed the life preserver and left it on the seat. He climbed out and the lieutenant shut off the engine and joined them on the dock.

'We left our phones and Natalya's bag in here,' he said in English to the lieutenant. He took Natalya's bag and his own phone out from where they had been hidden. He saw he had two missed calls and several texts and emails.

'Shall we go to the house?' said the lieutenant.

'Yes, of course. Come with me.' Scott went up to the door to the staircase and tried the handle. 'Sorry, I forgot. The house keys are on the *Salacia*, the boat that sank. The house is locked up.' Scott paused. 'I can call Dolors, the housekeeper. She can let us in.'

'Ok,' said the lieutenant. 'How long will that be?'

'I'll call her now.' Scott scrolled through his addresses until he found Dolors' number. He rang her home but the ringing went to answerphone. He tried her mobile number. She answered after a couple of rings.

'*Si, diga'm?*' She answered in Catalan.

'*Hello Dolors! It's Alejandro. Look, I've locked myself out of the house. Is there any way you could pop over to let me in?*' Scott remembered there being a spare set of keys in the office. He couldn't face telling Dolors about the events of the afternoon over the phone.

'*Hello Alejandro. I am in Begur shopping. I am at the butcher's. I will be back home later if you want to pop by.*'

*'Look, I'm in the boathouse. It's a long story. My keys are in the house. Is there any way you could come over here straight away? It is a bit of an emergency.'*

*'Ok Alejandro. Of course. I will come straight there. I will be with you in half an hour. All right?'*

*'Thank you. When you arrive, could you come straight to the boathouse and let me up. I'm downstairs.'*

*'Eh? I understand.'* She didn't sound like she did. *'I will come to the boathouse then?'*

*'Yes. And Dolors, I changed the alarm codes. So, come straight to the pool house. The alarm here is not on. Just in the main house. We... I am here downstairs in the boathouse.'*

*'I'll be there in half an hour,'* said Dolors and hung up.

'She will be here in half an hour,' Scott told the two policemen. 'She's in Begur.' Scott handed the lieutenant Natalya's handbag. 'I suppose you should have this.'

'Thank you. We need to head back to Palamós at eight o'clock. It's seven now. We could go to the site of the accident. We need to leave a marker for the crew to come to recover the boat,' said Robles.

'It's only the next bay along,' said Scott. 'We can be there and back by the time Dolors gets here.'

'You don't mind? It would help if you came.'

'Yes, of course. Come on, let's go.' Scott climbed back down onto the boat and the sergeant handed him the life preserver.

Once they had left the channel, the lieutenant gave the wheel over and came up to talk to Scott.

'Thank you for coming with us,' he said in English. 'It must be difficult.'

'Well...' replied Scott. 'Not really. It hasn't sunk in yet. Sorry. Bad choice of words. It seems surreal. Like it is happening to someone else.'

'She was your girlfriend?'

'No. Well, I suppose so. I only met her last week. We had spent some time together.'

'Very sad. I am sorry.'

'You are Lieutenant Robles.'

'Yes.'

'That's funny. I was going to call you. I didn't know I would be seeing you so soon.'

'I'm sorry?'

'Pablo Duarte told me that I should call you. About some research that I am doing.'

'Pablo. Sure. What did you want to call me about?'

'It doesn't matter. Not important. Just an article. Seems stupid now. It all….'

They had come round the point, past the lighthouse and the *Rusalka* which was moored offshore. They crossed over to the bay where they had dived that afternoon. In the middle of the bay was a cream and gold coloured tender. It had three people on board, one of whom had a wetsuit on and was in the process of putting on a tank and buoyancy jacket.

'What the …?' Scott shouted. The sergeant flipped a switch on the control panel and there was a whoop of a siren. The three men looked up. The police launch slowed as it approached the other boat.

'What are they doing? This is where she sunk,' said Scott, who had jumped to his feet. 'They are right over her. What are they…?'

'Ok, Alexander. Calm. Don't worry, we will deal with this,' said Robles.

Sergeant Puig steered the police launch up alongside the other boat. When they were alongside, he cut the engine.

*'Good afternoon. Please, you must leave this area. There has been an accident,'* he said in Spanish. Scott recognised one of the men as crew off the *Rusalka*. He was wearing a white shirt with what looked like sailor's epaulettes. Behind him was the looming Spralov.

'It's the crew from the *Rusalka*. The big ship we passed,' Scott said to Robles. 'That man is in charge of security for

234

the owner,' he said, pointing at Spralov. 'What do they think they're doing? They can't....'

'I do not speak Spanish,' said the sailor in heavily accented English to Robles. 'A boat has sunk. We are claiming salvage.'

Robles switched to English. 'As I said, there has been an accident. This is a police zone. Please leave.'

'We are claiming salvage. My associate is just going down to the boat to attach a rope.'

'The boat had already been registered as sunk by this gentleman here.' Robles indicated Scott. 'Salvage has been arranged. So please leave.'

'But we ...'

'Sir, I am asking you to leave, now. Or you will be obstructing a police investigation,' interrupted Robles.

The Russian shrugged his shoulders and said something to Spralov, then to the man in the wetsuit, who stopped putting on the equipment and put the scuba tank back down onto the deck. The captain started the engine and sped off, the wake rocking the police launch.

'What was that about?' Scott asked Robles.

'They were trying to claim wreck salvage rights. It is the law of the sea. If you help a boat in need or find a wreck you can claim a percentage of its value. I told him you had already claimed it. Vultures!' Robles looked over the side. 'So, where did she sink?'

'She should be somewhere around here,' said Scott, looking over the side. 'We were attached to the mooring buoy. I think it was here abouts.' Scott stared at the water. The sea took a few minutes to calm down and soon Scott could make out a dark shape beneath them. 'Over there.' He said pointing. 'There she is.'

'Ok. I see her.' Robles pointed to the right of their position and the sergeant steered the launch over the spot.'

'We will drop a marker. This is for the salvage ship. It also warns other boats of the wreck.' Robles took from a cupboard a green and white buoy, with a flag sticking out the top, with POLICIA written on it. It was attached to a small anchor and a long piece of rope. As they drove over the shadow of the *Salacia*, Robles threw in the anchor, followed by the rope and the buoy.

He turned to talk to Scott, whose attention was now on the shoreline.

'Could we go over there?' he said pointing to the rocks, to where he had swum dragging Natalya. 'I think I can see our diving tanks.' There was something bobbing in the water next to a large black rock. As they got nearer, Scott realised it was not black, but covered in dried blood. It was where he had tried to reanimate Natalya. Next to it, half submerged, were the two buoyancy jackets and tanks. Scott leant over the side of the police launch and pulled them in with the boat hook.

'Now she is marked, we must get you back home,' said Robles. 'I will call the salvage boat this evening.'

'When do you think they will be able to bring her up?' asked Scott.

'That depends. Maybe tomorrow. Maybe this week. Who knows. The sooner the better for the boat, for the pollution. Although I can see no oil on the water, that is good.'

'For the pollution?'

'Yes. And for you. If there is a gasoline leak you might be responsible.'

Puig pushed the throttle down and they headed back the way they had come.

'Will the salvage people find what sunk her?' asked Scott.

'As there has been a fatality, the boat will be brought to Palamós. There we will look at the boat to find the cause.'

'I know she was afloat and not taking on water when we started the dive. I want to know what happened more than anyone.' He paused. 'What will happen to Natalya?'

'There will have to be an autopsy. Then we can release the body. Do you know the, how do you say, next family?'

'Next of kin. No, I don't know who that is. There might be something in her bag. I can ask her work to get in contact if that will help.'

'Yes, thank you. We will try her phone. If it is unlocked sometimes the best thing to do is look for 'mother' or 'father' on a phone.'

'She talked about her mother. They sounded close.'

'Well, we will try her phone. I have a colleague who can speak Russian.'

'She is, was, Ukrainian.'

'Ok. Is there much difference? I don't know. Maybe you can get her work to call me? Here is my card.'

They were just arriving at the Can Daurat boathouse.

'Alexander, we will need copies of your documentation, the licence for the boat and the insurance.'

'Would it be ok to email you scans? There is a scanner here. It might take a while to find the boat documents.'

Robles looked at the sky and then his watch. 'Ok, can you email them to me. The email address on the card. We had better be off before it is too late.'

They bumped alongside the dock.

'The cleaner, she is here?'

Scott took out his phone and dialled Dolors, who said she was five minutes away.

'She'll be here in five minutes. Do you need to come up to the house?'

'No, that is ok. We will leave you here if that is all right with you? You will be ok?'

'Yes. Thank you. When will I know about the *Salacia?* The boat. Getting her out of the water.'

'I will speak with the company tonight. Please send me the documents. Of the boat. Can you give me your telephone number?'

'I gave it to the sergeant in the office,' said Scott indicating sergeant Puig.

'Ok. *Vale.* I will call you as soon as I know. Also, we will need a formal statement. About the accident. But that we can arrange later. Now you go home, get some rest.' Scott climbed out of the boat. Puig heaved the two tanks up onto the dock and Scott pulled them away from the edge.

'Alexander, I am truly very sorry about your friend. Natalya,' said Robles.

Scott watched the patrol boat reverse out of the dock. The launch's navigation lights came on. He gave a half wave as it turned and was gone.

Scott looked round the boathouse. It seemed an age ago that they had set out to go diving. He had wanted to keep an eye on the *Rusalka*. Natalya hadn't wanted to go diving. Not really. Why had he insisted? He'd thought a shallow dive would be fun. He'd told her that it wasn't dangerous. That she was with him. That she was safe. Stupid, cocky fool. It was all his fault. He looked down at the scuba tanks. There was something sticking out of a pocket. The dead starfish. He had wanted to give it to her as a memory of their dive. Maybe it had saved his life. There was something else in the pocket. The writing tablet. 'HAD FUN?' was still written in capitals.

The sound of footsteps coming down the stairs snapped Scott out of his guilt. He walked towards the door, there was a clinking of keys and it opened.

*'Hello Alejandro.'* Dolors gave Scott a kiss on each cheek. *'How are things? I came as quickly as possible. I haven't been into the house to turn off the alarm, just like you said.'*

*'Ok. I need to give you the new codes for the alarm. Sorry, I changed them the other day.'*

*'Where is the wooden boat?'* asked Dolors

*'Er…there was an accident.'* Scott didn't feel he was up to a full debrief with the over-emotional Dolors. *'The Salacia will be in Palamós for a few days. I was brought here but I left my house keys in the boat.'* He supposed that Dolors would soon hear about Natalya's death. Nothing stayed secret for long in these coastal communities, especially something as newsworthy as a

death, but for the moment, he just couldn't face talking about it.

*'Mr Franklin will be upset. He loves that boat. It's his pride and joy. Whenever he is here he goes out on it every day. Is there much damage?'*

*'I don't know. They will tell me.'*

*'He's is always so proud of that boat. He says...'*

*'It will be fine. I'm sure the insurance will cover it. If not, I will.'* He wasn't so sure if he would be able to cover any damage to such an expensive boat.

*'Be careful who you get to repair it in Palamós. There are lots of crooks about. I have a cousin there. He knows all the best boatwrights. Shall I call him? Mr Franklin always brings in his own mechanic to service the boat. From Italy I think. A nice young man. He stays here for a few days. While he services the boat.'*

*'Thank you Dolors. I have it under control.'* Scott tried to walk past Dolors but she stayed in the doorway.

*'Does Mr Franklin know?'*

*'I haven't had time to call him yet. I was going to call him now.'* Scott knew she meant well but he needed to get rid of Dolors. *'Let's go up to the house. I am sure I saw a spare set of keys in the office.'*

*'You don't want to leave your keys on the boat. Not in Palamós. Anyone could pick them up. They all know that boat. If they find the keys...'*

*'I'll make sure I get the keys back right away,'* interrupted Scott, who took the set of keys from Dolors' hand and started up the stairs.

*'Oh, you have been diving! I have never tried that. I think I am too old...'* He lost the remainder of what Dolors was saying as he mounted the steps. She would find out soon enough about Natalya and the sinking of the *Salacia*. He would just have to deal with her then. He rushed across to the main house. Once he had opened the kitchen door and turned off the alarm, he opened the office desk's drawers and in the second one down found a bunch of keys that

looked like Dolors' set. He walked back round the house and intercepted Dolors coming across the terrace.

*'There is a lot of diving that goes on here now,'* started Dolors, *'when I was young we didn't do much swimming. We went out on boats of course, but we hardly ever swum. Just to cool off. I learnt to swim though. I was a very good swimmer. I would have liked to have tried diving. Is it very good fun?'*

*'Sorry Dolors, I must start making some phone calls. Thank you so much for bringing the keys over. I must get on now. I will call you in the morning.'* He handed her back her keys and walked with her to her car.

*'Now, are you looking after yourself?'* She asked him as she neared the car. *'I know boys like you. You ...'*

*'I'm fine. Thank you Dolors.'* Scott said as he ushered her into the car, and shut the door. He walked back to the house, turning to wave at Dolors as she drove away.

The light was fading as he walked back into the house and turned on the kitchen lights. The dirty plates from their lunch were sitting in the sink. Scot poured himself a glass of water, drank it down, then went to a cupboard by the fridge and got out a bottle of J&B whiskey. He poured a couple of fingers into the glass and added a splash of water.

He went up to his room. In the bathroom, he peeled off the wetsuit that was now caked with salt and dried blood. He had a scorching shower, the pounding of the water calming his frantic thoughts. He dressed, then walked down through the house into the drawing room, turning on the lights as he went. He opened the doors to the terrace and walked out. The sun had set over the hill and while the sky had turned to night over the sea, in the west there was still the glow of the sun and a couple of wispy clouds burned a bright orange.

Scott sat at the iron table and got out his phone. He was relieved when Bill's mobile went straight to answerphone. He left a brief message saying that there had been an accident, he was ok, and that he would call in the morning

240

to give an update. Scott supposed he should call Natalya's work. Her mother needed to know. What a nightmare. He tried Santi and María but there was no answer and he didn't want to leave a message. He scrolled through his call register until he arrived at Saturday's entries. He had spoken to Camps just after speaking to Juan. He dialled the number. After a brief exchange, in which Camps told him Olenka was no longer interested in buying but that he would be happy to find another buyer, Scott managed to elicit a number for Olenka's office, and another mobile number for his assistant.

Once he had got off the phone with Camps, he dialled the office but there was no answer. He tried the mobile number.

'Si? Da?'

'Hello! Is this Dimitri Olenka's assistant?' Scott asked in English.

'Hello? Yes. It is?'

'Hello, this is Alex Scott. I met Dimitri on Monday in Barcelona. I am calling about Natalya.'

'Natalya is not here.'

'No, that is why I am calling. I have some terrible news.'

'Yes?'

'I was…We were…' Scott didn't know how to break the news. 'Natalya has had an accident. I am very sorry to say that… Natalya was in an accident this afternoon…She didn't make it. I'm so sorry.'

'She didn't make *what?*'

'I meant…' Scott felt sick.

'Yes?'

'I meant to say she didn't survive.' Scott took a deep breath and carried on. 'I'm afraid to tell you that Natalya died in an accident this afternoon.'

'She what? No, that cannot be. We have heard nothing.'

'It has only just happened. I… the police need to know…could you call the police? If I gave you their number, could you call them?'

'What? Yes. I can call them. You say it was an accident?'

'We were diving.'

'Diving?'

'Scuba diving. The police need to call her family. They have her bag, but they need to inform the family.'

'Well, I am not sure if I can help until tomorrow. We have the personnel files in the office in Moscow. Now it is shut.'

'Would you call them? The police? Please?'

'Yes, I will call them. But I cannot give them information on Natalya until tomorrow.'

Scott gave her Robles' mobile and landline number from the card and then hung up. She hadn't appeared very concerned that an employee had just died. More inconvenienced at having to call the police.

Scott went back into the house and into the office. After a brief search, he found a file with copies of all the car and boat documents. Thanking Manolo for being so efficient, Scott took out the *Salacia*'s registration document and the insurance papers. There was a scanner in the office but it wasn't plugged in, so Scott took photos of the papers with his phone. He emailed these to Robles, along with a photocopy of his passport that he had on file with a note saying that he could send better copies if needed. He added the number for Olenka's office and the assistant's mobile.

He went back out onto the terrace. It was now dark and the outside lights came on as he went down the steps to the pool house. He went into the bar and picked up the bottle of Lagavulin that he had found a few nights before. His phone rang, it was Juan.

'Hey, *mi amigo*. What's up?'

'Hey Juan. It's ... I've ....' Scott felt overcome with sadness.

'Are you ok, my friend? *Hola*, are you there?'

'Yes, I'm here. Juanito. Oh God. There has been an accident. We were diving. Natalya and I.'

'Hey, the blonde?'

'Juan, she died.' There was a moment of silence.

'What the fuck?'

'She died. I couldn't save her. She died in my arms. I don't...' Scott's voice began to break. He felt a tear trickle down his cheek.

'Are you ok? Where are you? I am coming now.'

'No don't worry my friend. I just needed to talk to a friend.'

'Tell me, what happened?'

Scott told Juan a brief version of what had happened, the accident, the boat to Palamós, the return to Can Daurat.

'I am so sorry, my friend.' Juan said when he had finished. 'I can't believe it. Listen, I'll come over. Or you come over to us. Come and stay the night. I will come and get you. You don't want to be alone tonight.'

'No. Really. Thank you. That's really kind. But I'd rather be alone. Honestly. Just needed to tell someone. I am exhausted. I am going to get an early night.'

'Look, if you need me, just call. Anytime Ok?'

'Ok. Thanks, my friend. *Un abrazo.*'

'*Un abrazo fuerte.*'

Scott poured himself another whiskey, and sat at one of the bar stools. It had been kind of Juan to offer to have him over, but he didn't want to spend the evening going over and over the afternoon. Going through it once with Juan had been bad enough. A few more whiskies and maybe he would be numb enough to sleep. His phone rang. A Spanish mobile he didn't recognise.

'*Si, dígame?*'

'Hello, is that *Señor* Scott? Alexander?' It was Lieutenant Robles.

'Hello *Teniente.*'

'How are you? Are you ok?'

'Yes, ok. Thanks.'

'Thank you for the documents. I have spoken to the *compañía de salvamento*, the...'

'Salvage company.'

'Yes, that. They are free in the morning. They can raise your boat tomorrow.'

'Ok, do I need to do anything?'

'No, they will bring it to Palamós, we have an inspector here.'

'Ok, thank you for telling me. I will tell the insurance. I spoke to Natalya's employers. They will call you in the morning with her next of kin.'

'Thank you, Alexander. I spoke to the hospital. They are performing the *autopsia* this evening. Will you be able to make a formal description of the accident? Is it possible tomorrow?'

'Yes.' Scott thought a moment. 'Shall I come over in the morning. At eleven?'

'We will be here.'

*'Hasta mañana.'*

*'Hasta mañana* Alexander.'

Scott poured himself another glass of whiskey. He carried his glass and the bottle back up to the house. He sat down at the kitchen table. Natalya. Probably on a stainless-steel slab. Cold. White. He didn't want to think about what was going on in the hospital. He picked up his glass and went into the little television room that was next to the sitting room. Maybe a film would take his mind off it all. He looked through the cupboard of DVDs. Most of them were ancient, and judging by the titles, probably bought by Charlie. Charlie. Another death at sea. What was it with the sea and people close to Scott? Did it have it in for him? He couldn't face watching a film. Scott went back into the kitchen and poured another whiskey.

# TWENTY-SEVEN

Bright sunlight coming through the curtains woke Scott. For a moment, he didn't know where he was. Can Daurat. His room. He had a raging thirst. Felt rather shaky. Must have been a big night. He got out of bed and lurched to the window. Another lovely day. Then memories of the previous day came flooding back. The accident. Natalya. She was dead. Images poured into his mind: her cold, lifeless body on the boat; the look on her face through her diving mask; her smile getting out of the car; the wetsuit oozing red blood onto the white of the boat.

Scott put on a pair of shorts and a shirt and went down to the kitchen. He made himself a coffee and started to make a list on the back of an envelope that was on the windowsill.

Call Bill; call insurance; call police. Then he added: go police Palamós 11. That was all. No need for a list. He felt the guilt of the responsibility over the accident bearing down on him, but he didn't have much to do. The police would contact her family today. He should write to them. At least tell them what happened. What had happened? How had the *Salacia* sunk? Had he done something wrong? He was sure there had been no leak, at least nothing he had seen. Should he have moved the boat when it was on Natalya's legs? He wondered if the boat would be badly damaged from the night underwater. God knows what would have floated away. It can't be cheap to refit a half million Euro boat. He'd call the insurance at nine.

To clear his head Scott performed his usual morning exercises and went for a half hour run. He climbed over the fence and headed south along the Camí. He didn't feel like going past the lighthouse. He might bump into Olenka or one of his men. It was Thursday. He had Taylor coming up to stay. He had completely forgotten. The plan to spy on Olenka had slipped his mind. It wasn't so important anymore. He would try to ring Taylor and put him off. So what if Olenka wanted to smuggle a load of drugs? If they poked their noses in too deep who knows what might happen to them. Was it really worth it?

By the time he got back from his run, Scott had decided to call Taylor and decline the offer to help. Taylor would understand. It didn't mean he couldn't spy on Olenka himself, just not at Can Daurat and without Scott. He came into the house from his run and tried Taylor. It went to answerphone. He left a message asking Taylor to call.

It was nine o'clock. Scott tried the boat insurance company. When he explained the situation, the receptionist took down his details and said he should call when he had the police report of the accident. He tried Bill on his mobile number but again it went to answer machine. He left a message for Bill saying he would call again.

At a quarter past ten, Scott gathered together his passport, the insurance documents and the boat papers and went out to the garages. One look at the Aston brought back memories of the trip to Barcelona: Natalya loving the comfort and the power of the huge car; their drive in the rain; the journey back in silence. He took the hire car.

On the drive to Palamós the accident repeated in his mind. Had it been his fault? Had he done something wrong on the *Salacia*? Natalya had said she had a PADI, but he had no idea if that allowed them to go diving on their own. He wondered if he could be held legally responsible. Had his efforts to free her caused her death? He was sure he did the right thing by getting the boat off Natalya, but would the police? He hoped he could give his account to Robles, he had appeared sympathetic to Scott.

He managed to find a parking space near the port and walked the remainder. As he came to the quay, he saw a small crowd gathered about a boat on a flatbed trailer and held upright by an enormous blue crane. It was the *Salacia*. The crane had put the boat onto the trailer with two huge canvass straps. There was green and white police tape wrapped about the cockpit of the boat. She looked much bigger out of the water. Her white hull gleamed. As Scott got closer he saw a head bobbing up and down on board. It was a green clothed Guardia Civil whom Scott didn't recognise. Feeling self-conscious as he approached the crowd, Scott headed for the door of the police building. Scott caught Lieutenant Robles' eye as he came in the door.

'*Hola* Alexander.'

'*Hola teniente Robles.*'

'How are you this morning?'

'Alive, I suppose,' said Scott, failing to keep the bitterness out of his voice. 'I brought the original paperwork. I see they have brought up the *Salacia.*'

'Yes, my *técnico* is having a look now.' Scott sat in the chair in front of Robles' desk. He took out the boat's paperwork and handed that and his passport over. Robles thanked him and took a scan of the documents on a scanner on the table behind him. Scott's phone started to ring and he switched it to mute. Robles came back to his desk with the passport and the copy. He put the passport on the desk, and opened a file on his desk.

'Thank you for bringing these. It is better than the phots you sent,' he said as he placed the documents in the file. He pulled out a typed form from the file. 'We have the results of the autopsy.' He looked up at Scott. 'I hope it helps, in

247

some way, to know that Natalya did not drown. I am sorry to say the cause of death was loss of blood.'

Scott nodded.

'The cut on her leg. That killed her. The femoral artery. I am afraid there was nothing more you could have done. I am told it would not have been bad. She would have felt little pain.'

Images of the black cloud of blood swirling round Natalya swamped Scott's thoughts. Putting on the belt as a tourniquet.

'I tried... I tried to stop the bleeding. With my belt.' Scott said in a weak voice.

'That was the right idea, but I am afraid the location of the wound... it was impossible. I am sorry Alexander.' Robles paused. 'Do you think you are able to give me a statement? If not, we can take the statement later?'

'No, let's do it now,' replied Scott.

Scott told Robles the events of the previous afternoon. Starting with their tying up the boat on the mooring buoy, their going for a dive. The boat coming down. Trying to move the boat. Getting Natalya free. The ascent. Getting to the rocks. The boat taking them to Palamós. Robles just listened and typed on his computer. Occasionally he held up a hand to ask Scott to stop while his typing caught up. When he had finished, he spoke.

'Ok. I have typed this in Spanish. You speak good Spanish, no?'

'Good enough.'

'Can you check this is correct, then sign it for me if you agree?' He had clicked on his mouse and a typed form came out of the printer. He handed it to Scott, it had all his details and a typed account of the accident. Scott glanced over it and signed.

'Would you like a copy?' asked Robles.

'Could you email it to me?' asked Scott.

'No problem.'

'What happens now? Did you get in touch with Natalya's family?' asked Scott.

'My colleague spoke to her mother this morning.'

'Oh, God. How was she?'

'I er...I don't know. I did not speak to her....'

'Poor thing. I can't imagine what she must be feeling...'

The Guardia Civil who had been on the boat leant in the door. He looked at Scott, nodded, then said to Robles:

'*Jefe... por favor?*' Indicating outside with his head. Robles stood up and said to Scott:

'Alexander, I will just be one minute.' And he went outside.

Scott looked round the office. On the wall to his left was a poster advertising missing persons. There must have been thirty or forty passport-sized photos on the A3 sized poster. Most were old men. A couple of teenagers. How sad, thought Scott. Next to it was a customs poster. It showed a list of prohibited articles. Nuclear waste, protected animals, arms and drugs. It asked for anybody with information on the smuggling of any of these items to contact the *Guardia Civil*. He thought of the *Rusalka*. He wondered if an anonymous tip off would have any effect.

Robles came back into the office and sat down. He looked grim.

'Alexander. My *técnico* has made the inspection of the boat.' He paused and looked at a sheet of paper in his hands. 'We are recommending the death of Natalya be investigated as a crime.'

'What? What do you mean?'

'*Cálmate.* Please. It is not against you. You were with Natalya underwater. She was killed by the boat falling on her. The boat did not sink by accident.'

'What? I don't understand.'

'The boat was sabotaged.' He paused. 'The intakes to the engine, the coolant, they were cut. Both of them. If it had been just one, well, yes, an accident, maybe.' He paused.

'But both? No, impossible. The pipes were cut. The engines on that boat are very big. It would fill with water very fast.'

'But who? How could they have been cut?'

'They are large, thick rubber pipes. They bring in cold water to cool the engines. My *técnico* says they are both open. Cut. Not broken from age.'

'But…but that's criminal… it's…'

'Normally this would be a civil problem. Maybe a problem with the insurance. But there has been a death. We have to open a criminal investigation.'

'Wait. Of course,' said Scott. 'I can't believe it.' He paused. 'The boat.' He looked up at Roble, who was looking confused. 'A few minutes before the accident. When we were swimming to the mooring buoy underwater. I saw a boat go over us. It was coming from the direction of the *Salacia*.'

'Ok, there was a boat. Can you tell me anything about it?'

'Sorry. Just that it was going fast.' Scott paused. 'What about the tender that we saw from the police launch? At the site. The tender from the *Rusalka*…'

'The *Rusalka*?' Asked Robles.

'You know, that big yacht moored off the lighthouse that we passed.'

'Yes, I have seen it.'

'The speedboat we saw that was over the wreck site, it was the tender from the *Rusalka*. It's been around the last few days. And I recognised the sailor and that man Spralov. It's a bit of a coincidence that it 'finds' the sunken *Salacia*. How did they know she had sunk there? Stupid of me. Why didn't I think of that yesterday?'

'Ok.' Said Robles writing on his pad of paper.' I can ask the *Rusalka*'s crew why they were there.'

'It must have been them. You say she would have sunk fast. Well, when we started the dive she was fine. So, someone must have come aboard, once we had submerged, and cut the pipes. When we went underwater there were no boats about. The nearest boat was the *Rusalka*. They could have seen us leave the *Salacia* unattended. And then you have my attacker of the other night.'

'Your attacker? What is this?'

'I was attacked the other night.' Scott gave Robles a brief description of the events of the other night. 'And there was a speedboat then too. Looked very similar to the *Rusalka's* tender.' Scott said as he finished the story.

'And you called the police?'

'Yes. I spoke to Inspector Matas from Begur. Do you know him?'

'Yes, yes of course. Have you any idea why these men would want to attack you? To sink your boat? Do you have a history with them?'

'History? No. Not at all? I only met the owner, Dimitri Olenka, on Monday night. I don't know him from Adam. Natalya was one of his employees. *She* told me he didn't want me snooping about.'

'Snooping?'

'Sorry. Investigating. Looking into him. As I am a journalist. She said he told her to keep me away from Can Daurat.'

'And why would he not want you at Can Daurat?'

Scott realised now he had to tell Robles about Taylor's theory.

'I have been talking to a fellow journalist. We think Olenka might be smuggling drugs.' Scott told Robles about the cranes, the forty-tonne cargo hold on the *Rusalka*, the secrecy over the lighthouse.

'I see your idea, Alexander, but…' Robles did not look convinced. Scott had to admit to himself that his explanation did not sound very convincing. 'Look. You have had a terrible shock. We have evidence that someone tampered with your boat. I think it is a bit early to make the connections with drug smuggling. A man strengthening his ship's hold does not mean he is smuggling. Let us make an investigation into this accident.

251

We will question the crew who we saw by the boat yesterday.'

'But we believe he is bringing in the drugs today or tomorrow. Can you not search the *Rusalka* when she comes back to shore?'

'Alexander, we cannot just search boats because of an idea. I will make some enquiries. If this Olenka is bringing in drugs, then someone will have said something. Believe me, we hear about these things. This amount you talk about, forty tonnes, this is an enormous quantity. Until now, I have not heard of this man in connection with any talk of drugs. We are not allowed to go searching boats on a, how do you say, 'whim?''

'I understand. But please, will you look into it? We, er... I, can keep an eye on him from Can Daurat.'

'Alexander, please. Do not get involved. If you are wrong, this Olenka could get very angry. If you are right, you could be in danger. You have told me what you think. Let us investigate. I will talk to inspector Matas...'

'I...' Scott faltered.

'Yes?'

'I think Matas might have a closer relationship with Olenka than...' Scott wondered how best to put this. He did not want to directly accuse Matas of corruption, he and the lieutenant could be friends. 'His relationship with Olenka might be a business relationship, if you know what I mean.'

'You are saying Matas is involved?'

'Well, no. Not exactly. We don't know for sure. But they are certainly close.'

'Ok Alexander. That is interesting. I have heard... Anyway. I will not talk to Matas. Please. Leave this matter to us. I will ask a few people. I will go and ask the crew of the...' He looked at his pad. 'the *Rusalka*.

'Yes, I will ask them about the accident. We will ask around if anybody saw anything yesterday afternoon. Please Alexander, stay out of this. I will keep you informed.

There will be a proper investigation into your friend's death. Now, as you are a witness in an active homicide, I will ask you formally not to leave the country...'

'Yes, of course.'

'And I will need to keep your passport for the present.'

Scott say goodbye to Robles and walked out onto the quay. Scott looked at his watch. It was half past twelve. He took out his phone. He had two missed calls from Taylor.

# TWENTY-EIGHT

Scott turned his phone volume back on and dialled Taylor as he walked back along the quay towards where he had parked.

'Hi Alex. I was trying to get through to you. I am just arriving,' said Taylor.

'Hi Peter. Look, something happened yesterday. I have just been at the police station. Heading back home now. I'll be a quarter of an hour.'

'What? Did…?'

'I'll explain when I see you. Be there in fifteen.' Scott hung up. He arrived at the hire car and got in. The fucking Russians. They had killed Natalya. And Manolo. They had attacked him. He had to do something. He and Taylor would get the proof. Give it to Robles.

On the drive back to Can Daurat, Scott developed and then discarded several plans to bust Olenka. The day he had met Taylor in Barcelona he had imagined that they would follow the *Rusalka* out to sea in the *Salacia*. That plan was now impossible. He wondered if he could get another boat. Juan had one. But then he would have to explain the reason he needed to borrow it. The jetski? If he remembered rightly it made a racket, and he doubted it could go that far away from shore.

He and Taylor must take photos of the *Rusalka* today. He wasn't sure but forty tonnes should make a difference to the waterline on the hull. Scott was pretty sure private boats didn't have those markers that commercial tankers have on their sides, but they could take photos and compare them to see if she was lower in the water.

He rounded the corner before Can Daurat and saw Taylor standing by a little black car on the driveway in front of the gates. Scott pressed the clicker on the car keys and the gates opened. As he drove past Taylor he waved and pointed down the drive. Taylor got into his car and followed.

Scott drove round the house to the garages and Taylor followed him.

'Wow. Quite a pad,' said Taylor getting out of his car.

'Hi Peter. How was the drive?'

'No problem at all. This is amazing,' he said looking about. 'So, you're the other half, eh?'

'If only. Usual abode a small hovel in Hammersmith. Just looking after this for a few weeks. And not doing the best job of it. Come and have a drink and I'll tell you what been happening.' Taylor took a holdall out of the car and they walked round the house to the pool terrace.

'Gets better and better,' exclaimed Taylor. They walked past the pool to the other side of the house and went in through the kitchen door.

'Leave your bag anywhere. I'll show you your room later.' Scott went up to the fridge and got out two bottles of beer. He opened them and gave one to Taylor.

'Right. Where to begin?' He paused. 'They killed Natalya. You know. The blonde from Barcelona.'

'What?' Taylor nearly dropped his beer.

'They killed her. They sunk my boat. Well, not my boat, but....'

'What? You're joking.' Taylor was staring at Scott with eyes wide.

'I wish I were. She's dead.'

'How? What?' Taylor looked stunned.

'We were diving. They came and sunk our boat. Why? Who knows? Maybe they didn't want me snooping around. We happened to be underneath her when she sunk. Came down right on top of us. Hit Natalya. Would have hit me too if I hadn't moved away.'

'But…But…' Taylor took a large gulp of his beer.

'I have just been with the police. In Palamós. They are opening a criminal investigation.'

'Jesus Christ.'

'I know, it's unbelievable.'

'And who was it? Was it Spralov? Did they get him?'

'No. They are trying to find proof it was them. They are asking to see if there were witnesses.'

'But if you were there…'

'I was fifteen metres underwater at the time. I only saw the bottom of their boat. I'd love to say that I was sure it *was* their boat, but I can't. But it must have been them.'

'Tell me the whole story.' Taylor said pulling out a chair from the kitchen table. Scott went through the previous day's events for the second time that day.

When he finished, Taylor sat for a moment in silence.

'My God, your poor bastard. What a terrible thing to happen. I am so sorry.'

Scott didn't know what more to say.

'Are the police going to arrest them?'

'That's the problem. They know it was sabotage. And they know it wasn't me, but proving who it was is a different thing. Peter, I am afraid I told the lieutenant, he's called Robles, I told him about the drugs.'

Taylor took a sharp intake of breath.

'I know we said we would keep it to ourselves until we had proof. I'm sorry, I told him. I think he thought I was just reacting to Natalya's death. But he said he will look into it. He said he hasn't heard anything to connect Olenka to any drugs. That normally he would have heard something. What we need to get is some proof. He said he couldn't just search the boat on a tip off… We need proof.'

'If Olenka catches wind of it…'

'I also told him about our reservations about Matas. He didn't seem surprised. I get the impression he will be discreet.'

'Jesus Alex. I hope this hasn't blown it. I so sorry for your loss. But I've been following Olenka for months now. If he gets wind that the police are on to him.' He took a deep breath. 'Well, we should know by tomorrow morning. I checked Olenka's two shipments. Or rather the container ships carrying them. Both are nearing this area this evening. Look, I'm sorry, you've been through enough. This afternoon I'll try to check the lighthouse.'

'I thought you said you didn't want to get close, as you had been hanging around there before.'

'Well, I don't, but I think it needs to be checked.'

'Yesterday I had a peek at the lighthouse. I bought a drone in Barcelona after I saw you. I flew it over the lighthouse. We can have a look at the footage now.'

'You got film of the lighthouse? Brilliant! I thought… I thought, what with the accident…'

'I flew the drone in the morning, before the accident. In fact, the drone itself is still out there. Somewhere near the lighthouse. I was bringing it back to me and it ran out of battery. Then a couple of Olenka's men came out, I think they saw the drone. Spralov was one of them. He had a gun. So, I hid and legged it. There should be the footage of the flight on my phone.'

Scott got them both another beer and took out his laptop. He found the right cable in his bag and plugged in his phone. He opened the video file from the drone flight.

'This is the drone taking off,' Scott said as the video began. 'I was on a rock about thirty yards off the path. Up, behind the lighthouse,' Scott said. The screen showed a blur of green as the drone flew over the thick scrub and trees. Suddenly the screen went blue as the drone overshot the cliffs. Scott gave Taylor a running commentary as the drone circled back and hovered over the lighthouse. They stopped the video when they had a clear view of the building.

'Jesus. It looks like he's demolished it,' said Taylor.

'There's not much left of the inside of the main building. And quite a bit of the outside wall is gone.' Scott said pointing to the gaping hole in the seaward wall. 'I'm not sure they are allowed to do that.'

'Why is he demolishing the building? It doesn't make sense,' said Taylor, then pointed at the screen. 'You can see, here, the top of the scaffolding and the crane. Maybe they want to offload directly onto a lorry. Maybe they want to drive a lorry into the building? Or through it. I don't know.'

'What have they done here?' asked Scott, pointing at a huge hole inside the structure.

'Looks like they have dug a large pit. They're not going to bury the drugs, are they?'

'It looks big enough.' Scott clicked on play. 'I rather overshot the lighthouse here… had to turn around…ok. Do you see… here? As the drone came back over …. there! There is another huge hole.'

'Why is he digging holes?'

'This is when they saw the drone.' The video had arrived at the part where Spralov and the other man looked up at the drone. The rest of the video was of the drone flying directly over the lighthouse then over trees and shrubs. After a few turns, the footage showed straight flight across the trees until it stopped.'

'I'm afraid that's it. It ran out of juice.'

'Not much to go on,' said Taylor, who looked deflated. 'Sorry, but I'm not sure that is really any help. Any chance we can retrieve the drone and use it when they come back with the drugs?'

'If we can find it. I know roughly where it fell. It's marked on the app on my phone. I'm not sure the camera will be much use at night though.'

'We'll need something to convince your man in the civil guard.'

'Any luck with any of your Interpol contacts?'

'The same I'm afraid. They all said this was pure speculation. Not enough to go on.' Taylor sighed. 'I can't wait for this to be over. I've been in Russia for ages, haven't been home for two months. Did I tell you about my boy?'

'I think you mentioned him.'

'A little boy. Ollie. I am dying to see him.' He took out his phone, scrolled through a few pages and showed Scott a picture of a toddler. 'Look, here he is.'

'A handsome boy,' said Scott. Who thought he looked like every other toddler he had ever seen.

'He's grown so much since I've been away,' said Taylor, his face beaming. 'I can't wait to get back and see him. Have just got to finish this Olenka article. I promised Judy that after this I'm through with the whole investigative reporter lark. Don't want to be running around the world chasing the stories anymore. Not if I'm going to see Ollie growing up. The FT have offered me a column. I need to wrap this up, as soon as possible.'

'Well, I think the drone is a bit of a no go.' Scott looked over at the end of the garden. 'But, we might have a solution…' He got up and walked across the terrace to the side of the pool house. Above him was one of the security cameras.

'A few days ago, I needed to change the passwords, so I had a read though the manual. To avoid burglars disabling the cameras by cutting the wires, these all have backup data SIM cards and batteries.'

'I don't understand,' said Taylor. 'How does that help us?'

'Well, it means these cameras can broadcast directly over the internet. If we can hide it somewhere where it overlooks the jetty, we should be able to see what goes on.'

'Ok, I see what you mean. But there are a few of questions.'

'Yes?'

'How do we know how long the battery will last?'

'Well, we don't. I'm sure they will last one night.'

'Ok, how do we record what is going on?'

'We can set it all up here this afternoon,' said Scott.

'How the hell are we going to get a camera installed over there at the lighthouse? We can't exactly waltz in there dressed in boiler suits and say we are the security experts come to install the cameras.'

'If we are right, and they are bringing in the drugs over the next twenty-four hours, all we need is footage of them unloading stuff from the boat. The cliffs where the jetty has been built have loads of little cracks and crevices – all we need to do is put one of the cameras in one of them. As long as it overlooks the jetty.'

'But how the hell will we get the camera there?'

'Do you feel like a kayak?'

'A what?'

'We could kayak over to the jetty.'

'Are you mad?'

'No. Not at all. There is a two-man kayak in the boathouse. It's only a few hundred yards. We wait until the *Rusalka* leaves, then we kayak across the bay. They won't see us in the dark. We can check the camera here this afternoon, then all we need to do it put it facing the jetty. On a rock somewhere, with a good angle on the spot where they will be unloading. We leave it there, and come back here. If, like you said, they come back in the night and start unloading, it should at least capture a bit of incriminating evidence. We can then send the footage to Robles and he can come round with the cavalry.'

Taylor did not look very enthusiastic.

'Honestly Peter, this can work. I can't think of any other way we will be able to get evidence for Robles. Not without our being there. That would be too dangerous. From what you have said of Spralov we want to keep clear of him. What do you think? Worth a try?'

'Well, we've got the afternoon to come up with something better,' said Taylor.

They sat on the terrace discussing alternatives to Scott's plan. None of which were any better.

Scott showed him to the room he would be staying in and they came back down to the kitchen where they made a sandwich and opened another couple of bottles of beer. Taylor talked mainly about Olenka, the difficulties he had endured in Russia collecting research on him. Scott found that he rather liked Taylor, there was something quintessentially English about him, with his outrage at impropriety and desire to see fair play.

In the afternoon, Scott found a ladder in the garage and managed to unscrew and unplug one of the outside security cameras. Scott spent an hour playing with the camera. With an app that he downloaded to his phone, Scott found he could remotely see a live feed, record video, and programme the camera. When the camera wasn't plugged into the mains, the power automatically switched to battery. The instructions claimed a battery life of seventy-two hours in standby mode and twelve hours of recording using the movement sensor.

Scott then went down to the boathouse to check the state of the kayak. It was an old fibreglass two-seater, and Scott was pleased to see it was still painted a dark naval grey from when Charlie had imagined getting up to all manner of secret escapades. Scott smiled to himself. Charlie would have loved their 'mission.' He tried the kayak in the water and it appeared to be seaworthy. He found a couple of oars in a cupboard.

He found Taylor sitting on the pool terrace with two fresh beers on the table.

'Right. The kayak is fine. The camera works. Looks like we are set.'

'Are we really going to do this?' asked Taylor.

'Yes, come on. Look, we'll be in and out of there in no time. You said the container ships will get here in the early hours of the morning. If the *Rusalka* heads out to sea this evening, we know we're onto something. At nine, nine fifteen it gets dark, so once we can't be seen, we can paddle over the bay, leave the camera pointing at the jetty and the base of the scaffolding and come back here. We'll just watch from here; wait till we see them pull up to the jetty. Once we have some video of them unloading anything dodgy I can send it straight to Robles.'

# TWENTY-NINE

Taylor had gone up to his room to check on the progress of the container ships on the internet when, at about half past six, Scott saw the *Rusalka* weigh anchor. He hadn't seen anyone go out to her on the tender, they had been checking on her position every few minutes and must have missed it. Scott had again failed to get through to Santi and María.

He called up to Taylor who came running down the stairs.

'She's off,' said Scott. They ran out on to the terrace and Scott handed Taylor a pair of binoculars. They watched the large ship turn towards the horizon, then the white wake frothed and she started to move away from the land. Only then did the sound of her engines reach them at Can Daurat.

'I would have thought she would be out of sight in fifteen to twenty kilometres. How far away did you say the containers were passing?'

'Between fifty and seventy miles,' replied Taylor.

'Ok, so if the *Rusalka* can make around twenty knots, it should take her between three and four hours. If, as we estimated, it will take a further three to four hours to unload forty tonnes, then we should have a minimum window of nine hours before they get back. The *Rusalka* should be back here between three and seven in the

263

morning. That leaves us heaps of time to go and place the camera.'

'When do you think we should go?' asked Taylor, who still looked very doubtful about the exercise.

'It's half six now, why don't we get ready at dusk, and head over just as it gets dark? In about three hours. They shouldn't be able to see us in that light, but if we can get there before it's pitch black it will be easier to leave the camera and head back.'

Scott went down to the boathouse to get them wetsuits. He couldn't help looking at the two scuba tanks and buoyancy jackets which were still on the dock. The tablet with 'HAD FUN?' on it was still lying next to them. Scott wiped the writing off with his thumb and put it back in the jacket pocket.

When he went back up to the pool terrace, Taylor had gone. Scott looked round the garden and saw him over by where the fence had been. Scott walked over to join him. Taylor was looking at the lighthouse through the binoculars.

'Oh, hi,' he said. 'There doesn't seem to be much movement going on at the lighthouse. Quiet as the grave.'

'That's a change,' said Scott. 'There has been banging and drilling noises going on for days.'

'What happened here?' Taylor said, pointing to the collapsed part of the garden. 'Looks like you've been digging holes like your neighbour.'

'It's a landfall. There used to be a tunnel that ran under that part of the garden. It's the path that runs along the coast, the *Camí de Ronda*. The path I saw you on the other day by the lighthouse.'

'Ok, yes, of course.'

'It collapsed the other day. I've been trying to get the coastal department to come and repair it but every department seems to deny responsibility.'

For the next hour, Taylor kept an eye on the lighthouse and Scott went back into the house. He tried to call Bill but again it went straight through to answerphone. Nor were Santi nor Maria answering their phones.

The sun had gone down over the hill behind the house when Scott called Taylor down to the pool house. Once in the boathouse Scott gave Taylor his wetsuit to get into.

'Is this necessary? Are we going to fall in?' asked Taylor.

'Not really, we shouldn't get too wet. But the water is cold, we'll probably splash each other a bit, and we'll be better off just in case we do fall in.'

They put on their wetsuits, followed by neoprene boots. Taylor's suit was too tall for him; the neoprene bunched at his wrists and ankles and was stretched taut over his belly.

'I feel like a penguin at a fetish party.'

'You look like one,' said Scott, laughing. It felt odd to laugh. Wrong. Scott's laughter faded. 'Can you give me a hand?' They placed the double kayak in the water.

'If you get in, I'll pass you an oar,' said Scott, kneeling, as he held the side of the kayak. Taylor put one foot in where the front seat was. Then, holding onto the side of the dock with one hand, he moved his other foot into the kayak, which started to wobble from side to side.

'Don't worry, I've got it, just get in and make yourself comfortable,' said Scott. He steadied the kayak. Taylor lowered himself down onto the front seat, his feet slipping forward on the fiberglass at the last moment. He landed hard on the seat and Scott had to fight to stop the kayak from tipping over.

'Right, try to keep your weight in the middle,' said Scott, thinking they should have taken the kayak out for a test run that afternoon. 'Are you ok?'

'Yes, all good,' said Taylor, still gripping the side of the dock.

'Ok, can you keep a hold there. I'll just get all our stuff and we can be off.' Scott went and retrieved the waterproof bag he had put together with the camera, his phone, some gaffer tape and a couple of torches. He handed Taylor an oar, placed the bag in the cubby hole behind the back seat, then got into the back of the kayak a lot more gracefully than Taylor had. He picked up his own oar which was on the dock next to him, and said:

'Right, off we go.' They pushed off from the dock. Straight away Taylor started to wobble and the kayak swayed from side to side.

'Wahey! Relax!' said Scott. 'Just sit straight. Don't worry about steering, I'll do that.' Taylor took a stroke with his right blade, then tentatively took another one with his left. Scott matched his strokes, putting a little more pressure on his left blade and they surged forward and right, out of the dock and into the sea.

It was very dark as they left the lights of the boathouse, but their eyes soon became accustomed to the fading light. There was a little bit of wind, and, once they left the channel, the waves were slightly bigger. Every now and then Taylor's oar caught a wave and sent water spraying all over Scott.

'I'm getting the hang of this.' Taylor said in a load voice over his shoulder.

'Great, but keep it down. Sound carries over water.' Scott whispered.

'Ok. Sorry.' Taylor whispered over his shoulder.

Once they were out in the bay they could see the hills around them silhouetted by the setting sun. The lighthouse had only one light on, but the scaffolding and jetty were still visible against the pale pink rock of the cliff.

The noise of the gentle wind and waves hid any sounds they were making, and with the wind behind them they made good time. After about twenty minutes of paddling they could see the cliffs looming. Scott kept the kayak pointing towards the jetty until they were twenty metres away then steered towards the left.

As they got closer to the rocks at the base of the cliff, Scott realised the waves would make it very difficult to get out. He wasn't sure how the fibreglass kayak would hold up to hitting the rocks. They were about five metres to the left of the scaffolding jetty. The slapping noise of waves hitting the structure masked their paddling.

'Peter. Stop, stop!' Scott hissed, as he paddled backwards.

'What?' Whispered Taylor over his shoulder, but stopped paddling.

The waves, over which they had been riding over when moving forward, were now bouncing them up and down. Scott fended off crashing into the rocks with his oar. He realised he would have to get out of the kayak to place the camera. That would mean leaving Taylor to keep the kayak afloat and off the rocks.

'Peter.'

'Yes.'

'Peter. I'm going to have to get out. Into the sea. Can you keep the kayak here? Where we are now?'

'Er…yes. But…Ok.'

'I'll get out, climb up those rocks and try to find a place for the camera. OK? When I get out it might rock a bit,' Scott whispered.

'Ok. Go ahead,' whispered Taylor.

Scott tapped Taylor on the back with his oar. 'Here, take this.'

Taylor reached back and grabbed it.

Scott placed both hands on the kayak's sides and lifted off the seat. He managed to get one foot on the seat. The kayak began to wobble.

'Peter! Try to keep us steady,' he whispered.

Taylor had one oar on the rocks, the other across his knees.

'Hold on with that oar.'

Trying to be a fluid as possible, Scott pushed up off the kayak and lifted both feet over the side. He reached out with his legs and felt them touch rock. He pulled the kayak in towards the rock a bit, until he could put some weight on his feet. Then he leant out towards the cliff, reaching out with his left hand until he felt rock.

'Done it,' he whispered. He managed to stand on a rock, up to his waist in the water, holding onto the rock with one hand and the kayak with the other. He gasped as the cold water seeped up the legs of his wetsuit.

'Right, I'll just climb these rocks and find a place for the camera. Are you ok here?' he whispered to Taylor.

'Yes, fine. All good. Good luck.' Taylor whispered back.

Scott retrieved the bag from the cubby hole and climbed up the rocks. He was only a few metres from the jetty, and in the remaining daylight everything was just visible. Scott climbed onto the rocks and felt along the cliff face. He soon found a crevice that was big enough to take the little camera. He took the camera out the bag, turned it on and placed it in the crevice pointing towards the jetty. It fitted well. No need for tape. Scott took out his mobile phone. He found the app for the camera, and pressed 'Live feed.' A dark window opened on the screen. As the camera adjusted its settings to night view, the jetty and the base of the scaffolding came into view. The view had a wider angle than Scott had thought, and Scott could see all of the jetty in the window in a green glow and could even see the front of the kayak. Scott turned off his phone and put it back in the bag, and turned towards the kayak and gave the thumbs up.

Taylor replied by putting down his oar and giving him the double thumbs up. The kayak lurched and the oar fell into the sea. The kayak started to wobble violently. A slightly larger wave came in and Taylor and the kayak keeled over. There was a large splash as Taylor disappeared into the black water.

'Shit!' said Scott, a little too loud. He jumped into the water, and, holding onto the rocks with one hand, managed to get hold of Taylor's wetsuit by the shoulder with the other. He pulled the spluttering Taylor into the rocks.

'Shit!' he whispered. 'Are you all right?'

'Ah!' Taylor coughed. 'Argh. Yes, all good.' He was floundering around on the rocks trying to find his feet.

'Here, hold on to the rocks here. There is a drop off. You'll have to climb up here,' whispered Scott. He helped Taylor to the rocks, then turned back to the kayak. It was belly up. Scott tried to right it but he couldn't get enough leverage to push it over. He grabbed an oar and passed it to Taylor. He couldn't see the other one.

'Fuck. We've lost on oar,' he whispered. 'And it's too heavy to turn over.' He looked at Taylor who looked comical in his wetsuit sitting on the rock with the sheer cliff rising up behind him. 'Can you give me a hand?'

They both pulled on the kayak, which slowly lifted then rolled back over the right way up. It sat low in the sea, almost totally filled with water.

'Shit! Shit! Shit!' whispered Scott. 'We'll never get the water out. We're going to have to get the kayak onto the jetty and get the water out there.' He made sure the bag with his phone in it was sealed, and went to the front of the kayak.

'Peter!' he whispered. 'Bring the oar. Can you take the back of the kayak? We'll swim over to the jetty.'

Taylor nodded at him. Scott started to swim to the jetty, pulling the kayak and his bag with his right hand. Although it was only a few metres, swimming dragging the flooded kayak was slow going and the waves kept breaking over his face.

The jetty was made of scaffolding bolted to the cliff. It was a platform suspended about thirty centimetres above the surface of the sea.

'Can you stay here while I get up?' Scott whispered to Taylor.

He held onto the jetty above his head but the waves were bobbing them up and down.

'And keep the kayak away from it. If it gets caught underneath it'll be smashed.'

269

Scott swam to the side of the jetty, and saw that next to the cliff the scaffolding came down into the sea. He used the scaffolding bars as a ladder and climbed up onto the jetty which was planked with wood. He was just walking over to the front of the jetty when he heard a load cracking noise. In the sea, Taylor was struggling with the half-submerged shape of the kayak, which was partly under the jetty. There was another cracking sound and Scott saw the kayak break in two.

'Fuck, Alex. I'm sorry. The waves, they pushed it under the....' said Taylor, as a wave pushed him under the jetty. Scott threw himself to the floor and just managed to grab hold of an arm. He just managed to stop Taylor from being washed under the platform.

'Here. Let me pull you up. Wait for a wave,' whispered Scott. Taylor reached up with his other hand which was still clutching the remaining oar.

'Here, take this.'

'Er. Thanks,' whispered Scott, who took the oar and put it behind him. As a wave came in, Taylor bobbed up in the water Scott reached under his armpits and pulled hard. He managed to get his upper body on the jetty and after a lot of squelching around Taylor got his feet up too.

'Fuck, fuck. Fuckidy fuck, fuck,' said Taylor.

'You took the words right out of my mouth.' Scott looked up at the scaffolding tower disappearing up into the gloom. From where they were, they could see no lights. The only lights they could see where Can Daurat's garden lights from across the bay.

'Well, it doesn't look like anyone saw us,' whispered Scott.

'How the fuck are we going to get back?' asked Taylor.

'We'll have to swim it. The cliff here goes on half way around the bay. We'll be better off swimming straight back.'

'Swim back there? You've got to be joking. We'll never make it.'

'It's not as far as it looks. Not even a kilometre.'

'A kilometre? At night? Wearing this?'

Scott looked at his bedraggled, soaking friend and realised Taylor would never make it across the bay in the best of conditions, let alone against the wind and the waves.

'Then up through the lighthouse it is.'

# THIRTY

'What? Climb up *that?'* whispered Taylor, looking at the scaffolding disappearing up into the gloom.

'It's either that or swim,' replied Scott. 'We haven't seen any sign of life. We've made quite a racket just now but no one seems to have heard. It doesn't look like there is anyone here. Anyway, what's the worst they can do? We just say we were in a kayak that sunk.'

'That's just it. The worst they can do. I don't want to be climbing cliffs around Mikhail Spralov.'

'Well, it's climb this or swim back,' whispered Scott. 'It's up to you.'

Taylor walked over to the edge of the jetty. The black waves were coming straight onto the cliff face, and the distant lights of Can Daurat seemed very far away. He returned to where Scott was standing.

'It looks a very long way to swim. I've never been a strong swimmer. Let alone dressed in this,' he flapped his arms. 'How will we make it up it?' he whispered, pointing up.

'I think there are ladders,' whispered Scott. He went over to the tower that reached up the cliff into the darkness. Scott took out one of the waterproof torches he had in his bag. Keeping his fingers over the end, he turned it on. By slightly separating his fingers he let out a small beam of light which he shone over the tower. It was about five metres wide and stuck out about two metres from the cliff. The outside was covered in net tarpaulin. Inside the scaffolding construction, he could see a ladder. He put his head and shoulders in and shone the light up. The ladder connected the base with a wooden platform a few metres above.

'Looks like there are ladders,' whispered Scott.

'Are we really going to do this?'

'We'll be fine. Just be as quiet as possible. If we take it slowly, and we don't make any noise.'

'How will we get out at the top?'

'Get out of what?'

'Out of the lighthouse compound,' Taylor paused. 'When I had a look at it from the path there was a wall around the landward side of the building. How will we get out of the compound?'

'I don't know,' replied Scott. 'There is a wall going all around it. But it's not in the best nick. The drone footage showed a few holes. I think I saw a place where we could climb over easily. We can't just stand here all night. And the wind is getting up a bit.' The waves slapping against the jetty had increased in size since the kayak had sunk. 'Let's get up there and see if we can't climb over the wall.'

'I'm sorry.'

'Sorry for what?'

'The kayak. I...'

'Look, don't worry about it. Let's try to get out of here without them finding us. We have rubber soles so we shouldn't make any noise. Just go slowly and test each step before you put your weight down. Try not to talk when we are up there. Try not talk at all. There might be someone we haven't seen.'

'Ok. You go first. What happens if we get busted?'

'We'll just have to ... If we can, let's try to avoid that result. Right, come on.'

Scott took the other torch out of his bag.

'Here. Take this torch. Just keep your fingers over the bulb if you turn it on. It will shade the light. Only use it if you have to.'

Scott handed the torch to Taylor, then pulled back the tarpaulin and climbed over a diagonal bit of scaffolding and into the tower. He reached out in the darkness until his hands felt the rough wood of the ladder.

'Try to follow as close behind as possible,' he whispered to Taylor who was climbing over the scaffolding. Scott placed a foot on the bottom rung and tested his weight on it. The ladder was tied in place and felt stable. He climbed up and arrived at another platform. As it was pitch black inside the tower, Scott took out his torch and risked another peek around. He was on a platform that was about half the area of the tower. There was another ladder going up to what looked like a similar platform. He went over to the edge and looked up. The other half of the tower comprised a vertical shaft which he assumed was for the crane. Taylor had reached the top of the first ladder and was climbing up onto the platform.

'Looks like this goes on right up to the top,' he whispered. 'You good?'

Taylor just patted him on the shoulder. Scott started up the second ladder and felt it wobble as Taylor started climbing behind him. At the top was another ladder. Then another. As they climbed the tower the noise of the waves diminished and Scott became more aware of the noise they were making. The creak of the ladders. Their breathing getting louder. The neoprene suit made climbing awkward and soon Scott was sweating. He could hear the more unfit Taylor's gasping larger breaths. After five ladders Scott decided to pause. He thought they were about half way up the scaffolding tower. When Taylor joined him on the platform he put a hand on his shoulder and whispered:

'Let's wait a moment and catch our breath.' Taylor nodded in agreement. The wind was stronger up here and there was an occasional flap of the canvas covering hitting the scaffolding. When Taylor's breathing had stabilised, Scott patted him on the shoulder and started up the next ladder.

They ascended five more ladders and Taylors breathing was once more getting increasingly laboured by the time they reached the top. At the top of the final ladder Scott came out onto a similar flat platform to those before but now, as he looked up, Scott could see stars in the night sky above and over to the west the horizon was a dull yellow. He could see the shape of the crane over the shaft and up in front of him loomed the outline of the lighthouse. Over to the right was the silhouette of some type of outbuilding and from a couple of windows shone a faint electric light.

Taylor reached the top of the ladder and Scott helped him onto the wooden platform. Taylor was breathing heavily. Scott put his finger to his lips and Taylor nodded. Scott could just make out what looked like planks that ran from the tower to the top of the cliff. He reached out and found a handrail. Very slowly, he put a foot on the plank and tested his weight on it. He put all his weight on it and it felt secure. He felt along the plank with his other foot, and tested the plank next to it. Both felt secure. Scott carefully walked along the planks feeling them bow a little under his weight. At the end of the planks he felt earth and gravel under his feet and realised he was on the cliff top. Behind him Taylor came across the planks, running his hand along the scaffolding handrail.

Suddenly everything exploded into brilliant light. Scott, blinded, raised a forearm over his face.

'You took your time,' said a familiar voice with a Russian accent. 'My God, you two must be unfit. We have been waiting for ever.' Scott, blinking, saw through half shut eyes that there were three figures standing about five metres away under two powerful spot lights mounted on the wall of the lighthouse. The clifftop between the lighthouse and the cliff was bathed in white light. As his eyes became accustomed, he recognised a flash of metallic material on the shoes of the figure in the middle. Olenka.

'Hello Dimitri.' Scott's mind raced as he struggled to come up with a credible excuse. 'We...' He looked at Taylor who had a startled expression on his sweat covered face. 'were out in the kayak. Stupid really. Out far too late.' As Scott spoke, Olenka nodded to one of his companions who took a few steps forward towards Scott. It was Spralov. 'We got into a bit of trouble. Thank God for...' Out of nowhere came Spralov's fist, smashing into Scott's face. He went straight down, reeling from the blow. He could feel the metallic taste of blood in his mouth and when he moved his jaw something hard came loose. It was sharp and Scott spat it along with a mouthful of blood onto the earth. It looked like half a tooth.

'What the...?' gurgled Scott.

'You can forget the phoney excuses, *A-le-han-dro*. I haven't the time for any bullshit.' Olenka said something in Russian. Scott looked up. Spralov grabbed him by the neck with one hand and with the other took hold of Scott's left hand. Scott screamed as an excruciating pain shot up his arm as Spralov twisted his hand, His neck was immobile in the Russian's vice-like grip.

Spralov released the pressure on his arm, and Scott realised he now had his fist around Scott's little finger.

'*Da*,' said Olenka.

Scott heard the crack as Spralov snapped back his little finger and screamed once again. Spralov released his neck and Scott fell to the ground cradling his left hand. He looked up and saw Olenka smiling, enjoying the moment.

'I hate you journalists,' said Olenka. 'You can't mind your own business. Always poking your noses into things that are no concern of yours. Well, now you will see how we Russians deal with the press.'

Scott's little finger was sticking out at an alarming angle. He wrapped his right hand around it and bent it back. He cried out at the pain.

Spralov was still standing above him, his attention was on Olenka. Olenka said something and indicated Taylor. Spralov took a step towards Taylor who stepped back, fear etched on his face. Scott sprang at Spralov with all his strength and crashed into him with his right shoulder. Spralov was larger than Scott and solid muscle, but the ground was uneven, the light bad and fortunately for Scott he stumbled.

'Peter, run!' Scott cried. Scott wheeled round and sprinted along the cliff towards wall that ran around the property. He could hear Taylor behind him. It was not more than a few metres. If he could scale the wall he could be away on the Camí. He saw a bit of the wall nearest the cliff had crumbled way and could be easily climbed. He just need to make it. His neoprene boots started to slip on gravel. His momentum carried him forward and Scott felt himself slipping down a slope towards the cliff edge. Scott threw himself to the ground and raked the ground with his fingers as he felt himself slip over the edge into the dark.

# THIRTY-ONE

Scott fell into darkness but almost immediately hit ground and the air was knocked out of his lungs. He began to slip down a steep slope. He dug his fingers onto earth, his nails ripping, his broken finger agony, flattening his body to try to stop. He struggled against the inevitable fall into the void. The rush of free fall. The impact of the rocks below. But he began to slow and then stopped. Terrified to move a muscle in case he began to slip again, Scott held his breath. His face was pressed against the earth, his sore jaw throbbing. Scott opened his eyes, and very gently started to breathe. He must be on a steep ledge of earth between the cliff top and the sheer cliff below. All he could see was black, and, as his eyes became accustomed to the dark, he realised his head was looking straight down at the sea. He was right on the edge of the cliff. He could feel the wind and hear the occasional crash of a wave far below on the rocks. Scott turned his head and could see a steep slope a few metres wide that fell off from the top. Thanks to the brightness of the spot lights the slope was in deep shadow.

He heard someone cry out something in Russian. It sounded very close, only a metre or so away. Scott dared not look in that direction to see where the man was. He was close. Someone else said something in Russian, but this was much fainter. He thought he heard Taylor's voice. He heard the owner of the voice near him walk away, all the while talking in Russian. Scott very carefully raised his cheek a couple of millimetres off the ground and looked up. He saw the back of the man walk away. He hadn't seen Scott.

He looked around. Ahead, along the cliff, he could see the clifftop and the scaffolding. In the corner of his vision, at a ninety-degree angle above him, he could just see a group of men, lit up by the bright spotlights. His black neoprene suit had not only saved his life in acting as a large rubber brake, but it's colour had camouflaged him from his pursuers.

The group of men had now come nearer to Scott's position, mid-way between Scott and the scaffolding tower. He could just make out Taylor between Spralov and the man who had chased him. They were holding Taylor's arms. Olenka was standing a couple of metres apart from them, away from the cliff. As they edged towards the cliff edge, Scott began to hear what they were saying. Olenka was talking.

'...to go the same way as your friend, *Al-eh-handro*. Nothing at all. In fact, we just found your bodies washed up at the base of the cliff. You had had an accident in your canoe. Maybe we don't find your bodies at all. Leave them for the fishes.'

Taylor stuttered: 'I saw it was an accident. Alex slipped. He fell. I will confirm that. There is no need to…It was an accident. Please. Or I can go home. There is no need for me to get involved. I'm sure you can inform the police. I can go…'

'Call the police?' said Olenka. 'Yes, that's good idea. I have already done that. When I heard trespassers on my property.' Scott didn't dare move a muscle. Any movement might make him slip over the edge. Or give away his position. Olenka took out his phone, punched the screen then put it to his ear. After a few moments Olenka spoke:

'Inspector? Where are you? Yes. Right away.' He paused. 'Well leave it. You can finish it later. I need you here now. I

279

mean now.' He hung up. 'These fucking Spaniards. All they think about is food.' He looked at Taylor. 'If you want to speak to the police you will get your chance.'

'Yes of course. Mr...er... My name is Franks. Peter Franks.' Taylor stuttered.

'No, Peter Franks is a character in a James Bond film. Yes, I know who you are Mr Peter Taylor of the Financial Times, London.'

'As I said, we were out kayaking, it got late...' Taylor's voice tailed off.

'That's why you came over to place a camera? To record our drug smuggling?' Olenka laughed. 'Where the fuck did you get drug smuggling from? You take me for a drug smuggler?'

'I don't... know... what...' stammered Taylor.

'Yes, I know all about your little plans to bust me. They are great, mobile phones. Aren't they? One simple program hidden in an email and we hear everything.'

'I...' started Taylor.

'I got that stupid bitch to open a special email and your friend's phone has been telling me everything for days. I've seen all your messages to each other. I could even see you on the GPS as you crossed the bay. I send my ship to the next bay and across you come, trying to spy on me. But I was already spying on you! The irony of it!' He held something in his hand, it looked like the bag Scott had been carrying. He pulled something out of it. 'Oh well, it has served its purpose, I suppose it had better follow him.' Olenka threw it into the dark void, then turned back to Taylor. 'So, Mr Peter Taylor, what am I going to do with *you?*'

'Mr Olenka. I have made a mistake. I'm sorry. I think I should go now.'

'You do, do you? You think I should just let you walk away?'

'I can just go home. You can have all my research. We haven't told anyone. I can just go home quietly and forget the whole thing.'

'You haven't told anyone about what? No, I'm not concerned about your little fantasy. But you have been writing bad things about me, Mr Peter Taylor. What did you write? 'Premier's poodle?' Wasn't that how you described me. Always nosing around my business. In Sevastopol. Moscow. Now here. Although where you got the drugs idea only you know.' He paused. 'No, I can't have you running to the police making up stories. I can't have them nosing around here. I think it's best you join your friend. It'll look just like an accident. By the time you are found, if you are found, I will be long gone. These are dangerous waters. No place to be out in a kayak at night.'

'There is a file,' blurted Taylor. 'If anything happens to me, there is a file of information that will go to Interpol.' Taylor paused, Olenka remained, impassive. 'We have told the *Guardia Civil.* If I disappear, they will know … they will come and investigate. You need me to tell them it was an accident.'

'You have told no one, you have told everybody, come on! Make up your mind!' Olenka took a step towards Taylor. 'A file full of what? Speculation that I am a drugs dealer? What a load of crap! Information that I have given bribes? That's not news! Everybody knows that! *Guardia Civil?* Do I care? The police are already coming.' Olenka looked over his shoulder. 'Where is that fucking inspector? Only lives a kilometre away. Greedy fucker is probably finishing his…' Scott could see headlights on the buildings behind them. 'Here he is.'

Olenka turned away from the cliff and disappeared in the direction of the lighthouse. Scott flexed his fingers, testing their grip on the ground. He had both palms flat and his fingertips dug into the ground. For the moment, it felt like he was safe and not about to go over the edge. His jaw and mouth were agony. He ran his tongue around his teeth and winced as it caught on a jagged, broken molar. He looked up. Taylor and his two companions were all facing the lighthouse. Taylor was still restrained by the other two.

'Peter Taylor, may I introduce Inspector Matas of the *Mossos d'Esquadra.*' Olenka and Matas walked up to the three at the cliff edge. Olenka said something in Russian. The other man let go of Taylor's arm.

'Thank you.' Taylor said to him.

'Say hello to the inspector, Mr Taylor.' Olenka said to Taylor. 'Inspector, say goodbye to Mr Taylor.' Spralov, who was holding Taylor's other arm appeared to grip it tighter, then suddenly pivoted, hurling Taylor out over the cliff. Scott saw Taylor briefly airborne, for a moment lit up by the spot lights against the dark night sky, then he disappeared into the darkness below. There was a feeble scream and a sickening thud as something heavy hit the jetty below.

'What? What have you...?' cried Matas. 'You mad...You ring me, you call me here to witness that?'

'Now you *are* part of the team,' said Olenka. 'Now you are an accomplice to murder. If you want your share, keep the police away from here. All police.'

'*Joder!* Dimitri...' Matas shook his head in disbelief.

'Make sure the body is well sunk by morning. And the other one? He must be somewhere down there. He fell...' Olenka turned to Matas. 'No, really, he did actually fall on his own.'

Matas said something to Olenka that Scott couldn't hear.

'If you want to collect your share you will shut up and do as you are told,' said Olenka. 'We couldn't have him or the other journalist nosing around anymore. They were about to go to the *Guardia Civil.* It will be difficult to explain a second accidental fall from a cliff. No, better to sink both bodies. A kayak accident. I just wanted you here. You seemed a little unconvinced last time we spoke.' Olenka took Matas by the elbow and they started to walk away from the cliff. 'We will find it soon. We *must* find it soon. I

282

need you to keep the police away, just for...' The rest was lost to Scott.

Scott felt sick. He had just seen his friend die. And he might easily be next. He saw two figures walk towards the tower. Two torches came on. They walked to the top of the tower and began to climb down the ladders. By slightly raising his head Scott could see their progress by following the beams of light. When they got to the bottom, the torches swept the jetty. They lit up a black shape. Scott realised it was Taylor in his wetsuit. One of the men went up to the black shape and pulled. Taylor's body flopped out across the jetty. The beam of light illuminated the black pool of blood that surrounded the end of the body with Taylor's crushed head. Scott closed his eyes at the horror.

The men began to shine their torch beams along the base of the cliff. They were looking for Scott's body. Scott was suddenly energised with the terror of capture. He dared not move for fear of falling, but he was terribly exposed just lying where he was. As if he had read Scott's mind, one of the men shined his beam up the cliff. Scott closed his eyes and pressed his face into the dirt. He prayed that the light would be too faint at that distance, that his neoprene suit would blend in with the shadows. Would his arm hide the white of his face? His whole body shook with a mixture of fear and exertion. After a few minutes, Scott risked partially opening one eye. There was no obvious beam lighting up his position. He raised his head. The two were still on the jetty but had stopped looking up the cliff. They were wrapping something around Taylor's body. When they finished, they dragged the body to the end of the jetty, and over it went. There was a large splash, audible above the noise of the waves. One of the men went to the landward edge of the jetty. The light began to wobble and shine in all directions. The man was traversing the rocks at the base of the cliff. After a few metres the light stopped. It shone against the cliff. The man reached into the light and pulled something out from the rock and threw it out to sea. The security camera.

As the beam of light made its way back to the jetty, Scott could here sloshing noises. He supposed the other man was washing down the jetty. The torch reached the jetty, and briefly Scott saw the outline of the two figures as they walked back to the tower.

Scott lay where he was, clinging to the top of the cliff. His mouth and jaw throbbing from Spralov's blow, his hand agony. How had he got to this terrible place? Yesterday Natalya. Today Taylor. While he clung to the patch of earth, his mind raced with all the things he would do if he ever managed to make it off the cliff alive. He thought about anything other than the rocks thirty metres beneath him.

The two men made it up to the top of the tower and Scott tensed, ready to try to flee if they spotted him, but they walked from the scaffolding straight towards the lighthouse without coming in his direction. After a few minutes the spotlights went out. A few minutes after that Scott heard voices, although not clear enough to understand their meaning. The voices faded, then there were a few thumps of car doors, followed by the noise of engines starting. Car headlights briefly lit up the top of the scaffolding tower, then all was quiet save the sound of the wind and the rhythmic breaking of waves on the base of the cliff below.

Scott wasn't sure how long he stayed in the same position, clinging to his little patch of dirt, listening for any sound of someone discovering his position, but it must have been at least half an hour more. In the end, he plucked up the courage to try to move. He very slowly loosened his grip on his left hand, which was furthest away from the cliff. His broken finger sent bolts of pain up his arm. When his body stayed where it was, Scott carefully extended his arm as far up the slope as he could reach. His fingers felt more earth and stones. He dug his working fingers in as deep as possible, oblivious to the pain on his ripped nails. Once he felt he had a secure grip, he tried pulling his body up the slope, pushing against the ground with his right hand. As he began to move, he felt his legs slipping towards the cliff. He dug the toes of his neoprene boots into the ground. When he had moved his torso a few inches up the slope, he slowly walked the toes of his boots up the incline.

Again, he dug his right hand's fingers into the earth as deep as possible and repeated the procedure. As he edged up the hill, the incline got steeper and it became more and more difficult to pull himself up. At last, his left hand felt the ground even off and Scott realised that he was at the top. With one last surge of effort he gripped the earth and pulled with his left hand, pushing his right hand and managed to roll his torso up the incline and onto the flat ground. He lay there for a few minutes taking deep breaths. He rolled over and got up onto his hands and knees. He was on the top of the cliff about half way between the scaffolding tower and the wall that ran around the lighthouse. As his eyes were now accustomed to the night, by the light of the newly risen moon he could see the crumbling wall that he'd been running towards when he fell. He looked at the slope which he had just come up. It was only a couple of metres wide. All that effort for less than two paces. He had been incredibly lucky to have stopped just where he did, it had saved his fall over the cliff and hidden him from his pursuer behind.

He looked around the walled compound. The wall ran from the cliff edge to some large gates then joined with the lighthouse building. The lighthouse itself was in darkness, but there was a single-storied outhouse next to it which had a light on in a couple of windows. Then the wall ran from behind those buildings to meet the cliff the other side of the tower. Scott was about to head for the crumbled bit of wall that he had seen earlier, when he noticed a car parked in the shadows between the lighthouse and the wall.

He walked over to it, sensitive to the slightest noise, his neoprene suit making a rubbing noise as he walked. It was a 1960s alfa Romeo Spider. He remembered Santi's car parked in the square in Begur, what seemed like months before.

While his instinct told him to get over the wall and get as far away as possible, Scott felt he had to check to see if Santi or María were here. He knew the lighthouse was just an empty shell, so he crept as silently as possible along the building towards the outhouse with the light. When he arrived at the first window he kept back in the shadows and slowly edged his head round until he could see into the room. There was a man sitting at a table facing away from the window. There was a bottle of beer on the table next to him, and he was reading a book or a magazine. Apart from the table and chair, there was a camp bed in the corner. There was a door behind him. Scott carefully felt his way along the wall until he got to the second window. Again he slowly edged his head round to see what was inside. The room was larger. There was a big wooden table on which were piles of papers. Some of which looked like plans. Sitting at a chair was Santi.

# THIRTY-TWO

Scott gently tapped on the window pane. Santi half turned towards the window, then went back to looking at some plans. Scott tapped again. Santi turned around. The Santi Scott had had a drink with a few days previously had been healthy, vibrant, with a sparkle in his eye. This Santi looked like he had not slept in days and had all the weight of the world on his shoulders. He was unshaven, had huge bags under his red eyes and his clothes were creased and dirty. He looked towards the window with a frown, and Scott moved his face into the light closer to the glass. There was a flash of recognition on Santi's face, replaced by fear and he put a finger to his lips. He pointed at the door to the next-door room.

Santi, all the while looking at the door to the other room, came round the table and approached the window. He was limping or dragging a leg. The window had bars on the outside but he opened it inward after very slowly opening the latch. The window made a slight creak while opening, so Santi stopped, and listened. After a few seconds, he pulled the window open a bit more and poked his head thorough, up to the bars.

'*Alejandro. Qué coño...?* What are you...? When...? What are you doing here?' he whispered.

'Santi. What is going on? What are *you* doing here? You look like shit!' whispered Scott. From the look on Santi's face he realised he probably looked not much better, if, indeed, a lot worse.

'What happened to your face? Why are you in a rubber suit?' Santi looked puzzled.

'Long story,' whispered Scott. 'Why are you here?'

'They have me here. There is a man next door. My guard. I am not allowed to leave. Alejandro, they have María. I have to do this thing.'

'What do you mean? They are holding you? Prisoner? We must get you out of there. Is there anyone apart from the guy next door here?'

'Here? Just the one guard.'

'Is there another way out?'

'No.' Santi looked once more at the door. 'Just through there. But Alejandro…'

Scott had already left and was creeping along the wall back to the other window. He slowly moved his head round until he could see the man sitting at the table. He couldn't see any weapon on the table or in the room. The man was older than Scott, in his fifties, and looked skinny. Scott thought that, as long as he didn't have a weapon, he shouldn't be too difficult to overpower. Scott crouched down and crossed under the window, being careful not to make any noise. He arrived at the door and waited. He could just make out which side the lock and handle were on. Scott dropped to his knees and felt around his feet. When he had come this way before, he had bumped into a few objects which had nearly made him fall. He felt around on the ground. There were various rocks but when he weighed them in his hand they felt light and puny. He needed something heavier. At last his hand scrabbled against something more substantial. It was a metal bar of sorts. He felt its length with his other hand. It was nearly a metre long, and heavy.

Scott carefully returned to the door with his bar and one of the rocks, and stood with his back to the wall on the side of the door with the handle. He hoped he would be out of the light when the door opened. He tossed the rock over onto the ground in front of the guard's window. It made a thud which wasn't very loud. Scott waited a minute. Nothing. He crouched down and felt around and picked up another rock. He threw it in the same direction. This time the rock must have landed on something hard because it made a much louder clack.

He heard the noise of a chair scraping across the floor. Scott took a deep breath and got ready. There was the sound of keys turning and the door opened. Partially blinded by the light, Scott held his breath while pressed against the wall. The man called out something in Russian. Scott could see his silhouette in the light coming from the doorway. He could hear his breathing. The man said the same thing again. Then he took a step outside. He was now standing next to Scott, just a few centimetres away, looking out towards the sea. He took another couple of steps and repeated what he had said. He now had his back to Scott. Scott raised the bar. The man was small, with a bald spot among his thin grey hairs, and Scott could see the bobbles on his grey cardigan and a hole in one of the elbows. Scott realised he couldn't hit him. Not on top of his head. He might kill him. He dropped the bar and threw himself on the man.

Scott's weight brought the two of them crashing down, but once on the ground the old man showed surprising strength. Scott had his arm around his neck and the man tried biting down, getting a mouth full of neoprene. As the old man struggled, Scott managed to get his arm further around the man's neck so that the crook of his elbow was at his Adam's apple. Scott had faint memories of a PE lesson in his childhood where an over-keen army type had shown the awe-struck adolescents ways in which they should under no circumstances try to "neutralise" an opponent. This had been one of them. Scott pressed with his other hand and held on as the old man writhed around. Suddenly the man went limp. Scott held his grip, thinking

289

this was a ploy. But there was no more movement from him, and after about a minute Scott relaxed his hold. The man was motionless. He hadn't made a sound.

Thinking he had possibly broken his neck, Scott put two sore fingers to the man's carotid artery in the neck. He couldn't feel anything. He put an ear to the man's mouth and heard the very faint sound of breathing. Scott grabbed the man under his arms and dragged him into the building. He laid him out on the floor and looked round the room. There was the table and the chair, the camp bed and a smaller table with a holdall on it. Scott shut the door. Behind the door was a toolbox. Among the tools was a roll of American silver gaffer tape. Scott used most of the roll tying up the old man's arms and legs. He put a strip around the man's head at mouth height. Scott made sure he was breathing through his nose and propped him up against the wall. He took another stretch of tape and used it to bind his swollen, broken little finger to his ring finger.

The door to Santi's room had two bolds locking it. Scott drew these back and opened the door.

'Alex,' said Santi, looking aghast at Scott as he walked in the room. 'What has happened to you?'

'Santi, I need to get you out of here now.'

'What? What have you done with...?' Santi looked past Scott into the next room. 'No, *no, no.* Alex no. They have María. What have you done?'

'What do you mean 'they have María?''

'Dimitri. He has María captive on his boat.'

'Santi, they just killed a friend of mine. Here. An hour ago. They threw him off the cliff. They think I am dead too. If they find me they will kill me. I need to get you away. Now.'

'Alex, I cannot. He has María. I must stay.'

'He's a psycho Santi. Come on. He'll hurt her whether you are here or not. You must come with me, now. We'll work something out together, but, at the moment, he has both of you. You can't help María locked up in here.'

There was a sound from the other room. Scott went back. The old man had opened his eyes and was looking at Scott. Scott tested the tape. Scott saw something in his pocket. A mobile phone. He took it out and pressed the screen. It wasn't locked. He walked back into the room with Santi.

'Ok, let's get out of here. We can be at Can Daurat in ten minutes. Come on.' He took Santi by the arm. Santi insisted on gathering up all the papers on the desk and rolling them up into a large document cylinder.

'Come on, we haven't time for that,' said Scott.

'No, we need these,' said Santi.

'Well, hurry. Or we could call the police now.'

'It's no use,' said Santi, 'he has the police helping him.'

'Matas. Yes. I know about him. But I was going to call the *Guardia Civil.*'

'Alex, we can't call them. Please. María is on his boat. He was not making idle threats. He said he'll hurt Maria. Give her to his sailors.'

'Ok, no police now, but come on. We are best off trying to work this out somewhere away from here.'

Scott pulled Santi by the elbow into the next room. The old man was still propped up against the wall. Watching them as they came in. Scott felt his restraints again.

'He not going anywhere. And we've got his phone. Do you think they will come back tonight?'

'*No lo sé* Alex. I don't know. He said they would come back in the morning.'

'Well, let's get out of here.'

Scott dragged the old man into the second room, turned off the lights and shut the door. He closed the two bolts. They turned off the other light and went outside. Scott waited a moment while his eyes adjusted to the darkness. Scott started walking towards the gates, but Santi veered towards his car parked next to the lighthouse.

'Santi,' hissed Scott. 'Let's walk. It will be quieter.' Santi joined him by the gate. The gate was locked but, by pulling up the drop bolt, Scott was able to pull both doors open. They slipped out and pulled the gate shut behind them. The tarmac path to the main road led straight off in front of them, but Scott indicated the break in the undergrowth that marked the Camí de Ronda.

The walk to Can Daurat took them a quarter of an hour, but it felt like an hour. They walked in silence. Scott noticed Santi was limping, so he took the folder of plans off him. On a couple of occasions Scott had to hold him to stop him from falling over. In the dark, it was difficult to see the path and the uneven ground made walking difficult. Scott thought back to his morning runs and what a different experience this was. His wetsuit, now dry and covered in salt, rubbed as he walked. His jaw and mouth ached. His little finger throbbed. His other fingers were smarting from when he had dragged his nails in the ground. He couldn't believe the events of the past couple of days. Natalya's death seemed like an age away.

When they arrived at the gate to Can Daurat, Scott realised he had left the keys to the house in the dock. He told Santi to wait for him there and climbed down to the shore. He crossed the rocks until he came to the channel that led into the dock. He lowered himself into the water, swam into the dock and climbed up the ladder onto the side. Still in the dark he managed to shut the boathouse doors before he turned on the lights. Scott found his keys then extinguished the lights.

He ascended the spiral stairs and crossed the pool house in darkness, squelching across the tiles in his wet neoprene. As he came out of the pool house the outside lights came on and bathed the garden in light. So much for stealth. Scott went over to the fence gate and let Santi in.

Once in the kitchen, Scott put the roll of plans on the kitchen table. He checked the time. It was a quarter to two in the morning. In the bright light of the kitchen he realised how exhausted and battered Santi looked. 'What is going on?' Asked Scott. 'Why were you locked up? Why has he got María? He said to Matas he was about to find 'It.' What is this 'it' he is looking for?'

'This is what is so mad. He is looking for gold.' Santi sat with his head in his hands.

'Gold? What? Here? On the Costa Brava?'

'Yes. And more importantly he believes I know where it is. Or rather, I can find it.'

'What, *gold?* As in gold in the ground? Here?'

'No. He believes my grandfather hid some gold. In the civil war. Somewhere here.'

'What? How does...? Why...?' After all the events of the past few days, Scott felt at his wits' end.

'Dimitri believes that his grandfather and my grandfather stole a lot of gold and buried it here. He believes it is in one of my grandfather's houses.'

'That's insane,' said Scott. Then he remembered the holes dug at the lighthouse. 'So, he's been looking for gold *inside* the buildings?'

'Yes, the lighthouse. Some other of my grandfather's buildings.'

'That's insane,' repeated Scott.

'Well, maybe not quite as insane as it sounds.'

'What?' Scott could hardly believe what he was hearing. *'You* think it's true?'

'I don't know if it is true. But it is certainly possible.'

'What do you mean possible? Who did they steal the gold from?'

'That's the thing. Dimitri's grandfather was captain of a merchant vessel the *Kursk*. The *Kursk* was one of the three ships that took the Spanish gold reserves to Russia.'

'Gold reserves? What are you talking about?'

'In the civil war, when the Republic feared it might lose, it gave the Spanish gold reserves to Russia, to stop them falling into Franco's hands.'

'Really?'

'Yes, really.' Santi sounded annoyed. 'For safe keeping. The gold went by train from Madrid to Cartagena then was loaded on three Russian ships. When those ships arrived in Russia, there were some boxes missing. This difference has never been explained. Dimitri says his grandfather stopped a night here, off the *Cabo de Begur*. That he made an agreement with my grandfather and unloaded some gold. They were to divide it up after the war. But Stalin killed his grandfather and Franco killed mine. He says the gold is still here.'

'So how much did he take off? Was it worth much?'

'Forty tonnes. Worth a fortune.'

'What the...? Forty tonnes of gold? And no one noticed?'

'They were in the middle of a war. Remember these were Spain's gold reserves. All of them. Centuries' worth of gold from America. Hundreds of tonnes. There was a lot of gold being transported. Dimitri believes the gold is hidden in one of my grandfather's houses.'

'Ok, but forty tonnes. You would have thought someone might have noticed if their house was made of gold!'

'Well, it weighs a lot but it needn't take up too much space. Forty tonnes is only two cubic metres of gold.'

'Santi, don't you think if your grandfather had had two cubic metres of gold he would have told someone. You grandmother? Isn't it more likely this is just a fantasy made up by Olenka?'

'I might have thought that, if not for this.' Santi opened the cylinder and tipped the papers onto the table. He rummaged around. There was an old piece of paper with faded writing. He held it out to Scott.

'This is a letter in French from my grandfather to his. My grandfather writes that 'it' is safe. That only he knows the location. 'It' is hidden in a 'project.' He wishes him well and says they will meet after the war.'

Scott realised he recognised the writing. It was the same neat scrip as that of the cookery book María had lent him.

'Dimitri only found that letter on the death of his father, six months ago. It was among the family papers.' Santi showed Scott another faded piece of paper with writing in

Cyrillic script. 'This is a note written by Dimitri's grandfather in which says he unloaded 500 boxes of gold coins. The Kursk was carrying a total of 4500 boxes. Dimitri came here and bought all the houses that he knew had been built by my grandfather. He was destroying one house without the right permissions, so, being the council planning officer, I went to stop him. During that meeting, I mentioned the house had been built by my grandfather. When he realised I was related he got very excited. When he found out I had the original plans he went *loco*. You saw me just before I brought him the plans.'

Santi put his face in his hands, then slowly looked up.

'After that he started to ask me about my family. Were we rich? Did we have many houses? When he heard the story of my grandfather being shot in prison, he seemed pleased. It was then that he told me the story of the gold. He offered me a commission to help him find it. Five percent of the value. Millions of Euros. Then, well, when we couldn't find it…Then he tried more forceful methods.' Santi pulled up his trouser leg. The skin was scarred with what looked like cuts and a few cigarette burns. 'He was like, like a spoilt child. Mad. He couldn't stop shouting. He let that monster Mikhail do this.'

'Is that Spralov, the large shaven-headed man?'

'That's him. When we had looked everywhere and still no result… He made me call María. He said I was useless, that I had no right to a share. He said if I do not find the gold he will kill María, then me.'

'You involved her in this?' Scott could feel his anger rise.

'I didn't think he would *hurt* her.'

'Santi, you idiot. What did you think he was going to do? We are going to have to get her back.'

'We must find the gold.'

'I think that is highly unlikely if you haven't been able to find it so far. You have no idea where it could have been hidden?'

'None at all. We have searched everywhere. All the houses that my grandfather built. Can Daurat was our obvious choice because of the name. Dimitri had been trying to buy it when I brought him the plans.'

'I was told it was called Can Daurat after the gold colour of the hill at sunset.'

'And it was. But I checked, and my grandfather did no work on the house. Only on the tunnel under the garden. So, Dimitri lost interest in the house. We dug the tunnel up a few days ago.'

'Yes, thanks for that. When I was attacked, were you there?'

'Of course not. I only heard about that afterwards.'

'What happened to Manolo?'

'I think that was Mikhail. Dimitri's head of security. They told me that they came over to have a look around the house and were surprised by Manolo, that he fell by accident. But I do not believe them.'

'Look Santi, we've got to call the police. We can't go up against this lot.'

'No Alex, please. You have seen what they are capable of. Dimitri meant it when he said he would hurt María. She is on his boat. We can't do anything. We *have* to find the gold.'

'You have checked everywhere? All the houses you grandfather built? Did he do any other works aside from the houses?'

'The tunnel under the garden here was the only other work he did in that period. I would know, I did my thesis on these buildings.'

Scott thought it unlikely that they would be able to add anything to what Santi and Olenka had already done. He had to try to convince Santi to call the police.

'Have another look through all the plans, I'm going to get out of this,' said Scott, indicating his wetsuit. Scott went upstairs to his room. He took off his boots. He unzipped the wetsuit and pulled the top half down. By standing on the arms with one foot he managed to pull a leg out. He then did the same with his other leg. Scott went into the bathroom and turned on the lights. He was greeted by a swollen faced ghoul. He had huge bags under his eyes and his unshaven jaw had swollen up. He looked at his hands. Half his left hand was covered in silver tape. His hands were encrusted with dried blood and dirt.

Scott turned on the shower and stepped in. The hot water stung his cold salt-covered skin. He stayed immobile for a few minutes, letting the roar of the shower drown out all thoughts and just enjoying the feeling of warmth and comfort. In the end, he snapped himself out of his trance. He needed to get back downstairs.

He dried himself and got dressed in jeans and a t-shirt. Every little movement hurt and he felt totally exhausted. He slowly descended the stairs and returned to the kitchen. Santi was still sitting at the table, but with his head in his hands, staring at the pile of papers in front of him. Scott went over to the table and sat down opposite him. He looked at an architect's plans of a house he hadn't recognise. He wasn't sure what he was looking for. Underneath was the letter from Santi's grandfather to the old Olenka. His French was clear and correct, but there was nothing in the letter to give away any hiding place.

Scott looked at the letter. The handwriting. 'You gave me your grandfather's cook book. It was written by him in prison. Didn't you say something about your grandmother saying how valuable it was?'

'What?' said Santi, lifting his head.

'The cookbook. That he wrote. I borrowed it from you to write my article on local food. You remember, in Begur, in the square. You said your grandmother always said how valuable it was. Could it have a clue in it?'

'What? Of course!' cried Santi, coming out of his daze. 'How stupid of me. Where is it?'

'I've got it. There might be a map or something hidden in it. There must be!'

'Get it! Get it!' snapped Santi.

Scott went to get the cook book. He ran upstairs to his room, but could not see it anywhere. He checked his bag, the cupboard, even under the bed. He came downstairs again and had a look in the office. It wasn't in any of the drawers. He walked back into the kitchen. Scott had a look around then went up to the bookshelf. There were thirty or forty cook books, maybe he had put the book there. Or Dolors had.

'Where is it?' asked Santi. 'You haven't lost it?'

'I'm sure it was here. In the kitchen. I think Dolors might have put it with the other books.' replied Scott. But it wasn't there.

Santi was now following him around the kitchen. He couldn't see it.

'Where did you put it?' Santi asked. 'If you have lost it, María's life…'

'I'm sure I put it down somewhere here,' interrupted Scott, who had no recollection of the little notebook after they gave it to him in Begur.

Could he have left it in the hire car? He tried to remember back to his first night at Can Daurat. It seemed so long ago. Had he shown it to Natalya? The thought brought on a wave of sadness. He tried to think. Which was difficult with Santi standing almost on top of him.

María had given him the book in the café. Scott walked to the window, followed closely by Santi. His jacket. He remembered putting it in his jacket. He brushed passed Santi and went out of the kitchen. In the corridor outside there were a few coat hooks and his khaki jacket was hanging from one. He felt it and sure enough, there was something in the inside pocket. He took out the small leather bound notebook and walked back into the kitchen.

'Here it is.' Santi hobbled over and snatched it out of his hands. He went over to the kitchen table, sat down and began leafing through the book. After he had gone through all the pages, he began at the beginning again.

'Anything?' asked Scott, resting his palms on the table.

'Just recipes. Give me a knife,' replied Santi. Scott went and got a small paring knife from the rack and handed it to Santi handle first. Santi began to cut into the leather binding. Soon he had taken off the leather cover. Underneath was just card and paper. Santi began cutting into the leather but there was no hidden compartment. There was nothing written neither on the leather nor on the material underneath it.

'Useless. There is no map here.'

'Could there be a code?' asked Scott, who had sat down opposite him. 'Somewhere in the text?' Santi began to study each page from the pile of cut out pages next to the ripped-up binding. He picked up each page, read carefully through one side, then slowly turned it over and repeated the process on the other side. Scott watched him for a few minutes, then said.

'No luck?' asked Scott.

'*Qué?*' said Santi as he turned around. 'No, no. Nothing. Stupid book. Just a load of recipes. Fucking stupid traditional recipes. Look.' Santi threw a handful of pages towards Scott's side of the table. 'Just pages and pages of recipes. At the start,' he picked up a page and showed it to Scott, 'he writes a dedication to my grandmother. 'Always remember the recipes'. He writes the 'wealth is in the snail.'

'What do you mean? The 'wealth?''

'Here,' said Santi, pointing out the text. 'Here. *La riqueza está en el caracol. Nunca olvida.*' He tells my grandmother the wealth is in the snail. To never forget. I hate snails. Then a bunch of stupid traditional recipes. He doesn't mention any house. Any project.'

'Wait a second,' said Scott, who had stood up, 'pass me the plans. Which are the plans for this house?'

'I told you, he didn't build this house. Just the tunnel under the garden. I went through all this with Dimitri. But we have dug all that up. There was nothing.'

299

'Show me the plans anyway. Are there plans?'

'Yes, of course. He always made very detailed plans.' Santi began to search through them. 'Here…here it is. See, he always made very detailed plans. You see there is the shore, the pool house, and this is the tunnel that goes under the garden. The area my grandfather rebuilt is here.' The area of the plans that covered the tunnel under the garden was more detailed than the rest which looked more faded.

'Why is this bit different?' asked Scott, pointing to the tunnel.

'This is my grandfather's work. The rest is copied from the old diagrams. The original plans of the building."

Scott looked carefully at the edge of the paper.

'There. The stairs.'

'What about the stairs?' said Santi.

'Look at these plans.' Scott said pointing. 'They show a room leading off the spiral stairs to the boathouse.'

'Yes?'

'But there *isn't* a room off the stairs. The stairs go straight down. Aren't spiral stairs called *escalera de…*'

'*Caracol.*'

'Snail. The wealth is in the snail.'

'I think you've got it.' Santi eyes were shining with excitement. 'But the room…? Let's go!'

'There is just a wall. An alcove. Come with me.' Scott ran out the kitchen and down to the pool house. He opened the secret door and went down the steps until he was standing at the tromp l'oeil. It was painted over a plastered wall. Scott hit it with his palm. It sounded solid enough.

'Alex. *¿Dónde estás?*' came Santi's voice from up the stairs.

'Down here!' shouted Scott. Santi hobbled down the stairs. 'Look. This wall is just where the room should be. Your grandfather didn't build anything here. He just blocked it off. I'll get a hammer.' Scott went down into the boathouse. In one of the cupboards he found a large metal tool box. It opened out into side trays with a large central space. In it there was a hack saw, a huge wrench, various screwdrivers and underneath them all a metal mallet and chisel. He took the last two back up to the mural.

'Well, here goes.'

The sound of the mallet hitting the chisel into the wall was deafening in the confined space. The first blow just dislodged some plaster. The second blow removed a bit more and exposed part of a brick. Scott worked along the edge of the brick, knocking off small lumps of plaster. Suddenly a large lump came away, revealing the brick wall behind.

'Try to get a brick out,' said Santi.

Scott concentrated on the mortar between the bricks. It was very hard and Scott was only dislodging pea sizes chunks at any one blow. After five minutes, covered in sweat and dust, he paused. Santi took the chisel and mallet from him and had a go. Santi put the chisel in the mortar and gave it lots of little taps with the hammer. This worked well and he ran the pick around the brick, gradually getting more mortar out.

When he had managed to remove about half the mortar, he lowered the pick and gave the brick a massive hit with the hammer. This had no effect other than to send a chip of brick flying back into his eye.

'Here, let me.' said Scott, taking the tools off him as Santi blinked. Scott put the chisel in the join between the bricks and gave it a few heavy blows with the mallet. The chisel went in by a few millimetres each blow, but on his fourth blow it went in by a few centimetres. Scott tried to pull it out but it was stuck. He hit it left then right and slowly he worked it lose. He pulled it out and looked in the hole.

'We're through!' he said. He could only see darkness. He started to chip away at the mortar and it came away more easily. After a few more blows he managed to remove the mortar from the bottom and sides of the brick.

'Here goes,' he said. 'Watch your eyes.' And gave the brick a hard hit. The brick disappeared, leaving a black hole. Scott put his hand in. His arm went in up to his elbow.

'There is definitely a space behind here.'

He worked on the mortar around the next brick. This came away more easily and soon there were two bricks missing. The third brick came away with just one blow. After that it was easy and soon Scott had pushed six bricks back in to the hole.

'Let me get a torch,' he said. He ran down to the boathouse and found a diving torch. When he got back Santi was banging away to remove another brick.

'Here, move aside. Let's have a look in there,' said Scott. He moved Santi to one side and shone the torch into the hole. About twenty centimetres in was something made of wood. He reached in a tapped it.

'A wooden box. Santi, we've found it!' he said clapping Santi on the back. They knocked away a few more bricks and soon could see that there was a stack of boxes behind the wall. Once they had removed enough brick to expose the top box, they reached in and pulled on it. It was wooden, the same shape but about double the size of a typical shoe box, but was very heavy. It had handles at each end and it took both of them to pull it out of the wall. They took an end each and carried it down to the boathouse. It was a rough wooden box with some stencilled numbers on the side. The lid looked as if it had been nailed shut and there was no lock or hinge.

'Quick, open it!" barked Santi.

Scott put the chisel in the join under the lid and gave it a blow with the mallet. The chisel went in. Scot wiggled the chisel up and down and soon the top and the nails holding it down came away from the base. A dark felt bag tied up with string filled the box.

Santi pulled at the string, and when he couldn't untie the knot, began to tear at the felt. The old material fell apart without any noise to reveal a pile of gold coins.

'We found it!' Santi said, picking up a handful of coins. He handed one to Scott. It was a mint condition gold coin with the emblem of the United States. Scott looked closely and saw the date 1918.

'How much did you say there was?' asked Scott.

'Five hundred boxes. That's what Dimitri's grandfather's note says.'

'Jesus Christ. Right, *now* we can call Olenka.' Scott watched Santi staring at the pile of coins. 'Santi. Hey Santi.' Scott snapped his fingers in front of Santi's face. 'Come on. We need to call Olenka. Get María back.'

'Maybe we should hide some...' started Santi.

'We haven't the time. When he finds out you're gone he'll go ape. It's almost dawn now. We've now got proof we have the gold,' said Scott holding up a coin. 'That's all he wants. He wants to load up with gold and be on his way. Let's just give it to him and get Maria back without getting all of us killed in the process.'

# THIRTY-THREE

They were back in the kitchen. It was five thirty in the morning. Scott had made some coffee and they had eaten some bread and cheese. Scott said to Santi that he needed to get something from the cellar. Santi followed him into the office where Scott picked up some keys and they both went down into the cellar. They walked along the rows of dusty bottles until they came to the green metal gun safe.

'I thought we might need some insurance,' said Scott. He opened the safe. He looked along the row of weapons. He selected a double-barrelled gun which looked like a side by side shotgun but with narrower barrels and a carrying strap.

'What's that?' asked Santi.

'It's an express rifle. Four seventy calibre, that's nearly a half inch diameter bullet.' Scott found a box of large ammunition on the top shelf of the safe and took out two ten-centimetre-long brass bullets. 'These are made to stop an elephant.'

'What…?' began Santi.

'I don't trust Olenka an inch. I very much doubt he'll let you and María go. For all he knows you'll go straight to the police. Despite the gold. Once María is off the boat and with us, I'll point this at Olenka and we can get ourselves out of there. No way he's going to argue with this cannon.'

'But if he sees that, he'll keep María on the ship.'

'Of course. I'm going to hide it in the boathouse. Once María is with us I'll grab it.' He saw the look on Santi's face. 'Look, it's the best we can do.'

He looked around the cellar.

'We're going need some boxes to cover up the hole in the wall. Can you bring some of those?' He said pointing to a few empty, wooden wine boxes. They took the gun and some boxes and set off for the boathouse.

They carried the crate full of gold from the boathouse back up the staircase to the alcove and pushed it back through the hole. Scott began to cover it up with the boxes from the cellar, a pile of lifejackets, some rope and other bits and pieces of boating equipment. He took out the bulb in the stairs that was nearest to the alcove and found a dustpan and broom and got rid of as many signs of rubble as possible.

He hadn't liked the way Santi had been staring at the hole as they closed it up. He had had to sit him down and explain the plan twice. María for the gold.

Scott got Santi to find Olenka's number on the old guard's phone and dialled it. It rang five times before it was answered. A very sleepy voice said something in Russian.

'Good morning Dimitri.'

'Hello. Who is that?'

'Good morning!'

'Hello? What are you…? Who is…?' There was a pause. 'Ahh, Al-eh-handro. So, you didn't die. We should have searched more. You have Nikoli's phone.' He paused. 'I presume you are with my architect.'

'If you mean Santiago, yes I am.'

'And Nikoli?'

'He is fine. Probably sleeping at the lighthouse. More than I can say for Peter Taylor.'

'That was a regrettable accident.'

'You can stop the crap, Olenka. I was there. I saw it all. Let's not pretend anymore. You have María on the *Rusalka*.'

'*Señorita* María is my guest on my yacht, yes.'

'I have something you want. We have found it.'

'You have found what?'

'What do you think. The gold.'

There was a rustling noise of sheets and Olenka spoke again, his voice stronger.

'You have found it. Where?'

'Wouldn't you like to know?'

'Bullshit. You haven't found it.'

'Five hundred boxes of gold coins. I am looking at one now,' said Scott and read from the coin in his hand. '1918 Liberty on one side, twenty dollars written on the other. Very pretty. Very heavy.'

'You found it. Was it all there? Five hundred boxes?'

'Well, I haven't counted them all. But yes, there are a lot of boxes.'

Olenka exclaimed something in Russian.

'This is good. Very good. Tell me where it is, and I will release the girl.'

'Yes, of course. Would you like my credit card details too?'

'Pardon?' Scott's sarcasm was lost on the Russian.

'We are going to do this my way. If you release María I will tell you where the gold is. On one condition. You leave fifty cases behind.'

'Fifty cases?'

'That is more than enough for us. It's just ten percent. A finder's fee. You can spare that.'

'Ok,' said Olenka. 'That seems reasonable.'

'Bring her to Can Daurat. To the boathouse.'

'All right.'

'Right. Bring her to the boathouse and I will tell you where the gold is. Once she is safely away.'

'How do I know you have found the gold?'

'You come and meet me here first. I assume you are still on land?'

'Yes.'

'You can come straight over here. I will show you some coins. Then you can call your ship. Get them to bring María here. When she and her brother have left, I will go with you and show you where the gold is buried.'

'Ok.'

'You take the gold, leave me fifty cases and you can sail off into the sunset for all I care.'

'Ok. I will come to your house. Give me an hour. Now remember, no police. No *Guardia Civil*. Or we sail away. With María.'

'Of course. I want to keep my fifty cases too. No police. There will be no tricks from us. We will see you in an hour.'

Scott hung up. He looked at Santi.

'Well, he agreed.'

'He'll never leave fifty cases.'

'I never thought he would. But if he thinks we are as greedy as he is it might give us an edge. Right, we've got an hour. You need to be ready to take María away.' Scott looked around the boathouse.

'We need to hide this somewhere,' he said, indicating the rifle. He opened a tall cupboard built into the wall of the boathouse. In it was a bunch of assorted water sports equipment: water skis; oars; life jackets. Scott placed the loaded gun in the corner of the cupboard.

He was about to head up to the house when he saw the open tool box and the hacksaw which he picked up and took with him. Santi followed him up to the house and Scott insisted he sit in the kitchen and have another coffee. Scott went down into the cellar and came back up fifteen minutes later with three more empty wine boxes to put in front of the hole.

An hour later the sky was just beginning to get light over the sea. They were waiting in the kitchen when they heard the buzzer. Scott went into the office and opened the gates. He saw a car come through the gates on the monitor and he closed them behind it. The car crunched along the

307

gravel and stopped outside the front door. There was the sound of car doors closing. Scott and Santi went out the kitchen door and round the house.

Olenka and Matas were standing by a black Audi A8.

'Good morning. Good morning Santiago.'

'Good morning.'

'Inspector Matas is here to make sure you behave yourself,' said Olenka and Matas pulled back his sports jacket to show his holstered gun.

'As we said on the phone. All we want is María back and ten percent. And we've got cameras to make sure you behave,' said Scott pointing to the security cameras.

'Show me the gold.'

Scott took out a gold coin from his pocket and tossed it to Olenka.

'My God. My grandfather's gold.' He said turning the coin in his hand. He looked at Matas, eyes shining. 'I was brought up with this story. We all thought it was a myth. A fable. Until I found that note. Imagine the balls. Stealing forty tonnes of gold from Stalin. And he never told.' He looked at Scott. 'You found it. How?'

'I'll tell you that when María is safe.'

Olenka and Matas exchanged glances.

'Ok. I will call the boat now. I have sent a man to collect her from my yacht. Where do you want her brought?'

'Here,' said Scott. 'To the boathouse. Shall we go there now?'

Scott led the way down the garden, through into the pool house. Olenka and Matas were looking all around as they walked through the garden.

'Don't get excited, the gold wasn't here. You won't see any hiding place here,' said Scott, hoping their job camouflaging the alcove would succeed. He led them through the pool house and down the spiral staircase. He forced himself to keep an even pace as he walked past the alcove and was relieved to hear them follow him without comment.

Once down in the boathouse, Olenka and Matas stood together, with Scott and Santi nearest the door. Scott went along the dock and opened the doors to the sea which looked grey and flat in the early morning light. Without the *Salacia,* the dock seemed very large.

'They can come in here,' explained Scott. 'Then Santi and María will leave by car. When they call to say they are away, we can go. I will come in your boat and show you where the gold is buried. It is near the sea. You will be able to carry it to your boat.'

'How do I know you will show me?'

'I'm not stupid. I saw what you did to Peter. Believe me I have no wish to die. All we ask for is our ten percent. No police. No tricks.'

Olenka took out his phone and had a conversation in Russian.

'Five minutes,' said Olenka.

'Why did you have to kill Manolo?' asked Scott.

'That was a regrettable...'

'I keep hearing about these regrettable accidents. María had better be ok or you'll never see your gold.'

'She is in perfect health,' replied Olenka.

'Who was it who sunk the *Salacia?* You? Spralov? And why?'

'We wanted to sink the boat, not hurt anyone, it was...'

'Yes, I know. A regrettable accident.'

'Hey Santiago,' Spralov turned to Santi, 'you found the gold. Good work. Don't worry, you'll get your ten percent. Your fee has gone up since you make friends with this *hack.*' Olenka almost spat the last word.

Santi looked warily at Olenka and Matas and said nothing.

A few moments later, they heard the noise of an engine and the *Rusalka*'s tender came round the corner. As it neared the boathouse Scott could see María held by the shoulders by Spralov. She looked terrified, the material on her shirt was bunched where his fingers dug into her arms.

The tender was driven by the sailor Scott had seen the day before. He had a worried expression on his face and kept glancing at Spralov. They came up the channel and into the boathouse. Scott caught a rope and tied up the bow. He then tied up the stern. Santi embraced María as she stepped off onto the dock. She was drawn and shaking, but looked in good health compared to Santi and Scott.

'Ok Olenka,' said Scott, 'let these two go, we wait until they call, and we can go and get the gold.'

'Nice plan Al-ee-handro,' said Olenka. 'But I think you will tell me where the gold is now.'

'Not until they are safe away,' said Scott.

'Inspector?' said Olenka, nodding to Matas. Matas drew his pistol pointed it at them.

'Show us where the gold is now,' repeated Olenka. 'Either that or the inspector will start by shooting Santiago. You *will* shoot him, won't you inspector?'

Matas nodded slowly.

'You forget, you're on tape.' Scott said, pointing to the security cameras.

'Oh dear.' Olenka said in mock distress. 'I'll just have to wipe the memory. *Again.* We hacked this stupid security system days ago. No, you are going to tell me where the gold is, now! First Santiago, then I'll let Mishka here start on the lovely María.' He said indicating Spralov.

Spralov grinned and made as to get off the tender.

'Ok. You win,' said Scott, holding his hands out with palms towards Olenka. 'It was here. It's here in the boathouse. Let me show you.' He started towards the tall cupboard. Matas still had his pistol pointed towards Santi and María. He felt all their eyes bearing down on him. He was only a metre away from the cupboard. If he could only grab the rifle. He reached out to open the cupboard door and Santi said:

'Alex, *no! ¡Por favor!*

'*Qué dice?*' said Matas '*Para!* Stop!'

'What the fuck?' said Olenka.

310

'Stop where you are!' said Matas, then to Olenka, he said: 'For some reason Santiago doesn't want him to go to that cupboard.'

Scott glared at Santi, but Matas waved his gun at him, so he stepped away from the cupboard. Matas handed his pistol to Olenka.

'Cover them, please,' said Matas to Olenka. Matas took out some surgical latex gloves from his pocket and put them on. He opened the cupboard door and whistled.

'Ahh, Mr Scott, so. This is where the gold is? Really?' he asked, reaching into the cupboard. He turned back to them with the elephant gun in his hands. 'Thinking of doing some hunting?' He opened the gun and took out one of the two bullets. 'I'm not sure we have any animals that would require something this big.' He held the huge bullet up in front of his face, rotating his hand and whistled. He put the bullet back in the gun. Then closed it. Olenka nodded at him.

'Or maybe we do.'

He put the gun to his shoulder and pointed it at María.

'Dimitri, please!' said Santi. 'That was not my idea. I didn't want...'

Matas pointed it at Santi, who was standing next to the water.

'Dimitri, it wasn't me...' Olenka nodded at Matas who pulled the trigger.

There was a huge explosion and a flame shot out the barrel. Matas rocked with the recoil and took a step backwards so as not to fall. Immediately after the shot there was another loud crack and a fizzing noise as the bullet hit the opposite wall taking out a large chunk of masonry, ricocheted off and went spinning out to sea. Scott looked at Santi. He had a surprised look on his face and looked down at the red mark in his chest. His legs began to buckle and he fell to his knees before slumping over into the water. María screamed and dived for the body but Scott caught her before she followed it in.

'Well, Mr Scott, it looks like you have just committed murder,' said Matas. He placed the gun on the workbench that ran along the wall and took off his gloves. Olenka was giggling. María was sobbing and Scott held her tight.

'That's not a gun, that's a cannon!' said Olenka, with awe.

'You murdering bastard,' Scott's voice was calm, hardly audible above María crying.

'It is you who will be charged with murder,' replied Matas.

The very unhappy-looking sailor on the tender stammered something in Russian and Olenka silenced him. Matas looked to Olenka, who nodded his head.

'Now, you will tell us where the gold is,' said Matas.

'Or Mishka here,' said Olenka nodding to Spralov, 'will violate your friend repeatedly in front of you before he kills her. And it will not be quick.'

Scott looked down at María. He looked up. Matas had retrieved his pistol from Olenka and was pointing it at them. Spralov got out of the tender and started to approach them.

'Where is the gold? Now. And no tricks,' said Olenka.

'It *is* here. In the boathouse,' said Scott, ashen faced. 'It's up the stairs.'

'Show me. Now.'

Scott walked towards the door to the stairs. They all followed Scott up the narrow spiral steps. He walked slowly, his mind racing.

They reached the landing with the trompe l'oeil alcove and the pile of boating equipment. Olenka and Spralov came past and stood on a step higher up. Matas was directly behind him.

'It's here.' Scott stood to one side. 'Have a look,' Scott said pointing to the alcove.

'You look,' said Olenka. 'Go on. Careful now.'

Scott pulled away the equipment with clattered on the floor. The hole they had made in the wall was exposed.

'Go on' repeated Olenka.

Scott removed one empty wine box and put it to one side. He began to lift another, and reached into it and grasped something inside. He spun round, letting the box fall to the floor.

The shot from the sawn-off shotgun hit Matas squarely in the chest. At the distance of half a metre it was impossible to miss. Earlier Scott had taken the hacksaw, cut the barrels and the stock off one of Bill's shotguns and had loaded it with SGS cartridges, then placed it in one of the wine boxes. Matas' chest was no match for the ball bearing-sized shot, made for hunting wild boar, fired at point-blank range. He was dead before he hit the floor. The noise from the blast in such a confined space was deafening, and it took a moment for Scott to recover. He looked around. Olenka and Spralov had gone. María was screaming a few steps down from the alcove, her hands over her ears. Scott shook her by the shoulders. She stopped.

'María. Are you all right?'

She nodded, looking dazed. Scott took out the mobile he had in his pocket and put it in her hands.

'Call the police. Now! Do you understand?'

She nodded. He could hear steps retreating up the stairs.

'Call the police. Go down to the dock and hit the red panic button by the light switches. Tell them there has been a shooting. Get everybody.' He looked up the stairs. 'They're trying to get away. María, did you get that?'

She nodded again.

'I'm going after them. Call the police.'

Scott felt in the fallen wine box and picked up a handful of shotgun cartridges. He opened the gun and a used cartridge was ejected past his shoulder. He put a fresh cartridge in and snapped the gun closed. He slowly started to ascend the stairs, pointing the gun up the stairs. On each step, Scott peered round the spiral steps, checking there was no one there. At last he reached the door to the pool house which was open. He crouched very low and edged his head round the door. No one. He stood and walked into the room. Empty. Scott walked across the room, keeping the gun pointed in front. At the door, he paused. In the grey morning light, he could see a set of tracks crossing the dew on the grass towards the trees by the cliffs. Scott looked towards the house, then followed the tracks. The tracks ended where the trees started and the dew stopped. Suddenly a figure broke from behind a tree and ran for the promontory.

'Stop!' cried Scott, raising the gun. It was too far to be sure of hitting him. He started to run after him. 'Stop, or I'll shoot!' The man looked over his shoulder but kept running. Spralov. Scott fired but he was too far away and carried on. Scott ran after him. They passed the landslide. He had made it to the promontory. There was no where he could go. Scott was closing the distance. Spralov reached the fence and launched himself onto it. He was half over it when Scott arrived at the fence and raised the gun. He couldn't miss. Scott realised he couldn't just shoot the man, hanging there in front of him. He dropped the gun and threw himself at the Russian. Weakened by the landslide, the fence could not take their combined weight and both they and the fence went crashing over.

Scott grabbed at Spralov as they fell and managed to get hold of a leg. As he felt himself slipping, he grabbed the fence with his other hand. Spralov had slipped off the fence and was now suspended over the cliff. He lost his handhold and fell another few centimetres. He reached up and clung to Scott's hand. Scott's broken finger sent new bolts of pain up his arm as Spralov's grip slipped.

'Help me, please.' Something in the 'please' reminded Scott of Taylor's pleading at the lighthouse. He thought of Taylor and his son. Old Manolo. Natalya. Santi. So many good people gone.

'Wrong thing to say,' Scott said, and shook his hand free. Spralov's scream only lasted a couple of seconds. Scott looked down. Spralov was splayed across the pink rock at the base of the cliff as a crimson puddle spread out beneath him.

Scott managed to pull himself back up the collapsed fence until he was back on flat ground. He heard a loud crashing noise from far away on the other side of the house. He looked around and saw the saw-off shotgun lying where it had fallen. He picked it up and ran towards the noise. He ran up the garden terraces and came around the garages towards the gates. He turned the corner of the drive and saw a black car crumpled against them. So, Olenka had tried to smash his way out. The car was still running but there was steam coming out of the front. The driver's door was open. Scott kept the gun raised and checked the car was empty. He could hear sirens approaching. The police could take it from here.

Suddenly there was a scream. A woman's scream. María. Scott ran back down the garden. There was another scream and a shot. Scott tore into the pool house. He raced down the steps and burst out into the boathouse. The tender had gone. He looked out of the dock doors and saw the tender reversing twenty metres out, Olenka was at the wheel and María was in the seat next to him. The sailor from the Rusalka was lying on the dock with what looked like a gunshot wound to the head. Olenka was steering with one hand and had the gun in the other, pointed at María. Olenka spun the wheel and the tender turned. He was going to make for the *Rusalka*. Territorial waters only extend twelve miles off shore. He could be out of the police's jurisdiction in half an hour. With María. Scott had to stop him.

Scott threw down the sawn-off shotgun and picked up the express rifle from where Matas had left it on the side. He opened the rifle, and an empty cartridge ejected. Only one bullet. He put the sling over his shoulder and ran round to the other side of the dock. He untied the jetski, got onto it and, praying the battery was charged, turned the key.

The jetski roared to life. Scott untied the rope from the cleats, checked the gun was secure on his shoulder, gripped his knees to the seat and gunned the throttle. The tender was now a few hundred metres away, going probably thirty knots. The Benelli Series R is the fastest production jetski in the world and when all three hundred and forty horses of its 2.3 litre supercharged V6 are all unleashed at once, it can accelerate to over ninety miles an hour almost instantly. And Charlie had had his upgraded.

Scott clung on for dear life as the violently powerful machine exploded over the waves. Although the sea was nearly flat calm Scott felt every tiny ripple that the jetski smashed into. The disappearing tender began to loom large, and Scott saw Olenka look over his shoulder and raise his hand. There was a flash. He was shooting at Scott. Scott wrenched the steering handles and veered off sharply to the right. He put the throttle on full. The tender was on the plane doing thirty knots but Scott blazed past as if it were stationary. He saw Olenka follow him with the gun, whether he fired or not would have been impossible to tell over the insane howling of the Benelli's engine.

Scott saw the *Rusalka* up ahead. She was about a mile away. The tender would be there in a couple of minutes. He had to stop Olenka getting Maria onto the ship. Scott flew across the waves until he got within thirty yards of the *Rusalka*. He was directly between the tender and the ship. He could see the crew watching him. The boarding platform was down, but she had her anchor up and the engines were running.

Scott wrenched the handlebars and spun to a stop. The craft settled quickly, the small amount of wake soon dispersed. Scott could see the tender coming straight for his position. He unslung the rifle from his back. One bullet. Second trigger. Scott stood up and put the rifle to his shoulder. He aimed at the approaching boat. He looked down the twin barrels. The far sight was a white dot at the end of the barrel. That fitted neatly in the 'V' of the near sight.

At three hundred metres, all he could see was the shape of the tender head on, moving up and down a little as it planed across the waves. At two hundred metres, he could see Olenka at the wheel. He was pointing the gun at María who was in the seat next to him. The boat came closer. Olenka got larger. The little white dot went from Olenka's head to his chest, to the steering wheel, to his chest, to his head, to his chest. As the boat came closer Scott forced himself to relax. To breath out. To keep the rifle on target. The jetski had settled and there were hardly any waves. Head, chest, middle, chest, head. Keep the gun on Olenka. The tender was eighty metres away. Seventy. Olenka pointed his pistol at Scott and began to fire. Keep calm. Impossible to hit a barn door at that distance with a pistol. Let alone on the water. Fifty metres. He felt something fly past him, close. Lucky shot. Keep calm. Breathe. Head, chest, stomach, chest, head. The tender was nearly upon him. Head, chest, stomach, head. Squeeze the trigger.

Scott nearly went over backwards with the force of the explosion. He just managed to keep his footing. His ears were ringing. Olenka had disappeared. The tender was nearly on him. Scott reached forward, wrenched the throttle and, with a roar, the jetski jumped out of the way of the tender.

'María. Jump!' shouted Scott. Olenka was down, behind the driver's seat there was just a spray of red over the white and beige upholstery. María was still in the passenger seat and the tender was heading straight for the *Rusalka* at full speed. Scott shouted for her to jump again. María must have heard him as he saw her threw herself off the boat into the water. The tender carried on straight at the larger ship. Scott could see the crew, who had gathered on the decks to watch, begin to scatter as the tender neared.

Scott, seeing María surface and raise an arm, accelerated the jetski over to her. The tender smashed in to the *Rusalka* at thirty knots. The bow of the little boat tore through the floor to ceiling windows of some stateroom. As the momentum carried the little tender on into the ship, there was a scream of grinding metal and crash of breaking glass.

Scott reached Maria and pulled her out of the water onto the back of the jetski. She was in shock, shivering and wide eyed.

'Alex. You…'

'Did I get him?'

'Oh yes, you got him.'

'Let's get you back home,' said Scot. There was a *warrumph* as the fuel of the tender caught light. Scott sat María on the back of the jetski and she put her arms around his waist. Scott just caressed the throttle and gently rode the waves back towards Can Daurat and the sound of sirens.

# EPILOGUE

Scott raised his glass.

The police had arrived ten minutes after María's phone call. The report of a shooting had brought five police cars, both *Mossos d'Esquadra* and the *Guardia Civil*. Lieutenant Robles had arrived by sea when he heard the report on the radio. The fire on the *Rusalka* had raged out of control and the crew had been rescued by the coast guard.

Scott and Maria had been taken to the police station to make statements. At first the police had arrested Scott for the murder of a police inspector, but the boathouse's security camera had backed up their version of events.

Maria had been allowed to leave at three that afternoon, Scott at eight. As the whole of Can Daurat had been closed as a crime scene, Scott stayed a couple of nights at Juan's hotel.

Two days later Scott accompanied María to Santi's funeral. It was Scott's first Spanish funeral and he was shocked by the emotion expressed. María clung to his arm throughout.

It took the police two days to organise transport for the 500 boxes of gold that were found in the bricked-up room off the spiral stairs.

Bill Franklin, who had been on business in Hong Kong flew in on the third day, and it was with him that Scott was sharing a bottle of champagne.

'Sorry about the *Salacia*.'

'Cheers!' said Bill, clinking glasses with Scott. 'Don't worry, the insurance will cover it. She's nearly fixed already. I'm more pissed off that you chopped up one of my hundred-thousand-dollar Holland and Holland 12 bores.'

'Oops. Sorry about that. Was under a bit of stress at the time.'

'Don't worry. I'll take it out of your share.'

'My share?'

'Oh! Didn't I mention it?' Bill was smiling.

'No Bill. You certainly didn't mention it. My share of what?'

'The Spanish government has offered us a reward.'

'Us?'

'Well, you found it, and it was in my house.'

'What is the reward?'

'Reward for finding buried treasure is five percent of market value, but as this was stolen property, albeit a long time ago, they have offered us two percent.'

'Jesus Bill, that's …'

'Twenty-eight million Euros,' said Bill with a huge smile on his face.

'You're joking?'

'I am certainly not joking. Well, I think my lawyers had something to do with it, but the government agreed in the end. That's fourteen million each. Yours is minus the price of a new shotgun, of course.'

Scott sat there in stunned silence. He would never have to work again.

'What'll you do with it?' asked Bill.

'I'd like to give Peter's family something, and María. I'll make sure Natalya's body gets home safely. Then I just don't know. Might write some articles. I suppose I don't need to anymore. I could write that book all of us have in us.'

Bill put down his glass of champagne.

'Well, if you have nothing better to do, I have various interests in Cuba. You speak Spanish. There has been a bit of an emergency and need someone to...'

'Thanks Bill,' interrupted Scott, 'I think I'll pass.'

\#

## About the Author

David Kennedy has lived all over the UK and mainland Europe. He is lucky to have the best wife in the world, a beautiful daughter and an ancient dog who all put up with the writing of this novel.

Costa Brava is his first foray into novel writing.

If you would like to know more or receive news of future works, please visit

www.davidkennedywriter.com